THE DEVIL YOU KNOW

A FICTION-ATLAS PRESS ANTI-HERO ANTHOLOGY

C.L. CANNON   K.A. WIGGINS   ZOEY XOLTON

K. MATT   K.R.S. MCENTIRE   LILY LUCHESI

SCOTT MOORE   KAT PARRISH   ANGELA KULIG

NICK EDINGER   J.M. RHINEHART   AMBER MORANT

FICTION-ATLAS PRESS LLC

THE DEVIL YOU KNOW

A FICTION-ATLAS PRESS ANTI-HERO ANTHOLOGY

CONTENTS

FOOL ME TWICE

BY C.L. CANNON

If you could walk a mile in someone else's shoes, it is often thrown around as a moral ambiguity to live your life by, but as someone blessed with some, shall we say, unusual gifts, not to mention an infinite life-span, I much prefer to infer meaning rather than experience it firsthand. As high as human highs are, their lows can be downright unbearable. They live, and think, and feel in extremes that I've long since sworn off. Their emotions have stolen more from me than they could ever repay. They are selfish, ruthless, and they thirst for power more than anything else. Of course, I know not all humans are inherently evil, and they can even be useful at times, but the majority place self-interest above all. I've also never met a human who couldn't be bought for one price or another. Their loyalty is paper-thin, and I intend to make them pay for their crimes against my kind. Their reckoning is coming. My plans are in motion, and I do not intend to yield. There's just one more cog in the wheel to lay in place. Athaliah.

When I first encountered Athaliah, I felt nothing. She was clearly human—small of frame, with unruly rust-colored hair, and eyes that seemed permanently pointed at her feet. I'm not sure that I noticed her as anything more than shabby décor littering the floor of the night club where I'd agreed to meet my contact. My mind was too transfixed on retrieving the information I needed to take account of the waitstaff. It wasn't until she looked me in the eye and asked for my drink order that I felt the spark of her power and a niggling in the back of my brain that reminded me of someone I'd long tried to forget. Perhaps she was a distant relation or even an illusion my mind had made up. There was a glint of emerald green in her hazel eyes, and the soft timbre of her voice sent chills down my spine. The possibility and potential of her scared me. It had been centuries since I'd feared another being or cared about one. Neither fear nor care had brought me happiness, and so this rare moment of recognition as I stared into her eyes sent me bursting from the scene, desperate to escape the past and unwilling to relive it.

My skin itched, and my breath quickened as I made my way through the heavy foot traffic of London. I preferred the black ink of night. Easy to slip through and to disappear in, especially with my talents, but on this night, the streets were crowded with merrymakers eager to celebrate the coming of the new year. Bodies pressed against me from all directions, making it harder to navigate the crowd without skin on skin contact. Finally, I managed to plod down a less crowded alley and gather my composure. I tugged unsuccessfully at my scarf, cursing myself for wearing it in the first place. After a few minutes of fidgeting, it finally loosed, and I leaned against the rough brickwork of the alleyway.

Who was that woman, and what connection did she have to my Ava? I would have to face her If I wanted to find out, not run away like a coward. Not to mention the fact my contact would have shown up by now with information I'd been waiting a lifetime for. I swallowed the lump in my throat and steadied my breathing. What was I doing? Forfeiting my one chance to find Ava because the ghost of her haunted me from every dark corner? In every scared human girl? There was nothing about this serving girl that could be more important than finding the location of the talisman. I had no idea the role she was about to play or the depth of her power and so, I took another ragged breath and steeled myself to battle the crowd back to the club. Things were so much easier to navigate when there were no prying eyes to witness me transform. Remaining in this form was tedious, but necessary for the time being.

A few moments later, I was once more standing inside the flesh fair of the club, which seemed to have doubled in occupancy as the clock drew closer to midnight. There was no sign of the girl from earlier. Edwin, my contact, stood toward the back left of the establishment, looking just as out of place in his detective garb as I must have in my tailored suit. The youth of the nineteen nineties were much fonder of acid-washed denim than I would ever be comfortable with. I carefully squeezed my way through the crowd to stand opposite Edwin, who greeted me with a nod.

"So, what did you find out?" I prodded.

"No definite sightings, but I've heard tell of a long-haired lad poking around where he shouldn't be, asking over a necklace. An old one. He's claiming it's a lost family heirloom, only no one's ever heard of the bloke or his family."

"One of their little gray cloak soldiers, no doubt. Perhaps if they'd never stolen from me in the first place, they wouldn't be exhausting such manpower trying to find something that's rightfully mine."

"Want me to put someone on this do-gooder's trail, sir?" I had many informants in all areas of the human world, but Edwin was one of my favorites by far. He was no-nonsense and direct.

"No, I think I should meet this young man face to face. He could have sensitive information. An address will suffice."

Edwin nodded before handing over a small envelope containing the address of the Arma boy's current accommodations. We parted ways with a promise to meet again in one month. I'd nearly forgotten the incident with the girl. It was a fleeting error in judgment. I'd let the promise of the talisman, the promise of being reunited with Ava, cloud my mind and befuddle with my senses. I made my way through the chaos of entangled bodies and through the back exit as the crowd began their countdown. Ten, nine, eight, seven… I let the heavy metal door bang behind me as I strode down the pitch back alley. A few seconds more and screams of pain rather than celebration drew my attention.

It was her, the girl from the club. Two rather large rubbish bags lay on either side of her, and two good for nothing men pressed her small body against the faded brick of the alley.

"Oh, come on, love, give us a kiss," the shorter man said, running one filthy hand down the girl's cheek.

"Get off her!" I growled. If there was one thing I couldn't stand about these mortals, it was the way they treated their women.

The tall tattooed man's head snapped to attention as I approached.

"What are you, her father?" he asked, side-stepping to block me from his friend. "Get lost, you knob. She's ours."

I felt my blood boil. I ripped my glove from my hand with my teeth and let my bare fingers wrap firmly around the tall man's neck. "I said, get…off…her!"

The tips of his boots scraped against the pavement as they struggled for purchase. One by one, the visions hit me. A boy who'd been handed the world and threw it away for amber-filled needles and empty company. A man who didn't know trust, or love, or friendship. An angry man who took what he wanted to feed his addictions. An ocean of blood on his boney hands.

Stubby hands grabbed at my collar, pulling me back to the present. The second man was cursing, unable to overpower me or free his friend from my grasp. I tossed the tall man roughly to the ground and turned, grabbing hold of the smaller of the two. This time there was pain as the images flooded my mind. A life of loss and poverty. Another user, but not a killer—not yet anyway.

"Please," came a small voice over my shoulder. The girl stood, shirt torn and arms bloodied, looking me straight in the eye again. "Please, just get me out of here. They're not worth it."

If only she knew how right she was. They were worthless, and yet there were a thousand other humans like them scurrying around this city, waiting for another innocent life to destroy. It wasn't the first time I'd been asked to spare the unworthy. Not the first time green eyes pleaded for the lives of the very men who'd hurt her.

The tall man had regained his senses and was shuffling backward across the pavement, forgetting his friend entirely. I released my hold on the second man, shoving him face-first into the alley wall.

"Leave," I commanded. "I never want to see either of you in this city again."

The short man clutched his bloodied head and stuttered, groveling his compliance.

I turned to the girl once more, taking care to push my fingers back into my gloves before stepping closer to her. "You're hurt. We should get you some help."

She glanced down at her torn clothes and skinned elbows with a shrug. "I'll be okay. Just a few scrapes. I'm miles better off than them," she said, gesturing in the direction the men had fled.

"Can I at least escort you to somewhere safe?" I asked. No use letting her wander the streets in such a state.

She smiled and forced her gaze down to her feet as she'd done inside the club. "Yes, I would like that very much."

We walked a few paces to the end of the alley, and I looked to her for direction. The club was bursting with drunkards and filled to the seams with sweating bodies, there would be no peace or safety for her there.

"My flat is this way," she said, seemingly reading my mind.

I followed her out of the alley to the right and down the main thoroughfare, still as crammed with people as it had been when I'd flown from the club earlier.

"Thank you," she practically whispered as I walked by her side through the masses. "I don't know what would have happened if you hadn't chased them off."

I nodded, silently acknowledging her and contemplating how I'd gotten myself into this mess to start with. I should be tracking down the Arma boy. Every minute he was out there was a minute he could find the talisman and slip back to the sacred city. I hadn't made it a habit of saving human girls or any human for that matter in over a thousand years.

A few more silent moments passed, and the crowd began to thin as we trekked further away from the middle of the city and into the residentials.

Finally, she spoke again. "I'm sorry if I offended you earlier. You left so suddenly." Her tone was apologetic, like that of a scolded child.

I stumbled over my words for a minute, trying to articulate a response that wouldn't leave her thinking I was some sort of mad hatter.

"I, no, that is to say, you did nothing you should be sorry for. You just remind me of someone, that's all."

Her brow creased as she took in this new information. Perhaps she was pondering my mental acuity after all.

I broke the silence before she could come to a decision. "Do you happen to have family in London? Or, while we're at it, a name?"

The girl blushed before gracing me with a sincere smile. "Athaliah, but everyone just calls me Atty, and I wouldn't know about my family. I grew up with my nan, but she passed a few years ago. I never really knew my parents, and she didn't talk of them."

"Ah, that's unfortunate. I'm sorry," I apologized.

"And what do I call you, sir?"

"Samael, and I'll spare you the names most people call me."

That little jibe elicited a genuine chuckle from her.

"Well, they can't be all bad. I refuse to believe such a brave man could be thought ill."

I chose to hold my tongue at that remark. To some, I was a demon, to others a mentor, and to one, equal parts cherished and damned.

We abruptly left the pavement to cut through what looked to be private gardens.

"Are you sure this is the w-?" I began but was cut short.

"Who is it that I remind you of?" Atty asked in a rush of breath. "Maybe you knew my mother?" she guessed.

There was no way I could have known her mother nor even her grandmother, but how could I explain away centuries of waiting? Year upon year of searching? Best to drop the subject entirely.

"Oh, I doubt it," I said, waving my hand dismissively in front of me.

"I've…been away from London for a long while now. Probably just a passing resemblance."

She seemed disappointed with my answer for a moment but then continued her questioning.

"Did this person hurt you? They must have done something terrible to cause you to flee like that."

That was a question I was not expecting. It was a complicated question laced with too many emotions and feelings I'd tried to bury for too many years.

"It was not her intention to cause me harm, and it was a long time ago," I said, trying to brush it off once more.

"Oh, I see. Did her family not approve? Was it a forbidden romance?"

The way her voice quickened, and her eyes sparkled with interest threatened to turn my stomach. She imagined a fairy tale instead of the hell I had endured.

"Or perhaps it's more tragic than that? Did she die?"

I swallowed the lump that had formed in my throat. This was not something I spoke about and most importantly, death wasn't permanent. Not always. I had a plan, and it was going to work.

"Atty, I don't wish to talk of this. Let's just get you home. Enough about me."

"I'm sorry. I'm always prying too deep. My nan used to say I could run off the dead with my prattling. Forgive me."

She was a rather awkward girl, to be sure, but I couldn't fault her for that. It was the unusual ones that had most interested me over the years. They had the queerest stories and, more often than not, the most talent. "It's quite all right. Why don't you tell me more about yourself?" I was curious to know more about that spark I had seen inside the club. I couldn't have imagined it. Every time I looked into her green orbs, I felt that familiar prickle against my skin. She had an energy, hidden potential, even if she hadn't learned to unlock it yet.

"Oh, I'm no one," she said modestly. "Just a girl with no past and likely no future if things keep going the way they have."

Now that was a strange thing to say.

"And why do you say that? Did something else happen to you before tonight?" I asked, curious to get to the bottom of her revelation.

"It's nothing," she said, trying to blow the comment off. "I just, lost something. A family heirloom. Some long-haired git nicked it from me this morning."

The Arma kid. Could it be? After all this time, the talisman had wound up in the hands of a girl who knew nothing of its power?

"What kind of heirloom?" I asked. I had to be sure. The coincidence would be far-fetched, but I couldn't quite let myself hope yet.

"Just an old necklace. My nan said it belonged to my mother, but who knows, I just felt something, when I wore it, you know? I felt like a part of her was with me, even though I never met her. Is that daft?"

Of course she could feel the power. If she was connected to Ava, even by a distant bloodline, it would still sing to her.

"No, not at all," I assured her. "What did this necklace look like?"

"I don't know. It was sort of a dingy silver I guess, with some weird symbols on it. Snakes and fire. Bits of gold leaves."

That was all I need. The symbols of our faith, the bond the three of us shared, molten into the necklace I'd made for her. Fire and snakes, the symbol of the Proelia, and the leaves I'd added just for her. The leaves that bound us all together. After all this time, I'd found it.

"Atty, I think you're more like me than you know. And I think perhaps I did know your family after all. We have to find that necklace."

"But how? And what does my necklace have to with it?"

"I made it a long time ago… to protect someone I loved. It's a long story, I'll explain fully later. For now, let's get you inside. How much longer till your flat?

"It's just …just around the hedge here, " she stammered, looking a bit unsure of her surroundings.

"Are you okay?" I asked, worried that I'd sprung too much on her in my excitement.

"Fine," she answered a bit curtly before moving on to her next question. "I don't get it. If it was yours to begin with, how did you lose it? And how can it protect someone? It's just a necklace."

"You're like me, Atty. You have a gift. I promise, I'll teach you how to use it. I'll teach you to reach your full potential. How to stop death, even, but first, we have to locate the necklace. As for losing it, let's just say, be careful who you trust."

I rounded the lot only to find myself staring down a corporate car park. We'd doubled back somewhere in our traipse through the gardens. And that's not all that was strange. Something was different. The girl's demeanor had abruptly changed as we rounded the last set of hedges. She was fidgeting more and looking over her shoulder. Had I frightened her with my plans? With my excitement? No, that wasn't it. She was looking for someone.

"I'm sorry, Samael, it's nothing personal. I find your offer pretty generous if you ask me, but I already have a mentor. "

It was an ambush, and I'd been foolish enough to follow her right into it. She'd accomplished just what the Arma boy wanted. I'd completely let down my guard for a poor defenseless damsel in distress and spewed my secrets only to find the damsel not so defenseless after all. The boy, Sydney, who would cause me immense frustrations in the coming years, stepped out from behind one of the parked automobiles. Five other gray cloaks flanked him—their eyes fixed on me and ready to attack if necessary. I sensed a fire wielder, a healer, and a traveler. The other two were harder to put my finger on. In a fair fight, I could hold my own, but seven against one was hardly sporting. Athaliah moved past me to stand at Sydney's side. I didn't miss the warm smile she gave him. How long had they been working together?

"Good job, Atty. Did you get the information we needed?" Sydney asked, not taking his eyes from me for even a moment.

"A resurrection talisman. He wants to bring the back the savior."

"She's not your savior," I protested. I'd always hated that title. They left a girl to die and made her a martyr—a saint. She wasn't theirs, and she never would be. She was a scared girl, a brave girl who didn't deserve the hand fate dealt her. And if it was the last thing I ever did, I would put it right.

"That's where you're wrong. She is our savior, the sacred sister of our forefather, and you will not desecrate her memory by raising a demon in her stead."

"Your forefather is the reason she's dead. Did you know that? Did you know Anso sacrificed his own sister? Abandoned her? For what? The humans?" I spat the words like venom, and as they permeated the Arma ranks, I felt the hiss in my voice grow, and my transformation take hold. It had been millennia since he'd taken the form of a snake. It was my least favorite animal to shift to, but desperate times called for desperate measures. While the Arma militia had been focused on enclosing my paths of exit from behind, they completely disregarded the rain gutter in the wall of the carpark. I slithered inside as quickly as possible, narrowly escaping capture.

"Damnit," Sydney cursed, grinding his feet into the pavement. "Peter is not going to be happy that we lost him, but at least we have the talisman. Atty, give me your necklace."

I watched with amber eyes as Athaliah pulled the talisman from her pocket. The whole time, my salvation had been an arm's length away. There was something about the way Athaliah handed the necklace over to the boy that made me think she didn't quite trust him with it.

"What are you doing?" she asked as Sydney handed the necklace over to the fire wielder.

"We're going to get rid of it. It's too risky to keep," he explained, placing the silver slab into his friend's already glowing hands. The blue hue turned to gold, and eventually, the flames sputtered to a halt.

"It's obviously protected," Athaliah said, snatching the necklace from the flame wielder. "We'll have to find another way. For now, I'll keep it safe."

Of course I'd thought to protect the talisman from Anso's fire, from any flame that could seek to destroy her soul and a thousand other means of magical harm. They wouldn't get rid of it that easily, and I had a feeling Athaliah hadn't been lying when she'd mentioned her connection to the talisman. I could see it now—a longing to understand the connection and a growing need to keep it safe. Perhaps tonight wasn't a total loss. I'd revealed more secrets than I'd ever planned, but I'd also gained a potential ally. I just needed to keep an eye out and bide my time.

Twenty years have passed since that night, and finally, my plans have come to fruition. It's time to collect. I watch from my perch as a middle-aged woman with wild, rust-colored hair shuffles across the walkway to sit on one of the abandoned park benches. Her steps are more deliberate now, and it seems she's found the confidence to stop staring at her feet. Her eyes are still dotted with emerald green. She darts them from side to side as she tries to detect my presence.

I glide down from my perch soundlessly, transforming from a raven into my human form in midair. My feet rustle in the autumn leaves as I land behind the bench.

"What have you done with it, Athaliah?"

The woman jumps, twisting around to face me.

"I always forget that you can do that," she says, clasping her hand over her heart. "It's creepy if you ask me."

"No one did. Now, where have you stashed the talisman?" I ask, growing impatient with her stalling. She obviously didn't have it on her. She's too smart for that.

"It's in a safe place. My son, who I believe you met earlier, gave it to his friends for safekeeping. Two little Armas stranded outside the sacred city. They shouldn't be too difficult to find."

"So, betraying your own kind now. Branching out, are we?"

"I am no kind, but my own. I don't belong to either of you."

I consider her position for a moment. How queer it must be to belong nowhere and inspire no one. As sickening as the Arma and their human worship was, at least they believed in something. My Gladios served me faithfully while also maintaining a semblance of freedom. They respected one thing, my power over and unwillingness to yield to the humans. Athaliah has none of that. She's been playing the sides against each other for too long, and her game of cat and mouse is about to abruptly end if I have any say in the matter.

"You know, you almost had me, all those years ago," I muse, walking slowly and deliberately to face her at the front of the bench. "I really thought you were just an innocent soul I'd saved from undue suffering."

She scoffs. "Oh, we all know you've always been weak to a pretty girl in distress, Samael. Isn't that what got you into this situation to begin with?"

She thinks she knows me after all these years. She's only seen what I've allowed her to see and only knows what I've allowed her to know. But I know far more about her dealing.

"I heard you made some questionable judgment calls yourself. Marrying that Arma boy, Sydney? Tell me, did you look him in the eye when you stuck the knife in his heart or where you too much of a coward to do it yourself?"

Her jaw clenches. That wounded her. "I loved Sydney. I did what was necessary, which is more than I can say for you. You could have anything you want, dominion over all, yet you waste your years on a glorified treasure hunt."

"My affairs are my own. At least I have a little thing called loyalty," I shoot back.

"You can keep your loyalty. And you can keep your savior. I don't care anymore. But you will allow me and my son safe travel away from all of this."

"And why would I do that?" I ask, curious to know what she thinks she has over me.

"Because I'm tired. I'm tired of running, I'm tired of pretending to be someone I'm not. You told me you'd help me unlock my potential. Turns out, I didn't need you after all. I know how to destroy the talisman."

"Impossible." There is only one other soul who knew how to destroy the talisman, and that soul happened to be trapped inside said amulet.

"I assure you, all things are possible. If you know who to ask."

A cold shiver crept up my spine as I stared into Athaliah's emerald eyes. Ava. She'd asked Ava.

ABOUT C.L. CANNON

C.L. Cannon is a USA Today Bestselling Author, publisher, publicist, editor, designer, and lots of other occupations with the -er sound at the end! She is a woman of many talents who never gives up or stops improving. She enjoys writing about love and friendship. She loves it even more when she can add fantasy and science fiction aspects to those themes! She's a self-proclaimed Harry Potter freak (Slytherin Pride people), lover of anything Joss Whedon (Spuffy forever), Tolkien fiend (who enjoys second breakfast), and addict of classic literature (Social class struggles turn me on... literally ;) yah see what I did there?) She spends her days trying to #bookstagram (and probably failing), helping other authors grow and succeed (I love my job), and loving on her two babes (velociraptors), Seth and Petey. She's also sort of a social media enthusiast! You can find her basically everywhere on the net (man I just aged myself). Or, you can visit her website or join her street team for more content!

https://clcannon.net
https://facebook.com/groups/clcannon

facebook.com/clcannonauthor

twitter.com/clcannonauthor

instagram.com/cl_cannon

BOY WITH NO NAME

BY K.A. WIGGINS

She's drowning under the weight of her ghosts, and all I can do is hold her up while she stumbles and gasps for air.

If I were less selfish, I would have left her to build a new life, instead of dragging her back where it all began.

But when you're nothing, you have to grab everything you can and hang on to it with everything you've got.

I step out of the shadows and into the path of the cloaked figure, capturing its narrow shoulders. "Where is she?"

I resist shaking Ange with each word only by the narrowest of margins. The slight woman breaks my grip with an ease that would shock those who know her only as my long-time and long-suffering attendant.

Her dark hood falls back, exposing startlingly bare features that might look delicate if they weren't fixed in an expression that rocks me back on my heels. I'm used to seeing her masked and painted, sharp gaze carefully downturned, pretending to serve while I pretend not to know where she goes and what she does when my back is turned.

I waver, suddenly unsure now our years of careful plots and counterplots have unraveled. This is new territory for both of us. But I don't have time to win her over, even if she could forgive all I've done —to her, to those she's loved, to the ever-growing list of those she protects. Including, it seems, Cole. The last person I can afford to lose.

"She doesn't want to see you." Ange's tone makes it clear the object of my obsession since childhood is far from the only one who doesn't want to see my face right now.

I don't blame Ange—I've given her more than enough reasons to think me the enemy. But I can't let it go, either. Something's wrong. I can feel it.

Or rather, it's what I can't feel.

The whole tower is achingly empty in Cole's absence. And not just the numbingly dull corridors of Refuge above, either, but also the seven glittering, decadent halls of my glorious "secret" club below its repressive rule, Freedom. Even the secretive pulse of the Underground Ange has built over these past six years into a hidden but powerful force to contend with my own domain holds no spark of Cole's distinctive, silvery light throughout its maze of once-abandoned tunnels. The horrifying sense of utter emptiness extends even beyond, through every drowned street of this haunted city right up to the dead silence of the boundary that keeps both the last remnants of humanity and the monsters who prey on us trapped within its sickly dome.

My whole world is hollow in a way I haven't felt for six years. Not since *she* came.

"I need to see her, Ange."

Ange turns her back.

I can't blame her. I've hurt a lot of people, but her more than most. Her, perhaps more than any living soul besides Cole. Somehow, the ones that matter the most are always the ones I hurt the worst.

If I were less selfish, I might do something about that.

It doesn't stop me from chasing Ange down the crumbling corridors as they give way to drained tunnels. Her narrow back grows more and more rigid under the long, hooded cloak that helps her blend into the shadows, her steps sharper, her balance careful and ready to throw off attack, a skill she learned first by choice and honed by necessity.

She doesn't like me following her, though we both know I've been aware of her not-so-little underground resistance for years. But now I'm upsetting the rules of our game, breaking character in this careful play we've put on for so long.

I couldn't care less.

I push past, ignoring the elbow she jabs into my side and the way her steps speed, until we're both all but running, jostling to be the first through the makeshift door to the infirmary, I have to assume houses the lifeless remains of the one person I can never afford to lose.

But when I shove the tattered curtain aside, the narrow cots are empty but for a stranger. He's solid, though not large, with the worn look of one who has spent much time outside the sheltering prison of the tower walls. Ange's hapless twin, Amy, and an open-mouthed, curly-headed child are at his side, tending to his wounds.

He's the one Cole was sheltering as the nightmares closed in. He was there, useless, a dead weight, as she struggled and failed to fight the monsters. As useless as I was to protect her. And now she's gone.

I ignore Amy's screech and the child's babbling to wheel on Ange, my arm raised. I don't know if I'll hit her or clutch at her to keep from falling to my knees.

She decides for me, wrapping one hand around my fist, and placing the other on my chest, holding me at arms-length with that surprising strength I always seem to forget about.

"She's not dead, just gone." Ange's tone is steady if a little breathless. "Cole's beyond your reach now. Go home, Ravel."

I tear out of Ange's grasp, wheeling to scour the room for evidence she speaks the truth. We've both spent so long lying to one another, after all. But there's no trace of Cole left in the tidy, threadbare room to confirm her fate one way or the other.

Amy cowers against the useless stranger, avoiding my gaze and dragging him down as he tries to do something foolishly heroic. Ange taps her toe and motions to the makeshift door. But the other one, the child, now she's interesting. She glares up at me and says, "You're the bad guy, aren't you? My Ash took her far, far away, so there."

―――――――

This is how I imagine the beginning, pieced together from what I know, and what I've heard, and what must have been:

The infant's dark eyes reflect Maryam's inhuman gold as her elegant hand trembles over the ink of his hair, the warmth of his skin, and withdraws. The Mayor of the Towers of Refuge turns away from the child she has brought into her broken, dying world.

This is me at five days old.

―――――――

To a small child of the Underground, I'm the bad guy. In the wild, hungry halls of Freedom, I'm the promise of everything they've ever wanted to have and be. But in Refuge, I'm something else entirely.

Too many things, if it comes right down to it.

To the mindless drones toiling away in the carefully choreographed tedium and isolation of the work divisions, I'm invisible—just another faceless, nameless body in the crowd. Mandated isolation has become instinct; it's rare for one to look up, blanched skin paling even more and leaden eyes widening as they take in the inhuman gold light of my eyes, the lesser gold of my still-human skin, just as alarming in this place where all color has been excised.

For the lucky few, the ones that do look up and don't look away, I'm something more: a whisper of temptation in a weak moment, a nudge in the wrong direction, a teasing glance, or an under-the-table deal.

To their grasping, jostling supervisors, to the poisoned and poisonous division heads and council members, I'm the shadow prince, heir to a throne that will never be vacated, stand-in for the untouchable golden beauty of the legendary woman who gave me life. And, just as important to their purposes if not more so, king of the black market.

I'm the one they go to when they want something—anything—and I always leave them wanting just a little bit more.

I know everyone's secrets, I hold all the keys, and my hand is in every deal worth making.

But to the Mayor of Refuge, the one they call my mother, I'm just a servant.

Once, I thought her experiments might change all that. Then, later, I thought building my own empire in the abandoned halls below the tower might make her look at me differently. No matter what I've tried, what I've done or has been done to me, I have never managed to please, disappoint, or horrify her enough to see me.

That's about to change.

This is what I dream:

The child I was wallows on the precious rugs and scoots, nearly but not yet crawling, across polished floors, drooling on the extravagant relics of a lost world. He chases the clicking of glittering stiletto heels, babbling and pawing at diaphanous skirts as they float past.

Maryam-mama forgets herself, inhuman gaze softening for a moment before cutting away once more.

It's not a memory.

It can't be.

Because this is what I remember:

I stand at attention in a crisp, black uniform, a motionless shadow waiting on Her Worship, Maryam Ajera, Mayor of the Towers of Refuge, Chief of the Council of Guardians, First Mother to the Citizens, and the Breath of Tower Regulation.

She is not to be called mother.

She has left this to others to make clear. She prefers not to speak to me at all. It is sufficient to simply gesture, to merely suggest her desires, so that her wishes might be met as if by magic.

I forget myself—only small mistakes—shifting to scratch an itch, drifting forward into her field of vision, running through the halls when I think she can't see me.

I'm banished to a lightless cell for two days for daring to peek back into her audience chamber when sent away. For much longer, when I'm caught in her forbidden rooms staring at an ancient photo of a woman who looks almost nothing like her holding an infant who looks alarmingly like me.

I cry out in the haunted dark as those as hungry for power as they are resentful of those nearest it paw at golden skin—as near to hers as they're ever likely to get—and nightmares whisper in my ears. It's only when I fall still and silent that I am released.

This is me at eight years old. Still nameless, yes, but learning.

Becoming.

The secret to getting what you want is knowing what everyone else wants before they do—and making them think you're the only one who can give it to them. But that only works as long as you make sure they never actually get it.

Maryam may hold the title Mayor of the "Towers of Refuge," but for the whole of my life, we've been down to just the one tower. The others fell—three before I was born and one soon after—to disobedience and insurgency, or to the corrosive poisoned fogs, or to the Mara, the dream-eating nightmares devouring every last soul. The whispered tales and official accounts never agree, nor do they detail exactly what happened. In any case, the council members remain. Five for each of the massive buildings that once stood, and every one of them jockeying for power as if they stand a chance of ever stepping into top spot. The mayor's is a lifetime appointment, and, based on Maryam's exquisite looks and apparently perpetual youth, her devil's bargain with the monsters comes with much more than a normal lifespan along with all the power.

The Council of Guardians meets once every four weeks, but each member sneaks in separately to see her at least twice as often as that, bringing petty grievances and scavenged gifts in pathetic attempts to curry favor.

It didn't take long to convince them there's greater benefit in trading with me first.

Today it's Shaughnessitu who steps out of the elevator, rat-like eyes gleaming under dual bands of gold woven for protection into the suspiciously shiny and soft-looking span of his hood, clearly not made of the coarse, standard-issue fabric. He plays at following regulation while skimming the best of the goods seized by Refuge Force, the guards-turned-military division he heads up for our supposed protection and defense.

I sweep him into Maryam's antechamber, ostensibly to await her attentions. But I'm the one he presents with his gift of the week—a pile of grimy golden chains, probably seized in a raid from some hapless scavenger clinging to life on the streets outside of Refuge's protective walls. It's astonishing the city ruins haven't been picked clean decades ago, though the towering ruins are admittedly vast, and the risks of moving through the waterlogged streets and toxic fog, considerable. The Mara aren't the only monsters who rose with the sea.

"Delightful." I stroke the links as if the slime doesn't repulse me, surreptitiously checking to see if the glimmering metal is solid or, more likely, mere plate. "Her Worship was just saying to me last week how she felt in need of fresh adornments."

"I always tell my men to keep an eye out for trinkets for Mayor Ajera." He winks. "But do they listen? Useless lumps. No, I'll have you know I collected these personally in a raid only yesterday. I do like to keep my hand in the game, so to speak. You'll put a good word in her ladyship's ear, I trust?"

"My pleasure," I murmur, draping the filthy chains over a satin cushion that is instantly in need of laundering. Or burning. "Her Worship is always most appreciative of your little attentions. Just as your friends will be tonight, I'm sure."

His ratty eyes twinkle at the thought of pleasures to come. Freedom provides escape for many, and though not all forms are to my taste, keeping a close, if hidden, eye on them is often to my benefit. At least I no longer have to personally cater to the desires of those I need power over.

I've come that far, if not yet far enough to treat animals like this the way they deserve.

If my smile becomes a touch fixed, the master of Refuge's brutal enforcers doesn't seem to notice, and I manage to herd him back to the elevator and away with enough time to "misplace" his gift before Maryam returns.

She will never see the chains. Another day, I might slip them to one of Ange's underground artisans to be cleaned and reworked into a usable form—adornments for a dancer in Freedom or threaded into Refuge's questionably effective wards against the Mara.

Today, I can't afford to be so charitable. I'll need every resource I can steal or scavenge to go after Cole and bring her back, and the longer I have to work to stockpile everything I'll need, the harder it will be to track her down.

I get to work, calling in favors, gathering supplies from the scavengers outside the tower walls, and the artisans below, and the manufacturing heads above. I weave web upon web of misdirection to ensure there's a nest to bring my prize back to, a reward that will satisfy, a supply chain that won't falter.

The witless leaders of Refuge are certain to try to seize my network and turn it to their own purposes if they realize I'm gone. Their counterparts in Freedom are probably too indolent to really make much progress, but I'll make sure they're occupied, nonetheless. Even Ange must be dealt with, cajoled and persuaded, and carefully steered to take the right actions at the right times. The Mara can't be manipulated or managed into compliance, but that can't be helped. They've been out of my control for a while now. I prefer not to dwell on the fact that I was ever so foolish as to think I had influence with the monsters in the first place. They're dangerous, but they're not my biggest concern, not for the moment.

It's hard enough work planning the rescue mission, nevermind a revolution to follow, but I am almost certain all will be well—just so long as I can bring Cole back with me.

Even an unwanted child has choice, and this is what I choose for myself:

I am disobedient. A disappointment.

The only time Maryam deigns to look in my direction is when I defy her. So, I do. Repeatedly.

It's a winning strategy, though not without cost. Every time I'm sent away to be punished, I wonder if it will be the end for me. Of me. Of the tenuous unspoken us, *she cannot fully erase.*

But time and again, I'm brought back to stand in the shadows behind her, to dance silent attendance on her.

I watch. I learn. I see the shame she hides, the sacrifices she makes, the flaws in her performance of beauty. The cracks in her perfection give me hope.

But I am still young and so alone.

If she would only turn and look, if she would truly see, reach out to me . . .

My waiting is not rewarded. She keeps her back turned. And so, she does not see the moment I give up on her.

I have never seen another child. But I know this one is something special from the moment I lay eyes on her. I feel it, just as I felt her and the others the moment they crossed the supposedly impenetrable boundary and entered the city.

She's dragged in with a dead man and a dying woman who flickers with a living mist that limns her skin and lights her eyes.

The child sees me hiding in the shadows. Her eyes, aflame with silver, lock on my dark ones. Desperate. Pleading.

When the woman dies, the mother, *the light goes with her. But though the child falls, her own light fading to nothing, she does not die.*

I knew then, just as I do now, that I would do anything to be seen by Cole one more time.

The worst moment is when I place my hand against the sick shine of the barrier and push, only to draw it back dripping with icy brine.

The barrier was supposed to be impenetrable, but Cole's family crossed it once, blinking into being on the crumbling streets that would prove their tombs. Just weeks ago, a new presence flickered to life inside my mind as Ash, another dreamwalker—for as near as I can tell, that's what they were—crossed after her. And now he's taken her away from here. From me.

But I know I can bring her back. The sense that brings the silvery magic of the ones like Cole to life like a beacon inside my mind is just one of the benefits of being the mayor's pet research project. Over the years, she's rewritten me into a creature as much like *them* as humanly —or inhumanly—possible. It only hurt most of the time.

So, when I square up to the barrier that has trapped ravenous monsters and panicked survivors together in a decaying arena of death for generations, crossing it isn't my biggest concern.

It's what's on the other side that terrifies me. I'll have nothing, but what I can bring with me into a vast and probably deadly world I know of only through century-old tales and crumbling records. I've prepared as well as I can, scrounging a battery-powered two-wheeled contraption that will supposedly draw power from the sky once I get it out of these tunnels for speed, and loading it down with as much food as it can take. I even have an old, rust-pitted knife, though such inelegant methods have never been my preference.

But it hadn't occurred to me until just now that I might have to swim my way out.

I march in circles puffing and wringing my chilled hand, trying not to think too much about the cold dark water. About how I'll be flinging myself out into it with no control over what I'll find in its airless depths. Or what might find me.

I'll dive in any minute now. Preferably, the next minute after now. Or the one after that . . .

I trip over a small pack sitting against the tunnel wall and give it a kick in petty revenge. It has extra sealed food and water, lights, and two sets of spare clothes—one in my size, a smaller set in hers, in case we need supplies on our return. I'm usually a good planner. I've had to be.

Enough feeling sorry for myself.

I pull a larger pack off the back of the bike and fish a map out of its depths. There's useless writing on one side of the yellowed paper, left over from whatever book it was I ripped out of, and on the other, my careful sketch of an even older map of the city, with the flooded bits shaded in.

One of the many secrets I've uncovered over the years is that the sea level has gone down a little since the worst of the flooding took the city. Not enough to clear the old, overland routes, though. I'm effectively stranded on an island.

This underground tunnel looked like it would get me nearest to dry land on the other side, but close doesn't count for much when the waves stand between. I examine the map, hunting for a better path in vain. Then I fold it and place it carefully in the supply pack, moving the whole thing further down the tunnel in case the sea tries to invade on my way out. A map of the city inside the barrier won't do me much good on the other side.

I wheel the bike back to the same point, a juncture where this tunnel joins another. Maybe if I hit the barrier at speed, the bike will throw me far enough through the water that I can reach the shore.

I lean in close, hugging the frame, and take a deep breath, cheeks, and chest ballooning as I hold it behind pinched lips and gritted teeth. Then I gun the engine and fling myself into the merciless ocean.

The secret to staying in control is never showing weakness.

I learned this from the woman who made me. She hides away when the Mara come and strip her of youth and beauty and the illusion of complete mastery she projects over every living soul in the tower. She makes her bargains in secret and shadows and emerges into the light only when her flawless image has been restored.

I learn a lot of things, watching from the dark and hidden corners. I learn about her deal with the Mara, about the lives she sacrifices to keep Refuge running, the orders she gives to keep each division operating with mindnumbing yet essential efficiency, the punishments she metes out to any who disrupt that rigid clockwork. I uncover more of her experiments, her research, her quest for more and different power, the quest that led her to make me and to continue striving to remake me into a more useful tool.

She manufactured me like she manufactures Noosh, but for a very different consumer. Only that experiment went wrong, and instead of a soulless and silent human-meal-replacement, she ended up with me.

I don't know if she ever tried again, or if there were experiments before me. Black-eyed brothers and sisters sent to the Mara in the place of her mindless serfs to protect the working drones in this hopeless hive of futile activity. If there are, she's hidden them well.

But in the meantime, she's found a new purpose for the failed experiment I became.

The tattoos started sometime after I learned to walk, and before Cole's parents were killed, and she was folded into the machine of Refuge like any other stolen child.

Black ink lines pricked into my body, one by one. I only screamed the first time.

It only took that first time, seeing the way Maryam's eyes shone, the way she watched so closely for days afterward. She started between my shoulder blades and worked her way out, so slowly, there was always time to heal, time to forget the full force of the pain, time to ignore the way the prickling sense of things unseen crept up on silent feet.

When the pattern finally wrapped around my shoulders and started creeping down my arms, I waited until she was out of the room, took off my shirt, and looked in her mirrors. The heavy black marks were sharp-edged, curving across the ridges and hollows of my flesh.

They looked utterly, tantalizingly alien—until that breathless moment when a family was dragged into Maryam's chambers with eerily familiar patterns of silver mist swirling across their skin.

I have many secrets from Cole. She already hates what little she knows of me; how much would her loathing grow if she knew I was the one who caused her parent's death and her own capture? My stolen, false power, my traitorous desire to draw Maryam's gaze, my unknowing words that raised the alarm and tore apart her world. Her self

My guilt, and fascination, and ignorance, and need, tearing her life apart over and over again.

This is me at thirteen years old, the year I named myself.

The barrier stings my skin like a thousand tiny pricks of a needle, stealing my air and heating my blood. But it's only a moment before the press of water shocks away that instant of painful heat.

Water sprays high on every side and drags at the wheels of my bike but does not engulf. The bike wobbles, engine whining, and I swing off to prop it up before it falls with me under it.

The water doesn't even reach my knees. I take one careful step—the ground shifts beneath me, soft, unseen, somethings brush my ankles—and then another, dragging the sinking weight of the bike through the uneven underwater surface. Only then do I trust my lungs to the open air, crisp, and salt laced.

I clamp down on the sudden urge to turn and dive back into my familiar, poisonous little world. The sky is too distant, the air too clear, the soft, familiar buzz of Cole's presence crushingly remote.

I climb the clinging, wet slope to the pebbled shore all at once, sucking back a cheer: Cole's *alive.*

I crossed the barrier. I can sense her, which means I can track her. And once I do, I'll do whatever it takes to bring her home with me.

Elation gives way to shivers. I rummage through the mostly-dry pack on the back of my bike, pull out a second map, sparing a just a thought for how miserable I would be right now if I'd lost the lot of it at the boundary or in the waves and had to swim my way free of the city.

Though, according to the map, I was still in the city. My whole world up until today had consisted only of a small peninsula jutting from the top of the dense tangle of streets on the map, a near-island of downtown core separated from a mass of once-occupied land so large I have no way of picturing it in my mind.

And beyond this city, another, and then another, radiating out everywhere that wasn't mountain or sea, and even in some spots that were, all the way to the edge of the map.

Cole hasn't been gone *that* long. So, hopefully, she's holed up somewhere in one of the closer cities with that useless sixer who stole her away. I can sense a shimmer of other dreamwalkers around her, but I'm not familiar enough with Ash's signature to confidently say it's him. Good news if they've separated.

The not-so-good news? She feels as distant as the stars, and all of the once-inhabited areas around here were supposed to have been pretty battered when the old world ended, so there's a strong possibility they headed up into the mountains.

That's on the third map, the one I traced last minute, just in case. The further from the coast, and the higher up you go, the fewer people-places there were . . . but these maps are over a hundred years old, and who knows what's out here now, besides monsters.

Thankfully, monsters have never shown much interest in me. Not as food, anyway.

They took Cole away from me, not knowing she was always meant to be mine.

They treated her like any other stolen child, strapping her to a cot and pointlessly wiping away all that made her, so she could be as blank and useless as any other drone.

I didn't understand why. Why, after all the effort to make me the perfect hunter for her kind, Maryam took away her magic the moment she got her hands on her.

I was younger, then.

It's as good an excuse as any: I was younger, and full of rage, and desperate to make a world that didn't hurt so much. A world where magic could live and breathe without its light being torn away.

So, I started building Freedom.

There were always underground parties, breakaway groups who snuck off into the abandoned lower levels to indulge in all the ways forbidden under Maryam's smooth, iron fist. It was dangerous and officially forbidden, but everybody with power knew about it, and the mayor tacitly permitted it with the understanding that if people wanted to go to such efforts to offer themselves up to the Mara, they might as well go and do it where she wouldn't have to clean up after them.

Her division heads and council members were less pragmatic when I approached them. More than one proved interested in an exclusive playground outside of her golden gaze. They gave me what I needed to bring it to life, in return for being and doing what they wanted—at least at first, before I clawed my way into enough power to turn the tables on them.

But Freedom was never just a private wonderland for dissipated fools. It was always meant as a challenge to Refuge. Instead of control and abstinence to keep from tempting the hunger of the Mara, every desire would be expressed and filled, without restraint or delay. No stray longing or craving could call the monsters if all that the people wanted or needed was provided.

And I was the one who would build it. Rule it. Challenge Refuge's dominion and bring it to its needs. When the world was safe for her magic once more, I would bring my silver-eyed girl out of her sleep and lay it all at her feet while my maker looked on in despair.

I was younger then. I knew of the Mara, but they had not yet come to me.

That changed.

I keep a brisk pace away from the ocean, the inky hairs on the back of my neck prickling as I imagine the waves and their sharp-toothed inhabitants surging in pursuit. But I hear nothing but my own damp boots squelch-crunching alongside the crackle of tires.

Cole is a vanishingly distant weight at the end of a line with its hook caught in my insides, and it's all I can do to keep from riding straight after her. But the cities-map of the old world shows a landscape hostile to moving in a straight line almost anywhere. There were inlets and huge rivers, and not-so-huge lakes and even a stream could prove an impassable barrier if I couldn't find a bridge still standing. Already I've had to sidetrack around piles of rubble and pits of cratered earth, and I'm still within reach of the rush and roar of the waves.

If Cole's in the mountains, I'll have to take a wide detour to climb out of the wide, deserted valley with its ruined cities. My steps slow, shuffling first one way, then another, hopelessly trying to gauge the best route as I crinkle the edges of the map.

In the end, I just get on the bike and follow the almost-painful tugging inside, day after day. I backtrack and circle and wait for the sky to clear so the bike can gather enough energy to go on, and then try all over again. And the whole time I wander, from coast to inland city to mountain ranges and beyond, I wrestle with how to get Cole to come back with me when I finally reach her.

She won't do it just because I ask. Any trust she might once have placed in me has long since shattered. Forcing the girl you like to participate in human sacrifice, even for a good cause, turns out to be hard on a relationship. I like to think that offering myself to the monsters in her place gained me back a little ground, but the last time I saw her, she was still glaring daggers, so perhaps that was less of a power move than I'd hoped.

Luckily, I don't actually need Cole's trust or her affection, not for this. All I need is leverage. The real question is: what does she want that only I can give her?

The journey through the mountains doesn't interest me. The answer to that question, though, that's what drives me through failing supplies and chafing skin and rivers frothing with monsters. It keeps me plodding onward even after the bike refuses to start, until I find myself, finally, at the end of the road with a wall barring the way.

The barrier back home is much taller, made of a sickly shimmering force instead of mere earth and wood and metal, but, at least to me, this lesser wall is far more impenetrable. And I've arrived with blisters and chapped lips and a savagely pinching belly, but no answers to that all-important question: what does Cole want?

So, I sit down at the edge of the road and stare at that rustic but formidable wall and the dreamwalkers' forest city beyond and wonder what I'll say or do when the gates open.

The Mara don't need tricks to get you to do what they want. They don't hide in the shadows—they are the shadows, and they're always listening. They know what you want before you do.

They didn't want my life—they wanted a direct line on the power I was building. Why, I don't know. They can take whatever they want, whenever they want. Whoever they want.

All our petty attempts at following the rules, protecting ourselves and each other, and it comes down to nothing more than the games they play behind closed doors. The deals they make. Maryam's deal—an eternity of youth and beauty and power over life and death, just so long as she filled her quota of lives sacrificed to the nightmares.

So, maybe I do know why they came to me. They devour life, more than the living. They crave the wanting, the desire, the longing, the struggle, the pain, the fear, the misery. All of it.

The price of opening Freedom, of mastering my own domain, was paid in blood. The same poisonous bargain as the woman who made me: blood in exchange for power. The chance to choose which lives to protect by choosing which lives to sacrifice and when, if not how many.

It was a terrible choice, but not an impossible one. I adapt. I survive. I thrive.

It cost me Ange's friendship, and Cass's before they took him right in front of me. She's turned out to have been more useful as a rival and leader of the Underground than a friend anyways, but Cass . . . Cass was . . .

Cass is too recent. Too hard to think about. But I can't stop thinking about it, because his death is where it all broke down.

The Exchange—that ritual sacrifice of one life for many, the public celebration of my absolute mastery of Freedom and, in the eyes of my people, dominion over the Mar—made powerless. The Mara flaunting their own power as mine shattered, betrayed for all to see.

It was very nearly the end for me, for all of us. It still could be.

The Mara made the rules, and now they're breaking them one after another. Killing at will. People only follow Maryam and I out of habit and *helplessness, but even if they did muster the strength to revolt, they have no defense against the Mara.*

They won't fight back, though. No, it's more likely they'll simply close their eyes and wander into death unseeing.

Unless we lead them in a different direction. A new direction.

If Freedom has taught me anything, it's that people want a leader.

They want to hope. They want more. And they don't want to die—at least, not in pain and horror.

They're mostly just not ready to do anything about it on their own.

And that's it—the key I need to get to Cole.

The people.

I take my time, despite what has to be a mounting death toll back home. I wait and watch from the forest for the perfect moment.

Even when Cole finally walks out of the city full of dreamwalkers and into the forest with only a powerless girl for company, I stay out of sight, trailing them in the shadows.

Cole looks different. Fuller, somehow, stronger, her expression less guarded, more open, though she bickers and pretends irritation with the short, round-faced girl—Grace, Cole calls her. It's adorable and unsettling, the way Cole growls and stomps and grumbles. I've never seen her so happy.

I hang back far enough only that unerring sense of Cole's presence keeps me from losing the girls altogether. When they stop and sit by a stream, I don't dare risk getting close enough to catch more than the odd word without giving myself away. I nearly fall off the log I've perched on, though, when powerless little Grace suddenly flickers to light, both in my mind and with that trademark silvery mist of dreamwalker shimmer. Thankfully, the small cascade they're sitting near seems to make enough noise to drown out my flailing.

I didn't know they could switch their power on and off like that. Apparently, I won't be able to rely on my senses to warn me if there are any of their people nearby . . .

I crane my neck, checking in every direction to make sure this isn't some kind of trap. No one's behind me, but I must have missed something important, because suddenly Cole is crashing past—thankfully, without seeming to register my presence. I barely have time to slip behind a tree before Grace chases her down, the both of them yelling and stomping.

I creep closer, trying to figure out what happened. Is this my chance? If that other girl would just give Cole some space to get good and angry on her own, I could sweep in and—

It's all I can do to stay silent when the monster comes to her.

It's not Mara—a formless nightmare of fog-shrouded claws and fangs. It's not one of the slimy, sharp-toothed things in nearly every body of water I passed on the way up, either. It's like nothing I've ever seen.

One moment, Cole's battering a poor, defenseless tree in a fit of anger over . . . whatever it is that set her off. The next, this huge fluttering, creaking tree-like *thing* is looming over her. And my beautiful, magical, impossible girl just picks herself up off the ground and starts attacking it before I can even think of stepping in.

Apparently, she's learned a thing or two out here, too. She's not standing at a distance fighting on the unseen plane like a dreamwalker, but getting right up in its . . . well, it doesn't have a face, exactly. Up in its bark? Up in its branches?

In any case, she almost looks like she knows what she's doing, using her fists and her feet to full effect. Not that it has much effect on the creature. She tires long before it does, and as much fun as it was seeing her attempt to literally kick a monster's ass, I have to wonder why she doesn't just use her powers to shred it into nothingness.

Then, without warning or apparent reason, the monster does disappear. I sneak closer on careful steps. How did I miss the moment she took it out? She shows no sign of the starlit glimmer of her power, but the treeish thing is definitely gone, and both girls seem to have come through unscathed.

I trail them back to the cascade, daring to follow a little closer this time. They're not paying the slightest attention to their surroundings, nor are they headed back to the safety of the city walls. Instead, and despite the recent attack, they settle peacefully on the bank of the stream, Cole holding a clump of something dark and solid in her arms, Grace empty-handed. Both girls close their eyes.

Grace's power switches back on, but Cole . . . she just sits there, dappled with sunlight through the leaves and reflections off the water. No silver mists her coppery brown skin, no longer tinged by the sickly gray of Refuge, nor does it glitter in her tangled dark hair. I ease away from the heavier shadows under the trees and take a deep breath—and dive for cover as she jumps to her feet and hurls the thing in her arms into the water with a low cry.

Not the right moment, after all.

Cole rocks on the bank for a moment, hands braced on her hips, and then stomps right into the water, sloshing in dizzy loops as the dark object bobs around in the current before cornering it against a tangle of roots on the far side. She slogs back to where she'd started and, drenched to the waist, stretches out in the sun, one hand on the thing she's just rescued from the stream. It shines in the sunlight, droplets glistening as they roll down its knotted sides. The color and texture look like wood, but the surface seems polished, almost silky, with neither the roughness of bark nor even of cut posts, though the form is knotted and whorled. I don't remember her carrying it before fighting the tree monster. Did she take it from the creature, somehow?

She sits up, running her hands over the bit of wood. It sits well in her hand, balancing easily on her upturned palm. Her shoulders soften, her face relaxing as she gazes at this strange object from the forest, and there's this moment where she looks so peaceful it makes my stomach twist.

A cold sweat prickles across my skin. The earth seems to drop out from under me. I've come all this way, given up so much, risked everything, really, to find her and bring her back . . . and it might just be time to accept that I haven't been waiting for the perfect moment to make my entrance, but for a sign—or even the slightest hint of one—that I won't be ruining her life by forcing my way back into it.

My mouth is dry, every muscle in my body knotted against the truth at this moment. It will kill me to walk away from her. I know it will. It will be the end of everything I have ever wanted and worked toward, everything I am.

If she doesn't come home with me, there's no point in going back at all. I'm no one out here, and I have nothing. I might as well turn and walk into the nearest river and flail around until the waters or monsters take me.

I fight the shaking, shove against the stubborn resistance in my very bones, and take that first step away from her. I've sacrificed more lives than I can count to make a place for her—and then, even more lives to keep her in it with me. Now there's only one life standing in her way, and I'm not about to start crying about it yet. I take another step, and another, always backward, so I can keep my eyes on her until the last possible moment.

Then Cole twists and is sick over the edge of the bank.

My heart stops. Maybe she was injured earlier or poisoned somehow. She needs help—

But before I can take more than a step toward her, she jumps to her feet and hurls the knot of wood right at me. I duck, flinging myself behind the nearest tree, and the projectile whistles past, crashing and rolling through the bushes behind me. I chase it on instinct, a half-formed plan whirling into place before my eyes as I shove that near-fatal moment of weakness as deep inside as I can.

Something's wrong. She's not happy here, despite all evidence to the contrary. She hasn't built a new and better life for herself. Oh, she's been trying. She's been trying so hard, it's, making her sick. But she can't just let go and move on.

I still have a chance.

I fish the oddly warm knot of wood out from under the bushes and stroll back through the undergrowth without bothering to soften my steps. And then I toss it right back at her.

"Really, flame?" I say, warm with confidence once more. "I thought you'd be happy to see me."

I'm not wrong.

I know I'm not.

She'd never have been happy there, not really. She'd never have been able to let go of the regret, never been able to forgive herself for giving up on our city, our people.

Even if they were always more hers than mine. Even if the way she felt every death was the only thing that made me notice them at all.

But the same ghosts who summon her back to the fight are wearing her down before she can get there, and all I can do is hold her up while she stumbles and gasps for air.

If I were less selfish, I would have left her to build a new life, instead of dragging her back to where it all began. If I had ever known, ever learned how to love, I might have turned that day and left her in the woods and never looked back.

But even when I try to save her from myself, it's only a ploy to make her care. Because when you're nothing, you have to grab everything you can.

And hang onto it with everything you've got.

ABOUT K.A. WIGGINS

K.A. Wiggins is a Vancouver-born Canadian speculative fiction writer, speaker, and creative writing coach. Her work explores social movements, environmental crises, and identity through intricate, dreamlike tales of monsters and magic. *Boy With No Name* takes place in her celebrated "climate change +monsters" *Threads of Dreams* series on a parallel timeline to book 2, *Black the Tides*.

Website: https://kaie.space

facebook.com/kaiespace

twitter.com/kaiespace

instagram.com/kaie.space

SON OF THE DEVIL

BY ZOEY XOLTON

Time is an illusion, it is said, the creation of man existent only to give meaning to the endless procession of days and nights through which we must march ever onward. Time, or more precisely, the lack of it, makes human life precious—our short years, the fragility of our form. From the cradle to the grave, the life of one man is measured in memories. Love, family, the fruits of his labors; these moments are treasured, etched into the mind, until the day that we breathe our last.

But...*what if your last breath never came?* What if the welcome embrace of death eluded you? What if you couldn't be killed? What if you were truly immortal? What of time? What of the burden of memory? I speak from experience when I say that the pain of loss only amplifies with time. I have heard philosophers and doctors of the mind say that it fades, leaving naught but a scar, a mere reminder of something that once was. However, I have found the opposite to be true. Perhaps it is an easy thing to say when one does not have to endure more than a single, solitary lifetime?

Through all my long years, through the centuries I have lived—if *lived* is what you would call it—the traumas of the past remain fresh and raw in my mind. Like festering wounds, they taint my thoughts and color my view of the world around me. The demons of eras gone by haunt me, forever reminding me of the mistakes I have made and what they have cost, not just me, but those I once loved.

Time has been no salve on my wounds, nor a balm for my heart. Time is all I have, and he is a cruel master. With each day that I exist, he continues to fuel my sorrow and the rage that I have carried for more lifetimes than any one man could ever dream.

I am Vlad Drăculea, once called Vlad the Third, son of Vlad Dracul the Dragon, and perhaps most infamously, I have been known as Vlad the Impaler. But most recently? Simply *Dracula*. I am what man calls a vampire. Once feared, a living nightmare in the shadows, a beast, and monster, a warrior on the field of battle...now, no more than a ghost. To the world, I do not exist. At best, I am a memory, a snapshot in the annals of time, a Voivode of ancient Wallachia; a man, some say a hero, who lived and died; a mortal man.

What I truly am has passed into myth and legend, alongside the werewolf and baba yaga, and yet here I am. Ever present, ever watching, as man marches to the steady, relentless beat of the drum. The world is more connected and more populated than it has ever been. The barriers of land, sea, and language? A thing of the past from which I was born...and still, I am more alone than I have ever been.

I miss my wife, my son, my country, and speaking my native tongue. I miss water and wine, warm meals, and the comforting sounds of a land still wild and untamed, not yet industrialized and deforested. My pain could swallow me whole, plunging my soul into eternal despair, were I to dwell on such things. Perhaps, if I were to share with you these memories, my story—of who I was and how I came to be—the weight of my burden would be alleviated, even if only for a short time.

Let me take you back to old Wallachia, to the ancient Kingdom of Hungary, when I was but a boy, and entirely mortal, when I knew not what bitter plans fate had in store for me.

"I am afraid, Father," I say, small fists clenched by my sides as the emissaries of the Ottoman sultan, Murad the Second, await me. My father, Voivode of Wallachia, holds my shoulders tight as he kneels before me, his heavy brows furrowed.

"Fear is for the weak, son. Do not be afraid. The people of Wallachia need a strong leader. They need the *dragon heart* that burns within you. You are a son of princes—descended from conquerors blessed by God himself. You will come to no harm under Murad," he assures me. "You are a token of my loyalty, and that shall never waver."

I feel hot tears well in my eyes, but by sheer force of will, I do not permit them to spill. I breathe deep and nod. "I will be brave, Father. I will make our family proud."

Vlad the Second allows his stern-lipped expression to soften just a little, just for me. "I know you will, my son." With that, he rises to his feet and, standing beside my mother, a grim mask upon his face, allows the Ottoman envoys to escort me away. I look back just once, as I am led toward what will become my new life and see the pain in my father's eyes. They say more than words ever could. I meet his troubled gaze with all the courage I can muster.

Swallowing my fear, I leave the lands of my forefathers and begin my journey to foreign lands ruled by war, strange Eastern traditions, and an altogether different god.

I am Vlad the Third, Son of the Dragon. I will be brave.

Wiping the sweat from my brow, I ground my stance, long spear at the ready. My sparring partner, Murad's own son and heir, Mehmed the Second, stands several paces away, his *kilij* sabre in hand. We are the same age, he and I, and I know him as well as I know myself. Raised in his father's house, he is more akin to a blood brother than the son of my father's enemy.

Mehmed dances forward, his movements flowing like water. He is an adept swordsman, and easily my equal in combat, yet I am his opposite. Where he flows—smooth, elegant and lethal, his command over his *kilij* as beautiful as a poet's command of the written word—I stab and strike, brutal and fast, like the cobra.

"Are you ready, Prince?" he asks as he twirls, the silver of his sabre glinting in the morning sunlight.

"Always," I retort, a wry smile stretching my lips.

It begins.

Mehmed is fast, his *kilij* slicing through the air, aimed at my neck. I raise my spear, deflecting what would have been a killing blow. Having trained with them myself, I know all too well the keen sting of Ottoman steel. Turn for turn, we engage and parry, neither one of us willing to concede ground or admit fatigue. War burns in our blood as bright as pride, and we fight until the high orb of the sun marks noon.

The Agha of the Janissaries, the commander of the sixty-one regiments of the sultan's extensive army, and our personal combat tutor, signals the end of our match for the day. I obey immediately, returning my spear to right, bowing to our senior as is military custom. Not seconds later, as I straighten, I feel the all too familiar kiss of the *kilij* against my throat. I turn to my brother in arms, my hand straying to my neck. When I pull it away, a trickle of blood stains my fingers.

"Do not drop your guard, brother," he warns, a broad, wicked smile upon his face.

The Agha does not discipline the prince for his transgression.

"You have drawn First Blood," I say. "It will be my destiny to draw the Last." I will never forget the moment his ill-gotten smirk of triumph turned to something more alike to cold disdain.

With the lands of my people a distant memory, my time spent with the Ottoman's continues. As each year passes, I become more certain that I will never see my father and family again. I feel lost, though no one would know it. I keep my despair and inner turmoil to myself. To display emotion is a sign of weakness, and I will not give the sultan the pleasure of my anguish.

In my own right, I have become a soldier of great renown. I fight side by side with Mehmed, and despite his great swordsmanship and his mastery of the tactics of war, it is my name that summons fear in the hearts of the sultan's enemies. For my brutal strength, and my penchant for running my enemies through with my weapon of choice, impaling them upon the field of battle, I am given the ominous cognomen: *The Impaler*.

When the Janissaries march, death flies upon swift wings. I am Murad's Angel of Death. At night, when I retire to my decorated barracks, I wonder if my father, *The Dragon*, has received word of my many exploits, and whether or not he is proud of the man I have become.

The year is 1447, and I am nineteen years old.

Before first light, the Agha announces himself. Rising, I rub the sleep from my eyes in the pre-dawn hours. "Come in," I call in fluent Arabic.

The Agha appears drawn, worry lines etch deep grooves into the corners of his eyes and his temple.

When did he get so old? I find myself wondering. "What is it, Agha?"

The Agha holds his head high, though, for the first time in all the years since I was taken hostage by the sultan, I see unmistakable fear in his eyes. I feel the hairs on the back of my neck rise. Something is not right. I can sense it in my bones.

The Agha clears his throat. "News has reached us that your father is dead."

All color drains from the world around me—all but red. "How?" I demand as evenly as my voice will allow.

"Your cousin, Vladislav the Second, is an ally of Hungary and a traitor to your family. In exchange for the throne, he assisted the Hungarian, John Hunyadi, in laying siege to the Court of Târgoviște last night. It has been said that your father died fighting in the Bălteni marshes as he attempted to save your elder brother, Mircea.

I turn my back on the Agha, pain and rage rising like a tide within me.

"The sultan offers you his condolences, Impaler, and would have you reclaim your ancestral throne as Voivode of Wallachia, in your father's place. You would have Murad's personal blessing in this."

If the Agha continues to speak, I am not aware of it. *My father is dead.* Those four words repeat over and over in my mind, a debauched mantra. The Agha must recognize my spiraling descent because he exits my tent, silent as a ghost. My world begins to spin, and I feel as if I have no control. The rage must be released, the fire extinguished. I throw my head back like a beast and howl out my pain.

I upend the furniture; tables fly, my cot upturned. I hurl anything and everything I can get my hands on. The encampment beyond is silent. The soldiers know better than to come near me. Grabbing my spear and *kilij*, I storm out of my tent and into the cool air. I feel every bit the dragon of my ancestry, my breathing heavy and hot. The darkness seems to envelop me, embracing me like a mother.

Mounting my horse in a single bound, I spur the elegant Arabian beast into flight. We tear through the camp and out into the wilderness beyond the firelight. Dismounting, I tie my steed's reigns to a gnarled tree and leave her to graze in peace. I need to be alone with the world that has forsaken me. Slashing at verdant brush as I go, I disappear into the ancient shadowed forests of the Carpathians.

The moon high overhead, I push through the dark hours of the morning and deeper into the heart of the primeval beech forest. Finding a clearing, I stand tall in the gloom and scream to the heavens. "Why? Why, God, have you forsaken my great family? We have served you without question! We have been your devoted subjects…and this is our due? Answer me!" The silence of the forest is deafening, and the fire within me burns like an inferno, desperate for release. I hack at several trees in rage, frustration, and despair, blunting my blade.

Having spent some of my fury, I drop to my knees, emotionally exhausted. A soldier forged in the heat of battle, beaten into submission, I can go days without sleep. I can march on command and fight until every muscle in my body weeps for reprieve. Yet, for survival, I have repressed all emotion for the better part of ten years. It feels cathartic, yet draining to let the torrent of my inner demons free.

Amongst the shifting shadows, beneath the stars and the rustling canopy of the forest, I feel bereft. A lone, mournful howl breaks the night and my pitiful reverie. My spine stiffens as I raise my head. In my blind fury, I failed to notice the beast's approach. Ahead of me, just hidden by the creeping fog that swirls by the tree line, a pair of golden eyes gleam back at me. Several more pairs reveal themselves, one after the other.

Every fiber of my being is suddenly alert and primed for battle. In the space of a single heartbeat, I am at the killing edge. My years of training have not failed me. Slowly, my fingers creep through the fallen leaves and mist to wrap around the hilt of my *kilij*. I draw it to me with a death-like calm, so as not to provoke them before I am ready. The alpha of the pack steps from the darkness and into the moonlight, and I find myself in awe.

This is no ordinary wolf. The wolves of the Carpathian Mountains are some of the largest anywhere. One alone would easily overpower most men, but I am not most men. This magnificent creature is twice as large as any I have ever seen. Its build is thicker, more muscular, and on all fours, it stands almost as tall as my horse. On its hind legs, it would dwarf me.

Rising to my feet, weapons at the ready, I consider my options. Fighting men is infinitely different to fighting beasts. I can deflect four incoming swords, but half a dozen or more monstrous, fanged jaws, each likely to target a different area of weakness? The odds are not in my favor. What I know to be mere moments hang in the air between us like an eternity. Any semblance of legitimate fear in me dies as my rage comes screaming back, rising like a demon. "What are you waiting for?" I shout in my native tongue.

As if the beasts understand, three wolves are given leave by their alpha to attack, one to each side, and one at my back. Their lunges are staggered, a fine battle tactic, each wolf giving the other the opportunity to make purchase before the next one launches. I spin, a whirlwind of blades. My aim is true, and my *kilij* slices through thick silver fur and soft belly flesh. The first goes down, dragging itself and a ghastly trail of blood into the shadows, whimpering as it goes. It will not survive.

As my blade follows its natural arc, it rends the throat of the second wolf, dropping the beast at my feet before it loses momentum. I follow through with my spear. Spinning on my knee, I brace myself as I drive it through the chest of the beast just as its leap reaches its climax. I use its momentum and my own strength to loose my weapon from its rib cage, and it crashes to the ground, swallowed by the mist with a mournful howl.

My face splattered with warm blood, my breathing ragged, I turn to face the remaining pack. The alpha pads forward and the other glittering eyes in the darkness fade away as they slink back into the black or night. "It's just you and me, now," I say as I catch my breath. "Let's end this."

The alpha circles me, and I pivot with him, never exposing my back. He is bigger than his betas, and no doubt, several times as strong. *Man, versus beast, a tale for the ages.* The wolf launches himself. I twirl— as is the way to fight with the curved Arabic sword—and to my shock, my swipe is too soon. I overextend. The alpha latches onto my upper arm, his finger-long teeth finding their mark. I roar as they sink in, before he swings his mighty head, thrashing me from side to side by my bloody limb.

With seemingly little effort, he swings and releases. I hurtle through the darkness, slamming into an ancient beech. I hit the ground hard, dazed. I rise with difficulty, using the tree for support. My injured arm is covered in blood, from my shoulder to my fingertips. The holes are deep, and the pain is raw. Blades sting, slice, and stab, but the tearing puncture wounds are something else entirely. *I'm going to lose my arm,* I think in horror. I clutch at my arm in a vain attempt to stem the bleeding.

Blinking back stars, it dawns upon me that I am without my weapons. My *kilij* lies discarded at the center of the clearing, and my spear is several feet in the opposite direction. The wolf watches me intently. If I didn't know better, I'd think that he was waiting, studying me—taking my measure. Wincing, I crunch to my left, carefully pulling a concealed dagger from my boot. In the style of the Janissaries, I wield the dagger, the crook of my elbow outward, the hilt of the dagger enclosed in a fist-grip, the blade outward, the pommel toward my chest; a defensive stance, a last resort.

In the battle-worn fog of my mind, I wonder if this is truly to be my end. The second son of the Dragon, the Impaler, Vlad Dracula himself, mauled to death by a wolf. Master of War, Angel of Death to the sultan of the Empire…brought down by a beast of the forest. Were the creature before me not so immense, I would feel shame. With the white fur around his jaws stained with my dark essence, his yellow eyes ablaze, he is the very embodiment of horror. *He is the perfect natural-born killer, more perfect even than I.*

Darkness teases at the periphery of my vision, and I feel faint. Glancing down, I see that I am standing in a pool of my own blood. *I am done for. There will be no justice for Wallachia. I will never see the lands of my home again. What a fool!*

The alpha paws at the earth, growling, he bares his fangs. Pageantry aside, he pounds forward before flying through the dark, a nightmare in flight. With my fast-draining clarity, I tell myself to hold. *Hold. Hold. Now!* Committed to his direction, the alpha's jaws spread wide as he prepares to lock his maw around my throat. At the last second, I twist around the beech, and the alpha makes impact with the tree, instead of me. I swivel back around to the front of the tree, and I stab. I stab for all I am worth, I land a frenzy of blows, again and again, striking like a cobra. I drive it in, hilt deep—into his flank, belly, shoulder, neck, wherever I can while eluding his flesh-rending teeth.

The alpha falls sideways as I land hit after hit. He scrambles away, snarling. I drop to my knees, the last of my energy exhausted. I have lost too much blood. Not even the best doctors in the Empire could save me now. I look the beast in the eye as he charges. He will have me, even if it's the last thing he ever does. As a fellow hunter of my own kind, I understand. I would do the same, given half the chance. *There is no room for mercy in war.*

I ready myself for the monstrous impact and the pain that will signal my end. He will tear out my throat, and I will lose consciousness instantly, dying several moments later. I close my eyes as he reaches the height of his jump—

"No!"

Am I hearing things—my mother's voice? I wonder. *Am I so close to death already?* The impact never comes, and my tired eyes struggle open as I sway on my knees. A woman, *a goddess*, stands on the opposite side of the clearing, arm upraised, palm outward, an expression of determination and power painted upon her beautiful face. My eyes follow hers, and I fall back on my elbows at the sight that greets me.

The alpha hangs, suspended in time, jaws frozen open, primal hatred tensing every muscle in its being. I hear a sickening crack, and the wolf falls, a broken beast, eyes blank. I allow myself to collapse to my back. Sprawled upon the earth, mist swirling around me, dancing stars fill my vision.

"You are he, the Impaler, the Prince of Wallachia," says the woman as her face swims into view. She is kneeling beside me, looking down upon me intently. Pale, white-blonde hair, tangled with fronds of bracken and braided with seasonal blossoms, spills over her shoulders. Upon her brow, she wears a painted, or carved star, I can't be sure, as she begins to fade in and out of focus.

"I am," I manage.

"Do you wish to live, Prince? Do you wish to protect your lands from the traitors and the foreign invaders?"

I try to swallow, my mouth dry. "It is over," I whisper.

"It is not over," she responds. "This is your *beginning*, Lord Dracula."

The ethereal woman draws a short blade from her boot, and I don't even have the strength to flinch. I want to ask, *'What are you doing?'* but I cannot. I feel dreadfully cold, starting at my extremities, like a living entity, it slides through my veins, spreading throughout my body until I understand the phrase 'as cold as the grave' intrinsically.

"I am Astrid, and I am going to save you," says my unlikely champion. Taking the dagger, she slices her palm, licks the blade, and begins to chant. Her words are foreign to my ear, though I recognize it as being one of the Northern tongues. Her voice rises and falls as she holds her hands above me, her eyes closed in concentration.

She is a witch! I realize. A heathen, working blood magic. Having been raised in the Light of God, I know witchcraft to be an unforgivable sin. *What is she doing to me? Will my soul be damned?* Her palms begin to glow a turgid red, and the swirling mist that envelopes us reflects the dark light. I feel a stab of burning ice in my chest, and I gasp, my body violently shuddering in response.

Astrid's voice changes, her feminine tone gone, as if someone or something—ancient and timeless—speaks through her. With all my failing strength, I will my eyes to remain open. Her head turns, cocking to the side to look me dead in the eye, an unmistakably inhuman movement. Her eyes are pools of black, gateways into the great Void beyond our world.

"Drink!" she commands in a deep, demonic voice. "Drink of the blood of the Dark One and live eternal! Seal your covenant, and each soul you take shall be mine!"

My eyes roll back in my head, and I blink repeatedly to stay conscious. Warmth spills into my mouth, the tang of iron strong. I cough, my entire body screams with pain.

"Drink!" The voice is that of the Devil.

I swallow, my throat flexing as I try to save myself from choking— from drowning on the blood that is being forced upon me. I feel the blood burn as my body accepts the dark offering.

"Astrid," I whisper with what must be my last breath.

Her eyes are ice blue once more, and with a stern, but comforting smile, she clutches my hand. "I am here, Prince. Sleep now, I will be here when you awaken."

Awaken? I'm dying...

I sit upon the throne of Wallachia, the rightful Voivode, my beautiful wife—the Doamna Astrid—by my side; the crimson, gold, and sapphire banners of House Drăculești proudly on display. Musicians and entertainers fill my halls, and Bran Castle resounds with joy. Today marks our son's tenth birthday. Mihnea cel Rău is the apple of my eye. Dark of hair, like me, but gifted with ice blue Nordic eyes of his mother.

Mihnea sits upon the steps of the dais, opening gifts presented to him by the Boyars, the nobles, of Wallachia, and Moldavia. Wine flows freely, and it seems that despite the terrors of my past, all is well.

"Father, Father!" says my son, as he comes to my side. "Look! My very own throwing ax. It even has my name inscribed! Can we go hunting soon, please, Father? I long to try my crossbow, too!"

I smile at my dear boy's enthusiasm, and I am taken back to my own childhood. "We shall go hunting in the spring when the deer are plentiful, and their numbers renewed after the long winter."

"Thank you, Father! I can't wait!"

I kiss my son on the head as he leans into me affectionately. "Go now, play with your friends. It's not every day you turn ten."

Mihnea goes to move when the ancient oak doors of my feasting hall burst open. I catch my son's wrist instinctively. A contingent of twenty-four soldiers, a half dozen bannermen, and two emissaries bearing the crest of the Ottoman empire march in, brazen and bold, fearless. I feel Astrid stiffen beside me, and her hand seeks my forearm in comfort and unity.

My men's hands rest upon the hilts of their swords, but they remain still, put to ease momentarily with a look.

"Would you have peace, brothers?" I ask evenly as the emissaries come to a halt at the foot of the stairs. I recognize them all. The one called Ekrem inclines his head, meeting my eye.

"We would have peace, wherever possible," he replies.

"It seems a strange way to keep the peace, and ill-mannered, Ekrem, to march in on a birthday celebration, unannounced, and uninvited."

"You have my personal apologies, master Drăculea. As you well know, I go where I am told."

I know why they are here, and every bone in my immortal body fills with rage.

The emissary continues. "We are here on behalf of His Excellence, the blessed sultan Mehmed, and son of Murad. Ten years have come and gone since you defected from his father's army, and by way of forgiveness, and to keep the peace, he would ask the firstborn sons of Wallachia, including your own, brother," he says.

My hall is silent, as if every last man, woman, and child is holding their breath. All eyes are upon me, hanging on the silence that precedes what I will say next.

"In the name of peace?" I ask. "Of course." I rise from my throne, and my eyes turn black. "Wallachia is no vassal state to the Empire, and we will pay no such tribute."

Ekrem's eyes are wide as he notices the none-too-subtle change. "You are a demon!" he accuses. "Blessed, Allah! Mehmed will have his price, whether it is paid willingly, or paid in blood."

I feel a deep, sadistic grin stretch across my face, and I take a step down from my throne. "If the sultan wishes blood, he shall pay with his own," I say. "Now go, bring word to your master that Wallachia will not bow."

"You are mad!" says Ekrem. "You know the might of the Janissaries, and we have only grown. There will be no Wallachia by the end of this!"

"We shall see," I say, my voice dripping with dark promise.

I watch as they turn and leave, my eyes returning to their usual dark green.

"You're letting them go, Prince?" one of my most loyal knights asks.

I sit back down and signal the entertainers to task. "I am, I will not spill blood this day."

He nods and resumes his place.

"Father, will they take me, like they took you?" Mihnea asks, his eyes full of concern. "I know what they did to you—"

"Quiet, my son. No one is going anywhere, least of all you. The sons of Wallachia will be safe, I promise. Do not let the foreigners spoil your celebration. Go now, make merry, and think no more on it. I will take care of everything."

"Yes, Father," he says, and the Bran Castle resumes its festivities.

"My love?" whispers Astrid. "You have just started a war with the Turks."

I take hold of her hand and kiss it. "I am ending a war that started long ago, my lady," I respond. "Do I not have your trust?"

Astrid's pale beauty overwhelms me, even now, ten years from the night that she called upon the Dark Lord to spare my life.

"You have my trust," she assures me, "and my heart. Always."

I lean in, as does she, and our temples touch, eyes closed. "I will save our son," I promise her.

"I know," she whispers back before she crushes her lips into mine, and for just a few precious moments, my world makes sense again.

The sun sets, and the stretching shadows of the evening melt into the complete, all-encompassing darkness of the night. My keen vampire eyes see as clearly as if it were day. From the balcony of the master chambers of Castle Târgoviște, I wait. The Ottomans are marching. I can hear them, their footfalls like the rolling of thunder through the valley.

Astrid appears silently by my side. "You will be victorious, my love, I have foreseen it," she says.

"I have no doubt of it," I respond. "The Dark Lord has given me more strength and greater powers than God ever did. I will slaughter them all, and never again will the Ottomans dare challenge Wallachia."

My beautiful wife is quiet. Something is amiss.

"Speak to me, Astrid. You are a witch, and High Priestess; what troubles your thoughts?"

She hesitates before she speaks, and I know she is lying.

"Do not worry for me, my love," she begins. "There is no matter on my mind but your safety and that of our son." She reaches out and touches my hand-wrought red armor, emblazoned with the likeness of demons and the scales of dragons. "The Dark Lord has assured me that the enchantments I have woven into your armor will protect you."

"Astrid."

She stands on the tips of her toes and silences me with a kiss. "I love you," she whispers.

When our lips part, I meet her eye, and she smiles.

"I love you, Astrid. I might never have said it before, but thank you —for the gift of this second chance to protect my family and our home. I'll never forget the moment I first laid eyes upon you. You were so strong, so powerful. I thought you a goddess."

"We were fated to find one another," she says simply. "We will always find one another."

Trailing her hand out of my own, she looks back just once, before she takes her leave, her emerald gown billowing in her wake.

I do not know what it is that she is withholding from me, but I have to trust that it is nothing of relevance to the impending battle. *If it were important, she would have shared it with me,* I assure myself. Turning back to the darkness below, I see the torches of war funneling through the pass and into the valley beneath Târgovişte. I can hear the steady beat of almost thirty thousand men's hearts. They seem almost to march in unison, following their feet, and their sultan's pleasure.

"I am coming for you, Mehmed," I say to the wind as it howls by, swirling into the pass, and through the black forests of Wallachia.

The castle is fortified, no one is permitted in—and no one allowed out. Even my most trusted harbor fear in their hearts. They will not say it, but they believe I have entombed them, given them no means of escape, should the siege reach the gates. My people, at least, those within my court, know the nature of the beast that I am. I have never kept it a secret, but I have never displayed the extent of my power, either. I have never wanted to rule with fear. To me, trust and loyalty have always been paramount. I would never use my darkness against Wallachia.

Tonight, however, the world will know of the insatiable violence contained within my damned soul. I will unleash the Devil, and blood will flow in rivers. I will create such a spectacle of the Ottoman Janissary army as to be remembered throughout all of history.

Thousands of torches light the night. The Janissaries are within the valley, and the only way up to Târgoviște is a long, narrow, and solitary winding road up the mountain. In the distance, an almighty rumble shatters the silence. Despite their discipline, the rear of the army turns as one. A great landslide is triggered, and the way is shut, filled with thousands of tons of earth and rock. I smile. They are trapped. My men did their job well.

I hear the change in rhythm of the hearts of the men. They are used to being in a position of power, unstoppable. Now, they are at my mercy, and I will give them no quarter. Spreading my arms like wings, I launch myself into the inky night, plummeting some two hundred feet before I channel my gift of flight. I draw level, just a foot from the ground, and smash thousands of unsuspecting soldiers off their feet.

Panic rises among the ranks as bodies fly, yet in the dark, the source of the attack cannot be seen. I plow through their ranks, like a warm knife through fresh butter. Screams rend the gloom—the sound of breaking bones and spilled blood thrills me, fueling my drive to destroy them. *Kilij* clash and arrows fly, directionless and pointless. Most of them killing their brothers in arms. I laugh, amplifying my own voice with dark magic, and it echoes through the valley, bouncing off the hills and back at the now terrified Janissaries.

I break them all, hundreds at a time, casting them aside like piles of discarded dolls. I could cut them down, slicing them in half. It would only be too easy…but I have something in mind, an homage to my reputation, and I need most of them whole, still in once piece.

Inside of an hour, almost thirty-thousand men are dead, strewn across the valley. Floating above the battlefield, or perhaps, the field of the massacre is the better description, I allow almost seven thousand men fleeing for their lives to scramble away. They will return to their sultan and their families, and word will spread of my terror. No one will ever dare challenge Wallachia again, and that suits my purpose. Ultimately, they will all be put to the sword. The sultan does not abide deserters. It is the very reason why he has come against *me* with such irreverent force.

The morning is still several hours away, which permits me more than enough time to orchestrate my greatest artwork of atrocity to date. It is likely another such scene will never be viewed with mortal eyes again. Through the dark hours, I work, and by first light, I stand before the gates of Târgoviște, reveling in the beauty of my masterpiece.

Word will spread like wildfire of my macabre spectacle, my Forest of the Dead. I smile. Twenty-three thousand, eight hundred, and forty-four Janissaries impaled. I have ensured that *Vlad the Impaler* will never be forgotten.

As my court begins to spill out of the castle, eyes wide, and hands to mouths as they drink in the horror in the valley, I head back inside. "Astrid! Mihnea!" I call. I stop one of my men as he moves to go past. "Have you seen my wife and son?"

"No, my lord. The lady barricaded herself in the Chindia Tower, the last I heard. She said she must not be disturbed."

The hairs on the back of my neck rise, and I feel my stomach drop. I run up the several flights of stairs that lead to the tower, a blur, or a trick of the light, to anyone watching. I reach the solid, iron reinforced door and knock, my heart thundering in my chest. "Astrid? Astrid, open the door." I wait but a few moments before I put my knee through the door and toss it aside. The sight awaiting me shatters my very soul in the space of a single breath.

"No! My love!" The words escape me without thought. I break the circle of blood, salt, and candles. Dropping to my knees, I lift her, cradling her in my arms. "Astrid, Astrid, wake up! Please, open your eyes!" Her beautiful face is pale, and I can hear no heartbeat. "No!" I sob, over and over into her white-blonde hair. "What have you done? Why?"

"She did it to save me," says a quiet, familiar voice, wracked with guilt. "You were protecting all of Wallachia...she did what she had to do."

"Mihnea," I gasp, tears carving a clean path down my bloodstained cheeks. "I don't understand. What happened here?" Then I notice the bloodstain on his shirt.

Standing, he comes to kneel before me in the broken circle. From behind his back, he reveals a bloodied arrow, then placing it in his lap, he opens his shirt, and there, directly over his heart, is an ugly, puckered red scar.

I reach out and trail my fingers across it, and my lips quiver at the terror of it.

"How?" I stress again. "You were safe. You were inside! I barred the doors."

Mihnea tilts his head, gesturing to the far corner of the room. "No one needed to enter, Father. They were already inside."

I follow his gaze and find my most loyal knight, Ștefan, slumped on the floor, dead. All of a sudden, the circle of blood makes sense.

"He told us that a separate contingent of Turks was scaling the mountain and would breach the castle. Then he raised his crossbow... and he shot me. I heard Mother scream, I saw a flash of light, and then, there was nothing but darkness. I think I died, Father. I do not know for how long I was gone, but when I awoke, Mother was dying. She told me not to break the circle. She said that she loved me, and that only life could pay for a life, and that the Dark Lord was calling her home. And then she—" Mihnea wipes the tears from his face with the back of his bloodied sleeve. "Father, she gave her life for me."

"Come here, son," I say, drawing him nearer. Together, temple to temple, we comfort one another and mourn the light of our lives; my beautiful Astrid, my wife, my priestess, the mother of my only child, and the very reason I'm alive. *She saved us both*, I realize. She saved us both.

A funeral is held for the lady of Wallachia, the only loss of life from the night siege on Târgoviște, aside from that of the traitor. How long had he been in bed with Mehmed? I couldn't know, but it sickens me to dwell on it. In the way of her people, Astrid is burned on a mighty pyre, the embers of her mortal beauty soar into the dying dusk. I cannot believe that she is truly gone. My heart breaks with each breath I draw, and I suspect it will, forever.

Then I remember her last words to me: *We were fated to find one another. We will always find one another*, and a small smile tugs at the edge of my lips. If anyone knew the secrets of life and death, it was my precious Astrid. I realize that she was trying to tell me that we would find each other again. I don't understand how, or when, but there was a time I did not believe in the dark entities of the night, so I know better than to question her arcane promise.

In the weeks that followed, I hunted down Mehmed with the passion and deranged fury of a madman. To his credit, despite all that he had heard of what I had become and what I had done, he faced me like a man. I toyed with him, gifting him the slightest of hopes as we dueled, as we once had, back in our youth. No matter how I threatened him, he would not repent for the murder of my wife. With defiance in his eyes, he swore to fight me until his last breath. My patience wearied, I tore out his throat, draining the monster until he was naught more than a husk. I mounted his corpse on a spear, as I had so many before him—a final warning to the Janissaries. No one was safe from my reach, not even the sultan himself.

What remained of the Ottoman armies retreated to the East, leaderless, and fearing the wrath of the Devil himself. I stayed in Wallachia until my Mihnea was a grown man, and I passed on the title of Voivode to him so that he might lead our people into an age of prosperity and joy, free of the tyranny of the line of sultans. Our son became a good man. His mother would have been proud. Though he was aggrieved to see me leave, I felt it was time to explore the world and gift Mihnea the opportunity to forge his own legacy, one outside the reign of blood that I had left in my wake.

With my enemies dead, and my vengeance wrought, I felt no less broken, but finally, I felt free. I had kept my promises all, and in my heart, I found a measure of peace. Though it was not to last...

In the year 1510, when my son was just fifty years old, he was deposed by the Boyars of Wallachia. In secret, they had forged alliances with the Ottomans. The Ottomans wanted Mihnea dead in revenge for my atrocities. With the promise of wealth, the Boyars gave up the independence I had fought so hard for. Wallachia once more became a vassal state, and my son sought refuge in neighboring Transylvania. Then, on the steps of the Sibiu Cathedral, he was assassinated, and I was not there to protect him.

The Ottomans had ultimately succeeded, and I fell into a deep despair. A despair so black and deep that I could not distinguish it from the burning hate in my cold heart. I traveled to the Middle East, and for a hundred years, I stalked, butchered, and drank of its people. A punishment for all that they had inflicted upon me, and my great family. I was never found and never stopped. I was a demon, and there was no escaping my wrath.

I ended the line of sultans, and with the aid of the Western influences, the lands of sand and sun were thrown into chaos, never to truly recover.

And now, dear friend, I am here. A shadow among the realms of the living, I travel from city to city, country to country. My Wallachia of old is no more. It is a once kingdom, now a part of modern Romania. My legend and legacy can be found in textbooks the world over, and my mythology endures, despite the death of superstition among mortal men in these eras.

I have sat in theatres and watched television shows of vampires, and not one, perhaps outside of Bram Stoker's *Dracula*, has managed to convey the true loneliness of an immortal life. In my search for hope, over the course of my long years, I have learned of all the religions and philosophies of the world, and most of them offer nothing more, or less than eternal servitude, or damnation.

Yet, the Buddhists of Tibet offer the concept of reincarnation, of the energy of one's soul living countless lives, learning, growing, and dying, only to be reborn again. This theory of belief offers me hope. Perhaps this is to what my beautiful Astrid had referred to when she said that we would find each other again? Perhaps, despite the hole in my heart, and the despair in my soul, I need only be more patient.

What if my beautiful wife is somewhere out there, just waiting to be discovered? It was she who found me fighting for my life that night in the ancient forest of the Carpathian Mountains. *What if this time, it is my turn to find her?*

Dear reader, I thank you for sharing in my tale, for allowing me to recapture what I had lost. For so long, I have tried to elude the demons of my past, when perhaps all along, I should have been embracing them. It seems that none of us can escape who we truly are, and it may be this very realization that is our salvation.

I am Vlad the Third, Dracula, the Son of the Devil, and I have all the time in the world. My story continues from here, with hope.

The End.

ABOUT ZOEY XOLTON

Zoey Xolton is an Australian Speculative Fiction Author who likes to daydream, and write stories about the beautiful and improbable, the dark and fantastical, as well as the adventurous and utterly romantic! Whether it's fairy tales, fantasy, horror, paranormal romance, urban fantasy, or science-fiction...she dabbles in it. She has been featured in over 100 anthologies to date, and she is currently working on progressively longer stories. She prays you enjoy, and fall in love with the deliciously tempting tales, and the characters that she brings into the world. Writing is her guilty pleasure...perhaps reading it will become one of yours?

Website: https://zoeyxolton.com

facebook.com/authorzoeyxolton

twitter.com/zoeyxolton

instagram.com/zoeyxolton

I AM A MOUNTAIN (Y ESTOY HUNDIÉNDOME)

BY NICK EDINGER

The nurse lady here says my health insurance doesn't cover what I call "getting my ass kicked by Beaver-Man." Unbelievable. Can you see what I have to deal with? I'm at the hospital's emergency room desk, and I gave this woman my name and ID. I'm in trouble if my wife looks up our medical records. And this broad don't even trust my word as a henchman. She didn't mention insurance, I had to bring it up, and I'm pretty one-hundred percent sure that's not how it goes, Okay? Who knows what I said through my searing leg wound? *Estoy a punto de llorar.*

Maybe you don't understand what I just said. Maybe you only speak English so far. Let's keep it that way. I'd like to have some thoughts for myself, and I let you into my head as a favor, *gracias.*

I'm staring at this nurse lady, the only white person in this whole building, by the way, and I point to my swollen leg because it's… well, the leg's actually not so bad. I've had worse. Tonight wasn't my first scrap with Beaver-Man, but if he sneaks up on me and my fellow henchmen like that again… you know, next time I see my boss, I'm gonna tell him my job is to design uniforms, not play cat and robbers.

The important thing is, I'm not crying.

I have a lot of ongoing missions:

#2: Defeat Beaver-Man, that costume creep who won't quit.

#3: Pay off my wife's college debt.

#4: Set up a savings account for my kid with the rest of my dough.

#5: Get back the beer money I gave Jack.

What's Mission #1? Don't cry.

At least until I'm on a rooftop or something. Jack, OddBo, Brianna, Narp, Otis… my fellow henchmen on the bench behind me ain't cryin'. And they all got beat up by Beaver-Man tonight, just like me.

There are henchmen in wheelchairs all over this lobby. I can tell they're henchmen 'cause they wear the black and gold three-piece suits I designed for them. Suits with their ties singed and cuffs ripped, with brown bloodstains, it breaks my heart.

Ripped and burned suits got it easy compared to the five mooks on the bench behind me. Otis whimpers when he shifts his weight, Brianna's arm swings limp from her shoulder, and OddBo… I think you're a little too young to hear about OddBo. Point is, although I've got a throbbing in my lower leg like an overheated motorcycle, I gotta be stoic. I can't cry. In fact, I love motorcycles. This pain, it's nothing. I got everything under my thumb.

All this time, the nurse yaps on. She rubs her eyes. She invites me to sit down at the bench across the room. I wait for her to bring me a wheelchair. After a long silence, she says that my injured companions have half the building's wheelchairs, while Labor and Delivery stole the other half.

So she hands me a crutch. Just one crutch, by the way. I've never used one of these before, but I know how they work. I just move it next to my broken leg as I walk back to the waiting room bench.

My leg flames up with each step. They must've given me a terrible crutch. It takes a few grunts, loud grunts, *gritos*, to walk to where my fellow henchmen sit. They stare at me. Don't know why. I make the same sounds when I deadlift. Narp points to my good leg, then to my crutch. He's always doing weird stuff.

Jack looks over his shoulder as if Beaver-Man will walk through the automatic doors any minute. That sap. He should watch the windows, like me.

I sit at the bench's end and start some rhythmic breathing. I ignore the fuzziness in my eyes. Jack, next to me, doesn't scooch over. I'm not asking him to. I can balance myself just fine on an inch of bench.

Jack's face looks like blueberry pie right now. He's got a foot over me in height. He threw me off the warehouse roof last week, and he could do it again. But I need my beer money back. I gotta confront him, and right quick too.

Jack's a mess, but the other henchmen on the bench remind me of something else. Sinister Sid talked about the five stages of grief when he hired me. What you need to understand is, when Sid's not scheming for world domination, he gives his employees something like a therapy session. Sid taught me to listen to all my voices. Voices that range from "rub your belly" to "rob a bank." And because of Sid's teachings, I see in this room the five stages of henchmen, or at any rate, the stages I went through as a henchman. Let's start with OddBo.

<u>Stage One (Denial)</u>: OddBo, with his last good eye, reads something on his phone. OddBo isn't a henchman, he'll always say he's an "entrepreneur's assistant," and he won't take our dirty henchman money to even buy himself a pillow. I said similar things my first week on the job.

Jack and OddBo, they sit next to each other and talk. Jack declares that if anyone gives him a hospital bill, he'll shove it down their throat. Jack didn't see my hand hover over his shoulder, about to tap him. I dart my hand behind my back. I'd rather go round two with Beaver-Man than face Jack on a bad day.

On my left, Otis writhes on the ground. He clutches his backside and looks to the sky. After tonight's encounter, he doesn't have much of a left cheek anymore. Either left cheek. He's bawling.

I hear a thump from the window. I leap up from the bench, raise my fists, cough as pain shoots through my bad leg. I turn around. Outside the snow-streaked window, there's a kid. The kid giggles as he folds up another snowball. He sticks out his tongue. I flip him off.

I sit back down. Breathe in, breathe out.

<u>Stage Two (Anger)</u>: Jack still rants to OddBo. At any given moment, Jack will complain about how Beaver-Man destroyed Sid's satellite, or how I never let Jack design the uniforms, or how Beaver-Man 'accidentally' (so say the papers) hit a kid. But it's cool. When my godfather got in that ranting mood, he got more results than anyone in the family, especially the women.

I almost forgot to say hello to you. Hello, Destinee Delgado. I'm your father, your Daddy. I suppose you wonder why your Daddy narrates his life to you right now, given that you're likely at home and are most definitely not in this bleached-out hospital with me. This hospital feels like the taste of all the medicine I hated as a kid.

First of all, don't call me Daddy. Call me César Thumb. I guess you can call me César Delgado, since that's my Catholic name and all, but never in public, all right? In fact, just call me *Papá*. Don't presume too much.

We only met once. You were just four months old then. It was the last I saw of you and your *Mamita*. You weren't old enough to remember anything I said, so don't act like you know me that well.

You, Destinee, are only present in my head at the moment. Here's the thing. The reason your *Papá* sends you all those dolls and dresses and American "soccer" balls for your birthday is this. Your *Papá* works for Sinister Sid. Who's Sinister Sid? If you only read the papers, which I'm not sure you can because you're only three, although I could read in Spanish at three but not in English until eight, so those *matones* running my school labeled me 'learning disabled' even though I could run the whole school better than… the point is, Sid gets a bad rap. Maybe it's the streaks of tattoos that cover all skin on him. Maybe it's the bald head like your *Papá* has. Maybe it's because he's a big guy, unlike your *papá*. Maybe it's because he summoned demons from another galaxy to help him in a retail scheme. Who can say? But anyway, Sinister Sid, one of the best men, the best. Took me in when I didn't have a job. Gave me a good salary. Most importantly, he helped me realize myself. Sid taught me this breathing technique where I breathe in until I feel the oxygen pulse through the tubes in my brain and breathe out until my shoulders fall back. He says to use these breathing moments to discern, without judgment, the true will of my inner child. I must follow that will without compromises. And when you see a guy who looks like Sinister Sid seem so relaxed, you know it's legit.

Otis forgot all his meditation lessons. He's up from the ground now. He talks with Jack about outpatients and bills.

Otis says, "Hey César, don't Jack owe you money or something?"

I shake my head so hard that my leg burns. Must be a homeopathic thing. Or was it holistic? Sid would know.

Breathe in, breathe out. Breathe in, breathe out.

Jack and Otis go back to their conversation. They don't even glance at me. I slink back like a child.

Sid once told me, "César, my friend, you must satisfy your inner child. Let go of society's expectations of yourself and be free to act on your own desires." That's what he said. Only thing is, I don't want to talk to my inner child anymore. I hate my inner child. That pussy (and don't let me catch you using that word,) that pussy needs to stop whining all the time. "I'm lonely! I'm scared! I miss my wife! *¡No puedo aguantar esta vida!*" Whine, whine, whine. I don't like whiners. I don't work with whiners. Now you, Destinee, when we met you, you were the quietest baby I'd ever seen. Absolutely wide-eyed, and absolutely beautiful. Smart, too. I'd rather hang out with you than glance at these frosty windows for when Beaver-Man's thick glove punches through them. One day I'll come back to you, Destinee, with a big wad of cash and an even bigger excuse.

I don't want to talk to my inner child. I want to talk to my actual child. Like nothing else. *Mi dolor es más grande que las palabras,* I suppose. I can't visit you anytime soon, I'm too busy, so I'll just talk to you in my head. That's who you are, my psychic link to myself.

I can see you now: puffy cheeks, peach fuzz hair, big eyes, eyes with tears in them. No, don't cry. Don't cry on me. I'm gonna look at you, and I'll do nothing else if you stop crying. I refuse to stare at these awful off-white hospital walls anymore. I breathe in, breathe out, breathe in gasps.

<u>Stage Three (Pleading)</u>: Otis haggles with the nurse from across

the room. He begs in a nasal screech to go next. The last time I cried like Otis, I got a good smack across the face and no supper. If Otis wants to make it in a world of superheroes, he's gotta do what I did: get a henchman name, lose some weight, stop answering his wife's calls.

Jack sniffs his nose and grimaces as if he smells something burnt. He looks at me. I hold my breath.

"I didn't expect to see you here, man," Jack says to me. His voice speaks with all the force needed to talk through a smashed nose and eviscerated— ah, almost let it slip there. I'll describe him to you when you're older.

"You gonna answer me or what?" says Jack.

I tell him, "Look, I'm only here 'cause my wife's always worried about my health."

That part's true.

I then tell Jack, "I barely feel anything at all."

That part is not true. There's, it's, it's like a singularity of sharpness at a point on my lower leg. It's like if the most cringe-worthy scene of one of those stupid telenovelas manifested as a parasite. It's like when Jaime Bosque stabbed me with a hot poker in third grade. That kid was strong.

Maybe if Jack got fixed up, he'd be inclined to generosity. I say to Jack, "Jack, let me take a look at your face, I know medicine." He squirms away from my outreached hand. I don't know why he's upset. The stitches I gave Brianna last year held on for five whole hours. Plenty of time to heal up on its own.

"If you knew anything," says Jack as he pushes himself against the other bench mates, "you wouldn't have led me under that fire escape."

That wasn't my fault.

I say to him, "Jack, if you want me to solve your problem, I'll do it: wear a helmet. Wear two, actually. I just blueprinted something like that. If you give me my money back, I might even make one for you."

His fists tighten, and his body tenses up. I wince.

"I don't see a helmet on your [shiny] head," says Jack.

Now that's uncalled for. He didn't actually say [shiny]: I just put that in my mind because I don't want my inner child to hear such language from a stranger's mouth. You like shiny stuff, right?

But anyways, talking to my inner child like that, who the fuck does he think he is? If Sinister Sid were here, he'd smile with his golden teeth and whisper, "Your emotions are never wrong. Let your desires guide you down every right path, for there are no wrong ones. And remember, if I am not good for you, you are permitted to kill me at any time." Well, Sid, I don't think you should be killed. But my emotions tell me two things right now. One, I want payback. Two, I want to give into my leg pain. I'm only gonna follow one of those things. I summon the sharpness of a hot poker to retort back with, "Go stick your head in a [magic mirror], you [pony]."

Otis gulps.

"Oh [frolic] you, you [princess]," says Jack. "I should be making the uniforms 'round here. If I designed duds, I'd have your suit stick your [Barbie doll] in your [play set]."

Now my actual inner child speaks up. My inner child tells to give Jack a big kick in the [play set] and pummel him until his face resembled Jamie Bosque's. And Jamie Bosque, let me assure you, don't look too good nowadays.

I give Jack a fast kick.

It is loud and painful.

For me.

I used the wrong [wishing] leg.

Everything in that leg seizes, and the nerves flare along with it. I regain my breath. Then I see Jack wind up his arm. It's aimed at my charcoal-colored jacket, in particular the forearm, in particular where my tattoo is hidden.

I punch him in the face before he gets me. He recoils back and collapses into the window behind us. The window wobbles. My knuckles sting, but it don't matter much.

Jack kicks his leg up in instinct. His leg hits Otis in his former left cheek. Otis falls on OddBo and cracks his phone when they hit the ground. They both yelp like a superhero punched their nuts. It's like our scrape with Beaver-Man all over again.

Two security guards hold Jack and me back as we shout insults at each other. OddBo, meanwhile, caresses his neck and calls out for a pillow.

As Jack and I spar in our deadly, verbal duel to the disgrace, the world moves forward. Narp, OddBo, and Otis all get called to the emergency room proper. Six more henchmen replace them in the waiting room. Jack and I don't let up our battle of intelligences. As my leg smarts from the kick, I notice my inner will (as Sid might call it) grows stronger. Instead of remembering how hospital bills can wreck a family, or remembering what my wife looks like, I just need to remember if Jack will know what *pinche puñetas* means. That's a good use of all the air I breathe into my brain. Plus, I usually don't like to brag, but I think I got the upper hand with a decisive "Eat a [Prince Charming]."

When Jack's name is finally called, the henchman sputters out a limp "Well, why don't you ask Beaver Man if that's what happened?" before the two security guards drag him behind the swinging doors to the emergency room. I lay my head against the cold glass behind me. That feels good. For a little bit, at least.

Now here comes the bad part.

Stage Four (Depression): Brianna didn't get called up. She's the only other person on the bench right now. She stares out at the walls. She rocks back and forth. Did the hospital forget her, or did she not hear her name? Sitting there feeling sorry for yourself is a good way to starve on the streets, as I told her before. And, let's be real, she's not the biggest tragedy in the Sid and Beaver beef. I don't even consider her worse off than the reporters who say "Beaver-Man" with a straight face every night.

Sinister Sid, man, he saved more than my life. When I work on a new uniform or engage in one of my many battles of wits against a vigilante, I forget what's going on in the world. All my problems vanish. But now I'm alone with all my bad thoughts. Thoughts about what my wife thinks of me and what my godparents would say. And I shouldn't think negative thoughts about myself. Sid wouldn't like that.

Back when my mother was around, she'd have looked at my injury and said *Sana, sana, colita de rana.* Whatever that was supposed to mean. She would've let me help her sew clothes, and everything would be better. If my father were around… well, let's not get carried away with this. I'm already imagining you, Destinee, and I'm not sure how many more people I can imagine alongside you without being the kind of guy that runs down the streets shouting *¡Oigo voces en mi cabeza! ¡Mi pensamientos me duelen!*

I'm not crazy, by the way.

And all this is fuckin' *arduo* right now. I clench my fists, I grit my teeth, I taste iron, I make faces that would make you giggle if you saw them. I refuse to ask for medicine. Not doing it. *Ningún medicamento me puede curar* anyways.

I'm like this for three agonizing, painful, excruciating, laborious, tormenting minutes. At least, that's what the clock on the wall says. I was probably waiting days for my turn.

A nurse arrives to escort me. He smells like ice cream, which brings me back to my childhood a little. Ice Cream Man (*paletero?*) leads me through big swinging doors and into the hospital hallway, where half the staff loiter and the other half rush gurneys down the lane. If I ran this hospital, you'd see these people put to work, I'll tell you that. Any one of them could be a decent replacement for this wobbly crutch. But I keep walking.

<u>Stage Five (Acceptance)</u>: Narp looks like a sage on a mountain as I pass by the open door to his room. He doesn't cry. We're both Mexicans, and he knows just as well as I do that there's no good reason for Mexicans to cry. Maybe for a mother's death, you can shed a tear, since everyone thinks you're a sissy regardless. But if you cry because you broke a leg or crashed a motorcycle or left your family, then you better not show your face.

The nurse pushes the door open to my white storage box of a room. I slam down on the bed and relax my leg. I take off my jacket so the nurse can wrap the pressure-balloon thing around my arm.

He takes my temperature, asks some questions, does some more vital-gathering, and then leaves. He closes the door and, you won't believe this, Beaver-Man was behind the door the entire time!

Where does this guy get off, huh?

That's only a subconscious thought. At this moment, I'm in panic. I bend over to cover my bad leg from this so-called superhero. He's still covered in dirt from our fight. Dirt caked on his running shoes, his brown sweatpants, his huge jacket, his motorcycle helmet of a beaver mask. But, come to think of it, blood turns brown after a while.

He takes a step forward.

I raise my fist but doing so must've pulled a string inside me or something, because my bad leg seizes up. Beaver-Man grabs my punching hand and holds it in place with the strength of a wall.

I shout, "Hey, you better watch yourself now, because now you don't have your windows and your grappling hooks, and you can't get away from me this time."

He brings his other hand to his utility belt. He opens it.

Now I'm screaming, I reach with my other hand, but its muscle gotta be twisted or something. I say, "If you tear a single seam on my coat, I'll have you know it's rigged to blow the whole building!"

Beaver-Man doesn't know that I'm lying. The coat's only rigged to set on fire.

Wait. I already set this coat on fire when Narp grabbed it this morning. I've been walking around almost twenty-four hours with a burnt coat. A burnt coat that's on the floor in a heap right now.

Shit.

If I survive this, don't let me catch you using that kind of language.

From his utility belt, Beaver-Man pulls out a packet of multicolored forms. He throws them on top of my bed. I sit stunned for a moment. Then I grab a form. It's got questions about previous work experience.

"There are several places that seek employees right now," says Beaver-Man. "Submit these forms to the addresses listed on top of each sheet. They will secure a job for you. None of these locations have qualms about employees with criminal records. If the wages provided aren't enough to support you or your family, I will pay for information on Sinister Sid's operations, hideout, and future plans."

I may be wrong, but it seems that Beaver-Man, if the voice is anything to go by, is actually a chick.

I know! Crazy. She punches harder than most chicks I know. I guess that's one way to keep a secret identity. Her getup is so baggy and loose that I can't tell what she really looks like. I bet you're happy, Destinee, because you've got a role model to look up to, I guess. Me? I know exactly what to make of this. Oh yes. No doubt in my mind.

Beaver-Man puts both her fists on her hips and looks as if she's staring at the goddamn American flag. All this time, I've been thinking, she's probably clueless to how this cops and villains game goes. Does she even know what "beaver" means this side of town?

"We'll call it a draw then," I say. "You know, a lot of these applications you gave me are for manufacturing and meatpacking. I've worked those jobs before."

"Then put that on your resume."

"As in, I got fired from them."

"They will disregard criminal history. They will also disregard previous work errors."

"I prefer designing outfits, thanks."

"There are clothing stores you can work for."

"Yeah, ones that don't let you sew brass knuckles in the sleeves."

"You can design a new outfit for me."

"Do you always have an answer for everything?"

"I will always fix what falls apart. It's in the name."

Christ, this is why the government tries to ban these wackos every few years.

I noticed something *extraño* about this chick, and now I've realized that the room smells like rotten sweat, if that makes sense. The smell's from her. She stinks. She can't have taken off her uniform in… well, that's ridiculous. She can't work all the time. She's probably got an old aunt to take care of or something. Why would anyone ditch their entire family for a whacked-out crusade?

I say to her, I say, "Then maybe you've noticed that Sinister Sid fixed me up good. Maybe you ought to learn something from him. I'm living my life. Not yours. Mine. I'm the Juan Lozano of henchman uniforms, and I'm not fucking going back to some woman shouting at me every day!

Beaver-Man leans forward. She grips my leg, the bad one, it flares up again. Her helmet is right in front of my face.

"Do you have a family," she says.

I know what she's implying. Sid wants to know all about Beaver-Man's… sorry, Beaver-Woman's family. Sid once told me, as he unloaded a rifle at our hideout's target range, that his inner child demanded he find Beaver-Man's family, pop them a couple questions. Beaver-Woman's got the same stance to her.

"No, no family," I say in the midst of a big gulp.

"That explains it," she states. "Until you lose everything, you will just be a tidal wave, wrecking people's lives until you fade away. You know nothing of sacrifice. It's that simple. You only do what feels good for you. And it would feel quite good if I took your leg and bent it until your toes touched your rib cage. Now tell me. Should I do what feels good?"

Here I am. I choke on my own heart and stain the bedsheet with my sweat. I fight back the chill on my skin to say the toughest thing I can say at this moment:

"…no?"

"And that's why I'm the hero," says Beaver-Woman. She looks at the tattoo on my forearm. "I appreciate your art," she says.

"Thanks. I got it in Japan," I say. "It's pronounced *Watashi ma nuke.* It means, 'I am the mountain.'"

Beaver-Woman straightens up. "I have one too," she says. "It says, 'For Stacie.'"

With a soldier's pace, she walks to the door, opens it, and marches out.

A doctor enters. She asks me questions about my leg. A nurse comes in too. The nurse takes me to an x-ray machine and puts me in. Throughout all this, I use the breathing techniques Sid taught me and I try not to pass out.

She takes me out of the x-ray machine. She puts me back in my room. The doctor comes back later to say I have a fractured fibula. Then the doctor slaps a bulky beige thing called an air cast on my leg. She gives me a painkiller prescription and a sheet with caretaking advice. She tells me to schedule a follow-up with primary care. She leaves. Throughout this, I'm using the breathing techniques Sid taught me, and I'm trying not to pass out.

I leave the room, less hazy now. I walk down the hospital hallway, under its oppressive lights, and past the beeping noises in the other chambers. I swing the crutch along. The air cast does help. I hear newborns from nearby rooms.

It's clear that Stacie was Beaver-Woman's baby girl. Beaver-Woman said her name like I say yours. She probably lost Stacie at some point. Did she never take off her armor since? Impossible... but so are a lot of things in this business.

The checkout desk is right next to the check-in desk, where the white lady talked to me about insurance. The checkout man chews gum with a strong jaw. In front of him, and behind me, is the rising winter sun.

As I sign the exit paper, the checkout man looks at my busted leg and says, "Broken, huh?"

"Yeah."

"You know, you didn't have to come here."

"Excuse me?" I say.

"You didn't need emergency medicine. The ER's a place for chest pain and gunshot wounds. You just need to rest and schedule an appointment for a permanent cast."

I snap back, "Well, what the hell do you know about medicine anyways?"

"I know you'll get quite a bill for it. So, I'll need your insurance ca— hold on," he says. He picks up the ringing desk phone and jabbers into it.

I stand there for a while. My jaw's open, my eyes are wide, all five feet five inches of me somehow feel smaller. Even worse, Jack runs up to me. He holds onto several job applications. His appearance hasn't changed.

I tell him, "She must've visited you too."

"Listen," says Jack, "the boss'll pay good money for dirt on Beaver-

Girl. Did she say anything that'll give her away? How about personal identifiers," he asks, dragging out each syllable of those last two words.

It doesn't take a second to recall: the tattoo! It may not lead to her capture, but it would lead to cash. My salary, the amount I don't send away, covers living expenses, not medical bills. Those bills are gonna go to my wife's house anyway. I could score some quick money... and I'd become the chump that Beaver-Woman said I was. If only I could run without screwing up my leg more. I want to survive, for you, my little *colita de rana*. But I want to be someone you can look up to.

Sinister Sid says to keep in touch with our inner child. Well, Destinee, now I'm asking you. Forget how much I love my job, forget all the B.S. I've said... I'm going to channel you for this one. I am a mountain, not a tidal wave.

I look Jack straight in the eye and say, "I'm going home."

And Jack, goddamnit, he gets such a stupid expression on his face that I have to laugh. "What're you talking about," he says.

I laugh harder. I say, "Sid says I can't tell you." I laugh harder still. I say, "I'm going to meet my Destinee." Now I drop, and I roll on the ground, busting a gut and busting up my leg even more. All the new patients in the waiting room look at me. And Destinee, after we have our first hug, I'm gonna tell you that it's not true how people can laugh so hard they cry. That never happens. I'm laughing. I'm not crying. I'm not.

ABOUT NICK EDINGER

Nick Edinger kicked depression's butt for good in 2018. He's not sure how he did it, but he's certain the mystery lies in fiction. He writes to help others surpass their own mental barriers through wit, wisdom, and challenge. Nick works as an editor in Austin. His writing has been published on Everyst, The Borgen Project, and several bathroom walls.

Find out more at nickedingerwriter.com

facebook.com/nickedinger226

instagram.com/onepicturebookreviews

OATHBOUND

BY KAT PARRISH

CHAPTER ONE

I was in the physick garden when the strangers arrived, three men and a boy riding the big war horses they breed only in West Themis and refuse to sell anywhere else in the realm.

Though the men were travel-worn and weary, their skin and clothes covered in grime, their hair unwashed and tangled, it was still possible to see how handsome they were, and how much they resembled one another.

They rode right up to the stone steps leading into the abbey and might have ridden inside if the iron-bound doors hadn't been closed.

Perhaps an hour later, as I was brewing a pot of butterbur tea Sister Ammelie had requested for a headache, Sister Klara approached me in the kitchen to deliver a message. The Abbess wanted to see me. I swallowed the ball of dread those words birthed in me, untied my apron and folded it neatly, then took a deep breath. I was not one of Mother Cassia's favorites. A summons into her presence was never a good thing. At the very least, it meant she had singled me out to handle some unpleasant chore. At worst? It meant I had displeased her in some way and was to be punished with a week of extra chores or deprived of food or other comforts for however long she felt it was necessary for me to learn the error of my ways.

I had once spent a month sleeping in the courtyard outside the main chapel because I had burned a loaf of bread.

She'd made me eat the bread, too.

To my surprise, when I entered the Abbess' reception room, I found two other Sisters there—Agnes and Beata—as well as the strangers from West Themis. Agnes nodded to me, her tension evident in the way her hands were clenched, but Beata simply gave me the aloof, aristocratic look she bestowed on everyone, no matter how high-born or low.

The tallest of the strangers was the first to speak, and he wasted no words. "By order of the Key of Justice, you three are hereby ordered to present yourselves to the court of King Kirle to face questioning by the Three."

"I am not a citizen of West Themis," Beata retorted. "Nor am I a subject of King Kirle. You cannot compel my cooperation." Rather than reply, the man who had spoken merely glanced at the Abbess. Mother Cassia cleared her throat.

"Sister Beata, these men carry a warrant signed by the Citizen. This is a matter of diplomacy, as well as one of justice."

Beata's lips thinned. "There is only the Lady's justice," she said. "And I serve Her."

Leave it to Beata to have the presence of mind to offer the perfect response, subtly reminding Mother Cassia that the abbey was a place of sanctuary while also challenging our visitors' right to order us around. While they might worship many gods in West Themis, here in East Themis, worship of the Lady was as ingrained into law as the rules mandating an election every ten years to select a Citizen to rule the country.

The big stranger smiled, an expression that did not reach his eyes. "Your piety is noted Sister," he said. "But your Citizen has no appetite for denying King Kirle's request in this matter."

That did not surprise me. Citizen Almase had long worked to unite the two nations sharing the island of Themis. Over the last several years, she had granted numerous concessions in hopes that diplomatic relations would resume and lead to eventual reunification.

But relations with King Kirle remained tense, especially since the steady stream of refugees who crossed the river border seeking sanctuary were opposed to his despotic reign. Many of those refugees were magic workers whose talents had been outlawed by Kirle, who feared a resurgence of the magical cabal that had put his predecessor, King Sestor, on the throne.

The Citizen was performing a delicate dance, well aware that King Kirle could order his armies across the river at any time, overwhelming ours with its superior numbers.

But what could King Kirle possibly want with us?

"We leave at sunset," the leader of the strangers announced, cutting off my speculation.

"Sunset?" I echoed because I couldn't help myself. "It doesn't seem terribly practical to travel at night."

Next to me, Agnes cringed. She'd always been a fearful sort, and, up close, these men were terrifying—their clothes bloodstained and their blades bright. She took a slight step away as the stranger turned his attention to me.

"And your name?"

I didn't answer. He was the one who had summoned us after all. If he didn't know my name, he could just guess.

"Sister Lina," Mother Cassia said in her sternest voice. I looked down, trying my best to appear meek. I looked at my shoes, their muddied tips sticking out from the hem of my robe. No sense in polishing them if I was going to be traveling. It was five hard days' ride from here to the river, much of it through marshlands. And then it would be another week to reach the capital.

"Sister Lina has been here since she was a child," Mother Diedre said. Her tone of voice left no doubt she would have preferred I had never been born at all, or at least never found my way to the pile of stones that was the abbey.

"We will travel at night until we reach the border," the man said to me, after giving me a long appraising look.

So, they don't want to be seen. That was interesting.

I made a show of looking up and staring at the big man's companions. The two other men looked back at me with disdain; the boy was wide-eyed with curiosity. Without looking at the group's leader, I said, "It's good to be so solicitous of your men, but won't your horses find it difficult making their way in the dark?"

Before one of the men could answer, the boy piped up. "Horses can see better at night than we can."

The big man started to admonish him, but I interrupted. "I did not know that," I said. "I have never seen a Themish horse up close."

"Sister Lina," Mother Cassia warned, and Agnes gave me an alarmed look. "Don't make him angry," she whispered, not quite quietly enough. But if the man heard, he gave no sign. Turning to Mother Cassia, he said, "See, they're ready to leave by sunset."

"Yes, Lord Berard," she said, then waited until he and his entourage had left the room before rounding on me in fury.

"How dare you embarrass me in front of foreigners?"

"What do they want with us?" Agnes said. "Are we to be hostages in some war?"

Beata gave her a scathing look. "If anyone cared about any of us, we wouldn't be here." Agnes recoiled as if Beata had slapped her, but what she said was only the truth. I'd been here since I was ten, and in the fifteen years since I'd arrived, not a friend or a family member had come to visit.

"Lord Berard did not share that information with me," Mother Cassia said, still angry.

I tumbled the name over in my mind. I knew something of the history of West Themis, but Berard was not a storied name.

"Why should we go with him?" Beata asked. "I have no ties to West Themis, none of us do."

It was "generous" of Beata to include Agnes and me in that statement, especially considering she tormented Agnes every chance she got. Agnes suffered from hunger as a child and, as a result, grows anxious on fast days and sneaks food to keep her from recalling those terrible days. Even Mother Cassia turned a blind eye to the small transgression, but Beata delighted in finding the food and destroying it while spouting pious nonsense. She's made Agnes cry on more than one occasion, especially with her insults about her thin hair, another result of the malnutrition she suffered.

If it had been either me or Agnes, who had challenged the Abbess, she likely wouldn't have responded, but she had a soft spot for Beata, often claiming the younger woman reminded her of herself. Beata always shuddered when she said this, for she considered Mother Cassia coarse.

"He invoked the Treaty of Haw-on-Necke," she said, referencing a thirty-year-old document that had ended the last war between East and West Themis. "Apparently, there has been trouble with Sestor's followers."

"But Sestor's been dead these many years," I said.

"There was an assassination attempt led by a second-generation born to his exiled supporters."

"Magic workers?" Beata said, looking interested. "I thought they were all killed when Sestor died."

I noticed she didn't say "was murdered," which was the dirty truth behind the official history. The king had been killed by Kirle, then a mercenary from Zoorea who spent five years earning his trust, only to betray him, to much rejoicing.

Sestor the Flame had not been mourned by many.

"His followers hope to rally behind Sestor's heir," Mother Cassia said.

Agnes, Beata, and I exchanged glances.

"She's been dead these long years," Agnes said.

"They never found Dalissa's body," Beata countered. "She could be hiding anywhere, gathering allies, biding her time."

"She disappeared fifteen years ago," I said—as much to myself as the others, the meaning of the unexpected visit suddenly becoming clear. "And we've all been here that long."

"They think one of us is the Heir?" Agnes said, horrified. I felt sick myself. Berard had said we would be taken before "the Three." That was what Kirle's notorious justice council was called. They were noted for handing down harsh sentences for the most minor crimes. If they felt they had the Heir in their hands and they could prevent a coup by Sestor loyalists, they would be merciless. None of us would survive their judgment.

"Two of you have nothing to worry about," Mother Cassia said, brightly, as if she could read my thoughts.

"This is a sanctuary," Agnes wailed. "They can't make us leave."

"Are you confessing?" Beata said. "It would save Lina and me a lot of trouble if you are."

Agnes burst into tears.

"If we're to leave at sunset, we should pack," I said. It would do none of us any good to have Agnes dissolve into hysterics.

"All we have is the clothes on our backs and this," Beata said, hooking her fingers through the chain she wore around her neck and pulling on it until it broke. Without a backward glance, she threw it on the floor and stalked out.

Agnes bent down to retrieve the small golden charm—a tiny hand —that symbolized the Lady's care for her subjects. She seemed completely distraught by Beata's act of defiance. "She didn't mean it," she said to Mother Cassia.

Yes, she did.

Beata was not being overly dramatic when she announced she had no belongings. The Sisters were not encouraged to cling to personal possessions of any kind. It was the work of only a few minutes for me to gather my sleeping shirt and inside shoes, a little book of poetry by the Tatov poet Renura, a small cache of herbs stored in little jars, and a pair of lumpy, hand-knitted socks. West Themis was a mountainous country, and cold this time of year, so I put my winter robe on over the one I already wore. I looked at the tiny room where I'd grown from child to woman and felt a pang. I had felt safe here, and now it seemed my life was no longer my own.

Whispering a prayer to the Lady, I picked up my bundle and went through the door, being careful as always to leave it open a crack, so if the Lady so desired, she could visit the room in the night to bestow Her blessings.

I knew I needed her blessings now, but she seemed to be otherwise occupied.

⁂

It was hot in the kitchen, with all the bake ovens roaring. Sister Madeline, the sleeves of her robe rolled up, and her hair caught back in a kerchief, was kneading a pile of dough as if punishing it, all the while muttering to herself in a most impious manner. When she saw me, she dropped the dough onto the counter and rushed to hug me, careless of the flour powdering her hands. "Lina," she said. "I just heard the news."

I disentangled myself from her embrace and kissed Madeline on her sweaty forehead. Old enough to be my grandmother, she had taken me under her wing like an orphaned chick and lavished love on me as if I were one of her own. It was a source of great sorrow to Madeline that all of her children had died of plague, taking their father with them. She had purchased a poison to join her family when the Lady appeared to her in her aspect as the Mother and convinced her to live.

Madeline had been an ardent devotee of the Lady ever since.

"What can I do?" she asked me, sounding distraught.

"We will need food for our journey," I said. "We'll be on the road for some days, and none of us have a taste for soldier's rations."

"If they even intend to feed you at all," she muttered darkly. Refugees from West Themis had brought stories of famine and widespread hunger in the country. With a sigh, she set out a large cloth sack and began filling it with provisions that wouldn't spoil.

I had just collected several skins of water when one of the other Themish men appeared at the doorway. He looked at the water skins and smirked. "Do you have anything stronger to drink than water?" he asked Madeline.

"Who are you?" she asked.

He looked surprised that she had admonished him for his rudeness. "My name is Danr."

'No, Danr, we do not keep spirits in this kitchen."

"Not even a cask of ale?" he said with a smile that was surprisingly charming.

"Not so much as a drop," I said and hoped he'd leave the matter alone. I knew the Abbess kept a small flask of brandy in her cell but did not think the strangers needed to know about it. It was such a little indulgence, and these men looked like they could afford to buy a drink from a roadside tavern if they needed something other than water to slake their thirst and wash the dust from their throats.

Danr stopped smiling. He looked over the small sack of provisions on the wooden table. "That's not enough for all of us," he said.

Madeline turned to him, her hands on her hips. "I will not allow my sisters to go hungry so that West Themish ruffians can stuff their bellies. This is a sanctuary and a refuge, not a public house on the road."

I was surprised that she spoke so harshly to the big man, but if Danr was offended, he did not show it.

"Think of us as pilgrims then," he said.

"Pilgrims ask," she said. "They do not demand."

Without even taking a breath, the man responded by holding out both hands, palms turned upward. "Take pity on me in the Lady's name, for I am a lost soul wandering in a strange land."

Damn you, I thought, because that was a pilgrim's plea the Sisters were sworn to answer. And from the looks of the man, he knew that too.

"And what is your name, pilgrim?" Madeline said seriously as if they had just met.

"Danr," he answered.

"That is not a name I know."

"It is not common on Themis," he said, "and nearly unknown elsewhere."

"Welcome, pilgrim," Madeline said. "You are welcome to bread and cheese and dried fruit."

"No meat?"

"We do not eat the flesh of creatures that walk or crawl or swim."

Now a slight smile was playing about Madeline's lips. Two can play this game, I thought, quite pleased that Danr had come out second best in the little clash of wills.

As I was adding some smoked cheese to my sack, I noticed the boy was standing in the doorway.

"Are you hungry?" I asked him.

He shook his head, perhaps too proud to admit it.

"Not even a little?" I said. "Because Sister Madeline has too much honey cake in the larder, and it would be a shame to waste it."

I knew Madeline wouldn't mind me feeding the boy. She had a soft spot for children.

"I've never had honey cake," he said.

"Would you like to try some?" I asked, exchanging glances with the cook.

The boy looked like he might be about to say yes, when Berard suddenly appeared in the doorway, his bulk nearly filling it. "Agi," he said, "come away."

The boy immediately scuttled to the man's side. Berard examined me with cold gray eyes. "Are you nearly ready?"

"There's fresh bread baking," I said. "Enough for you and your men as well." He looked annoyed by my offer, but I ignored his displeasure and added, "You must be tired of eating road rations and the meat you hunt."

He gave me a considering look as if weighing my words against my intentions.

"Fresh bread would be most welcome," he finally said. And with a glance to the boy, he added, "And perhaps a slice or two of honey cake."

I bowed my hand and turned away from the table to fetch the cake, pleased that the boy would not be denied his small treat after all.

Perhaps he is not as cruel as he appears, I thought.

It turned out I was wrong about that.

CHAPTER TWO

At sunset, Agnes, Beata, and I gathered outside the gate where Berard and his men were waiting impatiently. I carried the food Madeline had prepared while Agnes hugged a little bundle of books. Beata pointedly carried nothing.

Agnes looked at the horses in dismay. "I can't ride," she said.

"No need," Danr said. "You just need to spread your legs and hang on."

Agnes shuddered. But Danr wasn't looking at her.

He was looking at me.

Mother Cassia came out to the courtyard to say farewell, her features composed in a bland mask. Before she could say a word, however, Berard joined her on the steps and whispered something in her ear that shattered her calm. "No," she said aloud. "This is a place of refuge. It is holy ground."

"Gather your daughters," Berard said, this time loud enough for all to hear.

"What's happening?" Agnes whispered, but no one answered as the Abbess went back inside, and the bells began tolling.

A cold wind had kicked up, and I was glad to be wearing every stitch of clothing I owned. Danr saw me clutching my collar tight to seal in my body heat and grinned. "You'll be warm soon enough," he said.

I sent him a filthy look, which only made him grin wider.

About a quarter of an hour later, the Abbess returned, with all the sisters trailing behind her.

"Everyone is out?" Danr asked.

Mother Cassia nodded. Danr raised his arm and brought it down sharply, and in the next moment, a barrage of flaming arrows flew from the woods and onto the timbered roof.

"No," Agnes howled.

"Be glad you are not still inside," Danr growled. "In West Themis, treason is punishable by death."

"Treason is the crime of betraying one's country," Beata said. "As I have said, we are not citizens of West Themis, so therefore we could not have committed treason."

Danr was unmoved. "You have given sanctuary to assassins," he said. "You have protected the Heir."

"We would give sanctuary to the Unclean One himself if he asked for it," Mother Cassia said.

"And so, you have proved my point," Danr said.

"Enough," Berard said, and mounted his horse. He reached down to Beata. Giving him a contemptuous look, Beata ignored his outstretched hands, grabbed the reins, put foot to stirrup, and mounted as gracefully as if she had ridden every day of her life.

Trying to emulate her, I grabbed the reins of the nearest horse, but the stirrup was too high for me to step into it. I grabbed for the horse's mane with my free hand and tried to hoist myself up but felt myself slipping. Before I could protest, Danr cupped his hand under my rear and shoved me into the saddle.

Anyone but him, I thought as I saw the third man offer his linked hands to Agnes as a step. Danr could have done the same for me, but he'd chosen to humiliate me instead. I vowed I would not forget that.

As we rode away, the roof of the abbey collapsed. Most of the building was made of stone and would be undamaged, but the symbolism of what had been done was stark and a reminder that West Themis was more than twice as large as our prosperous little country and that if they chose to flex their power, there would be little we could do to stop them.

"There was no need to do that," I shouted into Danr's ear. I couldn't believe the Citizen would turn a blind eye to such a provocative action. But as Berard had said, she didn't have an appetite for war.

"No wonder people say that West Themis is home to barbarians." Danr's back stiffened, but he did not reply.

In the forest, we were joined by the small band of archers who'd been stationed out of sight. They were all young and looked malnourished. In the days of Sestor, when magic was allowed, farmers had relied on earth magic to sustain their crops. Now that such magic was punishable by death, Kirle's subjects were starving.

I wondered why his people hadn't deposed him and adopted the same form of government we had in East Themis.

As the night wore on, Berard led the way, followed by the man whose name I did not know, followed by Danr and me. Agi trailed behind, looking far too small to be riding such a huge beast. I noticed that Danr kept looking around to make certain the boy was still following. I wondered if he was kin to the child.

At dawn, Berard and his men stopped and made camp. Berard said something to Beata that made her frown, and soon after, she came over to me. "Lord Berard expects us to serve the food," she said.

"It'll be easier to ration it that way," I said reasonably. After all, we would have served them if they'd come to the abbey as pilgrims. "We only have about four days' worth of food. This lot could eat everything at a single meal."

Beata sniffed, but did not argue as I began unwrapping provisions. Just to be defiant, I served the young archers first. Some of the men shyly thanked me. Others simply started wolfing the food down, too hungry to be polite.

Beata and Agnes and I sat alone as we ate our meager fare.

"Berard is the leader," Agnes said. "Osgar, the man I'm riding with, is his cousin. Danr is Berard's brother."

"And the boy is Berard's?" I asked.

"Yes," she said.

I could see the resemblance.

"They're related to the King," she added.

"They have the Zoorish look," Beata said scornfully, "with that wheat-straw hair and those cold gray eyes."

At the abbey, we were not supposed to talk about our pasts, but that did not keep us from gossip and conjecture, as least about the sisters we found interesting.

And Beata was very interesting.

There were all sorts of rumors about her. One of the most popular was that her lover had died on a pilgrimage, and she'd cloistered herself out of grief. That didn't make sense, however, for she'd been at the abbey as long as I had, and I was only ten when I arrived.

It was fairly obvious that she had been raised in wealth. The quiet, contemplative life did not suit her. She complained about everything—the coarse weave of the fabric of our robes, the unseasoned plainness of our food, the uncomfortable mattresses on our beds—as if in her former life all she'd worn only silks, dined only on delicacies, and slept on mattresses stuffed with the finest goose down. In fact, it was hard to believe her grieving for anyone except herself.

I know that's an uncharitable thought, but I knew the Lady loved me despite all of my faults.

On our second night of travel, as we took a break to water the horses, one of the archers put his hands on Agnes.

"Leave her alone," I said.

"Just making friends," he said, one hand still fondling Agnes' breast as she trembled in his grasp.

Without thought, I picked up a rock and threw it at him. It connected with his left ear. 'You bitch," he roared and reached for the knife in his belt. Suddenly, Danr was there, standing between him and me.

"You were warned, Owin," he said sternly.

"She threw a rock at me," Owin replied, sounding like a petulant child.

Danr ignored the complaint. "Take the first watch," he said.

"But, Danr," the archer grumbled.

"I don't want to hear it," Danr said.

When the young archer moved away, Danr looked at Agnes.

"Did he hurt you?" She shook her head. "Good," Danr said and turned away as if that were the end of it.

"Aren't you going to punish him?"

He turned his gray eyes to mine. They were just as cold as Berard's but not as silvery.

"He is just a boy," he said.

"Then he should learn to be a man," I said. "If there is someone here who can teach him."

Danr's face shuttered.

"Is this how the sons of Themis treat women?" I demanded.

"Women," Danr said scornfully and spat. "You're all traitors."

"Danr," his brother said warningly.

I startled. I hadn't heard Berard walk up. He moved quietly for such a big man.

"You know it's true, Berard," Danr said. "Their order has harbored fugitives and revolutionaries. For all you know, they could have sheltered the man who would have killed father."

Father?

I had never heard that King Kirle had sons, but he was such a secretive, paranoid creature that little about him was known for certain.

Berard looked at me. "Tell your friend to stay close to Osgar, and she will have no further trouble."

That was not terribly reassuring, but I knew it was the best I would get.

As it turned out, Agnes did not seem to mind staying close to Osgar. Whenever I looked over at them, they seemed to be chatting. Beata noticed it too. "Agnes was always weak. Now she has a protector." It was a harsh judgment, but not untrue. By the third day's rest, Osgar had joined her, Beata, and me as we ate our frugal meals. He had dainty manners but an oafish personality.

He was also eager to be considered knowledgeable, so eager he answered all the questions we asked him.

Beata wanted to know the fate that awaited us in the West Themis capital.

"You'll be brought before the Three," he said, munching a slice of the now-stale bread Madeline had baked. "And whichever one of you is Sestor's daughter will be put to death."

"It's not me," Agnes blurted out.

There was no point in echoing her denial. It was clear Osgar didn't really care. The men had been sent out to fetch an heir, and they'd brought back three potential princesses. After that, it would be up to the Three to decide our fate.

Beata looked at Osgar with disdain. "I thought even your Zoorish-born king followed the doctrine that sin died with the sinner so that it could not be passed down through the generations."

"There's been a special dispensation," he said. "There have been omens." He looked at us meaningfully. "People have seen flames on the horizon and seen it as a portent."

Omens and portents. And they call us superstitious.

Agnes scoffed. "An ordinary sunset can look like flames on the horizon," she said. "How gullible are the people of West Themis?"

Osgar regarded her seriously. "It would be better if you didn't say such things when we arrive in the capital. It makes it sound like you think you're better than us."

"We are better than you," Beata said, throwing the hard crust of her bread on the ground before standing and walking away.

Osgar grabbed the bread and, without even wiping off the girt, bit into it without shame.

Agnes looked at him with pity in her eyes.

We were all saddle sore and weary and still a night's ride away from the great river when the food ran out. Several of the archers went out hunting, and Beata and Agnes showed Agi how to locate birds' eggs.

Owin, the archer who had assaulted Agnes, returned to camp with a brace of skinny rabbits and sat down beside me to skin them. "I'm sorry I frightened the girl," he said hesitantly.

"I'm not the one you should apologize to," I said, idly drawing his name in the dirt.

"Are you casting a spell?"

"No spell," I said. "I've written your name."

He looked at the letters. I could tell they held no meaning for him.

"This is an O," I said, pointing it out. "You are Owin of the ancient name. This is the first letter of your name."

He looked at me sheepishly. "I cannot write my name."

"Would you like to learn how?" I asked, impulsively. I was bored to distraction and looking for any sort of diversion.

"Why would you want to do such a thing for me?

"I am far from home, far from my friends, and this is a long journey."

"Far from your friends?" he said. "What about your companions?"

I smiled. "They are my sisters, but we aren't always friends. Do you have sisters?"

"Yes," he said.

"Then, you know how it can be with siblings."

He nodded then. My argument made sense to him. No matter how close or how loving they are, families are complicated. "Show me," he said, rather more arrogantly than I liked.

"Please," I said.

"I will not beg," he said huffily and turned away.

"Owin," I said. "I am not asking you to beg, merely asking you to be courteous. It is rude of you not to say 'please.'"

"I didn't know that," he said, and the admission staggered me.

"Well, now you do," I said. I picked up the stick I was using and drew another O in the dirt. "This is an O," I said. I handed him the stick. "Now, you try."

He copied the O and looked up for my approval. "Excellent," I said, taking the stick back so I could draw a W next to the O. "This is a double U," I said.

"It looks like you've drawn a mountain," he said, and I realized he was looking at the letters upside down.

"Come over here so you can see it properly," I said.

"Berard said we aren't supposed to talk to you," he said.

"Berard isn't here right now," I pointed out. Like the rest of the men, he'd gone hunting. "Draw a double U."

Owin took the stick and drew a double U.

"It should be sharper," I said and showed him again. This time he did it perfectly.

I showed him how to add on the I and the N, and by the end, when he proudly traced out the four letters of his name, I felt like I'd been awarded a medal. And then I noticed he was crying.

"Owin?" I asked. "What is it?"

"My father cannot write his own name," he said. "He is a fletcher, the finest around, but he cannot spell out his name."

"What is it?" I asked.

"Gidriz," he said.

I wrote it out in the dirt. "See there," I said, "you both have an I in your name." I wrote it again. "Practice writing it out, and when you get home, you can show him how to do it."

Owin looked at me as if I'd just given him the most precious gift he'd ever received. Perhaps I had.

"You're very clever, aren't you, Lina?" Danr said as he walked into the light with a small deer carcass over his shoulder. Owin immediately scrambled to his feet to take the deer from him. "Stay away from her," Danr said.

"Yes, my lord," he said as he turned away.

"I was just showing him how to write his name," I said indignantly. "A man should be able to write his own name. Or do the rulers of West Themis prefer to keep their subjects ignorant?"

"Who knows the ways of rulers?" he said.

'I would expect you and your brother to have some idea," I said, "since your father is King Kirle."

"King Kirle has many sons," Danr said. "He is not fond of any of them, and most don't even carry his name."

"Then why do you serve him?" I asked, genuinely curious.

"I am one of the king's rangers," he said. "There are perquisites to the position."

"Like better food?" I hazarded.

"More food," he said simply, "but not necessarily better." He looked at me sideways. "That bread you brought from the abbey is the best bread I've ever eaten."

"No one should ever have to go hungry," I said, and I meant it.

"You people in East Themis are soft," he said. "One day, we will cross the river into your land, and then we will feast on fresh-baked bread."

"We will fight you," I said.

"Will you?" He reached out one large, bloodstained hand, and pulled me to my feet, pulled me close enough to smell the death on his clothes and skin. His grip hurt. "I could break your wrist with a snap of my fingers." He put his other hand around my throat. "I can feel your heart beating beneath my hand. I could stop your heart beating with a single squeeze, and there would be nothing you could do about it."

"I believe you," I said. "Please don't."

"Please," he said with a bitter laugh as if I'd said something amusing. "Please is a word weak people use when they're not strong enough to take what they want." He began stroking my throat gently with his thumb. "The strong don't need to beg."

"Someone who takes what is not freely given is a thief," I said.

"Someone who teases a hungry dog is a fool," he said, bending to kiss me. I didn't realize what was about to happen until his lips actually closed on mine. I jerked away, but his hand was still around my throat, and he held me fast, forcing my lips open with his tongue. Instinctively, I bit down, and he broke the kiss, blood running from his mouth where his tongue was wounded.

"When you need a friend at court, come to me and say 'please.' See how far it gets you."

"Never," I said, and this time when I jerked away, he let me go.

We smelled the river before we caught sight of it, a nauseating stench of rotten flesh and marshy tides. As we got closer, we saw the river was choked with human corpses, some bloated and floating. Agnes gagged when she saw the bodies and turned away to spew bile. Osgar was quick to comfort her, and for some reason, that made me angry. I would have understood if she were simply trying to co-opt Osgar for her own protection, but she genuinely seemed to enjoy his company.

"Is the water poison?" I asked Danr, for it was an odd, yellowish-green color.

"No," he said shortly. "But the river is dangerous nonetheless."

"To keep your subjects from crossing to freedom," I said, and it was not a question.

"To protect our borders," he said. And just then, I saw a flash of fin as a monstrous creature rose from the depths to bite down on one of the floating bodies.

"The West Themis side of the border has a guard tower nearly every half-league," I said. "Was there really a need for you to seed the river with monsters?"

"That was Sestor's doing," Danr said. "The tyrant wanted to make certain that anyone who fled for the East regretted their disloyalty."

"That's terrible," I said.

"He was a terrible man," Danr said.

"How would you know?" I asked, for Danr appeared to be not much older than I.

"I was a ranger cadet when Kirle came to the island. I saw what Sestor and his magic had done."

"So Kirle murdered one tyrant and became another," I said. "How could he justify that?"

"Perhaps you can ask him when you meet," Danr said, and that was the end of that conversation.

We crossed the river on a wooden boat barely large enough to contain the humans and the horses. The river was choppy, and poor Agnes was pale and sweating by the time we got to the other side. I was nauseated for another reason. Now that we'd crossed the river, I knew we were just days away from our meeting with the Three. The thought of that dreadful reckoning terrified me.

CHAPTER THREE

I was in the middle of a fitful sleep when I was awakened by shouts. We had camped by a lake in the shadow of a small mountain, and the ground was rocky and cold. Danr was right. I was used to a soft mattress.

As I struggled into my heavy cloak, Owin passed by.

"What is happening?"

"It's Agi."

"What's wrong with him?"

"Milk fever."

That can't be. At this time of year?" I asked.

I looked toward the lake where Osgar and some of the archers were dipping the naked and shivering boy in the frigid water, water that was milky blue from glacial melt.

Oh no, I thought. Cold water was absolutely the wrong way to treat milk fever.

Without much thought, I walked toward the shore. "Get him out of the water," I shouted. The men turned to me.

"We do not take orders from you," Osgar said as Danr came over to see what the hubbub was about.

"Exposure to cold water will only make milk fever worse," I said. "Can't you see he's nearly blue?"

Without waiting for an answer, I waded into the water to wrap Agi in my cloak. The water was so cold I thought it would stop my heart. But then I saw the weeping sores on his torso, and my heart froze for another reason.

"He doesn't have milk fever; he has the spurge."

"You're wrong," Danr said, although with more hope than doubt, for everyone knew spurge was incurable and fatal.

"No," I said. "I've seen too many cases."

Desperate travelers had come to the abbey seeking cures, and despite our most earnest ministrations, only a few had survived.

Danr swore then, or perhaps it was a prayer he was uttering, but either way, I knew he was horrified.

"There's no cure for the spurge," he said.

I looked at Agi, who was trembling. He was trying so hard to be brave.

"Bring him to Berard's tent," I said, and I said it with enough authority that Dani picked the boy up. But Osgar gestured for his cousin to remain where he was.

"Why would we do that?" he asked suspiciously.

"Because there will be a fire going there," I said impatiently, "and he'll be much more comfortable."

"He's a son of West Themis. He doesn't need a woman cossetting him."

Danr said something to Osgar that I couldn't hear, then walked away, his strides so long I had to run to catch up.

There were two men outside the tent, guarding it, and they came to attention when they saw us but blocked our passage.

"Stand aside," Danr said.

"Lord Berard does not wish to be disturbed," the guard said.

"It's a matter of life and death," I said. "Please."

The guard curled his lip at my use of the word "please."

"Wait here," he said and disappeared into the tent, leaving the other man to stare at us as if he had no idea who Danr might be.

A moment later, Beata stepped out of the tent, wrapped in a fox skin, her dark hair tumbling down in disarray. She met my eyes boldly, as if daring me to judge her, then slipped away.

A moment later, Berard called out, "Enter."

There was a fire in the brazier that gave off a noxious smoke. I choked on it and began waving my hands around to dissipate the fumes.

Danr gently laid Agi onto the mussed-up cot his father had just risen from. Agi was feverish and seemed to be in severe pain. That was bad. The fever was a sign that the disease's end-stage was near.

"Are you certain the boy has the spurge?" Berard asked when Danr told him of my suspicions.

"Yes," I said.

He slumped then, this big man whose very presence filled up the space he occupied. He looked back at the boy, and all the tenderness he felt, but had not shown before, was in his face.

I took a deep breath. "There is a cure for it," I said.

He looked up at me, an unguarded expression of wild hope in his face, and then the implications of what I'd said registered with him.

"There is no known cure," he said.

"It was once known," I said, "but it has been forgotten." He looked skeptical. 'It's in the Black Codex," I said.

It was as if all the air had been sucked out of the tent.

"Sestor's grimoire?" Danr asked.

"It wasn't a grimoire," I said. "It was just a book of healing spells."

"You've seen it."

"It was in our library at the abbey," I said.

"Where is it now?" Danr challenged.

"Ashes dancing on the wind." I looked at him coldly. "Destroyed when you set fire to the abbey. The library was on the top floor, just beneath the roof."

I looked over at Agi. He was thrashing in his bed, soaking the bedding with sweat. "Please let me help him," I said. "Without treatment, he will die. And if we wait too long, even what I know won't help."

"Why would the daughter of Sestor help me?"

I sighed. "Just because I memorized the spells in the book, doesn't make me the Heir."

Danr looked skeptical. "I am an orphan," I said. "And sworn to help all those in need."

"Your father killed many people."

"I am sorry," I said but refused to engage that line of conversation. We were wasting time. "I have some herbs with me, but I'll need others."

"Melton," he called. The first guard instantly appeared at the flap of the tent.

"Yes, my lord?"

Berard turned to me. "Tell him what you need."

"It's a long list," I said. "Does anyone have any paper?"

Melton looked at me proudly. "I have a very good memory, my lady." *So, he couldn't read either.* That was unfortunate. I started naming the roots and barks and berries I needed, and the young guard nodded and concentrated hard. While he was gone, I stripped off Agi's wet clothes so I could look at his lesions. Several were already turning dark red.

"Do you have any sheep's wool," I asked.

Danr left the tent without answering and returned a moment later with a sack full of curly wool, clearly his pillow. The wool was pungent with rancid lanolin but also held a trace of his own musky scent.

I took the wool from him and used it to wipe Agi from head to toe, drying him off.

When the young guard returned with the ingredients for the medicine, I instructed him to put everything into a pot with some water and bring it to a boil. By now, curious people were gathering outside the tent, wondering what was going on. I saw Agnes, standing close to Osgar and whispering in his ear.

At last, the elixir was finished, a dull metallic green that smelled noxious. "I'll need a cup," I said.

Danr handed me the drinking horn from his belt. I carefully poured the concoction into the horn, being careful not to spill a drop.

"It smells terrible," he said.

"Yes," I said.

"But it will work?"

"Nearly always," I said.

"Nearly?"

"If an infant catches it, sometimes their little bodies are too weak to fight it off. That is true of the aged and infirm as well."

I could tell he was still wary of me using my potion on the boy. "I could drink it in front of you," I said, "and prove that there's nothing poisonous here, but we are wasting time."

Danr turned to Berard, leaving him to make the final choice in the matter. At last, his brother gave a short nod and left the tent.

"I have a bit of honeycomb I was saving," Danr said, surprising me. "Perhaps it will make the medicine more palatable."

"Give him a little bit before he drinks, and the rest after," I said. Danr nodded and pulled a scrap of leather from the pocket of his breeches, unwrapping it to reveal a sticky scrap of honeycomb.

"Agi," Danr said. "Open your eyes."

The boy obeyed. "Good boy," Danr said. "I have a treat for you." He broke off a tiny bit of the honeycomb and fed it to Agi.

"Is there more?" the boy said hopefully.

"There is more," Danr said, "but first, you have to drink something that tastes bad."

The boy frowned. "Why?"

"So, you'll feel better."

"But there'll be honeycomb after?"

"Yes."

"I'll drink the medicine," he said.

The boy nearly choked, but drank it all, down to the last dark green drop. Afterward, Danr gave him the honeycomb to wipe out the taste in his mouth.

Berard came back into the tent and watched grimly as the lesions on his son's skin started to fade.

"Will he live?" Danr asked.

"Yes," I said. "He's a strong child."

Berard stepped forward to touch his son's forehead. "His fever is gone," he said. "Just like magic." And before I could grasp what his intentions were, he drew his dagger and plunged it into my heart.

CHAPTER FOUR

I felt the blade slice through the muscle as if he were carving a joint of meat. I dimly heard Danr call his brother's name as I slowly pulled out the blade—still dripping with my heart's blood and threw it at his feet.

So much for hiding my true nature, I thought.

"What fell magic is this?" Danr whispered. A moment ago, we'd shared a moment of complicity as we fed the boy a sweet to reward him for being so brave as he took his medicine. Now there was nothing more than horror in his expression.

"It is not fell magic at all," I said. "You have heard the stories of Sestor's bloodlines, how he was descended from the Xtari."

"The Xtari never existed."

"But they did," I said. "And still do." *And I am proof that the bloodline still exists.*

"We can ransom her back to the Xtari," Melton said eagerly.

I had forgotten the young guard was still there.

Berard rounded on him. "The Xtari want to kill your king," he said.

"Kirle is not my king," Melton said. "He cares nothing for me and mine."

Berard was looking at me in a new light. A pitiless light. "She will return to her birthplace. And she will face the Justice of the Three."

My heart sank when I heard that.

"The verdict will be death," Berard sneered. "And it won't be an easy death," he added. "They'll follow the old ways."

I knew what that meant as well. The "old ways" meant that no blood could be spilled. I could be drowned or burned. I could be suffocated. I could be pressed. But most likely, the form of punishment was the "the phoenix cage," a torturous contraption in which the accused/condemned was put in a metal cage that was then heated. In the old days, they would have been burned by dragon's breath, but these days the executioners set a fire under the cage.

It was said to be extremely painful and take a long time.

"You will beg for death," Berard said.

"Enough," Danr said, looking at me. "She revealed herself to save your son. She could have let him die. You owe her thanks, not taunts."

Berard looked surprised that Danr had championed me. I was surprised myself. For a moment, we all stared at each other, and then Agi sat up. "Papa," he said, and held out his arms. And that was just enough of a distraction for me to escape.

I shoved Melton and scooped up the bloody dagger from where I had dropped it moments ago.

I ran past him, and as I came out of the tent, I flung a spell at the other guard so that he felt me pass but could not see me.

I didn't get far. Everyone in the crowd around me closed in—even

Agnes—and blocked my path, holding me there until Danr caught up to me.

I tried to cast a binding spell on him to freeze him in place, but to my consternation, it didn't work on him. I had used too much energy in the healing and the invisibility spell, and now I was defenseless as he dragged me back to the tent. The crowd around it had grown larger. Beata was there, bending close to Agnes. When she saw me, she sneered. "I always thought there was something strange about you."

Agnes was horrified. "You're Sestor's daughter?"

"He was my sire," I admitted, "but I disavowed him long ago."

"But he was a monster."

"Yes, he was."

I wanted to explain myself, tell everyone how I had witnessed his cruelties from the time I was too little to resist. But that would involve explaining how I eventually came to resist him when I came into the magic that I'd inherited through his bloodline. I had disavowed him, but was unable to purge myself of the magic in my blood. And wouldn't if I could.

I had confessed that to the Abbess and prayed about it all the time.

"They're going to execute you," Agnes said, and I couldn't help but notice that there was an edge of satisfaction in her voice.

I didn't understand it because Agnes came from the Principality of Kresh, whose ruler had been an ally of West Themis during Sestor's reign. They would have known of his excesses and turned a blind eye so that the imports of grain and meat and wine had continued to flow between the two countries. That trade had long ago dried up after Kirle murdered Sestor and began his own reign of terror.

What did I ever do to Agnes? I wondered. And then I saw her with Osgar. Their intimacy was obvious and a little shocking. She no longer seemed to be the timid little mouse she'd always seemed. *Protective coloration*, I assumed and wondered what circumstances had led her to the abbey.

Berard ordered me put in shackles for the rest of the journey. They were made of cold iron, which burned. My skin was red and raw and seeping from, and the pain was so severe I could neither eat nor sleep. There was absolutely no chance I could conjure a magic spell.

We no longer traveled by night, and Berard set a punishing pace. All the men were exhausted, and at night, they all fell from their horses and slept like the dead. I was still riding behind Danr, but he never spoke to me, nor responded if I spoke to him.

At night Agi would come and talk to me, squatting just out of my reach as I sat, chained to a tree and trying to keep warm.

"Danr says you used magic to save me," he said.

"Yes," I said.

"So, magic isn't always bad?"

"Magic is neither good nor evil," I said, "only the magic worker's intent."

"Papa says I shouldn't talk to you," he said.

"So, you are disobeying him right now," I answered.

His face screwed up with concentration. "Melton says you saved my life."

"I treated your illness," I said.

"My father hates you," he said.

'Yes, I know."

"He says you'll be put to death."

"He's told me that as well," I said.

"Agi, stop bothering her."

I turned my head. It was Danr. "I'm not bothering her," he said.

"Go on," he said. "Tomorrow will be a hard ride, but then we'll be home."

Grumbling, the boy walked away. Danr turned his attention to me.

"Get up," he said. "It's time to ride."

Sunken as I was in my misery, I was slow to obey. He reached down and grabbed the chain between my hands and pulled me to my feet. The action put pressure on the cuffs, and the searing pain was so intense I lost my breath and stumbled against him.

He pushed me away, but then caught sight of the festering flesh of my wrists.

"I thought you were a healer."

I caught my breath and replied, "The iron keeps me from using my magic."

Which is the whole point of binding me with iron. He looked like he was about to say something but instead, he surprised me by turning a screw that held the iron circles shut. The shackles fell into a heap at my feet. Almost immediately, the inflamed redness leached out of my skin as the tissues knitted back together.

He watched with an expression almost of wonder.

"Swear you won't try to run again, and I'll leave you free."

"I'm facing a death sentence," I said. "I'd be a fool to promise you that."

He studied me for a moment and then pulled his dagger—cutting two long strips from my cloak.

"Hold out your hands," he said. I thought he meant to tie me with the cloth but instead, he wrapped it around both my wrists, padding them before replacing the iron cuffs. They still hurt, but the cloth protected me somewhat.

"Thank you," I said.

"There's nowhere for you to run even if you want to," he said. Berard sent word ahead that the Heir has been captured. There's a bounty on your head. Enough silver to keep a family fed for a year."

"And how will you be rewarded for bringing me to justice?" I asked

"My father will be pleased," he said.

"You're easily bought," I said.

"Be quiet, or I'll gag you," he said.

I closed my mouth.

We arrived at the capital just as the moon was rising. The palace towers were visible all over the city. The bleached stone was marked by smoke damage decades old and rose out of a valley like an infected tooth.

We were greeted by what seemed a whole battalion of soldiers, but there was no sign of the king himself.

That's odd.

Agnes and Beata were taken away, presumably to be bathed and feted and cosseted, but I was taken immediately to an underground amphitheater that was already filled with spectators. They might as well have been howling for my blood.

Three women were waiting for us there. All dressed in black robes, their gray hair worn loose. All had eyes as gray as the men who had come to fetch me, and one wore a crude black iron key on a cord around her neck, signifying she was the one who held the Key to Justice.

She greeted Berard and Danr fondly, and I knew she must be a relative—an aunt or a cousin. Perhaps even a much older sister. Then she looked at me, her gaze so full of venom I could almost believe that she tainted the air with it and was surprised that I did not fall faint just from breathing it.

There was no pretense of even-handedness or even lip service to the idea that I should speak in my own defense. The woman with the Key greeted me formally as Dalissa of West Themis, daughter of Sestor the Flame, Heir to his magic, and also his actions.

It took less than an hour for the women to confer, and then the Key Bearer stood to state their judgment.

"We are agreed," the oldest of the Three said, and her speech had taken on a formal cadence. I tried to straighten my spine to show no fear as she pronounced the sentence they had decided.

As I had thought, I'd been sentenced to die in the phoenix cage.

Her words sent a shudder through my soul.

And then, as I watched, a fiery hole burned through her forehead, and she collapsed in mid-sentence.

I looked around to see where the attack had come from and saw three men wearing Sestor's sigil standing at the three doors to the chamber.

"Sestor forever," one shouted and sent another blast of fiery energy, this time toward Berard. He moved swiftly, but the magical attack still caught him in the torso. As if that had been a signal, suddenly, other magic workers burst through the doors. As they let loose their magic attack, it seemed as if the very air had caught fire.

"Stop," I cried. "Stop, in Sestor's name."

I didn't really expect anyone to obey my command, but the attackers were zealots, and they were committed to what they saw as my cause. The magic projectiles froze in place, then disappeared in puffs of glittering dust. Three of the young archers were dead, and Owin was badly wounded. Berard was still standing, but blood was flowing from his side, and his face was nearly colorless.

Danr looked at me, beseechingly. "Please," he said. "Please heal him."

Then, to my surprise, he dropped to his knees before me. "Please."

I looked at him for a long moment, weighing my options. Everyone in the room was waiting for my decision. I felt as if some weighty decision hung in the balance. "Remove my shackles," I finally said.

Danr reached up and unscrewed the tight pin holding the cuffs together. I almost staggered as my power came back to me, and I sent it in a rush toward Berard, staunching the bleeding, and then reaching deeper to pull the tissues back together.

"Burns," he said.

Good, I thought. *Now you know what it feels like.*

The leader of the Sestorians—the magic worker who had drawn first blood-stepped toward me. "King Kirle is dead, my queen. We await your command."

I looked at Danr, who still knelt before me, head bowed.

"I wish to call an immediate truce."

Danr looked up, surprised.

"I wish for a parley with representatives from both the Sestorian and the Kirlian factions. And I expect everyone to come to the table with honest intentions."

"But majesty—"

"This is my wish," I said.

The Sestorian leader looked at Berard and Danr. "We cannot negotiate with murderers," he said. "There must be blood before there is peace."

"No," I said. "There has been too much blood."

"Wait," Danr said. Everyone's eyes turned to him.

"What are you doing?" I asked, low enough that only Danr could hear me.

"Repaying a favor," he said and rose to his feet gracefully. "I am a son of Kirle," he said. "And the last of his line."

"Anyone can see, that's a lie," the Sestorian said. He looked toward Berard. "Anyone can see you're brothers."

But even as he said these words, Danr's visage seemed to melt. In an instant, he was no longer the fair-haired, gray-eyed man he'd appeared to be, but someone taller, leaner, with skin the color of lorch leaves in fall and hair as black and straight as a cat's whiskers. Berard looked at him in astonishment. "How?" he asked.

"I was Kirle's firstborn," Danr said, "a child conceived and born in Zoorea."

He glanced at me. "I favored my mother," he said by way of explanation.

"The Pirate Queen?" I asked.

"Her name was Lorolor," he said, and there was genuine affection in his voice. ."

"Kirle was my father too," Berard said, sounding aggrieved.

"No," Danr said. "When Kirle tried to steal my mother's throne, she cut off his genitals and fed them to the sea. He paid a loyal subject to perform his duty for him and then killed him to hide his secret."

"If the secret was hidden, how do you know it?" Berard challenged.

"He had me watch," Danr said. "To teach me a lesson. To toughen me up."

I caught my breath at that. Danr gave me a smile, an expression that was familiar on his unfamiliar face.

"My mother's father was a magic worker," he said. "She had the gift of shifting her features, and she passed it on to me."

"That's all very well," said the Sestorian, "but what is your proposal?"

"I offer you my life to end this feud."

No, I said, with more feeling than I would have thought I possessed.

"Yes," he said. Turning to the Sestorian, he added. "Once the stain of Kirle's blood is wiped from the land, you can remake the nation. Consider reuniting with East Themis. Grow prosperous, live without fear. Use your magic to grow crops rather than to wage war."

Danr looked around him, at the faces of the men and women gathered in the chamber. "It's a fair bargain," he said.

"I accept," the Sestorian said, and his people roared their approval.

"No," I said again, and this time my voice echoed through the chamber, amplified by my magic. "No one will die here today."

"My queen, with respect, the bargain is made," the Sestorian said.

"I agree," Danr said. He turned to the Sestorian. "What form of death will satisfy you?" he asked.

The Sestorian conferred with his fellows while I turned to the remaining Two. "Can't you do anything to stop this?" I asked. The woman who had taken the Key of Justice from the dead woman turned it over in her hands. "This is justice."

"This is madness."

"We choose milk of dreams as the method of execution," the Sestorian said.

I caught my breath. Distilled from a rare black flower that grows only on the island of Joxolo, milk of dreams was the most potent poison known in the realm.

"I accept," Danr said.

"Sentence to be carried out immediately," the woman holding the Key of Justice said. "Do you need time to prepare?"

"Danr," Berard said. "Don't do this."

"Calm yourself, brother. And abide by the new order."

In less time than I would have thought, a vial full of silvery gray liquid was brought into the chamber and handed to Danr. He held it up and smiled at me. "If only I had a bit of honeycomb," he said, and then drank it off in one gulp.

My heart seized as he convulsed and died.

There was silence in the chamber at the suddenness of it all. The

Sestorian stepped forward. "I am called Fentress," he said. "And it would be my honor to prepare this man for burial. He has done a great deed today."

I was in no mood to thank Fentress for his offer, but I knew what the moment required. "Thank you, Fentress," I said. "See that he has all honors."

"My queen," he said. "We will attend to it as soon as you are crowned."

"I'm not in the mood for ceremony," I said.

"I promise it will be brief."

Fentress was a man of his word. Within the hour, I was brought to the old throne room in the palace where everyone who'd been in the underground amphitheater had assembled, along with what looked like the entire population of West Themis.

The new Key of Justice—whose name turned out to be Sorala—placed a black-gold crown on my head and recited words that might as well have been gibberish. Afterward, my new subjects—Kirlians and Sestorians alike paid homage to me, pledging their fealty and offering their support for my wishes.

It can't be as easy as this, I thought. But perhaps Danr's death had served to lance the boil of resentment that had festered all these years. Perhaps West Themis was weary of their dreary existence. Perhaps there could be peace.

Finally, there was only one man left to pledge his fealty. I saw it was Fentress, and I saw he was smiling, which I thought wildly inappropriate given the events of the past hour. But before I could say something scathing, I saw another figure enter.

It was Danr.

"How?" I asked Fentress.

"Magic," he said. "I'm a necromancer."

"Why?"

"Because he sacrificed his life to make peace; it seemed only right to use my magic to bring him back. West Themis needs more peacemakers."

"I am in your debt Fentress," I said.

His smile broadened. "I will remind you of that one day," he said.

And then I turned my attention to Danr.

Once again, he knelt at my feet.

"I am your man," he said, "and always will be."

"Yes," I said. "You are."

ABOUT KAT PARRISH

Kat Parrish is an internationally bestselling author. A former reporter, she prefers making things up! An Army brat, her motto is "Have passport, will travel." She has lived in seven states and two foreign countries and would love to celebrate her 100th birthday with a trip into space. She lives in the Pacific Northwest near a haunted cemetery.

Website: https://kattomic-energy.blogspot.com

facebook.com/eyeofthekat

twitter.com/eyeofthekat

pinterest.com/kattparrish

PROWLERS

BY SCOTT MOORE

1.

It was hard to imagine what steel mixed with saliva tasted like, but Knox was lucky enough to experience it firsthand. If asked, he would have told anyone else it was quite unpleasant. He made sure not to move his lips. Best to avoid any unnecessary punctures.

"I would have thought the holy cloth prohibited you from killing anyone out of spite." Elena stood at the bottom of the red-carpeted stairs. If blood spilled, it wouldn't be hard to clean.

The priest flicked his eyes from Knox to his sister, Elena. Knox wished he would focus on holding the sword steady.

"You and your friend here have stolen from me for the last time. Maybe if I take off his nose, it will remind you where to keep it."

The priest sounded serious. Knox must have pushed him pretty far this time. Seven times in a single month may have been a little bit of an overkill, but the church had plenty, and he had none. How was that fair? Which god thought it was okay to push so much into his face and expect him not to jump at the first chance to take it?

"I thought your god was a forgiving god?"

Elena had slipped on the prayer carpets left out by some lazy worshiper. If not for that, they would have gotten away with the day's collection plate rather easily. As it stood, the priest heard the commotion, ran into the room with a sword, caught Knox off guard, and introduced him to the taste of steel—literally.

"My god is a forgiving god. Which is why I know he will forgive me for what I must do. An example must be made, and if I don't do it, then who will?"

Knox fumbled in his pocket. Elena hadn't expected the priest to have a change of heart. Maybe if this had been the first time they held up the place. Maybe even the second time. After a half dozen times, there wasn't hope of forgiveness. Luckily for Knox, they planned to get caught. There wasn't a way to know every attempt would go off without a hitch. Sometimes people were clever and caught them, and sometimes priests were stupid lucky, and prayer rugs caught them. Either way, they needed ways to get out then, too.

Knox grabbed the powder in his pocket, cupped it, and threw it in the priest's eyes at the same time as he backed away from the sharp edges of the blade. A miracle, overseen by the gods, saw Knox free himself without severing his tongue in the process.

Without time to celebrate, Knox reached down at his feet, grabbed the bag of coins, and made a line for the door.

"We are truly sorry!"

The priest stumbled on the stage and fell over the aforementioned rug. Sometimes the gods were cruel.

2.

The piers of Mocking Bay were some of the most beautiful sights in the city. The glass walkways jutting into the crystal blue waves were mesmerizing. Knox loved to go there after a score and think about all the promises of the world. Many of them would never be his, but these little spots were something not even the fates could take away.

"There are Acasia, Dason, and Kamari!"

Elena pointed to the far side of the piers where three youths splashed in the waters, their feet bare, and their faces filled with smiles.

Knox slowed, trying to put on an air of calm. He was the oldest of the group and wanted everyone to see him in that light.

Dason spotted them first. He ran over, grabbed Elena in a hug that brought her from her feet, and spun her around.

"The water is gorgeous tonight. Just warm enough, I am thinking about taking off my pants and hopping in."

Elena giggled. She had a thing for Dason, even if both were a bit too young to be thinking about it any further.

Knox walked past them toward the glass pier. Looking down, through the glass panes, he watched the waves lap at the underside. Imagining he walked on water made him forget about the struggles of life.

"Sun's about to set, I know how you like the colors." Kamari patted a spot next to her.

Knox flicked off his battered boots and slid his feet into the water next to hers. Kamari had been with the Prowlers maybe even longer than he had. He couldn't remember who got there first, but it had been before the summer sickness took his mother and father. It was definitely before Elena had joined him in the broken barracks.

"Did you get anything tonight?"

Kamari motioned for Acasia to throw her a satchel next to his thigh. Acasia didn't speak. An accident when he was young made it impossible for him to hear, and any noise coming from his mouth was purely accidental. He made it by without hearing just fine, but the group had to come up with special ways to talk with him. Kamari thanked Acasia with a quick flash of her fingers.

"We got two purses from the church in Meadows."

"The little churches?"

The Meadows were filled with trees and agricultural supplies. Many of the city's greenhouses set up there, keeping the air clean. At least the senators made them believe that was the case. For all Knox knew, they were just trees, and the churches there gathered money just like any other.

"The little churches got us enough coin to feed everyone for a week. What did you get?"

Knox didn't get to answer. Elena slid in, separating Knox from Kamari, and dunking her feet into the water.

"You are supposed to take off your shoes," Knox yelled.

"It doesn't matter. This way, I am ready in case we have to run."

There wasn't a point in fighting. Knox wished she would have picked a better spot to sit. After a long day, there wasn't anything he would have rather done than sit next to Kamari and compare hauls. Instead, Elena leaned in closer to Kamari.

"Knox almost got impaled by the priest up on Red Hills today," Elena whispered the words, but emphasized them enough for everyone to hear.

"You all went to Red Hills again? That is the... what... third time this week?"

Knox shifted uncomfortably. He had the bigger stash of coins. If Elena would have shut up, he could have had the bigger showboating. Instead, she opened her mouth and inserted his downfall.

"Yes, we have been there a few times this week. A few more times over the month. The hills bring a lot of sightseeing assholes, and I don't mind taking a little of their coin for myself." Knox pulled the sack of coins from his coat. "Not to mention, you all never complain about the food it buys you."

"What happens if one of these times they actually cut you down?" Kamari's dark face was deeper in color than Knox had ever seen it. He hoped that meant she feared for him because she would miss him and not because he was foolish.

"I am as careful as can be. I brought the coin, and we got out alive. I won't go back there for a few days."

Dason stepped to the docks. "You won't go there for months." His hands rested on his hips like his word meant more than drivel.

Knox closed his eyes and laughed. Leaning back, he gazed at the passing clouds. The purple, orange, and yellow of the sea and sky mixed above him. The world was grand on the piers at sunset. It almost made him forget about everything else in life. Almost.

3.

"Looks to me like Elena and Knox brought home the most coin again. Maybe you others don't enjoy eating? Maybe you would rather frolic about? Dip your feet in the waves and pretend nothing matters?"

Elena hid her feet behind an overturned chair. The watermarks from the entryway to General Fynn's desk were evident. There wasn't any hiding the puddles.

"We tried to hit someplace we haven't in a while. Tried to keep them guessing. Isn't that what you call good strategy? It is what you have taught us since I arrived. Keep them on their toes, and they won't know what hit them."

Kamari stepped in front of Dason and Acasia. She would take the brunt of the tongue lashing, she always did. Fynn didn't care who took it. His past as a general for the marching army made him hard and heartless. Still, he was the only reason any of them were still alive. Without his shelter and his guidance, they would have all starved to death a long time ago.

"I got lucky again is all. Hit the same place. I really messed up. We got lucky we didn't fail."

Fynn weighed the coins in his hand again. Dipping his hand into the bag, he threw two coins to both Knox and Elena.

"Keeping them on their toes. That is what I mean. Hitting them again when they least expect it. If almost failing feels this good, Knox, then keep almost failing and make sure to turn it into a victory." Fynn pulled his drawer open and shoved the coins into it. "As for the rest of you, maybe let Knox plan your route. You do a piss-poor job of it."

Fynn waved them from the office. Everyone clamored over themselves, trying to be the first out. Once the door shut, Dason let loose his displeasure.

"Oh, be like Knox. What a wonderboy Knox is. Barf!"

Knox socked Dason in the arm.

"Don't be pissed because you can't seem to understand more coins equals more rewards. Whose idea was it to pick the little churches?"

Knox regretted the words as they stumbled from his mouth.

Kamari's face belied the answer before he finished. She turned to storm through the barracks to her room, and Knox tried to stop her from reaching it and shutting him out. Leaving the others behind, he jogged alongside her.

"I didn't mean that. I was trying to put Dason down, not you."

Kamari stopped and turned toward him. Her eyes were narrow, and he readied himself for the tongue lashing.

"Maybe you should shut up and not speak before you talk out of your ass." She put a smile that showed no humor. "Then maybe people would like you more."

Kamari pressed Knox hard on the chest and turned away. He should have known to bite his tongue. Should have shut up, but it wasn't easy for him to do. He watched her walk away, knowing he had screwed up another shot at mending bridges with her.

"Do you think she will ever forgive you?"

Dason put his hand onto Knox's shoulder in a mock attempt at sympathy.

"Remove before I break." Knox pulled away just as Fynn opened the door.

"I think it would be best if everyone stayed in tonight. Dinner will be at the same time, and I have something for you all to do. I think you will enjoy it." Fynn didn't wait for a reply and slammed the door.

Knox knew better than to believe he would like it. Elena grabbed him by the hand and drew his attention.

"She knows you didn't mean to kill him. It was an accident and could have happened to anyone. She will come around." Elena squeezed his hand hard twice and then skipped away to follow Dason toward the eatery.

Knox had wished for almost a year for Elena to be right. He and Kamari had once been thicker than blood, but now it was a rare moment she even looked at him. What had happened hadn't been his fault. Elena was right, but he had made the decision that caused the accident. That much he had to take the blame for. One of the Prowlers had died on his choices, and there wasn't any way he could avoid the fact.

4.

Knox wasn't in the mood to eat anymore. Before going to the piers and watching the sunset, his belly had ached bad enough for him to eat enough to fill an army. Even after, while Fynn touted on him, he felt good enough to ravage the kitchens. Once Kamari reamed him for opening his idiotic mouth, he didn't feel much like eating ever again. Fynn had said he had something to request of them, though. No one missed a meeting with Fynn and stayed in the barracks.

Knox slid his plate in front of the pockmarked cook. The man was older than Knox by at least twenty years, but always made faces like he was a child. Knox wasn't so sure he didn't spit in all the food to boot. He had voiced this to the others a few times, but stopped when Kamira yelled at him for being mean. There wasn't any winning with her.

Knox turned from the line and looked over the tables. The Prowlers were a group of around fifty-five youth from across the world. Fynn brought them in from the far reaches of The Anvil Mountains all the way to the foreign lands of Ican. Mostly everyone conformed into groups and kept to themselves. Knox found Elena waving her hand like a madwoman trying to get his attention. He knew where to sit. He sat in the same place every night and had done since he could remember. He waved back to Elena to placate her. She sat again next to Dason, who shoved a big spoonful of what looked like mud into his mouth.

Knox slid onto the bench. He planned to talk to no one, listen to Fynn, and head to bed. Kamari came to the table last. She sat across from Knox, fiddled with her spoon, and spoke to no one. Knox watched her over the ridge of his eyebrows. Her fingers were filled with callouses from hard labor, her nails broken, and her cuticles dirty with who knew what. Still, they were the most beautiful hands he had ever seen. He longed to go back to a year ago when he held them in his own, and everything had been alright.

Knox went to open his mouth to apologize again for his comments outside Fynn's office, but the general walked into the room. Everyone scrambled to stand and salute as he walked to the head table. There wasn't anyone else permitted to sit with General Fynn, but there were always extra seats as if he would someday have a visitor join him. Knox got to his feet slower than everyone else, but Fynn didn't notice. His face was buried in a set of papers. When he got to his seat, he made to wave everyone down, not bothering to look up.

The noise resumed, and everyone sat, eating the rest of their meals. The cook brought out an extravagant cut of meat for Fynn and set it before him. Even in his state of pity, the cut of meat made Knox's stomach growl. He turned away, trying not to shake his head in disgust. Even here—in his own home—the world wasn't fair.

Knox pushed his own meal around with the side of his spoon. The thought of talking with Kamari had passed. She was in deep conversation with Acasia about what they thought the message was about. Their hands moved so rapidly Knox didn't even bother trying to keep up. The two could gossip so fast no one else could understand a thing they were talking about even in the middle of a crowd. Knox guessed that was one perk to having a made-up language.

General Fynn didn't touch his meat before pushing his chair back and throwing the papers onto the table before him. Again, everyone stopped chattering and turned their attention to him. This time no one stood to salute, but the attention went without saying.

"Let me be frank about something. Most of you came back with nothing today. You are lucky I don't throw you to the wolves in the city. How many of you would survive without these barracks to come home to? I think it very few. Still, many of you act like the privilege is a god-given right and not a luxury." Fynn shook his head in mock disgust. Knox knew it to be a show. Everything was a show with the general. "I have something to help you change your position in the barracks. Something that will make your world better and make your favor stand above even the highest coin earner. Which again is Knox and Elena, by the way."

Knox waved his hand. The stares weren't congratulatory. Still, Knox waved as if they had been. Fynn drew the attention back to himself.

"I have a simple request from everyone here tonight. I have papers brought to me by a friend in the marching army. They have gotten word of a weapon in the Red Hills, weapons that could change the face of our world, bring riches, and maybe even change the trajectory of history. If one could find these weapons and bring them to me, then I would be inclined to make them a very wealthy man or woman."

The general interlocked his fingers in front of his chest and peered over the crowd. Knox always thought General Fynn was a middle-aged man, but there were times when he could see the age lines across his face and knew he was much older than he put on.

"Where would we find these weapons, sir?"

Knox hadn't seen who asked, but the question made sense. If they were about to fly to the streets of the Red Hills, then they would need more to go on than weapons and somewhere. The Red Hills were gigantic. The red paved cobblestones dotted much of the western portion of the city. They towered so high they could be seen from almost anywhere, and on them were thousands of buildings, if not more. Many of them minor businesses and markets, but some were the homes of senators, government buildings, churches, and more.

"Good question and I am glad you asked it. However, I don't have an answer. That is the conundrum here. If you can find it, then you will be rewarded for your hard work, but it won't be easy. Not to mention, if you don't find it, and don't bring coin home..." Fynn clicked his tongue. "Well, we won't imagine you would do such a thing."

The message was obvious. General Fynn wanted the weapons, whatever they were, but anyone who slacked on their duties to get them coin would also be punished. Tomorrow, the streets of the Red Hills would be lined with Prowlers. Knox didn't envy them, because the taste of steel still hadn't left his mouth.

5.

Some parts of the city were situated over small heat vents trapped deep within the earth. On cool winter nights, it made for an amazing feature. In the summer months, when the air was already a hundred degrees, it made afternoons miserable, which was why Knox awoke before the first rays of the sun, pulled Elena from her covers, beat down the doors of the others, and made it to their first targets before it grew too hot.

"So, we are supposed to listen to the great and mighty Knox. What does he have to say? Where in the Red Hills are we going to search?" Dason ate his third wheat tart, leaving flecks of icing all over his brown shirt.

"We aren't going to Red Hills. I told you guys I wasn't going there for a month, and I meant it. We will hit somewhere else. Maybe try the archways. There were three new churches built there in the last year. I bet they still have some novelty effect on the people there. Everyone loves something when it is shiny and new."

Knox finished his coffee and chucked the cup into the alley. It clattered against the rocks and dirt and echoed back to them.

"You want to skip out on finding the weapons? This is right in your wheelhouse." Elena urged Knox, but he wasn't interested.

"Yeah, Knox. Don't you want to risk someone else's life for your own reward?" Kamari had eaten alone this morning. Knox hadn't been sure she would follow them, but hearing her voice bringing him down, let him know she had.

"Good morning, Kam."

"Don't call me that." Kamari pursed her lips. "Where are we going, Knox?"

"You want to listen to me?" Knox put on a mock expression of shock. "I can't believe you would trust me with such a task."

Kamari chuckled to herself. "Knox, I put up with you because you're a smart person. But you are also a smartass, and one doesn't cancel out the other."

Knox wanted to hit himself. Last night Kamari had almost been normal with him. She had almost treated him as a person again on the docks. What had he done to get in her good graces? He couldn't understand where he had gone wrong or what he had done right then. Whatever it was, the moment had faded, and things returned to how they had been for the past year.

"We are going to the Archways."

Knox turned, hearing Dason and the others sigh. They would follow him. None of them wanted to be left without the weapons or the coin.

The Archways were an hour's walk from the barracks. General Fynn forbade anyone to steal within a thirty-minute walk from their location. Said it was bad philosophy to work where you shit. Knox didn't know that it would matter. There were too many people in the city for anyone to remember a single face once lost in the crowd, but he followed the advice.

"Which church are we hitting?" Dason asked. His complaining about the weapons had been going on the entire walk, and Knox was happy to hear something else from him.

"There are three new ones, and I plan to hit them all. Elena and I will get two of them, and the third can be taken by you three."

Knox split the groups the way he needed them. In the past, he would have worked with Kamira, but that hadn't been the case in a year. Now his team only consisted of Elena. In many ways, it was for the better.

"You guys get two churches? Why? So, you can come home with more coin again?" Dason sounded incredulous.

"When you make up the plans, then you can call the shots."

Knox could see the archways looming in the background of three towering stone buildings. The churches always found a way to tower over everything. The money pouring into the system was enough to float the city down the sea on, but it went to only a few hands, hands of some very rich and powerful men and women.

"You three take the Sparrow, we will take the Eagle and the Hawk." Knox pointed to the churches in turn. There were symbols marking them on the glass decorative windows. Three birds for the three secrets of faith. All carried by messengers into the heavens. It was all total bullshit, but Knox didn't care about the messages. He cared about the coin the text brought in. "In and out, no funny business. There isn't anything else worth our lives in there. The collection plates on the dais and then out."

Each church was set up the same. Religious folk were very uncreative. They put the collection plate in the center of the dais at the front of the pews. No one stole from the gods. It was bad karma. Knox didn't care about karma. Karma didn't feed him. Knox grabbed Elena by the wrist and dragged her away. He could feel her other hand waving to Dason. He didn't turn back.

6.

Churches were the epicenter of culture in the city. If there was a real leadership, it lived in the walls of the mammoth structures. The senators were the face of power, but the priesthood was where the actual power lay. If a priest said to jump, the city asked in which direction they should leap.

It also made the churches the most lucrative businesses. Coin practically tumbled from the stained-glass windows. The priests jingled when they walked from all the coin. The next biggest structures in the city weren't the government buildings, they were the homes of the priest. Knox hated them. They were gluttonous and greedy. They claimed to have the favor of the gods, and millions of people believed them, but Knox wasn't one of them. He knew they were full of shit, but their open coffers were hard to pass up.

"Do you ever wonder if there is more to life somewhere else?" Elena asked as she practiced her rock kicking skills on the way to the church.

Knox didn't bother with much planning anymore. He hadn't been in this church before, but they were mostly all the same. There would be two altar boys inside the pews watching the coin pot. Both would be young enough to not run away with the coin and start a new life, but old enough to be curious about the outside world. Elena would provide a distraction with her presence, and Knox would provide the sack for the coins. Easy as that. Nothing to it if they did it right. A gambit they had pulled a thousand times. Don't fix what isn't broken.

"I don't tend to think of anything else. We aren't somewhere else, and pretending we are won't make it any better. I figure there is one way out of this, and that is death. I don't much feel like dying."

Elena wound her leg back and kicked the rock hard down the smooth, paved road. Knox watched it tumble through a grate at the side of the walkway and into the sewers below. Elena sighed.

"Dason says there are other cities around the world where we could be free from having to steal every day. Said he could get a proper job, something honest."

Knox laughed, imagining Dason doing anything that resembled an actual job.

"What is he going to do? He can't farm, can't sell something he doesn't own, and I haven't ever seen him craft anything with his own hands."

Elena's face scrunched. The soft spot for Dason would end up getting her in trouble one day. He wished he could tell her how it felt for the heart to be ripped from the chest, but she would have to learn it on her own.

"He can paint. We can sell his artwork. Dason says there are people across other cities that buy artwork for their walls."

Knox hadn't ever seen Dason paint, but he hadn't ever really been interested in Dason's talents either. The boy may have been good, but it didn't matter. You couldn't eat paint.

"I don't believe Fynn will give him the okay to scurry away."

Knox didn't believe Fynn would give anyone permission to do much of anything. They would be in his service until they got caught, Fynn grew tired of them and killed them, or Fynn died. No matter how old the general got, Knox couldn't imagine him ever dying.

"But…"

Knox held his hand up and stopped Elena. She could have her childhood fantasy, but at the moment, he needed her head in the game.

"The same plan as always, okay?"

Elena didn't look pleased with the subject change, but she nodded and allowed Knox to lead her up the stairs.

Once inside, Knox shut the doors to the outside. Allowing no other patrons into the church was step one. When Knox turned around, he didn't see an open dais. However, he saw four lances pointed straight toward his neck.

"Is there something we could assist you with?"

Knox swallowed hard and looked to Elena.

7.

Before the guards could react, Knox shoved both hands into his coat pocket. With a quick movement, he pulled out two sticks and cracked them over his knee. A loud bang rang into the church, echoing off the high ceilings. A second later, two more loud pops followed. They wouldn't hurt anyone, but they weren't meant to. Knox needed a distraction long enough to get out of the church alive. If they could get lost in the crowd, then they would be fine. No one could remember a single face in a sea of millions.

Knox grabbed Elena's hand and turned to run, but a guard had sneaked in behind them before Knox's trick. Knox turned to his left and pulled Elena hard toward the pews. Jumping onto them, he moved from one to the next toward the dais. There were windows in the back, and breaking one may lead to a lot of noise and attention, but he was running out of choices quickly. More guards came to check on the noise from the primary room. Knox was forced to turn before the dais and run into a swinging door.

It led them into a carpeted hall lined with paintings of serene land-scapes. Knox knew enough about churches to know these were the prayer boxes. He didn't know enough about churches to know how to get out from any other exit. Knox ran toward the open doors. Each was only a small cubicle leading to a single bench. Praying wouldn't help him now. He continued pulling Elena down the hall and came to another exit leading into a long corridor. There was a third door at the end with a nameplate. He didn't know if it would help him to get there, but maybe it had windows or an exit.

Knox ran hard, trying to think of what he would do if he were trapped or caught. He had other tricks in his coat, and if things got too serious, he had a knife, but those guards had lances. Knox barreled through the door without reading the nameplate. At the desk sat the priest of the church, fiddling with some papers. Knox pulled Elena into the room, turned, and slammed the door shut. He took a moment to find a chair and shoved it under the handle to wedge the door. Seven feet or so above the priest's desk was a small circular window. It wasn't wide, but Knox and Elena could fit through one at a time.

Knox wasted no time and made for the desk. The priest hadn't moved, his jaw open in shock. Knox waved Elena over, and together they moved the desk toward the wall. The priest shot from his seat and scurried over to the corner.

"Do you know what you are doing, young man?"

Knox didn't stop what he was doing. He didn't care about the priest as long as the priest didn't try to stop him. The desk touched the wall just as the guards sounded on the other side of the door. Knox picked up a paperweight from the desk and threw it as hard as he could through the glass window. The spraying shards flew outside with the weight. Knox wondered if there were people under them even now.

Knox turned to Elena and pushed her onto the desk. He followed and made a base for her to climb. The guards tried to open the door, but for the moment, the chair held steady. It wouldn't forever. Knox hoisted Elena toward the busted window. She removed her jacket and wrapped it around her hand before clearing the shards of glass remaining. Then she hoisted herself up and wiggled her body through to the other side. Knox heard her tumble through the air and come to a thudding halt on the ground outside.

"I am fine. Hurry, there is a crowd out here."

Knox planned to hurry. He looked back one more time to see the door wiggling almost open. Then he looked at the priest to wave goodbye before noticing something in his hands. The papers had plans drawn over them like those Knox had seen before in General Fynn's office. The schematics, as he called them, were for war weapons and alignments. Knox wasn't sure Fynn had ever been a general, but he did have a lot of war memorabilia.

"What is that?"

The priest looked at his hands and pulled the papers into his chest.

Knox should have run away. It was stupid to wait. The papers may have been something, though. Fynn had said Red Hill, but the Archways was where the church power shifted. Maybe he had been wrong. They didn't get any coin from this church, and they wouldn't be able to steal from anywhere else this afternoon. Maybe the papers would appease Fynn.

Knox bit his lip, jumped from the desk in a stupid decision and tried to grab the papers from the priest. The priest fought back, pulling away from Knox. The man wasn't strong, or large, and Knox decided right away to overpower him if the need arose. Knox drew his fist back and cracked his knuckles into the priest's nose. The audible crunch was barely heard over the screaming and crying of the priest. The guards had the chair leg broke by now. Knox grabbed the papers and ran for the desk as the door flew open. He jumped high, grabbed the ledge, threw the papers out the window to a worried Elena, and then wiggled through as the guards burst into the room.

Knox could hear the commotion and knew they didn't have much time. He grabbed the papers from the ground, shoved them into his pocket, grabbed Elena, and ran.

8.

Normally, after a score, Knox would have run toward the glass piers. It was where the others would have gathered. Instead, he pulled Elena the opposite way into the growing crowd of traders. They needed to meld into the crowd, get inside somewhere else, and take a few moments to breathe and think. Knox found his destination in the form of a small, rundown, back alley grocer. He slid into the establishment. The bell clanged over their heads to alert a single clerk to their presence. The clerk looked up from his book, thought about greeting them, then went back to reading as if they weren't there. Knox gave him a nod anyhow and ran for the back of the store. He stayed close to the long picture window that presented the outside. There were hundreds of people walking by, not paying a lick of attention to anything but their own problems. Knox pressed his back against the wall, away from the open view. He took a few deep breaths with his eyes closed.

"What took you so long in there? I thought you had gotten caught."

Elena huffed and puffed as much as he did. Knox pulled the papers from his coat. They were crumpled but still legible. He unfolded them and scanned the pictures. Elena scooted in closer. Knox watched to see if the clerk had moved, but the man was too invested in his story to care what they did.

"I found these in the priest's hand."

Knox thumbed a few of the pictures. The pictures looked like bracelets or rings, but Knox couldn't tell which because of the poor etching. Knox moved to flip the page, and there, taped onto the back, were two bands of pure red, gold. They were small rings with little weight to them. Knox picked the tape off with his nails and held them both in front of his eyes. Elena reached out and grabbed one from him.

"These are pretty." She held it to the picture window letting the light from outside refract from the gold.

It was pretty. Knox had to admit.

"Put it down," Knox said, pushing Elena's hand away from the window.

He spared another glance toward the clerk who still hadn't moved. The customer service in this store was poor. Knox pulled Elena behind the shelves.

"I wonder how much these are worth?" Knox flipped it over in his palm. It wouldn't fit over any of his fingers aside from the pinky, but it was solid gold for sure.

Elena took hers and slipped it over her ring finger. It almost looked like it expanded as she pushed it over.

"Is yours soft?"

Elena shook her head.

"No, it is real."

She sounded shocked it had fit her finger.

"You should take it off. We need to get it back to Fynn."

Elena nodded. When she tried prying it off her finger, though, it didn't budge. As easily as it had gone on, it refused to come off. Knox tried helping her, but it wouldn't budge for him either.

"Wet it with spit."

Elena tried sticking her finger in her mouth, but it didn't help. Knox pulled the papers back out from his coat and held them in front of the light.

"What does it say?" Elena asked, sounding more panicked than curious.

Knox saw nothing about the ring getting stuck. There wasn't much text on the papers at all. Mostly they were hand signs.

"I don't know, try one of these."

Knox flipped the paper. He hadn't a clue what he thought hand signs would do for a stuck ring, but he fed off Elena's panic and didn't think straight.

Elena curled her fingers into the position shown on the papers. As she did, a solid white beam shot from her hand toward the wall holding canisters of fresh milk. Three of the canisters exploded on impact. The clerk flew from his seat, Elena stumbled backward, crashing into a shelf, and Knox about pissed himself from shock.

"What is the hell are you two doing in here?"

The clerk ran back with a large stick in his hand. Knox didn't think the stick was for show. Without thinking, Knox slipped the ring over his pinky for safekeeping and moved to run out of the store. When he did, the ring latched hard onto his knuckle. Knox let out a squeal of pain. The clerk raised his stick high into the air, Knox went to block his face from being rearranged, and light shot from his hand, incinerating the stick completely.

The clerk stood there, holding his hands above his head, the stick's ashes floating in front of his face. Knox didn't test his luck. He ran forward and punched the clerk in the forehead. The clerk stumbled back, wishing he had stayed in his seat, reading his book, and fell to the ground. Knox ushered Elena toward the door, shoved the papers back into his coat, and went to the register taking all the coins with him. He should have felt bad, the poor clerk would get fired, and he probably wasn't any better off than Knox, but then again, he had tried to hit him with a stick.

9.

The smart thing to do would have been to go right to General Fynn and claim ignorance, but Elena hadn't wanted to do the smart thing. She wanted to show the others what the rings could do. Even though General Fynn had stated anyone who brought him the power would never work again, Elena had other thoughts swarming her head. Dason had made her believe there was another option to living.

"We show them, then we take them to Fynn, and that is my final word. I am only showing them if you agree to that."

Knox had tried to wiggle the ring from his finger the entire trip back to the barracks. It hadn't budged an inch. If anything, it felt tighter.

"We show them, and then we see what the world brings." Elena gave a smile and ran ahead of him before he could complain.

Sometimes her youth threatened to get them in trouble. Knox followed close behind, still reeling from the events in the shop. The rings were, for sure, the weapon Fynn looked for. The things they had done were amazing. There were other hand positions on the papers, but Knox hadn't dared to try them out. There wasn't a way of knowing what they would do. Not to mention, the church guards were out in heavy patrol looking for the two youths who had stolen from the Archways priest. Knox wasn't keen on getting caught and thrown into jail before he could reap the rewards from Fynn.

Knox wasn't so sure even Fynn could stop what would come down upon them, though. He had connections in the city, but how high up did those connections go? There wasn't a man alive more important than a priest to Knox's knowledge.

"Get your head out of your ass, Knox."

Elena pounded on Dason's door. No one answered.

"I bet they are at the docks. It is where they would go if they had gotten any coin. It is where we always meet."

Elena shook her head.

"They aren't stupid enough to stay on the streets with the patrol out as heavy as it was. Plus, they would have heard we almost got caught. They aren't still out there."

Elena thumped on the door again, and this time there was a noise on the other side. Dason flung the door open with sweaty hair plastered to his forehead and wide, shocked eyes bulging from his skull.

"I thought you two were dead or caught, or worse."

Dason's words came out in a spill and made no sense.

"What is worse than those two things?"

Dason took several deep breaths and then scanned the hallways as if he were afraid they had brought the patrol with them. He grabbed Elena by the arm and ushered her into the room. Knox followed and shut the door behind him. Dason flipped a few locks at the top of the door. There was no doubt he was spooked.

"What happened out there?"

Dason went to his wall and pounded on the brick with his fist three times. It was the signal for return. The others must have been listening for any news. Knox pulled Dason's desk chair from the corner and took a seat. Elena plopped onto the provided cot.

"We got a little sidetracked," Knox said.

Elena held her hand in front of Dason and pointed toward the ring. His eyes lit with excitement.

"That genuine gold?"

He grabbed Elena's hand and pulled it in closer to his face. Elena nodded vigorously.

"That's not all it is either. Want to see something amazing?"

Knox didn't like doing more with the ring. They weren't sure the effects, but there wouldn't be a way of talking Elena out of this, so he moved from the direct path. Before she could do the hand-gesture, there was a knock on the door, and Kamari's voice followed.

Dason ran to the door, threw off the lock, and let in Acasia and Kamari. Without missing a beat, he threw the door shut and flicked the lock back into place.

"They found proper gold rings."

Kamari and Acasia ran toward Elena, ignoring Knox in the corner. It was fine. Knox didn't feel much like showing off anyhow. He wanted to get to Fynn, get the ring off his finger, and forget he had ever seen them.

"Can I see it?" Kamari asked, holding out her hand.

Elena mimicked, trying to pull it from her finger.

"See, that is one of the weird things about the rings. Once they are on, they don't seem to want to come off."

She pulled hard to emphasize her point. Then she held her hand out for Dason to give it a go. Struggle as he may, Dason didn't even so much as turn the ring.

"She is right. It isn't moving a bit."

He sounded perplexed but also excited. Knox wished he could find the joy behind the fact the rings weren't coming off easily. Fynn wouldn't find it so funny.

"You said one of the weird things," Kamari said.

Elena smiled. She wanted the question to be asked. Knox had heard the bait from the initial reply. She would show them the powers no matter what Knox had said about them. At least it was almost over now. The others would realize how smart it was to go to Fynn and get this over with.

Elena shooed everyone to the side. Then she focused on a small cup in the opposite corner of Knox. Doing the hand movement from the paper in Knox's pocket, Elena shot a beam of light that incinerated the cup to ash.

There wasn't any commotion. Knox could have heard a needle drop. His heart hammered. Even seeing it again a third time made him feel uneasy. These were powerful weapons, and they had no business playing with them.

"Okay, you showed them. Now let's get them to Fynn." Knox stood and moved to grab Elena, but she shrugged out of his grip.

"Aren't these amazing?"

No one replied. Elena looked at Dason longingly.

"Elena, these are not toys. They need to be put into the right hands." Knox went to grab her again, and again she pulled away.

"Do you not see we could use these to be free? To leave this city and live somewhere else. All of us together."

Kamari spoke first. Her tone was low, and obviously a little frightened.

"Maybe Knox is right about this one."

Knox jumped on the encouragement. It wasn't often anymore that Kamari agreed with him on anything.

"You see, Elena. Let's just give them away. Stop thinking about childish dreams. This is our lot in life, and we are doing just fine. Maybe Fynn will give us the reward he promised. Wouldn't that be nice?"

Elena shook her head and pleaded with Dason again. Dason didn't look sure. Honestly, he looked afraid and for excellent reason. The rings had literally shot a beam of light that melted objects from existence.

"I don't know, Elena. I want to go, but I don't know about those things. Maybe Fynn will give us enough coin to live off, and we can be free that way. I don't know what we can do with these things, but what if we kill ourselves with them?"

Elena was obviously frustrated. She stomped her feet into the ground. She looked to be ready to argue further, but Knox got a hold of her this time.

"I let you show them. Now we show Fynn."

Knox pulled her to the door. Everyone moved from his path. They all knew it was the right thing to do. Fynn may not have been anyone's favorite person, but he would do right by them. Plus, he could show them how to get the rings from their fingers.

Everyone followed behind Knox as he dragged Elena behind him toward Fynn's office.

10.

Fynn sat behind his desk, surveying papers. Knox didn't know what Fynn did with most of his time. Those living in the barracks provided the coin, they cooked, they cleaned, and they ran errands.

Fynn mostly sat behind his desk and looked busy. Knox hadn't ever braved, asking him what the papers said, and he wouldn't start today either.

There wasn't a need to knock on the door as it stood wide-open. Fynn had office hours during the evening for the patrons to bring in their daily scores. Knox cleared his throat to alert Fynn they had entered the room. The general looked up from his shuffling and plastered a smile across his face. Knox was always his top earner, and it provided Knox with a better relationship with the general than others had.

"What have you brought me today, Knox?"

The general shoved his papers to the side and out of the way. His expectation was for Knox to throw a sack of coins onto the desk. Knox didn't have coin today, but he still felt good about what would happen when Fynn saw the papers.

Knox reached into his pocket and threw the folded packet onto the desk. Fynn looked confused and then grabbed them. Seconds later, he stood, knocking back his chair into the wall.

"Is this all of them?"

His voice had raised to a higher pitch than Knox had ever heard. The excitement was obvious. Knox let his heart settle. There had been a part of him that was nervous about how this would go. Seeing the obvious elation made Knox calmer and more sure.

"That is all we were able to gather. We found them in the Archways Church of the Eagle. A priest there read them in his office. I noticed them while we escaped from his window. I think there will be some commotion across the city for this one."

Fynn shook the papers and slapped the back of them with an open palm.

"This is what I have been searching for these last few months. This is the golden ticket. I am sure there are more out there, and I will let the commotion die down some before searching, but this will pass the time. Was there anything else with them?"

Fynn's reaction made Knox almost forget about the ring attached to his pinky knuckle. Then Fynn looked expectantly to Knox and saw the gleam of the gold. Knox saw his eyes land on the ring and pulled it in front of his face.

"There were these rings attached to the papers." Knox held his hand out for Fynn to see.

"Take it off, let me see it."

Knox bit his lip. This would be the sticky part of this transaction. Knox hadn't found a way to take it off yet.

"You see, there is a problem. Elena and I have put the rings on for safekeeping, and they won't come off."

Knox made a show of pulling on the golden ring. Fynn's eyes narrowed.

"They won't come off?" Fynn's voice lowered.

His walk around the table seemed to stretch into hours. Knox's heart hammered again. The next few seconds would determine how much praise Knox would get or how much trouble he would be in. Fynn took Knox's hand in his own. There were hard callouses along the pads of Fynn's fingers, and they scratched as they ran up and down Knox's.

Elena stepped forward and drew Fynn's attention.

"They have closed around our hands tightly. I don't know why."

Knox wished Elena had left well enough alone. Let him take the brunt of the punishment, and then they could have figured things out later. Fynn turned his attention and held his hand out for Elena. She placed her small hand into his. The contrast of size was enormous. Fynn was an imposing man. Elena was a small youthful girl. Knox came to stand by Fynn and peered over his forearm, trying to draw the attention back to himself.

Fynn ran his finger along the ring on Elena's finger. There was a compassion there like a father stroking his daughter's hand. Knox thought everything would be alright. Maybe he had panicked for nothing. Fynn was happy to see the rings. Even happier to see the documents.

Fynn stopped stroking and tried with a gentle pressure to pull the ring from Elena's finger. Knox saw the pressed lips and concentration along the general's features.

Fynn dropped Elena's hand, walked back to his desk, and waved her over to him. She came without pause. Everyone was taught from a young age to respect Fynn's request like they were those of a god. Knox couldn't react without making Fynn angry. Elena paused in front of Fynn and waited.

Fynn looked to Knox, drew in a deep breath, sighed, and then reached forward, grabbing Elena by the wrist. It happened in a flash, and there was nothing Knox could have done to stop it. One moment, Elena stood calm and watchful. The next, she screamed as Fynn pressed the tip of his dagger into her skin, severing the finger from her hand.

Knox heard Dason crying behind him and turned to see Kamari holding him back from attacking the general. Acasia vomited. Knox felt like his world had come to a sudden stop. Nothing moved right. Everyone looked to be in slow motion. Before he noticed what he was doing, he raised his hand with the ring, pointed it at Fynn's chest, and permitted the beam of light to come from his hand. Fynn ducked from the pathway, but behind him along the wall, a hole burst into existence.

Knox reached behind him, grabbing Kamari by the hand and rushing forward. There was only one thing to do. He bull-rushed the desk, knocking into Fynn with all the force he could muster. The ring flew from Fynn's hand and landed on the desk with a clatter. Fynn fell backward from shock, trying but not able to correct his footing. Elena screamed from pain, blood gushing from the spot where her finger used to be. Knox grabbed her by the opposite hand and pulled her toward the hole at the back of the wall.

Dason and Acasia followed close behind. Fynn moved to regain his footing, but before he could, Kamari grabbed the ring on the desk and moved to put it onto her finger. Knox reached out, grabbing her fingers and folding them before she could. With his ringed hand, he held his palm forward to show Fynn he would use the power on him. Fynn stayed put, having seen what the beam had done to the wall.

"You don't want to do this, Knox. I will still make you a rich man. Your sister can still heal from this. I will even let you keep your ring. Just give me the other."

Knox shook his head. There wasn't a point in trading requests. Fynn would kill them all if he got the chance, Knox knew that. He ushered everyone through the hole, keeping his palm facing Fynn to show his very real intent.

Once everyone was out, Knox thought of ending Fynn's life there and then, but Kamari pulled him hard by the wrist, and he turned, running as fast as he could toward the front gates of the barracks.

11.

The barracks were in the rearview. Knox continued running long after they faded out of sight. Fynn would have a party looking for them in less than an hour. Coupled with the guards always on the lookout and there was double the trouble. Knox turned in toward Statue Park. There they could at least find a crowd to blend into. No matter the time of night, there were always people milling about between the statues of the eagle, the hawk, and the sparrow. The symbols of religion were what the city, and the country ran on.

By the time Knox reached them, he was pulling air in big gulps through a wide-open mouth. The itching at the back of his throat made him wish he had grabbed water before he left. Who would have thought of something like this hours ago? Knox had been sure at the start of the day he would die in the barracks as an old man.

A quick headcount told him everyone had arrived with them. Each huffed and puffed themselves. Being a thief meant they had high endurance, but it was for quick, momentary burst of energy. They weren't conditioned to run thirty minutes across the city.

"How is everyone?" Knox asked, stupidly.

Dason had already taken the initiative to grab Elena and wrap her hand in a torn sleeve of his shirt. Knox grimaced at the sight of blood seeping through the fabric. He hadn't forgotten about his sister's finger, but in the rush, he had let it slip to the back of his mind. Now that they had all stopped, he could see clearly the extent of the damage done.

With a gentle push, he moved Dason to the side and grabbed

Elena's hand in his own. She looked up, expectantly toward him. When they were smaller, after their parents passed, Knox had always sung to Elena when she was hurt. It had helped her simple scrapes and bruises feel better. There wouldn't be any amount of singing that would make this go away.

"We are going to have to find someone to help us." Knox rolled Elena's hand around. Her arm pulsed and felt tight in his grip.

"With what money? Who? We can't sit in a hospital, Fynn will find us." Kamari paced along the multicolored stones beneath her feet.

There were hundreds of people about the park. The twin moons were coming up from the horizon and would provide enough light soon to see by. In the city, it was never truly dark. Knox bit his lip, concentrating on what they could do. Whatever they decided, it would have to be quick. Elena wouldn't have much longer before she bled out or risked infection.

"I have the coin from Fynn. The coin he gave me yesterday for being the highest earner. I also have coin from every day before that. In total, I think I have enough to encourage a doctor to keep quiet and help, but you're right. We can't do it in the hospital."

Knox looked around. Statue Park wasn't a brilliant place to hide. It was a splendid place to get lost in the crowd and provide some cover, but it wouldn't provide any alone areas.

"Why don't you all run toward the granite mausoleums. No one likes to visit them while the sun is down. I will find a doctor and convince him to come with me to meet you."

Elena moved to protest, but Knox stuck his hand into the air.

"I will be fine. Better off even. If we aren't in a group, we are more likely not to be seen. I will find the doctor and meet you there."

Knox moved to take off down the path. There were hospitals across the city. He would find the closest, convince a doctor with his coin, and then get them back to Elena before things became too dire.

"I will go with," Kamari said before Knox took two steps.

He paused. "I think you should go with them." Knox couldn't handle the lashing he knew Kamari wanted to lie on him. Whatever had happened here, she would blame him. Even though it hadn't been his fault.

Kamari wasn't taking no for an answer. Knox bit his lip again. There was another reason he didn't want Kamari to come. There may not have been enough coin to convince any proper doctor to follow him. The power of the ring surely could make up for whatever the coin lacked. Kamari wouldn't like it. She was a thief, but she still had a moral compass.

"I am going, and you can allow it, or I can just force it. Every second you wait is a second we can't get back."

Knox didn't have time to argue.

"Fine. Come, but if things don't go your way, you can't say I made you join me."

Knox turned around again to make for the closest hospital. The others made off in the other direction. He hated leaving Elena in the hands of Dason and Acasia, but he had no choice. With everything left in his gasping lungs, he turned and ran.

12.

There was something advantageous about the empty streets of evening. Unless running through the entertainment centers, the rising moons normally thinned the streets. It was a blessing in a time like this to not have to press through the crowd.

It took five minutes still to reach the closest medical center. It hadn't been the extravagant hospital Knox hoped for, but the medical symbol above the door of the small clinic promised an easier target. Without the added security of hospital guards, this place promised to be a straightforward solution.

"I am going to go in, do you want to keep guard?" Knox pulled up short of the door and turned to Kamari.

With a shake of her head, she let him know her intentions. "I want to make sure we get this done right."

What that meant was obvious. She still didn't trust Knox, even if it were his own sister in the thralls of death. Blaming him for things out of his control was the new normal for Kamari, though. Ever since the fateful night a year ago. It hadn't truly been his fault then, and it wasn't his fault now, but there wasn't time to argue it. Elena may already be in the clutches of trouble, and he didn't want to waste precious time.

He turned toward the doors and pressed them open, entering a well-lit waiting room. Several men and women gathered with minor injuries or coughs. Knox avoided their stares as she made quickly for the window. The nurse behind the glass stood, alarmed by Knox's frantic display. With a quick pull of the glass, she opened the window.

"Emergency?"

Her voice showed genuine concern.

"I have a big emergency. I need a doctor to follow me."

The nurse hesitated and looked around the room. All she saw behind Knox was Kamari. Her earlier anticipation of trouble wavered, and the nurse turned to confusion.

"Where is the patient located?"

"She is in the cemetery. We have coin." Knox pulled his sack of coins from his pocket. The display didn't look to appease the nurse's concern.

"We don't do house calls or cemetery calls. I am sorry, but you will have to bring the patient into the facility, but maybe you should bring her to a true hospital. We aren't equipped for life-threatening emergencies."

The nurse moved to shut the window. The conversation was complete in her mind. Knox shot his hand out and grabbed the frame. With a little resistance, he stopped the nurse from closing him out.

"We can pay," he said again.

The nurse shook her head.

"It isn't about the coin. Now, if you would please vacate the premises, I would appreciate your compliance."

Knox couldn't comply. He didn't have the luxury of forgetting what he had come here for. Elena's pained face flashed before his eyes. Knox didn't look back to confirm his plan with Kamari. She would give him a lashing later for his decision, but it was all he had left. Knox pushed the window open fully and jumped onto the counter. With a gentle shove, he pushed the nurse from his path.

Kicking papers, folders, and other items over, he jumped from the desk toward the door leading to the patient rooms. He heard Kamari coming in after him and apologizing to the nurse. The nurse yelled for both to stop and return to the waiting room, but Knox didn't pay any attention to the request. He threw open the door into a stark white hall with no paintings or decoration. The only item he saw aside from the swinging lights was a scale for weight. He ignored it. He made for the doors lining the hallway. In one of them would be a doctor, and he would force the man or woman to follow him to the mausoleum.

The second opened door revealed a middle-aged man hovering over a small girl with a broken leg. The girl winced as the doctor wrapped her leg in the white plaster of a cast. Her parents sat in chairs in the corner with concerned looks across their faces. Knox burst into the room, grabbed the doctor by the arm, and ignored the yells from the parents.

"I need your services now!"

The doctor straightened and turned to Knox, pulling his arm free with a little twist.

"I am with a patient." The doctor's fists clenched.

There were no guards here, but the doctor looked ready to defend himself.

"There is someone who needs you more. I can pay you whatever you need. This girl will survive the length of time it takes for you to help me."

The girl's parents didn't seem to agree with Knox's assessment. They yelled and screamed for him to stop, but Knox ignored them.

"I will go nowhere with you. I am requesting you leave this room now."

Knox grabbed the doctor's hand again and turned toward the door. He would drag him kicking and screaming if he had to.

The doctor broke the hold with another twist and struck Knox in the side of the jaw. The flash of pain made Knox stumble backward. The doctor knew more than medicine. Knox rubbed the side of his face and watched the doctor go into a fighting stance. Knox laughed at his predicament. The only fighting doctor in the city and Knox had to find him.

"We can find someone else, Knox."

Kamari grabbed Knox by his hand and guided him toward the door. Knox would have gone if there had been another solution. There were more doctors in the city, but wasting more time may cause further complications. Knox looked at his hand in Kamari's grip. He had longed for her touch for so long now, but he had to pull away.

The hand had something new on it that would help them. Ignoring the doctor's prowess for fighting, Knox held his own hand out before his chest. The gold ring gleamed in the light. The doctor took this as a challenge and moved forward. Knox didn't plan to fight. He turned his palm away from everyone and shot a beam of light from the weapon on his hand. Everything stopped. The adults no longer yelled, the doctor didn't move forward, and even the concerned young girl went silent.

"Knox!"

Kamari yelled, but Knox ignored her. He reached his hand forward again and grabbed the doctor.

"You will come with me, or I will make the next hole in your chest. Do you understand?"

The doctor stared at the newly formed hole in his wall. Then, without reluctance, he followed Knox from the room. As Knox turned and passed Kamari, he could see the disgust forming in her eyes. It didn't matter. There was only one thing that mattered right now. He had to get back to Elena and make sure she was okay.

13.

The doctor didn't struggle. There wouldn't have been any benefit for him to. He had seen what Knox could do with the weapon. Any sign of defiance and he knew Knox would strike him down. The prospect of kidnapping someone hadn't thrilled Kamari, but Knox didn't care. She already hated him. What was adding one more slight onto the mix?

At the mausoleums, Knox called for Dason. His head stuck around a concrete structure standing twenty feet high and topped with the crest of some rich family. Knox didn't know them and didn't care to.

"Is she okay?" Knox asked.

Dason moved to the side to allow the doctor room to work.

"She hasn't said much. She keeps staring at her hand and moaning, though."

Over her fingers, still wrapped tightly, was the sleeve from Dason's shirt. The doctor, seeing the genuine emergency, plopped to his knees. His displeasure at being kidnapped faded.

"How did you get him to come?" Dason hovered over the doctor's shoulder.

Knox didn't answer. Admitting to kidnapping wasn't something he was about to do right now. Maybe later, once this was over, he would tell everyone the story. Maybe it would be funnier then. Right now, he needed the doctor to focus fully on what he had in front of him. The sleeve unwrapped, and the doctor dropped it to the ground. Elena's hand was dark red, and the missing finger stood out like a light beacon.

Knox couldn't stomach to look at it, and so he looked away.

"Do you still have the finger?" The doctor looked to the others.

No one had thought to grab the finger from the desk. Kamari held out her hand. She had pulled something from her pocket. Knox remembered she had stalled and picked up the ring from the desk. Still attached to the ring had been Elena's ring finger. Kamari held it out to the doctor, who grabbed it and inspected it thoroughly.

"If we can get to a hospital, they can save this." He said, sounding very sure of himself.

"You can't save it here?" Knox urged.

"With what tools would you suppose I do that? Unless you have forgotten, you didn't give me time to grab even a medical bag. What you thought I could do with only my hands; I do not know. This is your screw up not mine."

Knox blew a loud sigh past his lips. The doctor was right. He hadn't put too much thought into any of this. How did one even bother to think during a crisis such as this?

"We can't go to a hospital," Knox said.

Kamari stepped in front of him.

"We have to go to save her finger, Knox."

Knox shook his head. "She will have to lose it. It is that or her life."

"Do we not even give her a choice?" Kamari placed her hands on her hips.

"The choice is made…"

Knox didn't get to finish his sentence. Elena uttered the words through her pain.

"He is right, but can I have it?" She held her good hand out toward the doctor.

The doctor tentatively gave the finger, with the ring on it, to Elena. She took it in her complete hand and looked it over. She moved it to the space it had used to be as if the wonder of it was too much. She didn't press the useless digit into her hand, but she held it over as if to imagine what once was. Without warning, the ring glowed. Then a small light emitted from the band and caused everyone to turn away from the sheer force of the brightness.

Knox looked back after the light faded. Little black dots swam around his vision, but there was no denying what had happened. Back where it should have been, on Elena's hand, was her finger.

Elena squeezed her hand shut and stared at the ring with a mixture of excitement and horror. Everyone else had their jaws wide open in shock. Then the doctor stood and ran. Knox thought about chasing after him, but paused. It didn't matter anymore. There was no more need for him.

14.

"How do you feel?" Knox made his way to his sister. The kidnapping may have been unnecessary, but he wasn't about to tell anyone that. He would focus his attention to Elena and hope the others forgot the doctor had been there.

"I feel just fine. It is like the finger was never gone." She flexed her hand to show the truth to her words. Her finger moved with the rest of her hand like it was fully healed. There was no scar. No evidence of detachment.

"Okay, I see everyone is just going to pretend we didn't watch a finger reattach itself to Elena's hand. I am okay with the result. Like, I am happy it happened. I am maybe the happiest of us all, but I still just watched a finger pretend it had never been chopped off. What the hell is going on?"

Dason looked far from happy. His face was blanched white in panic and shock. The quiver in his voice told Knox he was more than a little frightened at what he had just seen. He had every right to be. What they had all just witnessed was an amazing feat. The ring had somehow melded Elena's skin together as if it were magic. Was it any more fantastical than the fact it shot beams of light capable of incinerating anything?

"I don't know what happened. I don't believe we should stay here, though." Knox stood and turned away from Elena. They would still have to find somewhere to hide for now. Soon they would leave the city, but for now, they needed a place to stay the night. Someplace away from prying eyes and nowhere, Fynn could find them.

"Why don't you tell them what you did first." Kamari stood in front of him, looking displeased with Knox's life choices.

"This isn't the time for your morals and your worries. I did what I had to do, and if you can't handle it, then when we get out of the city, you can go on your own way."

Knox didn't truly feel that way, but everything weighed on him like bricks. What he wanted to do was embrace Kamari and tell her how glad he was she was with him. What he did instead was push her away. He couldn't keep taking these verbal beatings. She wouldn't let up on him, and right now, he couldn't take it. His emotions were too frayed.

"Now is the time, and they should know who they are traveling with."

Knox chuckled. "I am not a monster. I wanted to save Elena."

Kamari pressed her hands into Knox's chest. "Just like you wanted to save Lash? Is it that way, Knox?"

Knox tried to bite back his retort. There wouldn't be any good from it.

"I didn't force Lash to come with me. He knew the risks, and so did you. Everyone knew them. I thought it would go as planned." Knox had said these words a hundred times over the last year. It hadn't been his fault. Lash was older than he was. Lash had always been the leader.

Lash had also been Kamari's brother, and her vision of the situation would never be the same as Knox's.

"He wanted to do what was right for us all. You came with this plan knowing it was a foolish scheme. You wouldn't try it now, would you, Knox?" Kamari's tone brimmed with an accusation of ill intent.

Knox doubted she truly believed he wanted Lash dead. If she had believed that much, she wouldn't have stuck around. She only needed someone to blame. Here in this death yard, she was scared and needed someone to punch. Knox would be the punching bag. He had been for over a year. Maybe it was not because she blamed him. Maybe she needed him to be stronger than he was.

Knox stepped forward and grabbed Kamari by the shoulder. She struggled to break free, but he held her hard. Knox wasn't a sizeable man, but he had enough weight on Kamari to hold her in place.

"This will be okay. We will get through this." He tried to keep his voice steady. He didn't know if the words were true. How did they get out of the city? Once they did, how would they survive? Knox pulled Kamari into his chest, and she didn't resist.

Had this been all she needed since the beginning? For Knox to understand her needs?

"Aw, how sweet. I am almost loathe to break up the show." General Fynn stepped out from behind another stone grave. He wasn't alone. Others from the barracks flocked to him and fanned out surrounding Knox and his friends.

"We still have the rings." Knox raised his hand as a reminder of what had happened in Fynn's office.

"I see that. I also see they are more powerful than I first assumed.

Elena looks all better. Maybe I overreacted back there. Maybe there is still something we can work out."

Knox didn't believe him.

"How did you find us?" Dason asked. His face still lacked its normal color.

"Hard to miss a screaming nurse in the middle of the street. Knox here made quite the showing it seems. The good doctor pointed us in the right direction soon after."

Knox sighed. Maybe he should have tied the doctor up.

"You let us go, and we will not shoot a hole through your chest." Knox positioned the ring right at Fynn.

Fynn held his hands out in a placating show of acceptance.

"Listen. I know we don't want this to turn into a war between us. Knox, you know how hard it is to survive alone. Remember after your parents died? Before you came to live with me full-time. You don't want that again, do you? Especially not having to watch for me over your shoulder every waking moment." Fynn took two steps forward toward them. "I am offering you a truce. You keep the rings you have. I only want the rest of them. Work with me and not against me."

"I am never going back with you. No matter what, I will never go back." Elena stepped in beside Knox and held her own ring toward Fynn's chest.

This time Fynn looked more hesitant to continue his approach. If he thought he could convince Knox, he didn't feel the same about Elena.

"How about I leave you alone then? How does that sound? I let you both go. I will even provide the transportation."

"I want nothing from you!"

Elena would shoot Fynn. Knox could see it in her eyes. He lifted his opposite hand and pressed her wrist down. If looks could kill, Elena's eyes would have struck him dead.

"What do you want, Fynn?"

Knox understood the magnitude of this moment. If they killed Fynn, they would have to kill everyone else in the barracks before they were free. Maybe it was possible, or maybe they would fail, but no matter, the group would never be the same.

"I want the weapons. The Arches have them, and I want them. You bring them to me, and I will let you all have those you already have. Once it is over, you can go. I won't stop you."

Knox thought about it.

"As easy as that?"

Fynn shook his head. "Nothing more."

"I won't work for you." Elena tried to raise her hand again.

"You don't have to." Knox let her hand go but stepped in front of her and in front of Fynn. "I will do it, and then you leave us alone. As a show of good faith, I will go with you, but you have to let Elena and the others walk away free tonight."

Fynn thought about it. Knox had always been the best thief in the barracks. He received the reward for most coins every night and had since he came into the custody of General Fynn. It wasn't a hard choice. If anyone could find the weapons, it was Knox.

Fynn agreed. "Let them go."

The boys and girls from the barracks opened a hole for the others to walk through. None of them moved.

Knox turned to Elena. "Please go. I will catch up."

"We can just kill him," she pleaded.

Knox shook his head. "No, we can't, and you know that. There are others and killing everyone will destroy you. You aren't a killer."

"And you are?"

Knox chuckled. It wasn't a humorous chuckle, but one of pure nervous tension.

"I don't know. I will do whatever it takes to save you, though. So, you take the others and protect them."

Elena bit her lip. Dason came to her side and grabbed her hand.

"Come on, let's go before he changes his mind."

Dason was referring to Fynn, but it was just as much a direct hit to Knox. Elena didn't look ready to go, but Dason was probably the only person in the world who she would listen to aside from Knox.

"I won't leave the city without you," Elena said.

"I will finish what is needed and come find you."

Elena drew in a deep breath and then let Dason pull her toward the hole in the group. Acasia trailed after them, and only Kamari didn't move.

"I am going with you," she said.

Knox didn't have time to protest. As soon as she said the words, the hole closed. Fynn clapped his hands together.

"Great, we will plan in the morning. Nothing makes a man more tired than potentially getting his head blown off."

15.

The journey back to the barracks was quiet. Knox had nothing to say to Kamari in front of the others. He definitely had nothing to say to Fynn. So, he kept his mouth shut.

He worried about Elena out there alone in the world. Would she be okay until he could finish this last task? Had he been stupid to agree to this? The answer to that was probably a resounding yes. What other choice had he had? He couldn't let Elena become a killer.

As the barracks came back into view, the thoughts melted away. Fynn said nothing to him as he made for his office. Knox figured the general had nothing to worry about. They could still find Elena if things went sour. Then, they could force Knox into doing the deed. Better to do it now and get it over with.

Knox would find some solace in sleep, and then in the morning, he would go to the meeting and listen. It had been his intention to go to his room, shut his door, and forget the world behind him. It hadn't been Kamari's intention to allow him to do that. She followed him to his room without saying a word. Then she shut the door behind them.

Knox whirled around on her. He wasn't angry, but the words came out harsher than he intended because of his fear.

"What are you doing here? Why would you follow me?"

Kamari didn't even flinch. Determination sketched across her face. Something he hadn't seen in a long while. Not since before her brother had died, and she started blaming him.

"I am capable of making my own decisions. I am not going to let you get yourself killed."

Knox wished he wouldn't have said the next words, but they skipped from his mouth before he could control them.

"You haven't cared about me in over a year, why care now?"

Kamari's mask slipped.

"I have cared about you more than I have cared about anything else. You are the reason I haven't melted into the cracks of this world. Do you think I could have made it through a single day without Lash if I didn't have you to worry about? You're too stubborn to realize that. You only see what is right before you."

Kamari tensed and resembled a statue in the park. Knox closed his eyes tight. He was tired of being an idiot. She was right. He needed to stop projecting himself onto her. He had moved away from Kamari just as much as she ran from him. It was too much to think about. Lash had been more than Kamari's brother; he had been a friend.

"I am sorry," Knox said.

Kamari shook her head. "Don't be. It was never your fault. Lash was a person capable of his own decisions too."

Knox stepped forward. He would explain himself. He would make things better between them. If tonight was their last night alive before Fynn changed his mind or sent them into certain death, then he would leave this world knowing she had his side of the story.

"I only want you to know..." Kamari's lips cut Knox off, pressing into his own.

The sudden tingle running through his body made Knox's legs wobble. He stumbled backward into his bed. Kamari followed him and leaned her body into his. Knox couldn't think anymore. The ecstasy running through his skin was almost too much to handle. His heart beat far worse than it did before any thievery mission. His entire body shook from nerves. His fear threatened to overtake him, then Kamari pressed her lips into his again, and he forgot about everything except for her.

He let himself breathe deep her scent. Let himself feel her soft caresses on the back of his neck. Her lips were wet with saliva, and he tasted her tongue as it flashed over his. Everything in his body went from nerves to pleasure in a matter of moments. This was the way the world should always be. Moments like these were what the world's joy came from. He closed his eyes and let her take him away. Whatever the morning brought, he would accept it, but tonight he would remember just why he lived.

16.

Before breakfast and before he could talk with Kamari about what happened the night before, there was a knock on Knox's door, waking them both from their slumber. The knock came again and again until Knox yelled his answer. The voice on the other side told him to skip the mess hall and go straight to Fynn's office. Knox had expected as much. No need to waste time on frivolous activities such as eating. The faster he could get this done for Fynn, the faster he could find Elena and leave the city for good.

Knox changed his attire and put two shirts on. This way, when he left, and Fynn didn't allow him back into the barracks, he would at least have a change of clothes. Knox then followed Kamari to her rooms to do the same. Neither of them discussed the previous night. Both were too nervous about meeting with Fynn to say much of anything. Kamari kissed his cheek before they entered the office. Knox had an agreeable feeling about things. This didn't have to be all bad. Maybe this had been just the thing they needed to get them back on track.

Fynn was behind his desk, poring over the same papers he always pored over. Knox stayed about ten feet from the desk, standing with his hands in his pocket. The ring was still there on his finger, and if he needed it, then he could still use it.

Knox couldn't help but take a moment to stare past Fynn into the hole behind him. The perfect circle looked like it belonged there in the concrete wall. Knox had blown it out to escape after Fynn went crazy and chopped off Elena's finger.

Fynn lifted his head and smiled at seeing Knox and Kamari.

"I am grateful you both came back to finish this last job for me. This will be the most important thing you ever do. This will change the world. I guarantee it."

Fynn looked so overjoyed he almost bounced on his heel as he walked around the desk. Knox had never seen Fynn show so much emotion. Whatever he wanted the weapons for was enough to make Fynn almost dance.

The feeling in the pit of Knox's stomach told him giving the weapons to Fynn was probably a mistake, but what other choice did he have? Elena was still out in the city, waiting for him to find her. After that, they would get so far away Fynn would never find them. Whatever he did here wouldn't matter once they left. Let Fynn have the weapons and the city. Knox didn't want either of them.

"Where do you need us to go?"

Fynn leaned against the desk and interlocked his fingers, letting his index fingers rest on his chin.

"I see you are ripping to go. No time for chatting. I am glad. There isn't a lot of time left before they ship the weapons to a vault and store them away. Once they are there, it will be much harder to get to them." Fynn turned and reached behind him for a paper sitting on the desk. When he turned around again, he handed the paper to Knox. "I want you to read over this. It is a transmission found by one of the other boys in the barracks. Says the Church of the Sparrow will move their shipment of weapons this afternoon during the service of worship. The crowd will be a barrier between the city and the weapons. The gathered crowd will provide the cover, but I want you to find the weapons and bring them to me." Fynn clapped his hands so loud it made Knox jump.

The hand, with the ring, shot into the air. Fynn laughed, but he moved from the direct path. He was confident, but not stupid.

"I am leaving now. I will bring these back, and then you will follow through with your end of the bargain." Knox let the paper in his hand fall to the floor.

Fynn nodded. "I am a man of my word. You do what is needed of you, and I will leave you be. Travel the world, see it for what it is. I will have no reason to stop you."

Knox didn't know if he believed Fynn, but he would worry about that part later. He had to do his part to make sure Elena was safe. After that, he would figure the rest of this out. Knox grabbed Kamari by the hand and walked forward around the desk. He didn't bother taking the door. He wanted Fynn to remember what he was capable of, so he took the hole in the wall as his exit.

17.

In some parts of the city, there was so much overcrowding homes stacked onto one another higher than the naked eye could see. Their windows packed with a dozen smudged faces looking out into the packed streets. The Archways were not one of those places. To cozy up here, there had to be some coin.

In the Archways, coin was only second to the churches, and it was close. Those who were the most religious, preaching the word of the gods, often had the most coin. Therefore, they had the nicest homes. Knox understood the way the world worked, but it didn't make it any easier to swallow.

"Do you ever wonder what it would have been like to be born in the home of a priest? More food than you could eat. More coin than you could ever dream of spending. Thousands of men and women racing to line your bank vaults with more every day in the name of an invisible being in the sky."

Kamari had spoken little since leaving Fynn's office. Her cheeks were rosy from the brisk wind, and her eyes were distant. She didn't look angry. She looked afraid and worried about what the world would drop on their plates this afternoon. Knox tried to imagine it would be an easy score. Find the moving crates filled with weapons, remove them from the hands of strong-armed church guards, and get them back to General Fynn all before being caught, strewn up, and thrown into the cells.

Knox saw the gathering church crowd long before he reached the

Church of the Sparrow. It was the smallest of the three figurehead churches. Which is why Knox figured it made the most logical sense as a hiding spot. What thief would hit the smallest target? Not that many people stole from the churches. Most clamored to give their everything to the priest and their word. Only Knox and the other wards of Fynn took from the churches. Even then, only those with the nimblest fingers survived long enough to do any real stealing.

"Do you think we could get to Elena and get away? Before getting the weapons? Maybe we just run and never look back."

Knox had thought about that too. It was an alluring prospect.

"Fynn would never stop hunting us. What would we do if he caught us? What if he has friends wherever we go? He is always talking like he knows people across the entire world. Do we want to risk it?"

Kamari's face didn't change from the look of worry she had been wearing. If anything, it looked more strained than it had before.

"I just don't feel right about giving him these weapons. What is he going to do with them?"

Knox didn't think it mattered. Not really. Weapons in the hands of one man or the other, they were still weapons, and dangerous.

"I figure he won't do much different from the church. What does it matter if Fynn runs the city or if the priests do? It is all the same to those on the bottom."

Knox must have made a convincing argument because Kamari said nothing else. She tucked her chin into her chest and watched her feet.

Knox watched the growing crowd. There were a good four to five hundred churchgoers for the Sparrow alone. There would be more men and women gathering at the Hawk and the Eagle. This was a small sample of those in the city who would be out, making sure the gods saw them worship in the sun's light.

Knox pushed through the growing pockets in the crowd. There wasn't an actual reason to go inside the doors. Fynn had said they would move the weapons from the church to the Red Hills. If they did, there were only so many paths they could take but seeing them come right through the church would make things much easier.

Halfway through the noisy bunch, Knox heard someone speaking over a sound system speaker. There had to have been a microphone connected somewhere in the church. Knox moved over to a nearby food cart and climbed the axle to see over the heads of the crowd. There, on the top of the concrete stairs, was the young priest Knox had stolen the rings from. His disheveled appearance topped off with messy hair and wrinkled robes. To top it off, he looked nervous. In his free hand, the one not holding the microphone, he held a gigantic bag. Knox couldn't see what filled the bag, but he didn't have to wait long to understand.

"Thank you for waiting patiently. Normally, we would love for you to fill our pews. Normally, I would have a wonderful sermon for you from the gods. There has been a change of plans this morning, however, a slight blip in our regularly scheduled worship services. The Red Hill has called all of us into a gathering this morning. Everyone in the city who worships here at the Sparrow is requested to stage a march to the Red Hills. There is something special the Red Hill is calling us to do." The priest pulled open the bag. His fingers fumbled with the cord for a few seconds, struggling because of the microphone in his other hand. After a lot of static, loud bumps, and frustration, the priest pulled the bag open. Knox could still not see the inside. "The contents of this bag are an offering from our small church to the gods that watch over us every day. A small march from our backyard into the hills to gift them with the rings of worship. A symbol of unity between our congregation and the gods. The ring represents a bond unbreakable. The journey up the hills shows a passion unwavering. Together, the ring and the journey offer us never-ending salvation." The priest opened the bag further and dumped the rings onto the top of the stairs.

"That is the rings, and those are the weapons." Knox motioned for Kamari to join him. She climbed the wheel, unsure what he spoke of. From her vantage point, she could not see the rings. When she stood tall enough to see over the heads of the others, her jaw dropped.

"What is he doing?" Kamari sounded as confused as Knox felt.

"He is gifting the weapons to the crowd to carry for him. If they think they are for the gods, no one will steal them. If the rings are all transported from each of the churches in the Archways, then there will have to be a mass of soldiers carrying them. If they get the people to do it for them, then it may take weeks to move the rings, but no one will be the wiser. They are moving weapons under our noses."

Knox thought it ingenious. He was shocked the churches would think of something like this. Make it a ceremony, and no one would ever question the event.

"Who will march with me to everlasting freedom?" The crowd roared in delight at the prospect. "Then come forward and grab only a single ring. Wrap it in your palm and do not let it slip onto your finger. This is not a ring for you, but a ring for the gods."

Knox knew what would happen if the rings slipped onto even a single man or woman's finger. The church took a colossal risk, but it was less of a risk than having all of their guards moving large crates of weapons and scaring the senate into calling the army's power into use.

"What are we going to do?"

Knox thought about the question. Kamari sounded defeated, but Knox wasn't so sure. They couldn't get all the weapons, not the way Fynn had wanted, but they could get enough to make Fynn happy with the results. Then Fynn would leave them alone. Knox could take Elena, Kamari, and the others away from here. They could live a better life.

Knox took a deep breath. There were a lot of decisions in a person's life. Many of them were mundane. What to have for breakfast. Where to head on the evening walk. Sometimes, though, the decisions were life-changing events. Knox figured this wouldn't be as simple as what kind of jelly he wanted on his toast. He took a deep breath, jumped from the axel, and decided he would do whatever it took to make sure they could get away today and never have to look over their shoulders.

He wouldn't tell Kamari that, but she had forgiven him once. Maybe she would surprise him a second time.

18.

Knox didn't head toward the top of the stairs to claim his ring. The one on his finger would be enough. He would have to make it work. Knox waited for the crowd to gather in procession. They would march one right next to the other in a dramatic display. To them, it was a ceremony. To Knox, it was his life on the line.

"You don't have to come with me for this part." Knox turned to Kamari and helped her from the wheel. She allowed him to take her hand, and he gave it an extra squeeze.

"I am going with you. It is why I stayed in."

Knox wished she hadn't stayed. Last night had been the greatest night of his life, but he wished it hadn't happened. It made everything harder for him. Seeing Kamari beside him made the tough decisions tougher. He wanted her to only see him in a pleasant light, not to understand the darkness that sometimes roiled around inside him. There wasn't an uncomplicated way to make the rings come out of the hands of the people here. They would need to succumb to fear, and to create fear, Knox would have to put on a dramatic showing. This was for Elena. It was for Kamari, and he had to remind himself of what was at stake. It wasn't because he wanted to do this, it was because he had to. At least it made him feel better to think in those terms. If he was saving those he loved, then taking from others became easier.

Knox turned from Kamari. He couldn't look her in the eyes and do what he had to do. He would hold the image of her from the night before in his mind. That is what he would see when he did what he had to do next.

Kamari had once been Knox's partner in crime. She had stolen with him and Lash for years. One thing they never let her in on was the more extreme jobs. The ones where people didn't always make it out in one piece. Lash wasn't a saint like Kamari believed. It had been him that killed the first man Knox had ever seen. It had been him that ripped coins from the purses of women in the parks. Do whatever it takes to be on top. That is what Lash had instilled into Knox. Once Lash died, Knox had taken up Elena as his partner. The major jobs were taken up by Knox alone, but he made Elena believe the coin had always come directly from the church. It was easier than her asking questions. It was easier than him having to tell everyone about who he became to keep everyone safe and full.

Knox stepped into the moving crowd. He wanted to get out ahead of them. Some would scramble when the commotion started, but if Knox played it right, then he could get a lot of the rings before things went too far south.

As the people merged from the top of the stairs, Knox found himself at the head of a column. They waited for the signal from the priest who waited on the bag to empty. Soon the festivities would begin. Knox raised his hand and looked at the ring. He knew the trick behind the power of the beam already. His mind raced, and he gave another look toward Kamari. This would be the last time she saw him as the young, innocent boy she had fallen in love with. Whatever pleasure he had gained from her last night was the last he would ever receive. He knew this. He also knew it was a necessity. Bring the weapons back to Fynn or allow Fynn to kill everyone he loved. Being shunned wasn't the worst thing that could happen to him. Maybe in time, everyone would come to understand what he did next. It was out of love. That is what Lash always said to him. *This is for love, and that makes it okay. Whatever someone does for love is minimized because love is the strongest emotion of all.*

Knox turned his palm outward and flicked his finger into position. The beam of light struck the first man in line square in the chest. Knox ran forward and pulled the ring from his palm. He shot twenty more beams into the air before anyone understood what happened. He could hear Kamari screaming, but he unleashed the beam again and again. This wasn't something he enjoyed. It was something he had to do, and for this, he felt nothing of it. Only the hope he could get enough rings to make Fynn happy.

Knox turned and shot so many times he lost track. He kept Kamari in his vision as he moved around the crowd. She hadn't moved, her face slack with fear, and her mouth agape. Knox couldn't keep his eyes on her long. As long as she was safe, that is all that mattered. He didn't bother to stop and collect the rings. No one stuck around to gather them. He could collect them later, after this was over.

There was so much noise surrounding him, but Knox zoned it all out. The footfalls only guided him where to shoot. Everything else was a background noise he pretended didn't exist. The screams weren't from actual people. The cries were not real. Everything except for the rings was an illusion. Only they mattered to Knox. Everything else was a casualty of love.

Knox shot the beam over two hundred times. Only the one man died, Knox had been careful. Later, when he collected the rings, he would feel some remorse, but more than that, he would feel relief. Relief Fynn would be satisfied with his actions here today. The spectacle and the results would be enough for two things. One to show Fynn what Knox was capable of when pressed against a wall and two, a show of peace by handing over the weapons. Let Fynn destroy the city. It didn't matter to Knox. He would move on to the next city. Move on to the next gambit.

Knox finished and wiped his brow from the sweat forming across the creases in his forehead. He looked for Kamari, but she wasn't anywhere. It took almost an hour after he collected the rings to find her hunched behind a small overturned cart of food. She jerked away from his grasp as he reached for her. She struck him and cried, tears streaming down a red face. She wouldn't look at him as he tried to take her away with him. His words of love meant nothing over her screams. Eventually, she collapsed from exertion, and Knox carried her, along with the bag of rings, back toward the barracks.

The priest had run away before Knox could subdue him. Fynn wouldn't like that, but Knox would leave it out of the telling. Looking down one more time into the closed eyes of Kamari, he sat her down onto a cart filled with hay. He wouldn't bring her with him. Elena, Kamari, and the others could be safe now, but not with Knox.

The genuine tears and pain etched across Kamari's face made him realize something more about himself. He loved this woman more than he loved anything else in the world. He would have killed everyone in the city for her, but he also was broken in some way. He had felt nothing for killing the man and scaring the others. It had almost been like a dream.

He was worse than a monster, and he understood that now. In Kamari's eyes, he had seen his exact thoughts the first time Lash had killed someone in front of him. Fear, sorrow at death, and a lack of understanding of what the world made people do to survive. Over time, Knox looked up to Lash, but somewhere he had also lost track of what was right and what was wrong.

Knox left Kamari there on the hay and walked away. She would wake up and hopefully find Elena. They could wander off into a new city and find a fresh life. Knox would allow them that much. Knox had one more thing left to do.

He threw the bag of weapons over his shoulder with a clanking of metal. Then he turned toward the barracks.

19.

Leaving Kamari behind had been a tough decision. Letting his sister wander into the world alone was even harder, but he had to finish what he started. Years ago, Lash had told him he stayed with Fynn because there had been no alternative. Stay and do the general's bidding, or fade into non-existence through starvation or worse. Lash had kept coin to himself during those times. He hadn't always given the full share to Fynn. Knox had never braved keeping any of the coin for himself, but he respected Lash for his bravery.

What he planned to do today would make Lash's attempts at rebellion look like child's play. Knox walked into the barracks with the rings over his shoulder. There were people milling about, back from their thievery for the day, none of them attempted to go outside their means. Fynn wouldn't ever praise them, but they lived a simple enough life without his praise. Knox should have been one of these men and women. Instead, he had Lash rope him into the ploy to be the best. That brought him here today.

Knox walked up the back path. He wouldn't bother walking through the barracks. There was a perfect hole right into the office he needed to be in.

Knox made no pretense about stepping right behind Fynn, who had his back toward the hole. Fynn had no fear inside the barracks. Everyone knew their place in the hierarchy and feared the wrath of

Fynn. The man had no forgiveness or pity. There had been several kicked from his good graces into the streets. Fynn killed no one with his own hands, but that didn't mean his hands were clean. Sending a child into the streets was about as effective as a slash across their throat. Starving was probably a worse way to die than bleeding out on the office floor.

Knox walked around Fynn and tossed the rings onto the desk. Before Fynn could reach out to grab them, Knox grabbed the general's hand. The shock evident on Fynn's face almost made Knox jump backward. Then he remembered Fynn chopping the finger from his sister's hand and squeezed harder. With Knox's other hand, he held the ring outward to show his serious disposition.

"What is this?" Fynn's voice was steady.

He didn't believe Knox would follow through with any attack. Why would he believe that? No one had ever bothered to attack him before. He had trained the obedience into every soul inside the barracks. There was nothing to fear, or so he thought.

Knox's hand didn't waver. He had enough time on the walk over to steel his nerves. It didn't mean he felt good about what planned to do. It just meant he would follow through.

"I have decided I don't like the deal we discussed."

Fynn let a smirk creep across his face.

"You want more coin before you go?"

Knox wondered if coin would be enough to thwart the attempts of Fynn and his men. He doubted it. He would need a lot of coin to buy the amount of protection he would need. Knox would need to rest and sleep sometime. He had no desire to run forever. Had no desire to see his sister caught and flayed alive for Fynn's amusement.

"I don't think there is a bargain in this deal for you, Fynn. I have something else in mind."

Fynn's face scrunched in confusion.

"Do you want to die, Knox?"

He asked with a certainty of the end game. Fynn didn't believe this would end with his brains smeared onto what was left of his wall.

"That is not how this will go, Fynn. I have something else in mind altogether. Would you like to hear the new deal?"

Fynn leaned back, letting Knox keep hold of his wrist. If Fynn moved too suddenly, Knox would blow him to smithereens. Fynn at least respected the weapon, even if he didn't respect Knox.

"What deal would that be?"

Knox guided Fynn's hand to the desk and held it there. Fynn's palm was flat against the surface, but he didn't look to his hand, he watched Knox's eyes. That is why the sudden shock of a dagger to his ring finger caught him so off guard. The scream permeated the office like a wild animal's howl. Knox stared Fynn straight in the eyes. The general pulled his hand away, blood spurting from the nub where his finger had been. Knox reached to the desk and pulled the hairy knuckled finger from the surface. He held it up in front of Fynn's face.

"I thought about taking this as the deal. I thought maybe it would make you realize how serious I was about this. Then I thought, your finger would eventually heal. You would want more, and you would seek revenge on what I had done. So, I thought I probably needed more."

Fynn pushed the chair back and stood. He reached for his own knife at his hip. Knox wasn't afraid. He held his hand with the ring up. The Archway squares had made him realize another body on his conscious wouldn't matter. His soul was damned, but he would save Kamari and Elena. They would live free from fear.

"I am going to kill you, Knox. Then I am going to rip your sister and your little girlfriend to shreds."

Knox winced.

"I just don't believe you will do any such thing. Knox aimed the ring toward Fynn's thigh and shot. The instant hole took a moment for Fynn to register.

The next scream was a scream so loud Knox flinched. Fynn fell to the ground, and Knox walked around the desk, standing over him. Fynn's face had lost all color, his eyes streamed tears. The pain forever etched into his face was about as real as it got. Knox let him feel it as he bent next to him.

"I thought about you coming for us. Thought about what you would do." Knox aimed the ring at Fynn's forearm and shot again.

The scream came again. Fynn's body convulsed. Knox wondered if he could even hear him anymore. Fynn was beyond talking now. There wasn't any going back on what Knox needed to do.

He grabbed Fynn by the shoulders and, with some effort, dragged him from the hole in the office wall. Knox dragged Fynn until he was in the common area of the barracks. A place where everyone would see the general. Knox walked to an outside table where everyone would congregate as they came home for the night. With a struggle, Knox pulled the body of Fynn onto the table's surface. By this point, Fynn had almost faded. The moans had faded. Knox stood over Fynn one last time and stared at those already home for the day.

"I will expect the same respect you showed to the general. Those who believe they are special, different, or above what I say will join Fynn in the halls of the gods."

Knox leaned in close to Fynn. The man was probably already dead. It was hard to tell.

"Enjoy the afterlife," Knox whispered.

Then he shot a final beam of light for everyone to see right between Fynn's eyes. There was no sound from Fynn, but everyone gathered to let a gasp escape.

Knox tucked his hands into his pocket and walked back to his new office. Things may not have turned out as he imagined, but his sister would live. Kamari would be free. And General Fynn was dead. Maybe it wasn't exactly a happy ending, but it was one he could live with.

ABOUT SCOTT MOORE

A mere 31 years ago, Scott Moore was born into a small family in Odin, IL. Growing up; he realized there was nothing special about his town or the people in it. Normalcy caused him to play a lot outside with his imagination, read hundreds of stories, and to write his own. At 22, Scott became a first-time father and raised his son as a single parent. He also decided to go back to school, to help others who did not have a voice of their own. Scott graduated from the University of Illinois in 2015, with his BS degree in Psychology. Since then, he has worked with the developmentally disabled and helped them live their lives to the fullest. In 2018, Scott got engaged to a wonderful woman and inherited 2 children. Several months later, he found out that a 4th child would soon join the family. Now he is hoping to compound on that excitement by sharing his stories with the world. If you are interested in Fantasy such as Brandon Sanderson, Scott Lynch, or Brian McClellan then check out Scott Moore's similar books!

Website: https://mishmashers.com

facebook.com/scottmooreauthor

twitter.com/SkodtM

ORPHANS AND KINGDOMS

BY K.R.S. MCENTIRE

CHAPTER 1

The hour-long walk between Lady Esme's cottage and the village market was my favorite part of the workday. Between the warm rays of sunlight that teased my skin and the much-needed solitude, I wished the cobblestone path toward town was just a tiny bit longer.

The gray, litter filled streets of my birth city's prison district were a distant memory now. I never saw foliage or flowers back then. Just dirt and death.

I felt safe out here in the forest, beneath trees that hunched over me like the guardians I'd never had. Whenever the wind whistled through the weathered branches and teased my hair, it felt as if the universe was comforting me.

I held Lady Esme's shopping list in one hand and an empty wicker basket in the other. Crickets hid in the thick green foliage and lulled me with their rhythmic chants while birds chirped proudly as they soared through the azure sky. But it only took the sudden, sharp snap of a twig to bring back the survival instincts I'd acquired in the prison district.

My hand fell to the dagger at my waist as chills shot down my spine. I dropped the basket. The sound had been too close. Someone or something was right behind me.

I raised my blade as I spun on my heels to face a tall figure in a hooded cloak. My heart pounded in my chest, but I knew better than to run from a threat. Running is what rabbits do before being devoured by wolves. It's what children do before their orphanage's headmistress chooses to beat them till they're black and blue. If I wanted to survive, I knew it was best to stand tall and fight.

I grunted as I lunged forward with my dagger aimed at the stranger's heart. With a swift and graceful movement, the stranger pulled a longsword from under their cloak and parried my attack.

I lost my grip on the dagger when their blade collided with mine. All hope for survival left me as I watched my weapon fall to the ground.

If I bent down to pick it up, I'd be defenseless against my attacker. I stepped back and lifted my arms in surrender, finally peeking at my assailant's face.

A black hooded cloak covered most of their forehead and draped down toward their eyes, but the thick, red hair that fell from the hood and the red lips twisted in a grin were familiar. I let out a breath as I realized who it was.

"Thalia?"

Her grin widened as she pulled off her hood. "We didn't get the best training on manners growing up, but even *I* know that stabbing your sister isn't nice."

Thalia wasn't my biological sister. We'd grown up together in Moonshire's orphanage. That hell hole for children was located right next to the city's prison and was equally as horrific. In an orphanage full of abandoned children, I was the outcast among outcasts, but Thalia took me under her wing. She had a natural inclination toward magic, and therefore the adults feared her.

At seventeen, we decided to escape. We took on one of the few professions that girls with no money and little education could find—

conning rich men out of their coins. Due to Thalia's unique powers, getting by was easier for us than most.

"By the Gods, Thalia, you scared me half to death!" I playfully punched her shoulder.

She snorted. "Since when do you worry about the Gods?"

"How did you find me?" I asked. It had been over a year since I left the city of Moonshire to seek out honest work.

"You're not quite as stealthy as me," she said. "You're easy to track down. Besides, you didn't go very far."

I was asking the wrong questions. If Thalia had come all this way, she needed me for something. I wasn't sure I wanted to know what that something was.

"So, Rachel, what are you doing in Riverdam besides taking in all this natural beauty?" she asked.

"I've been working a lot, keeping my head down," I said. "Just trying to save up enough coins to enroll in the Mage's College…"

While those who practiced natural magic were branded witches and killed by city guards, the study of magic was permitted at the Mage's College if you paid enough coin. It was hypocritical if you asked me.

Thalia snorted a laugh. "College? Oh, come on, Rachel."

"Why not?" I asked. Back at the orphanage, I'd always get high marks on my schooling. The headmistress once said I might make it in life if I stayed away from witches like Thalia.

"Girls like us don't go to any type of college," she said.

I picked up my dagger and sheathed it, ignoring her statement.

"That's for girls with money, connections, or at least families," Thalia continued. "How much have you saved up?"

"Twenty-five," I couldn't hold her gaze as I admitted to such a small number of coins.

Thalia's eyes grew wide. "Twenty-five gold? After working for a year?"

"Twenty-five silver," my voice was weak.

"Oh, Rachel, we made more than twenty-five silver in one night back in Moonshire!"

"As thieves," I reminded her.

"Damn good ones," she said. There was confidence in her voice when she spoke. "I have a proposition for you."

"Of course you do." I sighed.

She lifted a finger and waved it in my face. "Don't dismiss me just yet."

I knew she wouldn't let up until she told me why she was here. "Okay, I'm listening."

"It seems the Jarl of Moonshire's son has turned up missing."

"Ethan?" I raised a brow. I remember seeing the young boy, who had to be about eight now, around town. "I'd like to say it's shocking that someone would harm a child, but after what we've been through, I'm not surprised."

The headmistress ran the orphanage more like a business than a charity. The needs of the children were not her top concern, to say the least.

"It's shocking that someone would harm a wealthy child," Thalia corrected me. "A child with parents who care about him. Well-connected, powerful parents. There are easier targets for people who are simply sadistic. They are targeting this child for one of two reasons: money or revenge. And seeing as no one has asked for any ransom, I place my bet on revenge."

"So, what's that gotta do with me?"

"Rachel, remember your manners. If you play your cards right, you might be able to afford your fancy college in this lifetime. The Jarl is offering a fifty-thousand gold reward for whoever helps find his son."

My mouth fell open. "Fifty-thousand gold?"

"The best part is, I've already figured out who's done it."

"And who might that be?"

"Picture this. Kaldar Juther, the Jarl of the Runetree province, comes to town." Her hands were animated as she spoke. "He's never been to our city before. Just shows up on business a week before the child goes missing. He's rented a huge manor right outside of the city gates. Has his own personal guards. Why does he need a huge house for himself? Why not just stay at an inn? I think he's hiding something, or rather someone, in the house."

"And Moonshire's Jarl does not suspect him?"

"Kaldar Juther is not some peasant off the street. Our Jarl is being smart about this because he knows he can't accuse Kaldar without evidence. The reward money motivates people to talk," Thalia said. "We'll find the evidence, bring it to the Jarl, and walk away fifty-thousand gold richer."

"But I can't just leave. I have a job here."

"Right. Making twenty-five silver a year."

"That's just the amount I've been able to save." I put my hands on my hips. "It's a start."

She moved closer, her eyes widening with excitement, "Rachel, If we do this, we'll never have to work again in our lives. I wouldn't have come here if I didn't think this was the opportunity of a lifetime. But time is of the essence. There are others looking for evidence as well. Now come on, we have to acquire some steads and get going."

Without another word, she took off toward town, compelling me to follow.

CHAPTER 2

I gripped my reins for dear life as I balanced on the horses back, adjusting to his stride as he trotted through the dense woodlands. I'd never ridden a horse before, and I didn't like the lack of security that came with my feet no longer being firmly planted on the ground.

I ducked under a low-hanging branch as my horse made a swift turn in the wrong direction. Thalia's black steed walked ahead of my brown one with confidence, but my horse stopped to graze.

"Just give it a kick if it slows down," Thalia instructed. "Use the reins to guide it."

I looked down at the animal that was twice my size. "I'm not kicking it! How did you get these anyway?"

"I batted my eyelashes at a stable boy," she said, but I knew it was more than that. Not only was Thalia drop-dead gorgeous, but she had a natural inclination toward magic. Most people studied years at the Mage's College to acquire half of her skills.

Thalia had the ability to manipulate moods. She could make you sad or happy or angry. I once saw her make our headmistress go into a rage and start banging her head against a wall like a maniac. But Thalia's favorite trick was her ability to lull people to sleep. Let's just say robbing wealthy men is a whole lot easier when you don't have to follow through with whatever promises you made before you were invited to their room.

I looked around the forest. Every direction mirrored the others, an endless loop of trees. I wasn't sure how Thalia knew which direction we were moving.

There was a dirt road that led from the village of Riverdam to the city of Moonshire, but we knew better than to take the beaten path. The village guards, or as I liked to call them the village idiots, were likely looking for two women on horseback. I'd rather face the bears, wolves, goblins, and trolls in the forest than risk getting thrown in jail.

My horse continued to snack. I knew I needed to do it. I squinched my nose and tensed my muscles as I gave the horse's butt a firm kick, bracing myself for it to take off running or try to buck me off its back. Instead, it lifted its head and allowed me to guide it back toward Thalia.

"I can't believe I came with you," I grumbled at her.

"I can." Thalia snorted. "You must have been bored to death in that little village."

"I actually liked it." I pointed my nose in the air. "Maybe the simple life is the life for me."

"Life will be a whole lot simpler with fifty-thousand gold," she reminded me. I shrugged in agreement.

She nodded her head toward something in the distance. We had only been riding for a couple of hours, but I could see the stone towers of Moonshire's palace peeking over the trees and reaching proudly toward the clouds.

"We are closer to Moonshire than I thought," I admitted as I pulled my reins to slow my steed.

"Riverdam and Moonshire aren't that far from each other. It only takes a day to walk here on foot."

"It just feels like worlds away, I guess," I said. "While we're out here, can you tell me a little more about this job? If you know who stole the boy, what do you need me for?"

Thalia halted her horse and turned to look back at me, her long, red hair blowing in the breeze. "I wasn't able to sweet talk my way into the target's house. I'm guessing I'm not his type."

"You are every man's type."

"Not this one," Thalia said, the frustration in her tone was apparent.

The Thalia I knew could sweet talk or scam her way to anything she needed. If all else failed, she would use her magic. I wasn't sure why she didn't do this job herself and keep the gold rather than splitting it with me.

"I think I was too aggressive. Maybe I made him suspicious? But you've got that sweet, innocent, I'm-walking-through-the-forest-with-a-wicker-basket charm about you. If anyone can do this, you can."

I rolled my eyes, but I was grinning on the inside. The worst and best years of my life had taken place by Thalia's side in the city of Moonshire. The first sixteen years, when I lived in the orphanage with Thalia as my only friend, were the worst. The two years after Thalia and I ran away were the best. Sure, I was a thief, but for the first time in my life, I was in control of my destiny. I was free.

As we trotted through the heavy foliage toward Moonshire, I thought about times when a robbery went bad, and I had to defend myself with my blade. My hand twitched toward my dagger, like an addict desperate for another hit of adrenaline.

"I knew it," Thalia said in a singsong voice. "I see the glint in your eye. You can take a girl out of the prison district, but you can't take the prison district out of the girl."

"Yea, yea," I rolled my eyes, but my lips twisted into a grin. "Let's just get to the city. You have to introduce me to my date for the night."

CHAPTER 3

The city of Moonshire had only two taverns.

The Deranged Drake, in the prison district, was where commoners gathered to drink away their woes and gamble away their money. When I lived in Moonshire, it was where Thalia and I would find our targets. Even commoners had more coins than two orphan girls.

Claws, in the palace district, was where Moonshire's high society gathered. Thalia and I avoided the place, assuming they'd smell the poverty on us before we made it through the door.

But Claws was where Kaldar Juther, my target, would be tonight. If I was going to get in, I'd need to look and play the part. That's why, from the cramped and dirty prison district shack that Thalia called home, I allowed her to transform me into Kaldar's dream girl.

"Hold still," Thalia said as she adjusted my silky, sky blue dress. The dainty gown she'd stuffed me in was a size too small and likely cost more than a year's worth of my meager wages. She tightened the corset-like ribbons on the back to give me a more defined waist.

"I can't breathe," I complained, straightening my back and sucking in my stomach.

"You don't have to breathe," Thalia said. "You just need to look pretty and get the job done."

As she worked on my dress, I looked around the small, messy bedroom. This was once *my* bedroom, and most everything looked as I remembered it. The dresser still had a few missing drawers, and the mirror was just as dirty as I'd left it.

A sense of nostalgia swept over me as Thalia's cat walked over and rubbed its head against my ankle. I looked down, alarmed, hoping the animal didn't get hair on the expensive dress.

"Get out of here," Thalia shooed the cat away. Looking back at me, she laughed, "I think she missed you."

At that moment, I heard three loud thuds from what sounded like another part of the house.

I glanced back at Thalia, but she continued fiddling with my dress as if she did not hear the sound.

"What was that?" I asked.

"That damn dog. I locked it in my room because he doesn't like the cat."

I raised a brow. "I thought you hated dogs."

She shrugged. "You know how it is out here. I'm trying to save coins, and no one is afraid of a guard cat."

Thalia pulled me over to a cracked, dirty mirror, and I took in her work. My lips were painted cherry red, and my curly dark hair had more bounce and shine than It ever had before. I could hardly believe it was myself in the mirror. I looked immaculate.

I resisted the urge to ask her how she acquired this dress. Most of our past targets had been men. I figured Thalia schemes are adaptable.

"Perfect," Thalia said. "Remember. Tall. Dark hair. Short black beard."

"How do you know he'll even take me to his home?" I asked. If he didn't go with Thalia, why would he go with me?

"It's your job to ensure that he does," Thalia said. "I'll meet you at the target's house later tonight. And stay safe."

The streets of Moonshire were dark, damp, and gloomier than I remembered. The oil lamps that typically illuminated the streets had burned out, and wet roads hinted that it had recently rained.

On my way from the prison district to the palace district, I decided to walk past the orphanage. It was getting pretty late, and I doubted anyone would be outside, but if I was in Moonshire, I figured I should stop by the place I'd once called home.

Inside the gates of the orphanage, a young girl of no more than seven was sitting alone in the dark. Her oversized gray dress looked wet and hung limply on her small frame. My hands balled into fists. I was ready to attack whoever left this child out to freeze in the cool night air. But as I approached, I realized there were no adults around.

"Hey there." I locked eyes with her and offered a warm smile, but she didn't smile back. Her eyes widened in fear at the sight of me. Before I could say another word, she ran away from the gate to hide.

As I continued down the road, I couldn't get the girl's face out of my mind. Her tired eyes looked like they belonged to someone with additional years. I said a silent prayer for the child to the Gods as I made my way to the palace district.

Claws Inn and Tavern was a stone's throw away from Moonshire Palace, and it stood almost as tall and proud as the palace. The two-story stone tavern was rumored to serve the best food and drink in the whole kingdom, and judging by the large crowd, the rumors were likely true.

A city guard in chainmail armor stood outside the entrance to Claws with sword and shield in hand. Heart aflutter, I took a deep breath and walked to the entrance with my head held high. I flashed the guard a smile, praying that if I acted as if I belonged here, he would believe it.

"Good evening, s…" I resisted the urge to refer to the guard as 'sir." Would people who frequented Claws call him, or anyone, 'sir'?

"Good evening, my lady," The man opened the door, letting me in without a second glance. That was a good sign. I figured I looked the part.

I walked inside and took in the large space. I had to struggle to keep my mouth from falling open. It was *so beautiful*. The most interesting things to look at in the Deranged Drake were the sweaty, drunken fist-fights. But here, the guests were engaged in polite conversation. Fire from the hearth warmed the room, and the savory aroma of stew and roasting meat made my stomach grumble.

Tavern maiden's carried steins full of mead to guests and flirted as they worked—I guess a pretty face makes it easier to part with your coins. However, as I entered the room, more than a few male eyes drifted from the maidens over to me. I recognized the familiar faces of the palace district's aristocracy, but judging by the curious looks on their faces, none of them seemed to recognize me. It helped that I'd been gone for a year and that I'd always been a nobody.

A handsome redheaded man in a black tunic gave me a smile. A man with deep brown skin and chiseled muscles winked at me as I walked by. I thought about how easy it might be to rob these men blind, but I needed to stay focused on my main mission: to figure out which one of these losers was Kaldar Juther.

I made my way to the bar. A couple of men with backpacks and accents were engaged in conversation with each other.

I climbed on the barstool and watched the men from the corner of my eyes as I looked ahead. The taller one with dark hair and a short beard matched the description of Kaldar that Thalia had given me. I'd need to play it cool and figure out if he was the correct target.

I saw his eyes drift over to me. I glanced at him and offered a coy smile before looking away. If this man didn't like how forward Thalia had been, maybe it was best I play shy. He observed me with interest but turned away.

The tavern maiden came over to me. Her hair looked frazzled, and mead covered her dress. "May I get you something?"

"Long day?" I asked her.

"We are very busy tonight, as you can see," she sighed. "People are coming in from all over the kingdom in hopes of finding the Jarl's son."

"Wine, please," I placed two silver coins on the table.

She gave me a curious smile. "I've never seen you around here before. Are you seeking fortune as well?"

From my peripheral vision, I noticed the bearded man lean closer to me. He wanted to hear my answer over the voices in the noisy tavern.

"No, I was born here." I was careful not to say exactly what part of town I grew up in. "I moved away when I was young. Came back because my old village was taken over by witches and unsavory sorts."

She poured me a cup of wine and slid it across the bar to me.

The bearded man turned to me and let out a hearty laugh. "Plenty of those sorts here in Moonshire."

His deep, gravelly voice caught me off guard. I swallowed as I studied the handsome features of his face and gazed into his hazel eyes. Damn. Why didn't Thalia warn me that he was so attractive?

"Just don't go to the prison district at night," he warned. "That's where all the crazies stay."

That one line was all it took to break my crush. It was an extremely unattractive trait to think you're better than others simply because of where you are from.

I forced out as carefree of a laugh as I could fake. "Oh, I've heard all sorts of horrible things about that place. Full of criminals, drunks, and witches."

"Witches are becoming a problem in all the provinces, actually. Never thought it would reach Moonshire." He reached out and shook my hand. The bearded man had the assured grip of a Jarl, but the calloused hands of a man who did manual work for a living. Maybe I had the wrong target? I glanced around the room for other men with black beards until he spoke.

"I'm Kaldar," he said. My life at the orphanage had given me the best poker face. I keep my expression neutral as I imagined the twenty-five thousand gold coins I'd soon acquire.

"Rachel," I said.

"Where is your husband? It's a little odd to see a lady such as yourself out at a tavern alone." He took a sip from his mead.

"I had one. When the witches brought plague to my city, many men, including my husband, died."

"I'm sorry to hear that," he said.

"How about you? Do you have a wife, children?"

He shook his head. "Not yet, unfortunately. I'm a Jarl of a struggling providence, and by necessity as a trader. I move around a lot to make coins and trade for resources that I bring back to my city. No wife or children, but I'm sorry that you've had to deal with witches. In my travels, I've seen the destruction that witches bring. They need to shut down the Mage's College as well. We don't need magic in this kingdom."

"Agreed," I lied.

"Well, as nice as this inn is, it's no place for a lady such as yourself." He reached out to me, brushing his thumb against my hand. "I'm renting the lakeside manor right outside town. I have a maid, a butler, and a spare bedroom. You could spend the night with me."

I couldn't help but grin. "I'd love to accompany you home."

CHAPTER 4

The field outside the city gates stretched for miles and miles. I held Kaldar's hand as we strolled toward his lakeside manor. Fog filled the air, and a heavy, ominous wind rattled the trees and bushes in the meadow.

"Why did you rent this place rather than staying at the inn?" I asked. If I could get him to talk, maybe he was foolish enough to give me a clue about the missing boy.

"I've always enjoyed my privacy," Kalder said. "Don't get me wrong, I can socialize with the best of them. But at the end of the day, I've always liked to have my own place to retreat to."

"So, am I imposing on your solitude?" I locked eyes with him and grinned.

He shook his head. "By no means. You're the best type of company."

Then he brushed a stay strand of my dark, curly hair away from my face and leaned closer. I panicked for a second, forgetting how to breathe. It had been over a year since I kissed anyone or had any type of romantic feelings. And even though I all but hated this man for kidnapping an innocent child, I knew I needed to play the part to get into his home.

He made it extremely easy to fake it. His lips were velvet against mine—pillowy soft. For a moment, I forgot that this man had stolen a child, that I was trying to find evidence of his crime. I was consumed by his kiss, all other thoughts erased from my mind.

"Rachel..." his voice was low and growly, his lips still inches from mine. "I'm sorry if that was too forward, my lady."

"Don't be sorry," I whispered. Then, to assure him, I leaned in and gave him another kiss.

He took me by the hand and led me toward the manor with a

newfound pep in his step. Before we made it to the front door, he paused.

I could hear his breathing getting quicker and heavier. His hand, still linked with mine, started to tremble and sweat.

"Is something wrong?" I asked.

"I... I..." he stuttered.

I let go of his hand and moved a couple of inches away from him. His eyes widened in alarm as he looked at me.

"By the Gods!" he said. I noticed tears leaking from his eyes, but anger flashed through his tears. "You demon! Are you bewitching me?"

"No... I..." I glanced around the field to the nearby trees and bushes but couldn't see through the fog. Thalia must be altering his emotions somehow. When I turned to look for her, Kalder grabbed me from behind, and I felt the cool metal point of a blade on my neck.

"I know you are enchanting me!" he said through tears. His trembling hand caused the blade to scrape against my neck. I swallowed as I reached into my pocket to find my own blade, but it was no longer at my side. My heart raced faster. Where was Thalia? She was supposed to be here.

Kaldar released me, dropped to the ground, and continued sobbing. I stumbled away from him and saw that it was my blade in his grasp.

He clasped his hands around his knees and started rocking back and forth to comfort himself. "Stop it, witch, please stop," he begged me through tears, eventually laying on his side. His eyes fluttered shut, and in seconds his sobs turned to snores.

Thalia emerged from behind a nearby bush with a smug expression on her face.

"By the Gods, Thalia, you were supposed to put him to sleep! I feel like I just witnessed an exorcism."

"It's fun to toy with them a bit." She shrugged. "Besides, we have bigger fish to fry. Go in there and find the boy or proof of the boy. I'll stay out here to make sure he stays asleep."

I took Kaldar's key, and a few gold coins, from his pocket and rushed to the front door. My hands trembled with nerves as I struggled to get inside, but eventually, the door opened.

I stepped into the manor and took in my surroundings. From the weapons decorating the walls to the tall marble statues to the fine furniture, everything in the home looked expensive. My fingers twitched with the desire to grab as much as I could and run. I forced myself to stay focused on my mission.

"Ethan?" I called out. My voice echoed through the large, empty house. "Ethan, it's okay, I'm here to help."

No answer.

I rushed from room to room but saw no boy and no evidence that a boy had ever been here. The only room I wasn't able to enter was the cellar. Even though my key would turn inside the door's lock, it felt as if something was pressed against the door to keep it shut. I grunted as I tried to push the cellar's door open, but it was no use. I decided to double-check the rooms I'd already searched for additional clues. I was starting to think I traded my job for a stay in Moonshire's prison when I tripped and stumbled to the ground.

"Rachel?" It was Thalia's voice. She raced over and pulled me up. "I can't make him sleep forever. Have you found anything yet?"

"No…" I frowned, rubbing the new bruise on my head.

"Rachel, you've gotten clumsy," she said.

"I tripped over something." I looked back to see what had caused my fall.

My mouth fell open at the sight of a child's black leather shoe.

CHAPTER 5:

Beads of sweat dripped from my forehead as Thalia and I raced over the drawbridge that led to the palace.

Dirty and weary, I held the leather shoe tightly in my hand. A palace guard unsheathed his sword as he watched us approach. I knew we were a sight to see: two bruised and deranged women in dirty, ripped dresses running toward the place in the middle of the night.

"We need to speak to the Jarl," I demanded. "It's urgent."

"Leave now," the guard said through gritted teeth.

"It's about Ethan."

The guards' expressions softened. "What news do you bring?"

I held out the shoe to show the guards. "I think it belonged to him."

"Where did you find that?"

I opened my mouth to speak but felt Thalia's hand on my shoulder.

"We would rather share that information directly with the Jarl," she said.

"Right this way," the guard said as he unlocked the place doors and led us toward our fifty-thousand gold reward.

EPILOGUE

His son's shoe was all the proof the Jarl needed to arrest Kaldar.

Under the cover of the night, the Jarl sent his guards to raid Kaldar's manor. They arrested him, ignoring his claims that witches had cursed him and caused his misfortune.

The guards found Ethan trapped inside Kaldar's cellar. The boy didn't say much about his time with Kaldar. The townspeople who saw the boy said he looked spooked and would need time to process the ordeal.

As promised, we were given fifty -thousand gold as a reward. I convinced Thalia to move to Riverdam with me and give up her life of crime. We'd purchase an estate even larger than Lady Esme's and make an honest name for ourselves.

Today would be our last day in the city of Moonshire.

"Rachel, why are you keeping that jewelry?" Thalia asked as we packed. "We can afford nicer things now. Honestly, we should just burn this place to ground with everything that's in it."

"Some things have sentimental value," I said.

"What do we have to be sentimental about?"

"Just let me look around your house first," I said. "This was my home, too."

When I went into Thalia's room, I didn't see the dog she mentioned. The unmade bed, piles of clothes, and makeup scattered around the space were to be expected. But while looking through the room, I found something else that caught my eye.

A small black leather shoe was hidden under a pile of clothing. It was the same size and style of the shoe we found at the manor, but this one was made to fit the left foot rather than the right.

I remembered the sound I'd heard while getting ready to go to the bar. Was it the boy, rather than a dog, that she had hidden in her room? It was odd that she needed me to bring Kaldar home without her. Maybe she needed time to put the boy in Kaldar's Manor? It made sense now. Thalia kidnapped the Jarl's son and orchestrated his rescue. This had been one elaborate con.

I sighed as I put the shoe back under the pile of clothes and pretended I never saw it.

The sun was bright, and the sky was clear on the day we planned to leave the prison district for good. I stood outside of Thalia's home, talking in the city responsible for the worst and best years of my life.

Three giggling children chased each other past Thalia's home. Despite their bare feet and tattered clothes, there was joy in their eyes. Their laughter rivaled the sweet music of the birds and crickets in Riverdam's forests.

I took in my surroundings. These rundown buildings and littered streets had a soul of their own. It made sense that so many people from the prison district had been labeled witches. In order to survive at a place like this, you learn how to create your own magic. You find your worth from within and foster your own joy.

"Admiring the prison district's natural beauty?" Thalia quipped from behind me. I had been so engrossed in my thoughts that I didn't hear her approach. "Gods, Rachel, I didn't think you'd actually be out here crying over having to leave this dump."

Was I crying? I lifted my fingers to my cheek. Sure enough, they were damp.

"You're the most sensitive outlaw I know," she said with a laugh.

I wiped my tears away. "We need to make one last stop before we leave."

She raised a brow in confusion but followed me as I took off toward the orphanage. I'd find the girl whose tired eyes reminded me of so much of my own. I'd give her a proper home and take her on walks down Riverdam's cobblestone path. She'd have every bit of love and protection that I never had growing up.

It was time to do some good with our ill-gotten fortune.

ABOUT K.R.S. MCENTIRE

K. R. S. McEntire lives on a healthy diet of fiction and tea. She loves art, photography and travel because, like books, they allow her to explore new worlds. She lives in Indianapolis with her husband and runs the Facebook page Diverse Fantasy and Sci-Finds, where she shares book recommendations with other bibliophiles.

Website: https://krsmcentire.wordpress.com

facebook.com/KRSMCENTIRE

twitter.com/KeshiaIsWrite

instagram.com/krsmcentire

AYAKASHI BLADE

BY AMBER MORANT

CHAPTER ONE

It was dark inside the empty room. The sun had set long ago, leaving the dim light of the moon to peer inside from the singular window. Two lit candles remained of the hundred in the opposite room. The tatami was clean and fresh. The men who hired Hayashi claimed the building was meant to be a new temporary home for traveling samurai with their daimyo, but he doubted even they would stay in something so small.

"When the boy turned around, the ghost of his mother stood there with her head tilted and a smile sliced across her face."

"Oh god, this is so exciting!"

"And out creaked the words 'would you rather a red kimono or a blue kimono?' The boy answered with red kimono, and in an instant, she sliced his head off his body!"

Screams filled the small room at the sudden exclamation to the story. Hayashi rolled his eyes. They had told at least ten different variations of that same story all night. None of them were original, yet it still scared the villagers each time.

The young man that told the story stood up and walked over to the paper shoji. He slid it open and froze just before going into the hall. The others in the group didn't notice and instead were deep in discussion with one another to calm themselves down.

Hayashi took a step toward the door and reached for his sword. "What's wrong? Why aren't you extinguishing the last candle?" He tightened his grip around the handle when the man didn't answer. "Speak!"

The man turned around. His face was sunken in and pale. He shook his head slowly before turning back into the hall. One step after another, he found his way into the opposing room and flicked out the candle. One remained, and he didn't return.

Hayashi grunted and released the hold on his katana. Silently, he walked over to the shoji and closed it shut, sealing the now remaining few into the room once more.

"We have one last story to tell, and then Aoandon will appear." Hayashi sat down in the circle. He took one last look behind him but didn't see the shadow of the missing member of their group. Another victim to the yokai.

"Will you be telling the final story?" An older man in the circle asked. He leaned forward and smiled in the darkness. "You must have so many stories to tell."

Hayashi smirked and nodded. "I do. But the best story I can tell is one that fits our evening now."

Everyone leaned forward, listening intently.

Hayashi cleared his throat. "When the Hundredth flame goes out, Aoandon comes to collect. Speak of the devil, and the devil shall appear."

Everyone was left in silence. It wasn't the usual ghost story like the others. His was a warning and announcement to welcome Aoandon to the home.

The room grew cold, and the candle outside of the room flickered in the distance. Unlike the others who had to go out to diminish their candle after a story, he didn't hesitate. She would be here soon, and if he wanted to avoid more casualties and receive his payment, he needed to finish this quickly.

He opened the door into the hall and stepped into the opposing room. All the candles stood in a circle, still having streams of smoke billowing out of the wicks. He stepped over to the far candle that was still burning and shook his head in amusement. All of them had claimed they were brave, yet none of them chose to go to the furthest candles. Instead, each one chose the closest one, still burning to extinguish.

Hayashi bent down and pinched the flame between his forefinger and thumb. He released the candle and looked up. The light from the moon turned a slight blue, and the sounds from the others in the group went silent. She was summoned.

Steps echoed in the hall. Hayashi pulled his katana out and silently walked back toward the other room. No one was there.

"Shit! She's here! It's true!" One of the men in the other room screamed.

Hayashi ran into the room. Hovering in the center of the group was a woman wearing a light blue tattered kimono. Her skin was translucent. The only light that echoed through the room was the blue that burned from within her own body.

Years ago, Hayashi would have been just as terrified of the creature standing before him, but now she was no different than any enemy he once faced on the battlefield.

Aoandon hissed at Hayashi, bearing razor-sharp teeth. She flew at Hayashi and swiped at him with elongated nails that resembled more like claws. She let out an audible screech.

Hayashi stepped out of the way of Aoandon and let her fly through the paper wall and into the hall. "Get out of here! All of you." He pointed at the window to indicate their means of escape.

None of them argued with his command and climbed through the window and into the forest beyond. They didn't leave the sack of money they promise to Hayashi's frustration. He would see them again for their payment.

He turned back to the door and smirked. "You yokai are all so predictable. You want to kill me, yet you can never seem to touch me."

Aoandon screamed and flew back into the room. "I will kill all of you humans!"

Hayashi readied himself, putting one foot back to maintain his balance. He waited for her to get closer until he could see the whites in the yokai's eyes. He sliced through the air. The blade never slowed as it flew through Aoandon.

She fell to the ground and turned back to look at Hayashi. She hissed in pain and swiped at the air. "How? How can you hurt me, human?"

Hayashi stepped up to Aoandon and smirked. He held out his katana in front of him. "A monk blessed my blade long ago, Aoandon. A blessing to kill any yokai that dared to harm me or any that I loved again. Sadly, there isn't anyone I love, so I'm glad you decided to attack me."

"Filthy human. We won't stop hunting you for this. Every yokai will know your name if you kill me."

Hayashi tilted his head. "Will they now? Hard to believe since you are the hundredth yokai I've killed with this blade, and yet you all are still foolish enough to attack me. So, I doubt your death will let anyone know about my existence to hunt me down."

He thrust the blade into Aoandon's chest and twisted.

"Jorogumo will find you. I promise you that."

The blue light faded away from Aoandon's body, and she closed her eyes. Her body went lax, and she slumped onto the ground for a moment before dispersing into a blue smoke that engulfed Hayashi. It swirled around him before floating away into the night sky.

Hayashi stood back up and sheathed his sword. The silver blade glistened one last time before hiding away in the shadows for good. He pulled out a small, thin blade and placed it against his skin. Ninety-nine other healed slices in his skin puckered outward. Each one a light shade against his tanned skin. Another ghost of a reminder.

With one practiced movement, Hayashi slid the blade across his skin and let the blood flow freely down into his hand. A flash of a smile appeared before his focus returned to his environment.

"You have been avenged, my love," Hayashi whispered.

He wiped the blood off the blade and slid it back into his belt. The cut wasn't deep enough to hurt him or weaken him from the blood loss. Eventually, it would begin to clot over, and he would just need to wash the blood from his body. It was how all the other cuts were.

"Now, to collect my payment."

The walk back to the main portion of the village wasn't long. But it was also late, and everyone would most likely be asleep. He didn't care who was asleep or awake. He just wanted the money he was promised. They hired him to stop the yokai that was haunting their village, and he did just that. Then again, the Aoandon was just one of many that would take the place to go after children that decided to tell the hundred ghost stories. Hers was just more violent than most.

He found the house that belonged to the Shoya. It was a little larger than the others, nothing extravagant for a village of farmers, but enough that it would provide bragging rights amongst his peers.

Hayashi rapped on the door and waited outside in the cold. No one answered except the shuffling of feet on the other side. He knocked again. This time there was someone shushing inside and bumping into an object.

"Shoya, I know you're in there. Pay me like you promised, and I'll be on my way." He raised his arm into the air. "Or would you rather I stay out here and attract yokai with the scent of my blood in the air?" It was a lie, but all villagers were superstitious enough to believe it.

More shuffling, and then the door cracked open. "I thought you had died in there, rōnin."

"Would you rather I died and let the Aoandon free?" Hayashi asked and tilted his head to the side to get a better view of the leader. "If you want, I'm sure I could summon another for you and just leave."

"No!" multiple voices called out from inside.

The Shoya coughed and shook his head. "No, that won't be needed." He turned around and whispered something inaudible to someone inside the home. When he turned around, he had a small sack of rice in his hands. "As promised."

Hayashi took the sack of rice and weighed it in his hand. "Seems about right."

He stopped before putting it away and opened the bag up and frowned. There was rice inside of the bag, but in the center of it was a large rock adding weight to it. Hayashi growled and dumped the entire bag onto the ground, scattering the rice in the dirt.

"You expect to fool me like this? Give me the bag I was promised!"

The Shoya went pale, watching the rice fall away, then shook his head to pull himself back into the present. "Yes. Right away. Of course." He turned back into the house and started yelling at someone inside about failing. After a few moments, he was back with a new bag of rice. "This one is just rice. We promise you. Now go! We don't want you in our village anymore to curse us," he hissed and slammed the door shut.

Hayashi took a step back and sighed. The Shoya was at least telling the truth with the new bag. It did have rice in it, and he shoved the small package of rice into his larger bag. He didn't feel bad for wasting so much of their rice. If the Shoya just paid like they agreed, he would be gone already.

"Hope you idiots all summon Aoandon again. Next time I won't be so courteous, and I doubt you will find anyone willing to rid you of her again," Hayashi grumbled and set off on the road and away from the small village.

CHAPTER TWO

Hayashi stared across the table at the empty spot in front of him. All the other tables had friends and family amongst them except his own. The smell of soba was the one thing there to keep him company.

He rubbed his fingers across his arms. It had been years since he last scratched one of the lines into his own flesh. Now so many were already fading into the wrinkles in his skin or so thin now they were impossible to notice. Still, he always kept the small blade and his katana by his side.

His eyes wandered down to the cushion next to him, and grimaced. A small spider no bigger than his fingernail crawled toward him. He pulled off his shoe and slammed it atop the spider. It missed, and the spider scrambled under the table.

"Disgusting. Can't even eat in peace without some filth bothering me now."

He slid the shoe back on and dove into eating his noodles. Those that sat near him had their eyes on him in concern. The village wasn't too small, but it was big enough to recognize a samurai. More importantly, they were big enough to know he wasn't one anymore and hadn't been for a long time.

"Is he here?" a man asked out loud to one of the workers in the restaurant.

"Is who—" one of the workers attempted to ask.

"The rōnin! I was told he would be here and could help us."

Hayashi sunk into himself more. It was a hundred yokai, and yet his fame followed him even after all these years. He didn't want to be seen. Enough people came looking for his help killing some random small yokai that was bothering their people, and each time he turned them down. It didn't matter how much money or food they offered. It wasn't important to him anymore. He had enough to last him until he died. Which he hoped was soon.

The man pushed past the waitress and into the dining area. He scanned the different tables and shook his head, acknowledging none of them were obviously rōnin. He finally stopped at Hayashi's table and smiled defiantly. Just as Hayashi had expected, the man wore a cheap kimono tied off at his knees. The color was faded from use in the sun. His eyes were covered by a wide-brimmed straw hat tied underneath his chin. He was not from the town and most likely traveled a short distance.

"I knew I would find you here." He sat across from Hayashi. "I heard you kill yokai for a price."

Hayashi grunted. "That was years ago. I'm not for sale anymore."

The man leaned forward. He smiled, revealing most of his teeth missing, and the others already tainted yellow. Hayashi couldn't help but lean back to avoid smelling his breath. "I want to hire you to kill a yokai for me. I can pay you well."

"Pay me well in what? If you had those funds, you could pay for new clothes. Or at least something to make your breath better." Hayashi scrunched his nose. "I'm not for hire. So, get out."

Another spider crawled across the table. Hayashi slammed his hand and squished the insect. He wiped his hand on his side, then looked back up at the man. He wished he could squish him too and be done with it all.

"You haven't even heard what the creature is. How can you just say no?"

"Because I can. Now leave." Hayashi pushed himself up from the table and turned to the exit. "If you have so much money to afford me, you should have enough to pay for my meal you ruined with your disturbance."

"Jorogumo!" The man yelled out. Everyone in the room fell silent. "It's a Jorogumo. No one else would be able to kill it." He stood up as well and pulled out a large sack from inside his kimono. It jingled with the movement. "There's more at our village if you come with me."

Hayashi paused and looked down at the bag. It made no sense that the man looked so poor, yet carried so much money on him. He reached out for a moment to take the bag and accept the offer but pulled away quickly.

"I'm sorry," he muttered. "I can't take the job." He pulled his sleeve up to show some of the marks still visible on his arms. "I already killed all that I needed to."

The man slumped his shoulders and walked out of the restaurant past Hayashi. "I understand. Perhaps someone else will come by and be able to help us."

Hayashi frowned as the man walked out. From behind, there was something odd about him. Underneath his clothing, something moved. Just before he walked out, a spider popped out from the man's collar.

"Wait! There's a spider—" Hayashi tried to call out after him.

The villager didn't respond and stepped out of the restaurant. Hayashi ran after him. The man was gone.

"Where did he go," Hayashi muttered.

He walked around to the back of the building and stopped. On the floor was the man's clothing crumpled into a ball with the hat sitting on top. Around the clothes crawled hundreds of small spiders like the ones he had killed earlier.

"Disgusting," Hayashi growled and covered his mouth with his sleeve. "What happened to you?"

A pile of spiders crawled toward him. They made a hissing noise. "Poor little rōnin. You scratched and scratched yet never got your wife back." The spiders piled higher until they were as tall as Hayashi. "Too bad you never found the one that killed them"

Hayashi brandished his katana and swung it at the spiders sending them in different directions. "Do not taunt me, demons."

They swirled at his feet and chuckled. "Taunt you? We tried to tell you the truth earlier in a form you would accept, and you brush us off. Now we bring our message in our true form. Jorogumo is coming for you."

"Who is Jorogumo?" Hayashi growled. "Why does she want me?"

The spiders piled up again, each one moving individually up and down the pile to aid in the growth until they formed a humanoid shape again. They separated to form a mouth and smiled. "She was the cause of your wife and young boy's demise."

Another group of spiders piled together, forming the shape of a woman and child embracing one another. The spiders screamed in unison, mocking his wife's and son's death.

"It was such a sweet death. Their blood was delicious for Jorogumo. Their screams music to her children's ears." They all laughed in unison and collapsed the form of his wife and son. "She yearns to taste your flesh as well, human. We hunted you for so long, and now we have found you."

The spiders in the humanoid form in front of Hayashi collapsed onto the ground and scattered across the ground. As quickly as they had appeared, the creatures disappeared into the cracks of buildings and into the distance.

"We will wait for you in the South."

"Jorogumo." Hayashi pulled his sleeve back up to look at the scars. None of the yokai were responsible for killing his family. He knew that much. He looked back up into the sky. "I will find you."

He picked up the straw hat from the fake human and put it atop his own head. He didn't know how far it would be of a walk, but he would at least make sure he was ready. It had been too many years since he had truly used his blade against a yokai. He would be ready.

CHAPTER THREE

Hayashi sighed and fell on top of the futon. He dragged his hand against the cool tatami floor. Just below him was a yokai living life as a normal human would. It disgusted him, but he already killed enough yokai for his taste. There was one left for him.

Floorboards squeaked outside of Hayashi's room. He turned his head to see who it was. A small light from a candle danced across the thin screen wall. Outside, a woman walked down the hall. Each step was taken with ease and careful consideration until she stopped in front of Hayashi's door.

"Am I beautiful?" The woman asked.

Hayashi sat up and growled. "Damn it, Rokurokubi. I'm not here to watch you flaunt your body again. I don't want to see it!"

The woman didn't move. "Do you think I am beautiful?"

He narrowed his eyes and stood up. The voice wasn't the rokurokubi's voice. Hers was much huskier. Familiar. This wasn't her. He reached for his katana that was leaning against the wall.

"Who are you?"

The woman giggled and slid the door open. Hayashi stood his ground and pulled the sword out.

It was dark, but the candle the woman held illuminated her face. Her mouth was sliced open, so she eternally smiled with slits running up her cheeks. Her teeth were yellowed from old age despite her skin as smooth as a young woman's would be.

"Kuchisake Onna," Hayashi hissed.

"You think I'm beautiful, don't you?" She didn't move her mouth as she spoke.

Hayashi took a step back. "No, you're hideous. Just like all the other yokai."

The Kuchisake Onna opened her mouth and let out a gargled laugh from deep in her throat. Her tongue lolled out the side of her face. "Then you will die, human!" The yokai shrieked.

Her fingernails grew exponentially until they were as long as her hands and as sharp as claws. She took a step forward. Every joint in her body moving as one, cracking like sticks in a storm. Another low cackle gurgled from the back of her throat.

Before Hayashi could react, the Kuchisake Onna fell. It didn't stop her. She pulled herself forward with her nails. The yokai lifted her head and gurgled another laugh.

"Stop right there!" Someone snapped from the doorway.

Hayashi looked up. The Rokurokubi stood in the hall with a knife panting. Kuchisake Onna turned to look at the other yokai and hissed. She pulled herself back into a standing position and lunged.

"I'll kill you," Kuchisake Onna screeched.

Rokurokubi sidestepped, letting the slit-mouthed woman run past her. In a flash, she pulled out a kunai and thrust it into the Kuchisake Onna's side.

"Not if you're dead," Rokurokubi said and smirked while she twisted the blade.

Kuchisake Onna's body turned into ash and fell on the ground in multiple piles.

Rokurokubi grimaced at the sight and walked over the body. She stepped over to Hayashi and gave him a weak smile.

"Why? That was one of your own," Hayashi asked. He stared down at the piles of ash on the floor, impressed at the fact that she could kill another of her kind.

Rokurokubi shrugged and slid the kunai back into a small loop on the inside of her kimono. "It's far easier to clean the body of a yokai off the floor compared to the flesh and bones of a human."

Hayashi stifled a laugh and shook his head.

"You look tired, rōnin. You should get some sleep."

"Not after that attack. If she tried to assassinate me, there's going to be more coming after me."

Rokurokubi tilted her head and winked. "Then be glad you have one of those demons on your side. I don't sleep, and I can stretch my neck out the window to keep my eyes out for any others that try to come here. As I said, it's easier to clean that than blood."

"Fine," Hayashi grunted. "But don't expect this to mean you're staying with me for long."

Hayashi laid back down on the futon and held onto his sword. Even if she promised to protect him, he felt far more comfortable with a weapon in his hands ready to use. He watched out the corner of his eye as Rokurokubi stretched her neck out. It wrapped around the room in a large circle while her head darted in different directions.

She moved her head, so it floated above Hayashi. "You should get some sleep. The night will be long."

"And what will you do once your master learns you revealed you were a yokai?"

She bit her bottom lip and twisted away. "Most likely, I will be removed from the inn. Even if you promised not to reveal who I am, he wouldn't care. It's part of my contract with him. If anyone learned who I was, then either he would kill me, or I would need to leave before he found out himself."

Hayashi grunted and turned away, so all he could see was her neck wavering through the air like waves. "Where will you go?"

"I'm unsure. Perhaps I will follow you until I find a new purpose. You obviously will need to continue to sleep every night, and I can keep you safe in exchange for your company."

"I'm not sleeping with you."

"That's not what I said!" Rokurokubi snapped. She fell silent for a moment. "I'm sorry. I shouldn't raise my voice. Sleep now, rōnin. Tomorrow we will discuss this."

Hayashi grunted again and pulled the blanket up further. "You can come with."

CHAPTER FOUR

Hayashi adjusted the bag on his back. After he had awoken to the sight of two additional ash piles awaiting him near the window and door, he doubted he wanted to be without Rokurokubi now. At least, not until he killed Jorogumo. After that, he didn't even care if she died.

Most of the bag was filled with supplies he acquired while at the inn. Some were foods the master provided him while others he managed to take with him, including the money he used to pay for the room. Rokurokubi walked a few steps behind him with her bag of belongings. Like his, most were stolen from the inn or her room that she felt she needed to keep with her.

"How much further?" Rokurokubi called out.

Hayashi shrugged. "I would say less than a day's walk. We should arrive before evening."

"But, Haya, my feet are—"

Hayashi raised a hand to silence her. "What did you just call me?" He growled.

"Haya. I'm sorry. You just seem like a Haya. Did I... Did I say something wrong?"

Hayashi glared at her and stepped closer to her, so all she would be able to see was his face. "The last person who called me that died. Do you understand me?"

Rokurokubi nodded. "Yes. I'm sorry. I didn't mean to insult you."

Hayashi sighed and shook his head. "You didn't insult me. My wife was the last to call me that. She died years ago."

Rokurokubi lowered her gaze. She bit the corner of her lip as if trying to think of something else to say. The hydrangea rested above her ear, now wilting with her emotions. For a moment, Hayashi had to blink to adjust his vision. The way she pouted now in the sunlight reminded him so much of his wife. He wanted to embrace her and kiss her, but resisted the urge, remembering who he was looking at was a yokai and nothing more.

"Let's get going. I don't want to delay anymore."

"Of course!" Her gaze brightened and sped her pace up to match Hayashi's.

Just as he predicted, the two arrived at the village before dusk. The sun wasn't directly above them anymore and cast long shadows across the multiple building sitting against the mountainside. Spider webs covered all the trees and houses like prey.

"Spiders?" Rokurokubi muttered and walked over to one of the webs.

"Jorogumo. Her spiders did this to the people."

"What happened to everyone?"

Hayashi shrugged his shoulders and walked into the village. There was no sign of anyone being in the village for a long time. No spiders were walking on the webs.

"Something is amiss here."

He walked over to one of the larger buildings and picked up a stick lying on the ground. He pushed some of the webs aside and furrowed his brow.

"This was a restaurant before."

He stepped inside. Unlike the outside of the restaurant, the inside was almost completely untouched. The only webs he found were giant piles in different areas. He walked over to one of them and brushed the webs aside. Pearlescent fear-induced eyes stared back at him. The skin was pulled tight against the person's bones.

"So, that's where the villagers went." He turned to the door. "Rokurokubi, stay out there. You don't want to see this."

She didn't respond at first. Something was scratching on the other side of the wall.

"Rokurokubi!" Hayashi yelled out.

He ran out of the restaurant and turned his head to look for her. She was a few feet away and surrounded by thousands of spiders crawling over one another. They resembled black thunderstorm clouds rumbling through the sky.

"Whatever you do, don't touch them." Hayashi held a hand out to pull Rokurokubi's attention away.

"Too late for that," Rokurokubi whispered. "I accidentally stepped on one of them, and then they swarmed around me instantly."

Hayashi looked around. There wasn't much he could use as a weapon against so many spiders. He looked down at the stick still in his hand and smiled.

"The only one here killing yokai is her and I."

He reached into his bag and pulled out a pair of fire starter stones. He struck them thrice before the stick alit with flames. They weren't the strongest, but it was enough. He lowered the stick near the spiders and watched as they scattered. They screamed in pain from the heat and bright light. Within an instant, the flames created a thin path for Rokurokubi to dart through.

"Jorogumo waits for you in the caverns. Don't you dare come back into our home," the spiders hissed.

The cluster of spiders gathered again and crawled toward Rokurokubi and Hayashi. Their high-pitched hissing sent shivers down Hayashi's spine.

He reached for Rokurokubi's hand, and they ran toward the mountains.

"Caves. They said caves are where she is hiding." Rokurokubi gasped. "Let's just pick one and get away from here."

They reached the edge of the village and turned around. The spiders all stood at the border of the village, hissing and pacing back and forth. Some climbed atop others before collapsing on themselves again.

"I don't think we will be able to get back in there," Hayashi grumbled and turned to face the mountainside. He expected a few caves to face the village. Instead, there were at least ten. "Want to take a guess?"

Rokurokubi looked at them and stretched her neck out to listen for any sounds from within each cave and still stand next to Hayashi. Finally, she returned to her body and shook her head.

"They're all silent."

"Then we'll just choose one and hope for the best."

Hayashi stepped closer to the cave directly in front of them. It was too dark to see further in now that the sun was on the other side of the mountains. He kicked a stone inside and listened.

Scuffling echoed back to him like more insects. He shivered at the thought of dealing with the spiders in the dark. He had the fire starter stones, but the light wouldn't be enough, and the smoke would be too thick for them to continue with the flame if the cave shrunk in size.

He turned back to Rokurokubi and sat in the soft grass. "We'll wait until the morning."

Rokurokubi looked up at the cave. "Do you think it's more spiders?"

"Possibly." He dropped his bag and put his head on it to use as a pillow. "For now, let us get some sleep. Those spiders want me to see Jorogumo, so I doubt they will kill us before then."

Rokurokubi sat next to him, staring at the cave. He sighed heavily then turned on his side away from her. He wasn't used to a yokai, and with the sky darkening once more, the shadows would just play tricks on him once more and make him imagine he was looking at his wife. He didn't need any more reminders beyond the demon that awaited them in the cave.

CHAPTER FIVE

Hayashi woke with the sun rising and blasting into his eyes. He squinted, covering his eyes. "What time is it?" he grumbled.

"Just after dawn," Rokurokubi hummed.

Hayashi groaned. It was too early to be happy right now. "What about the scratching?"

Rokurokubi shrugged her shoulders. "Almost all night. It got louder for a moment, but I couldn't see anything when I looked in there. I don't think it was a spider, though. The scratching sounded too much like a single creature walking around."

Hayashi stood up and brushed the dirt off his clothes. He looked out to the village. The spiders were nowhere to be seen, but he knew better than to try to walk back that way by himself. As soon as he stepped in, the spiders would try to come after him again.

"Are you sure you still want to come with me?"

"I have nowhere else to go."

"You realize you might die in there, right?"

Rokurokubi smirked and shook her head. Hayashi rubbed his eyes again. There were just too many similarities, and once he was done killing the yokai, he would need to figure out why she looked so similar to his wife.

The two walked over to the cave entrance and listened. There was no sound this time. The light poured into the cave illuminating the walls. They were coated in slime and shimmered.

Hayashi walked into the cave and swiped a finger across the slime. As a clear coating and smelled horrible. "You are right that it wasn't a spider. But, you're not gonna like what it actually was."

Rokurokubi looked at the slime on Hayashi's finger. "Then, what was it?"

He didn't answer her and continued his trek down the cave. The sound of the creature got louder again. He placed a hand on the wall. It was vibrating from the creature's movement. Wherever it was, it was close, and they needed to be careful.

After a few turns down the cavern halls, they found themselves in an open room. In the center was a large pillar that touched the ceiling high above them. The slime was thicker on the pillar in the center compared to the walls at the entrance. Hayashi pulled out his sword and took a step forward. Rokurokubi reached out and grabbed Hayashi's sleeve.

"What is this place?" she asked.

"This is its den."

"And you're both just in time for my breakfast," a deep voice hissed from the darkness of the ceiling.

Hayashi looked up. Something was crawling against the wall. As the creature moved, it opened holes in the ceiling to pour light into the room so they could see better. The light bounced off the walls of slime and onto the body of the creature. It was a giant centipede with the face of a human. It smiled down at them and clicked its pincers that jutted from its mouth. Omukade.

"Get behind me," Hayashi ordered and pushed Rokurokubi back.

The omukade smiled down at Hayashi and dove toward them. It turned before reaching them and wrapped around until Hayashi and Rokurokubi were surrounded by the insect's body.

"Jorogumo said there would be a human coming here, and I should leave them to her. But she didn't say anything about the yokai."

"She didn't tell me anything about you either," Hayashi growled.

The omukade laughed and lifted its head. Its pincers clicked together, adding to the eerie sound of laughter echoing against the walls. "You are a funny human. If she didn't want you, I would've loved to eat you. I'm sure you taste delicious, but she wants to devour you herself, so I'll just have to suffer from eating the yokai instead."

The centipede struck at Rokurokubi and lifted her into the air. Hayashi slashed his katana through the air, cutting one of the omukade's limbs off. It screamed in pain, throwing the yokai into the air before catching Rokurokubi again.

"How dare you!" He shook Rokurokubi, and she screamed in fear. "You dare attempt to hurt me? I have lived over a thousand years in these caves. Many have attempted to kill me. But you, you are so insolent that you don't even respect the fact that I am killing one of your enemies for you."

"She's not one of my enemies," Hayashi barked.

The centipede laughed a deep guttural sound like he was underwater. "Not your enemy? Then you must have taken her for a slave." It dropped Rokurokubi on the other side of his body and leaned down to smile at Hayashi. "Or perhaps you just like to fuck her."

Hayashi roared in frustration and thrust his sword into the underbelly of the creature. Blood splattered across his face ad he pulled out the blade and struck again.

"Damn you, rōnin! Slice me again, and I will kill your beloved monster in the worst way I can." Omukade lunged back and circled around Rokurokubi. "Leave now and face Jorogumo, and perhaps I will consider giving her a quick death." In a flash, the centipede dove at Rokurokubi. Her screams filled the cavern like a chorus of death. When omukade pulled away, blood dripped from his mouth. He smiled, revealing razor-sharp teeth stained red. "Let this be your warning."

"Hayashi!" Rokurokubi screamed.

Hayashi averted his gaze, trying to shut out the screams. Those same screams from his wife. He gritted his teeth. "Shut up already."

Omukade leaned closer to Hayashi. "What did you say, human?"

Hayashi turned and stared up at the omukade. "I said, 'shut up' and just die already!"

He jumped into the air and sliced the centipede's face. Blood splattered across Hayashi. The metallic scent making him gag.

The omukade screamed in pain and scurried back. Hayashi stepped toward the yokai, but it didn't bother staying in the large room and hid within one of the smaller caves.

"You will pay dearly for this, rōnin. Jorogumo does not take kindly to those who hurt her subjects." The scratching of his feet on the ground disappeared into the darkness.

Rokurokubi lay on the ground, her chest heaving. Hayashi ran up to her and collapsed next to her. He brushed a piece of her hair out of her face.

"You were a strong warrior, Rokurokubi," Hayashi said in a calm tone.

She gave him a weak smile and closed her eyes. "You were stronger still. Though, I don't understand why you attacked him. He could have killed you, and you should have let me die."

Hayashi shrugged and grasped Rokurokubi's hand. It was cold from the loss of blood, and already her skin was turning a light shade of blue. He had always killed a yokai instantly and never imagined they could bleed out from a slow death like this.

"You reminded me too much of my wife. I don't think I could have faced myself knowing I failed twice."

She pulled her hand free and touched his cheek. "Your wife seems like she would have been a nice person. Definitely not your type." She laughed through a cough. "I know you said you don't want to kill me, but would you do me the honor?" She reached out for her kunai, which was now soaked in blood, and placed the tip over her heart. "I'd rather die an instant death by someone that is seeking retribution than becoming that things meal again."

Hayashi nodded his head and grasped the dagger in his hands.

Rokurokubi opened her eyes for a moment and nodded her head to acknowledge Hayashi. Together, they thrust the blade into her chest. The air in her lungs escaped one last time with her eyes perpetually on Hayashi. In the brief moment, before her life ended, her eyes shifted, and once more, he was looking at his wife.

"Rest in peace, Rokurokubi," Hayashi murmured, and closed her eyes. "May your next life not be haunted as this one was." He pulled the dagger back out and put it on his belt.

He stood up and looked at the cave omukade escaped into. He was now ready to take his revenge. Rokurokubi's body turned to ash next to him, and he walked into the depths of his hell.

CHAPTER SIX

It was too dark now that there were no holes of light above him, which forced Hayashi to light his makeshift torch. The smoke wafted up and back, dancing through the occasional spider web that lined the walls.

The webs became more frequent the further he walked through the cave. Omukade's body lay trapped in a cluster of webs to the side. So much of his lower half was eaten away already by the spiders, leaving the creature's torso still wriggling in pain. The centipede's muffled screams were like a war cry for Hayashi.

"Jorogumo!" Hayashi yelled into the darkness. "Where are you, demon?"

Laughter surrounded Hayashi. Spiders crawled near his feet, avoiding being stepped on, but nuisances all the same.

"You want to find our mother? You walk to your death so easily," the voices taunted.

"Get away from me!" Hayashi yelled and lowered the flames from his stick near the ground. The spiders scream in pain and scatter into the dark corners of the cavern walls.

A hiss pulled Hayashi's attention back in front of him. "You dare hurt my children in front of me?"

Hayashi took a deep breath and walked forward into a large room. The floor transformed into a large, thick sheet of webs that wrapped around themselves and folded up the walls. There were no small spiders like the caverns behind him.

"Show yourself, Jorogumo!" He pulled Rokurokubi's dagger out of his belt. "You wanted me to face you, and here I am."

"And here you are," Jorogumo purred.

Hayashi looked up. Jorogumo lay on the ceiling with her arms crossed to let her head rest on her hands. Her torso was more like a human woman's while the bottom half was a snark as large as a horse. Her multitude of eyes looked down at Hayashi, and she smiled at him.

"I can see why she chose you so much, rōnin. You are delectable to look at."

Hayashi threw the dagger at Jorogumo. The spider caught the blade in her hands and stabbed it into the web above her. Thick, silken web slid out from behind her so she could lower her body. She twisted around until she landed in front of Hayashi.

"Interesting choice for your first weapon. Was that from your first or second wife?"

Hayashi pulled out his sword and dropped the flaming stick. It burned away the cobwebs on the edge of the room, lighting the walls in a dance of fury. "I only had one wife, and you murdered her. Now I'm here to kill you."

Hayashi charged at Jorogumo and swung at her. Again, she stopped his blade from hitting her using her hands. Her skin was far thicker than a human. She pushed the sword aside and smirked.

"Only one? Poor Rokurokubi. She worked so hard to win your favor too."

Hayashi ignored the taunting and swung again.

"You know what happens to humans who die because of a yokai?"

"We die. The end. Not like you."

"Not. Like. Us." Jorogumo chuckled and shook her head. Half of her eyes blinked. "You are more of a fool than I expected. No, you are exactly like us." She took a step back. "The dear yokai you had as a companion was your wife. I'm just sorry I couldn't kill her for myself so you could watch your loved one die at my hands again."

"You lie!" Hayashi screamed and lunged forward.

Jorogumo jumped into the air, dodging his blade and grabbed Hayashi's collar, pulling him backward. He fell to the ground with a soft thud. The small spiders climbed up to Hayashi. All of them giggling in delight.

"Vile demons," Hayashi growled and kicked some of them away.

He wasn't able to extend his leg because of the webs trapping him in place. He attempted to pull himself up, but the strain of the spiderwebs kept him close to the ground.

"You call us vile, yet you are the one destroying the lands. You call us demons for killing humans, yet you kill others as well. We kill to survive." Jorogumo walked over to Hayashi's legs and used her web to tie his legs together. "Even your beloved understood survival when she turned into the Rokurokubi."

Hayashi grunted and pulled against the webs to no avail. "I will kill you."

Jorogumo didn't respond. Instead, she hummed to herself and continued at her work like an old mother sewing clothes for her children.

He looked up at the ceiling, focusing on the dagger. He couldn't reach his sword or the dagger at this point. An idea popped into his mind. He smiled. "Jorogumo, you say you're better than us humans?"

"We are."

"You're no better than even the true spiders. Your nests scatter everywhere, and you choose to trap me on the ground instead of like the spiders you claim to be."

Jorogumo stopped weaving her webs and lowered her face to Hayashi's. "We don't compare ourselves to the insects you ignore so easily. I am a yokai."

"Is that what you say to your children?" The small spiders murmured to one another and climbed across the walls. "They're just spiders you've given the gift of speech. Or are they just filthy insects just like you?"

The spiders hissed at Hayashi and filled the room. He watched as a group surrounded the kunai. The dagger wiggled from the weight and then fell next to Hayashi with a soft thud. He turned back to Jorogumo and smirked, keeping her attention on him.

"You're not worthy of being called a yokai."

Jorogumo hissed and raised one of her legs. "Enough of this. I will kill you now and not waste time on these webs for you anymore!"

Hayashi forced himself as far over as he could to avoid the yokai's strike and grabbed the dagger on the ground next to him. He twisted his arm back and slammed the blade into her leg.

Jorogumo screamed in pain and collapsed under the injury. "Damn you, human," she hissed and snapped at him. "Children, kill him now!"

The spiders crawled off the walls and toward Hayashi. He didn't have time to wait and twisted more into Jorogumo's leg so he could reach her and stabbed her in the heart.

"That is for killing my wife." He pulled the blade down. It ripped her breast open. "That is for destroying her again." He pulled it out, letting the blood pour out.

Jorogumo collapsed, reaching for the giant hole in her chest. "Bastard!" She screeched. "I will kill you." She pulled herself away from Hayashi. "My children won't let you live in peace!"

"And neither will I."

Hayashi tilted his head up and sliced his hair to free himself, then removed his outer garments, leaving them on the ground. The fires at the edge of the room were now closer, the heat warming his skin.

Quickly, Hayashi grabbed his sword and walked up to Jorogumo. A multitude of small spiders crawled up his legs, biting into his flesh. He ignored the pain, kicking off a few of them as he walked forward. Finally, he reached Jorogumo and frowned.

"I hope you never come back and suffer worse than anyone you have dared to harm."

In a single flourish, Hayashi sliced Jorogumo's head off. Blood splattered his legs. The spiders scattered back against the walls to avoid the blood.

He turned back to the walls of spiders. "Your mother is dead. If you dare cross me again, I will make sure you all burn just like your home burns now."

The spiders didn't respond. Instead, they scattered into crevices never to be seen again. Hayashi smiled at his success and fell to his knees.

"I did it. I avenged you both. Now I can rest easy." He closed his eyes and took a deep breath.

CHAPTER SEVEN

Hayashi stood in front of his wife's grave. It had been weeks since the battle, and still, the scars covered his body from the spiders eating at his flesh. They no longer hurt as much.

"I did it." He placed a small bundle of hydrangeas on the grave. The same ones his wife loved and Rokurokubi wore during their short time together. "Would you be proud of me?" He wiped a tear away from his eye. "I guess you would be. You did follow me into death a second time after all."

Hayashi sat down and crossed his legs. "Before this all happened, I would have stopped hunting yokai for good. Almost did and let myself die in there." He pulled out his katana and placed it in front of himself. "I guess what I'm trying to say is, I'm going to keep hunting. Not just yokai this time. The humans hidden as demons too."

He pulled his sleeve up and held Rokurokubi's dagger against it. "Three slices this time." He didn't wince from the pain as he crossed it against his arm. "Omukade. Jorogumo." He paused and stared at the dagger for a moment before beginning the last slice. "Rokurokubi."

Hayashi looked up past the graves at an older man waiting for him. His next contract. He pushed himself up with a grunt and let the sleeve fall and cover his arm once more.

"Money is calling, and so is death."

ABOUT AMBER MORANT

Amber Morant grew up in the strange state of Ohio where nothing and everything all exist as one. She loves the darker side of fantasy where dragons and rogues are aplenty in a world that's unlike our own. When not writing, she spends her time playing video games, watching anime, reading, and trying to prove that aliens and dragons both exist.

Website: http://ambermorant.com

facebook.com/author.ambermorant

twitter.com/ambermorant

instagram.com/ambermorantauthor

TO STEAL A KEY AND KINGDOM

BY J.M. RHINEHEART

It was the shoes that caught Pen's eye first. That was how she'd known who she would rob.

All right, so it looked like an easy mark and a good take. None of the Emperor's guards to be seen, just a few people walking through the streets of Silve Hollow. The beginning of the lunch hour meant there were plenty of vendors around, and that meant a few easy purses to take from the nobles who came wandering by. It wasn't as if they needed all of that silver. Pen could think of other applications. Her own person came to mind.

Like those shoes she'd seen somewhere in the marketplace, the ones that had caught the vague amount of sunlight from above and sparkled. She didn't want the shoes themselves, more what they entailed. Those were expensive shoes. Expensive shoes meant an expensive purse.

The main marketplace stood in shadow from the tall, tilted buildings above, making it easy to keep herself mostly hidden as well. Above her, the buildings almost swayed in the breeze. Even the sun couldn't get through to the cobblestone despite it being midday, as tall as the structures were. Nowhere to go but up anymore, and those with more gold and favor with the Emperor got the best view of the sky.

It wasn't like they were untouchable, though. Pen got in and out of their dwellings just fine to *liberate* some of their items. She was doing them a favor, honestly, better to keep their homes lighter, so they didn't come crashing down. That was what they got for building their homes with brick and stone. Much easier to scale.

Another wanted poster with a vague, hooded form depicted on it briefly caught her eye. "The Ghost" was a horrible nickname, but it wasn't like she'd given it to herself. It made her grin to look at it, and she thought about adding it to her collection back in her den.

In her search for the shoes, she spotted Magnus perched against a wall, pretending to be all nonchalant, but his tapping foot gave him away again. The stupid kid was going to get himself caught one of these days. She shouldn't have taught him how to pick a pocket, especially since he wasn't particularly good at it. It reflected poorly on her. She'd just felt sorry for him, that was all. She rolled her eyes when he waved at her.

With Magnus in the mix, her eyes roamed over the marketplace again. A man with a nice pocket watch, two women with their hair done up with gaudy gold beads. Their purses were stowed in obvious places, hanging from their elbows next to their fans, fastened on to a thick leather belt that Pen personally thought adorable. As if something like that would stop her.

Then her eyes caught the sparkle of the shoes again, and she saw *her*. Plain clothes, but they were thick, nice, clearly tailored, not meant to draw attention. A shawl wrapped around her head, just hiding the golden necklace and earrings that glistened from a distance. Oh yeah, this one would have coins for the taking.

And there were the shoes. If Pen knew anything, it was that shoes like that were clearly handmade and meant for the individual that was wearing them. These, they'd fit like a glove. Green shimmering fabric, golden threads: rich without having to flaunt it.

That purse was hers.

It wasn't like sneaking up on the woman was difficult. Pen knew how to make herself disappear in a crowd, even one as thin as this one, and she moved herself closer and closer. If a stray purse wound up in her clutches as she went, well, no one else was the wiser. The two women, in particular, didn't even notice her coming and going, and the man's belt made it easier still to tug his leather pouch free.

The woman with the green shoes kept on going, and Pen came up behind her, eyes on the suspicious lump tucked under her belt. One quick slip of Pen's wrist and the lump came free in her hand. It didn't even so much as jingle, but she felt the hard edge of the coins all the same.

Three seconds later and Pen found herself airborne, tossed down one of the nearby alleys. A large man stood beside the woman, and he flexed impressive muscles as he glared at Pen, teeth bared. "I'll deal with her, your majesty," he growled. "She won't try to steal from a princess again."

"Stop," the woman, *princess,* said, holding a hand up. "We needn't harm the pickpocket."

Of all the things Pen expected to do that day, talking to a princess wasn't one of them.

Apparently, however, that was how things were meant to go: her backside sore, her feet, unable to find themselves beneath her, and overwhelmingly insulted by royalty. "Pickpocket?" she said derisively. "I'm not a *pickpocket.* I'm a thief!"

The princess raised a golden eyebrow, and she even had the gall to smile. Like Pen was a child she was indulging. "Oh? Is there a difference?"

Pen got to her feet and moved forward. One growl from the huge man stopped her, but she still crossed her arms and scowled. "A large one, yes. I can do more than just pluck a purse: I can get in and out of places where no one else can go." Including the tallest buildings that nearly hung over the castle itself. She'd earned herself quite a bit from one of the houses with some absolutely horrific-looking sculptures of the Dragon Emperor himself. Still, Roche had taken them and traded for some *very* shiny coins.

A thought came to her then, and she took a step backward. "Why haven't you gone for the guards yet? I mean, I did take your purse."

"Which you ain't returned yet," the lumbering giant snapped, and Pen instinctively held the purse closer.

"Peace," the woman said, holding her hand up again, and surprise of all surprises, the man settled. Pen felt like sticking out her tongue. "I have no intention of calling upon the guards." Her face shifted into what looked like disgust, which, all right, Pen could understand. It wasn't like royalty were any more popular than a local commoner with the Emperor. "I'd actually like to speak with you."

"We're speaking right now," Pen pointed out.

The princess chuckled. "Speak further, then. I believe there's a tavern not far from here where we could find some privacy?" With that, she turned and continued heading down the street, like it wasn't a big deal that Pen had taken her purse, that she'd lost... oh, that was a fair amount of coins in there, too. Even the giant man moved off after her, silently becoming her shadow again. Their leaving would've let Pen disappear off to wherever she could want to go.

So why Pen was following the woman instead, she had no idea.

The tavern turned out to be Billie's place, *The Sparrow's Rest*, and Billie herself was behind the bar. Clearly, Pen wasn't the only one who thought the princess daft: Billie gave an incredulous look at the woman, but finally nodded to a vacant table along the wall. Thank goodness the place was empty; Miss Fancy Shoes stood out like a sore thumb, her giant of a friend even more so.

Princess. What had Pen gotten herself into?

With the princess and her friend's backs to her, it made it easier to stash the various purses Pen had collected into the safer location of her own clothes. She didn't wear scarves across her chest for looks. The purses fit in nicely and didn't so much as make a jingle when she moved. Billie raised an expectant eyebrow at her, having caught sight of the purses, and Pen just made a face but nodded. She'd be pulling the purses back out to settle her tab before she left, or Billie would haul out that awful griffin's bone from behind the bar and threaten to beat her with it. The horrid thing still had a hind claw attached.

When Pen finally got to the table herself, the princess didn't look surprised to see Pen had followed, which was sort of vexing. She threw back her hood and irritably brushed away a few black strands of hair that had come loose when she'd been thrown. She'd probably have to redo her whole braid at this point.

"Anything you'd like," the woman said generously, lowering her headscarf and revealing golden curls everywhere. It would make a horrible mess if she tried to do any sort of running. Pen expected that as a princess, she probably didn't have to do a lot of running.

Pen smirked at her. "I think I ought to be paying since I've got your purse."

"That's very gracious of you, thank you," the woman said with a smile. Pen stared and her jaw dropped before an amused snort from the man made her close her mouth. The nerve of royalty…

Which, speaking of, how on earth was there still royalty floating around? "So…you come from a long way off?" Pen asked. "Because there's no king or queen anywhere nearby. It's just—"

"Emperor Sagum, yes, I'm aware," the princess said. She made another face of disgust, brow pinched, and tiny nose scrunched up. She still looked dainty doing it. "That's sort of the problem. Isn't it? Because it should be my family on his throne."

It took a minute for that to sink in. "I thought you were all dead or exiled," Pen said, stunned. "So, if you're the Princess—"

"Yes," and the woman sat up straight as if she were about to hold court. "I'm Catadina, Princess of the Silvelands."

She nodded to the man beside her while Pen tried to find her voice. "This is my loyal companion and bodyguard, Gart. It's been the two of us traveling, looking for those who would stand against Sagum and his regime. We intend to take back what he stole sixteen years ago. We intend to return the lands to the people and the royal family."

"No tall order or anything," Pen muttered. Where was Billie with a drink when you needed one? If ever there was a time for getting drunk, it was now.

Overthrow Sagum. Overthrow the man who'd seemingly appeared in the dead of night with a host of mercenaries that he called guards and killed the king? Overthrow the despot who'd executed anyone remotely loyal to the royal family and famously sent the queen and her two children running for their lives? Overthrow the tyrant who'd cruelly pinched every ounce of money he could from those who were barely making ends meet and imprisoned anyone who dared oppose him?

"I see you're no admirer of him either," the princess said quietly.

Pen glared at her. "Of that nasty piece of work? Not a chance. Every single one of us would gladly see him run off. Or better yet, as dead as the people he hangs from the castle walls."

Catadina's eyes widened in triumph. "So, you'll help then?"

Wait. What? "What do you mean, help?"

"Help us remove him from power," Catadina said as if that were the most obvious thing in the world.

Pen stared at her before snorting out a laugh. "What's so funny?" Gart snapped.

"You're insane, that's what," Pen said, still snickering. "That's a fool's run. There's been plenty of rebellions, and not a single one's worked."

"Why have they failed?" Catadina asked. She still didn't look disappointed, merely calculating.

Maybe she didn't know what a failure her attempt was bound to be. Not that it was Pen's responsibility to tell her, but she *had* taken the woman's purse, and it'd be a shame to see the poor thing executed. Pen hated the execution days. "Not a single one's breached the walls. I'm not talking about the outer walls, I mean the inner walls, the actual castle itself. They've made it to the courtyard, the gardens, all of that. But no one's gotten inside. It's impossible without that key."

"Key?"

"Where have you *been*?" Pen asked incredulously, shaking her head. "The Dragon Claw key! Four long dragon claws on the end that opens all the locks he installed. It can't be replicated. They've tried. Iron and steel aren't strong enough: a dragon claw's the toughest material you can find. They're unbreakable. Dragon bones and claws aren't difficult to find if you know the right person, but for some reason, even when they have the claws to make one, all of the replica keys have failed. It's a lost cause."

Catadina slowly began to smile, and Pen suddenly realized that the princess had known all of that already and somehow thought she still had the answer. "That's why I need you," she said. "That's why I need a thief."

Oh. Oh, no. Oh, *no*. "Not a chance," Pen said, shaking her head.

"I'll give you five times the sum of the purse you took from me," Catadina said without hesitation.

"No."

"Six times—"

"You can give me all the coins in the world, and I'll still say no," Pen said firmly. "It's not worth my life." That was a fast way to have your head removed or your neck decked out with a pretty rope.

The princess pursed her lips. "I'll give you anything you want. Anything at all. If you get me that key, I promise you that I'll give you your heart's desire. Even if it's a crown upon your own head."

Pen stared, mouth slowly dropping open. Gart didn't look surprised, but he made a face all the same as if this was something the princess did all the time.

Anything she wanted? Oh, but that was a tall list, and Pen couldn't even come up with half of it at that very moment. Even a *crown*. Her mind spun at the possibilities.

She could have as much silver and gold as she could carry. She could have a home all her own, not her cavern den beneath the streets but somewhere with access to the sky. And it wouldn't be at the top of a bunch of homes like the nobles, precariously perched and swaying in the breeze, but a real place, somewhere with grass and maybe even a *tree*.

She could find Cam.

"You can't just pickpocket a key like that," Pen said weakly, her last defense to this insanely dangerous and deadly idea, this stupid idea that she was, for some reason, *considering*. She was actually thinking about trying to steal the Dragon Emperor's *Dragon Key*.

Catadina just smiled. "That's why I didn't want a pickpocket. I need a thief."

It was flattery, and normally it would be well-deserved flattery, but it helped give Pen a dose of reality too. The Dragon Emperor had his nickname for a reason: though she'd never seen it for herself, some said that he was part dragon, part person, and he could change at will between one and the next. What she did know for certain was that he was vicious, he was ruthless, and he killed without mercy or fair trial. His guards were no better. Any run-in with the guards could be your last.

It was that thought which pushed away her dreams and made her slowly shake her head. "No. I can't."

Catadina blinked, clearly surprised. "I wish you the best of luck," Pen said. "Really, I do."

"You told us you loathe the Emperor as much as we do," Gart said angrily. He began to rise from his chair, but a hand from Catadina kept him held back.

"And I do," Pen insisted. "I hope he rots down in those secret prison cells of his. But I haven't gotten this far in life by being stupid. And that is, ultimately, what your plan is: ridiculously stupid. I'm not dying for your cause, Princess. Find someone else to martyr."

Catadina's cheeks were beginning to turn a bright cherry red, the first sign that she wasn't exactly unaffected by Pen's words. "We ain't lookin' for a martyr," Gart snapped. "We were lookin' for a damn good thief. Looks like we only found a coward."

Pen flew to her feet, nostrils flaring in her own rage. "You have *no* idea what you've found," she said, voice dangerously low. "None."

Gart reached for his weapon, but Pen was done. "Good luck on the suicide run," she said, and she pushed away from the table. She didn't look behind her, and nothing sounded like it was coming for her, blade, or person. Good.

Billie stood at the edge of the bar, her dark eyes probably seeing too much. "They're paying their own tab, whatever they order," Pen muttered, but she pulled out one of the purses and counted out the money she owed. She handed it over and went to leave, but Billie caught her by the elbow. "What?" she snapped irritably.

"What did they want?" Billie asked.

"To get themselves killed," Pen said. She yanked her arm back and headed out.

The vendors were in full swing now, stalls packed together, voices clamoring to be heard. Nobles walked around with jewels and purses on full display, but for once, Pen wasn't tempted. A few would've been so easy to lift, too, but her mood was far too foul to focus properly.

"Coward," she muttered under her breath as she walked away. "What does that ass know about me? I'm no coward." No, a coward didn't take risks or sneak in places like she could. She was the farthest thing from a coward. Just because she was smarter than they were didn't mean she was a *coward*.

The word dug at her, deep into her ribs, and settled like a barb around her heart. She snarled and drew her arms around herself, leaning against a nearby wall. Her day had started out so good, too.

Stupid royalty. They were no better than the Emperor: their way or no way at all.

A shout drew her attention. Down near one of the vendors, the guards had gathered, and she rolled her eyes. Good, let them bother someone besides her for a change.

"No, I didn't, I swear!"

Pen froze. The voice, the one she knew so well, yelped again. "I didn't take her purse! Honest!"

"He's been skulking around all afternoon," a feminine voice said. Pen shoved herself off the wall and hurried to join the crowd that was forming. She found herself shoved between two vendors as she fought to see what was going on.

A woman stood, glaring at two guards. No, she glared at the person being held by two guards: Magnus. "I'm telling you, I *didn't*," he pleaded. "I swear!"

The woman huffed, and another woman came up beside her. "I saw him! I saw him wandering around like a vagrant! Clearly, he took her purse!"

"We found two purses on 'im," one of the guards said. "But you said they weren't yours."

"Well, clearly, he's stashed it somewhere!"

Pen stared. Magnus hadn't taken her purse: *Pen* had. It was one of the two women she'd filched from as she'd headed after Catadina and her shoes.

Magnus's eyes widened even more, fear evident. "Look, I'm tellin' you I didn't take her purse!"

"But I bet you know who did," another guard said, this one with gold tassels on his shoulders. Of all the luck, of course Magnus had to get caught when there was a captain skulking around. The captain peered down at Magnus with a toothy grin. "Tell you what. You tell me who *did* take the lady's purse, and I'll let you go."

Magnus bit his lip and glanced around. His eyes locked with Pen's, and she found herself without breath in her body. His eyes pleaded with her, but she felt like a statue, completely frozen in place. She couldn't have moved or spoken, even if she'd wanted to.

Slowly Magnus looked back up at the guard. "I don't know who did," he said. "But it wasn't me."

The captain's grin fell away into a snarl. "Take him away," he ordered, and the two guards restraining Magnus began to drag him off. Magnus kept pleading the entire way, insisting he was innocent, and Pen found herself wishing he'd just name her. *Come on you fool. Tell them it was me. You know it had to be me. Tell them it was me.*

With a sigh, the captain turned to the woman. "Sorry about the purse. If we find it, we'll let you know."

The woman gave a sniff. "It's just a purse, honestly. But these pick-pockets need to be taught a lesson."

The captain gave a short nod and headed after the others. Magnus's voice had all but faded from earshot.

Slowly the crowd dispersed. Pen's shoulder got jostled by someone, and it broke her from her paralysis. Numbly she walked away, anywhere, somewhere that wasn't watching Magnus get carted off. The vendors had already returned to their stalls, and everyone moved as they had before. Nothing to see, just another person going to be taken to the prisons, hung or decapitated on the next execution day.

He could've named her. Why didn't he name her?

"You little fool," she hissed angrily, her nose stinging. He'd probably felt some moral duty to protect her, since she'd protected him all that time ago, and he was keeping his mouth shut out of *nobility*.

You didn't stay alive by keeping quiet; you stayed alive by spilling on the next person. How hadn't he figured that out by now?

Why hadn't he named her or pointed her out?

She realized her face felt wet and that, to her horror, her eyes were filling. Furiously she dashed her hand over her face, wiping away the tears. "Stupid *kid*," she muttered.

The purse hung heavy in her scarves. She wasn't a fool: even if she'd given it back, they still would've taken Magnus, taken her. They'd probably been hoping it *was* her. She was the one that they hadn't been able to catch yet, a thorn in their sides, and they would've known that their Ghost Thief wasn't Magnus. She'd stayed alive by being smart, by being quick. Being silent.

Magnus was loud and brash. He enjoyed every minute of it and thought it was a game. He deserved to be caught.

He was also young. And now he was going to die, rotting in the cells until an execution date was called. Probably by the end of the week. He had five days, most likely.

She stopped, eyes suddenly narrowing. No. *She* had five days. It wouldn't be a rescue; rescuing was for ridiculous royals who thought they could win back a throne through hard work and noble effort. She wasn't noble in the slightest.

But steal him back…that she could do. She had to.

Guilt didn't taste very good, and right now, it was sitting in her belly like a rancid stew. She owed him her life, and she didn't like being in anyone's debt. Still, getting into those prisons was going to require a key. And not just any key: the Emperor's Dragon Key.

Lucky for her, someone else needed that key, too.

Her feet carried her all the way back to *The Sparrow's Rest*. Billie startled when she slammed the door open and stalked with determination to the table. Catadina and her giant were still there, and both looked surprised to see her.

Pen crossed her arms. "I'll outline what I want as a final prize at a later date," she said firmly. "For right now, I want ale. And food. And for you to do whatever I need you to do."

Catadina slowly began to smile. "Absolutely."

"Just t'be clear," Gart said slowly. "You're in?"

Pen's lips turned up into a smile. "Oh yeah," she said. "I'm in."

Catadina's plans weren't what Pen would've described as dreadful. They were solid, clearly thought out, knowledgeable of the castle, and working to utilize every single resource the princess had. Unfortunately, there wasn't much in the way of resources. Or any real working knowledge of the guards.

"A distraction is all you need," Catadina insisted again. "I have the people to carry that out, waiting for my command."

"No, you've got people willing to martyr themselves for your cause," Pen said in reply. "The problem with every single rebellion is that they're all very loud, very easy to spot, and *very* easy to remove."

They were in the backroom of Billie's, sitting on various crates and casks around a makeshift table. For someone who was supposedly royalty, Catadina hadn't so much as batted an eye at the surroundings and had simply sat herself down, then thanked Billie for her help. Billie, for some reason, had merely nodded and left them a large bowl of bread and cheese.

Pen had never *known* Billie to be so agreeable. Perhaps Catadina had some magic of her own, to make Pen follow her and Billie offer up her back room.

Gart scowled at her. "No one's going to be a martyr. Quit with it already. We don't want deaths."

"But that's what you'll have anyway, whether you want it or not," Pen argued. How could they be so dense? "And I'm sure they'd love to say they died for their fair princess, but I'm not looking to be one of them."

"No loyalty amongst thieves," Gart muttered, and Pen stiffened.

"You asked for my help, and that's what you're getting. Did you want me to do this or not?"

Catadina held up a hand, and they both fell silent. Seriously, magic. "I wanted a thief," she agreed. "I merely wanted to offer you the best help I can give you."

"And the best help you can do is let me do what I need to." Pen raised an eyebrow. "You need to give me the item I've asked for and then follow my orders. If you can do that, we've got a chance of this working."

There was a snort from Gart, and Pen crossed her arms. "Problem?"

"We're trustin' a thief," he said. "Of course I have a problem with it."

She gave him the broadest smile she could. "You're the highest bidder."

"You haven't told her what you want—"

"Believe me. I'm looking forward to getting my payday for this idiocy. One that you'll pay handsomely for, but that's what you get for putting *my* life on the line." She glanced at the princess. "Fair?"

Catadina just merely nodded. "Then tell me your plan."

Grin widening, Pen clapped and rubbed her hands together. Finally. "Here's what I want you to do."

Gart didn't like it. Catadina herself didn't look too sure, which was worth it to see the princess looking uncertain about something for a change. But in the end, they both agreed, and Pen headed out to get the rest of what she needed.

The streets of Silve Hollow were mostly empty by the time Pen made her way back to the lower end of the town, as far from the white-walled castle as one could get. She passed by the bulletin board as she went, and her eyes drifted across the parchment. There was another Wanted poster for "The Ghost" with yet another menacing scribbling of her faceless self, but, for once, it didn't make her grin. Her eyes went instead to the list for executions.

Sure enough, there was an execution set for the end of the week, and two names were written in: Simms for disturbing the peace, and Magnus for petty theft.

Four days. She had four days to get him out. As quietly as she'd come, she drifted back down the street, avoiding three guards as she did so.

The numerous nobles' homes situated on top of other buildings cut out any moonlight she could've used to guide her path, as there were no lanterns out this way, but she knew her way through these uneven cobblestone streets well enough. The buildings got closer together, and the streets were narrower in the lower part of town, and Pen knew them all like the back of her hand.

First, to her den. After ensuring that there were no guards around, she quickly darted down one of the alleys. It was getting narrower by the day, and she raised a wary eye straight up. If they built any more housing for the nobles above the lower buildings and shops, she'd never be able to get in. How high could they even go, she wondered, before the bricks and metal of the shops and homes on the ground gave way?

Still, she'd rather her home be down here than up there. She'd gone stealing from a few of the nobles up above enough to know how windy and unstable it felt up there. They could keep their clear view of the sky: at least the solid ground beneath her feet was, well, solid.

She lifted a steel sheet away from the side of the nearby building and glanced inside the dark hole. The hole itself was big enough to fit her and maybe one other person at a time if they both crouched and held tight to each other. She reached inside for her candlestick: right where she'd left it.

A quick flick of a match lit the candle, letting her see the rough-hewn steps leading down. She slipped inside and set the sheet back behind her. The boards that made the ceiling creaked and let a little dirt fall down, causing her to pause. When there was no rushing foot-fall or more dirt falling, she continued on.

The tunnel wound further down until it was simply dirt and stone around her. Only then did it open into a larger cavern, and she felt herself truly relax for the first time all day. This was her kingdom, her safe haven. Maybe some wouldn't like a cavern with rock formations and little puddles of water, but it was cool, and it was quiet, and it was all hers.

She set the candle into a nearby candlestick and slid herself down into her hammock. The old cave had a few stone formations that made for nice chairs, tables, and shelves, but none of them were particularly good for sleeping on. They did, however, work for hanging a hammock across. The candle's light flickered across some of the formations, making shapes dance on the far wall. Sighing, she settled back down into her bed.

Magnus's face appeared behind her eyelids, desperately pleading for help. She opened her eyes and sat upright, any chance of relaxing gone.

Damn the kid! Hung or beheaded simply because he'd kept his mouth shut and only told the truth. He was going to die for some ridiculous notion of honor, for *her*, and her stomach twisted. She never should've taken him on. She'd only been trying to help keep him fed, tried to help a skinny, starving kid. It only proved the notion that doing good things was never worth it in the end.

"Then what are you doing now?" she muttered. Helping a princess reclaim her throne from a tyrant was definitely one of those noble, good causes. And even though she was considering a hefty price for her efforts, well, it was still going to be one of those do-gooder types of things that always came back to bite her in the end.

This was why she never helped anyone.

Helping people usually helps us in return, Penny.

There was Cam's voice, right on cue, the memory of her big sister drifting through like a cloud. She could even see Cam smiling, her two braids swinging as she walked away.

Pen settled back into her hammock, no longer relaxed but determined to get some sleep anyway. She'd need all her wits about her to do what she needed to do.

The next day dawned bright, once she stepped outside of her den. She made her way down the street, hood up and on guard. Her scarves weighed heavily against her chest, making it all the more pertinent that she get to Roche's as fast as she could. She wasn't the only thief on the streets.

She was just the best. Who else got a nickname like "The Ghost"?

All right, it was still a rotten nickname. Wasn't like she could offer up a different suggestion, though.

After taking a few back streets to avoid guards that were looking for trouble, she hurried down the lane to one of the stone houses. The front steps were clean and spotless, an iron railing neatly polished. The blue door matched the stones around it and looked like a properly maintained dwelling.

She immediately darted down the alley next to it and went to the side of the building. One of the stones came loose in her hand, and she reached in to ring the little bell inside. Even as she replaced the brick, a small door opened in the stones.

Roche waited until she was fully inside before closing the door. "Appointments are preferred," he said. "You know that."

"You should know better than to open the door without looking," she shot back. "I could've been anyone."

He waved her off and went further into his basement. With a roll of her eyes, she followed him in.

The upstairs made for a tidy house, but it was the basement that would've had Roche executed on the spot. A black-market warehouse sat, full of goods and…*acquired* merchandise. Pen came in the side door like the rest of the thieves.

The nobles came in the front, all looking for that "special something."

"One of these days, you're going to find a noble willing to turn you in," Pen said. Roche took a seat behind his desk. His long gray hair draped behind him in a small ponytail. For some reason, he thought it made him look tougher. She thought it made his face look swollen.

Roche just shrugged his broad shoulders. "They all know I keep meticulous records. If one of them squeals, I squeal back, and I'll do so far louder than they would. Now tell me why I let you in so damn early and quit pretending you're worried about me."

"I *am* worried," Pen insisted with a broad grin. "Who else would I fence to if not you?"

She got an eye-roll for that. Fine. She had other things to do yet today. Carefully, she pulled out her merchandise and settled it down in front of him.

Roche's eyes roved over all of it, and his eyes settled on the glitzy bottle of perfume, just like she'd thought they would. Marina was an avid fan of perfume, and Roche knew his wife loved the ornate ones: the prettier, the better. The woman's purse from yesterday had coughed up a few prizes, in the end, and Pen had instantly known which ones Marina would want.

He noted the few other items she'd plucked: a golden statue, a golden watch, some crystals and jewelry, and a beaded headband. "You've been holding out on me," he said at last. "I've not heard of anyone getting knocked over recently. Which means you've been keeping more than you've been selling."

"I don't have to sell you *everything* I lift." In truth, she mostly did because the items were far less valuable to her than the coins she got for them. She kept some of the crystals and jewels: they glittered in the light of her candles. "But I need something for these."

He raised an eyebrow. "My coins aren't good enough for you anymore?"

Pen stared at him stonily, giving nothing away. This was the risky part of her plan, but there was nowhere else she could go for these items. There was no one else she could ask. "I need dragon claws."

He sat in silence, eyes widening in obvious surprise. It wasn't often she got to see him startled. This time, however, it didn't bring her any satisfaction. She held her breath, forcing her hands to be steady. Easy; she needed to be easy about this.

Finally, he rested his hands on top of the desk and raised a single eyebrow. "You're not the stupid sort, Pen."

He knew. Or at least, had a guess. "Look, no one lives forever," she lied as nonchalantly as she could. "I can't help but want to try. The amount of gold that the Dragon's hoarding is supposed to be unbelievable."

"You're a fool," he snapped. "And when you get caught, not if, *when,* who'll you tell them gave you the pretty dragon claws?"

Relief flooded through her, but she kept her face as blank as she could. "I don't snitch," she said. "I wouldn't do that."

"They all snitch, in the end," he said darkly. "You won't get them from me. Try elsewhere."

Pen pursed her lips and reached into her scarves for her last item. It was one she'd withheld for a long time, but desperate times called for desperate measures. "You wouldn't give them to me for this?" she said, and she set the book down on the desk.

Roche went still. Slowly, as if afraid to breathe, he reached out and rested his hand atop the book. The gold filigree on top and along the edges wasn't worth as much as the book itself, and he knew it. "Where?" he rasped.

"Four dragon claws," she insisted. "And a set of those wax seals."

He paused, and she reached to draw the book back. His hand instantly clutched at the binding. After a tense moment of glaring at each other, Pen finally drew her hand back, allowing him to keep the book. He reached beneath his desk and brought up a steel box. The top held a dazzling amount of coins, and for a moment, the urge to lift them pulsed through her strong enough that her fingers twitched.

He did something with the lock that she couldn't see, but the top of the box opened, and her lips parted in honest surprise. There, nestled inside, were five dragon claws, along with a few vials and some herbs wrapped up in a white cloth. Pinesbury, she realized, and her blood froze in her veins. "Where did you get that?" she whispered, stunned.

He said nothing, simply pulled four of the claws out and then, after a moment, handed her one of the vials. "For you," he said. "On the house."

"What is it?" she asked.

He gave her a sharp and toothy grin. "Pinesbury melted and mixed with some selkie blood. Drink it when they catch you. It'll be kinder than what they'll do to you."

Wasn't that charming. She gathered up the dragon claws and wrapped them neatly in one of the pouches, then settled the vial in beside it. The wax seals were also handed over, six neat and soft columns in blood red.

"Pleasure doing business," she said cheerfully, and Roche glared at her.

"Get out. And I hope, for my sake, you manage to do whatever you're looking to do."

She took her leave quickly and darted back out. Roche wasn't likely to be happy with her for a while: she'd have to bring him something else worth his time. Hopefully, not another book, they were scarce as it was after the Emperor had ordered most of them burned. She only had two more back at her den, and she was saving them for a "get out of town" run.

The vial rested against her skin, the glass cold, even through the pouch. She headed back to her den to drop off the dragon claws, then, after a moment's thought, the vial as well. She could do this. She *had* to do this.

And it would look a lot worse on her if she came in with a vial of poison.

Which reminded her: she needed to drop a lot of other things while she was at it. She needed to look like anyone else, non-threatening. That meant a costume.

The hooded coat went, as did her scarves. She felt naked without them, but they'd only make her look suspicious, and suspicious, she couldn't do. Her boots were traded out for a delicate pair of shoes that she'd nicked from a noble. A skirt went over her leggings, and she tugged her braid out, then pulled her hair up with a simple clasp. Nothing fancy, just a silver one with a pretty design on the back. She made sure it was fastened securely before stepping over to a nearby pool of water and checking herself over.

She'd pass muster. Time to present herself.

By the time she'd walked over to the front of the castle walls, the sun was high in the sky. She cleared the last line of buildings that sat not too far from the castle and headed down the single lane towards the front gate. The white, high walls of the castle above her reflected the light enough to make her wince against the glare. It was better than looking up at the multiple bodies that the Emperor hung as a warning and reminder.

She immediately found herself face to face with a few of the guards waiting by the front gate of the castle. She gave them a broad and cheery grin as they pulled their swords out, then lifted the purse she'd stolen from the noblewoman. "I was told there was a reward for this?" she asked.

The inside of the castle wasn't anything near as fancy as she'd been led to believe. From Catadina's description, she'd expected an orchard, neatly manicured hedges, flowers, and open sky.

Well, there was plenty of open sky. Enough for her to see the skeletons and half-fleshed corpses still hanging from the walls. And she'd thought there were plenty of bodies hanging on the outside. She forced her unease down and stood, pretending to be interested in the statues around her. It wasn't hard, as they were everywhere, and every single one was either of a dragon or the Emperor himself. Any shrubs were merely there to decorate the statuary, and she couldn't see any trees.

None of this looked anything like Catadina had described, and Pen was grateful that she'd ignored the princess's ideas. She never would've gotten around the courtyard with those plans.

The guards beside her glanced at her warily, and she gave them a brief, sweet smile. Nothing to see here, just a woman turning in a valuable purse for a hopeful reward. Let them think she was just a commoner in search of a quick money grab. That was all they needed to think at this point.

"You take anything?" one of the guards asked. She realized a moment later that it was the captain who'd interrogated Magnus on the street. He kept combing through the purse but kept his eyes on her.

Pen gritted her teeth but managed to provide an earnest look. "No, sir, I wouldn't do nothin' like that! I just heard about a missin' purse, that's all, and I was hopin' to see it reunited with its owner. That's all."

"And the reward didn't hurt," the captain said with a nasty grin.

"Don't you worry, the Emperor pays his dues for those loyal to him." His hand paused, and he glanced inside the purse. A moment later, he froze, and his grin dropped away in an instant.

So, he'd found her surprise, then.

She tried to look confused when he rounded on her, fury in his eyes. "Where did you get this?" he snapped.

"I just found it in the marketplace, underneath a vendor's stall, that's all! If anythin's missin', I didn't have nothin' to do with it." She put a little bit of anxiety into her drawl, holding her hands up in a placating gesture.

Predictably, he didn't buy it, and his frown only deepened. "Can I go now?" she asked. Better to not seem too eager in the face of such clear outrage.

The captain glanced briefly at the other two guards on either of side of her, then gave them a short nod. Then he turned back to her, and his smile was wide and insincere. "Before you get your reward?" he said sweetly. "No, I wouldn't dream of withholding a few coins from such a *respectable* sort such as yourself. You'll wait, and I'll get your reward for you." It wasn't a question.

He spun around and headed immediately for the main tower of the castle, and Pen watched him go intently. He didn't try to open the door, simply knocked four times, and the door opened for him. So, Mister Head Guard didn't have a key, either. It made sense.

It also made her life more difficult, if even the Emperor couldn't make duplicates of his own key, but since when had any of this been easy?

The two guards immediately caught hold of her elbows and guided her further into the courtyard. Her eyes took it all in as they went: old stone benches, a fountain that hadn't run in forever, wilted plants, and shriveled up trees. There had been an orchard here, once. Not anymore. The Emperor had other things to spend his time on, including executing anyone who disturbed his paradise.

Another door sat in the base of the exterior wall, solid and imposing wood, and the guard to her left knocked three times, then once. That meant each door had its own code, or perhaps each person did. The door opened after a moment, and they led her inside to a dark hallway that smelled like mildew and cold stones. Another guard waited until they were through and then shut the door tight behind them.

Her pulse jumped in her throat, and her mind instantly began making plans on how to get out. It wouldn't take much, just a simple twist of one arm and then a kick with her opposite leg, straight between the legs. One hand to slam into a throat, another to pull a sword free, and she could be back out into the courtyard in seconds—

No. No, if she wanted her prize, she had to let them take her. This had been her plan. She had to see it through. All the coins she could dream of and more besides. Catadina would give it all to her, that was for sure. And Magnus would be free.

She just had to remind herself when the urge to escape kept growing.

They brought her to the end of the hallway, opened the wooden door at the end, and threw her into a small room. The room itself was cold and dismal, and a wooden chair sat with chains wrapped around it. How cozy. They sat her down in it but thankfully didn't make a move towards the chains. She would've had to inform them of what a terrible idea that was.

A door on the other end had a few slats cut into the top, providing a window in and out of the room. There were no windows or other doors, but plenty of candles to help light the room sat in sconces inside the stonework. A few old tapestries hung from the wall, and she watched as the middle one fluttered briefly. Interesting.

Before she could take in much more, the door at the far end opened. The captain came in, followed closely by—

Pen froze. Coming face to face with the Emperor had been an idea, but not something she'd considered a real possibility. Yet here he was.

He stood above her, tall and imposing, dark hair framing his sharp jaw. His eyes were a deep yellow that bore into her. His skin looked rough and scaly, but it was pale, almost paper-thin. She could almost imagine the scales hiding somewhere under the skin, ready to burst out. Her eyes drifted to his hands, but while they had long nails, there were no claws.

But behind his hands was a thick jeweled belt, and hanging from the belt were four twisted white claws hanging from a single, solid bar of iron.

The Dragon Key.

She whipped her eyes up and found him staring at her, eyes burning through to her core. "Yes," he said, and his voice was a low and throaty growl. "I do have claws, little one."

She managed to bow her head in a sign of respect. "Your majesty," she said. The key was so close she could almost feel it brushing her head. She could touch it.

And she would lose her head an instant later.

"I hear you've been most gracious in returning a purse," the Emperor all but purred. "Such diligence deserves a reward."

His hand caught beneath her chin, the long nails cutting into her skin, and she forced herself to let him move her. He smiled at her, and his teeth were bright and sharp, almost fang-like. "Tell me, little one: where did you find such a purse?"

"Beneath one of the vendor's tables, your majesty," she said. "I swear, I've not taken anything out of it."

"Or put anything in it?"

His other hand came over and opened before her. There, nestled inside, was the prize she'd offered up to him: a broach with the old royal symbol of a tree and a golden sparrow sitting on an apple. A token Catadina had kept on her that she'd not been particularly willing to part with but did all the same when Pen had asked for bait.

"Do you know what this is?" the Emperor asked her.

Pen shook her head. "A…broach?" she replied, feigning confusion. "It's very lovely, your majesty. I've never owned anything near that lovely."

He chuckled, low and reproachful. "That remains to be seen. But I would never doubt the…integrity of my people. So, I'll ask one more time: where did you find the purse? And did you find the broach within it?"

"I found it beneath the marketplace stall. I didn't touch the contents—"

The Emperor suddenly dropped the broach back into the purse, then snapped his fingers. The guards grabbed her by her arms and dragged her off the chair. He turned and began to walk away as they hauled her towards the middle tapestry. "But she did," she said hurriedly.

Slowly the Emperor came to a stop. The captain glared at her and cleared his throat. "Your majesty, I wouldn't trust the likes of her—"

"If your men cannot find the woman I seek, then clearly I cannot trust them either," the Emperor snapped, and Pen felt her skin crawl at the pure rage within his voice. She could've sworn steam came from his nostrils. "It appears they've not done their due diligence, and I'm left to handle matters on my own. This is how I must do so: do you have a problem with that, Captain Jorel?"

"None at all, your majesty," Jorel said immediately, but he kept glaring at Pen. Pen resisted the urge to stick her tongue out at him.

Slowly the Emperor stalked back over to her, and the urge to offer a defiant response died a swift death. His eyes would haunt her for nights to come, and there was fire hanging within their depths. "Who was she?" the Emperor asked.

Pen let a visage of fear cross her face. "I don't know who she was. She said she needed my help to deliver a message. That's all I know. She tucked the broach inside, said to hand it in, to get a few coins for my trouble, and just deliver a message all friendly-like. I didn't understand it none. I'm not a learned sort like the nobles."

"What did she say," the Emperor said. It wasn't a request.

She forced her tongue to trip over the words to embellish her terror. "The tree shall b-bear fruit again. It seemed a bit odd, 'cause, of course, trees bear f-fruit all the time, but she said it was real important to give to you."

The Emperor leaned forward, eyes piercing through her, and Pen forced herself to look as open and frightened as she could. Honest, she needed to look honest and easy to read, which was ridiculous. She'd never been honest or easy a day in her life. If she wanted her life to go past today, however, she'd have to pull it off convincingly.

After a moment, the Emperor pulled away from her. "Where did she give you the broach and message?"

"On the west side of the main marketplace," she said in a rush. It was the farthest place she could think of from Billie's and Roche's. And as far from Catadina's real location as she could muster up. If they caught a few of the other thieves that frequented the western marketplace, well, she wasn't responsible for them.

Jorel immediately grabbed the purse from the Emperor and took off with the second guard behind him, leaving Pen with just the one guard and the Emperor. The door slammed behind them, and all right, maybe Pen felt a little bad about the wave of guards that were about to make someone's life a little worse. Still, they'd be nowhere near *The Sparrow's Rest*, and that was all she cared about.

The Emperor watched after Jorel and the other guard until they were gone, then glanced down at her, still taller than her even while she stood face to face with him. Pen meant to bend her head down, meant to play her part, but when he smirked at her, something inside of her couldn't help but meet his gaze evenly. *I'm not afraid of you.*

She might be a thief, but he was the monster.

"Ah," and the Emperor showed his teeth in another fanged grin. "I'd wondered why the fire in your eyes didn't match the fear on your face. You're quite the unique sort, little one." His long fingernails clicked as he tapped them against each other, feigning patience.

She didn't say anything, which was probably the deadlier option, but the Emperor didn't seem to take offense. If anything, he seemed all the more amused. "Since you seem to be quite the messenger, would you be willing to, say, pass on a message back to her?"

"I might," Pen said after a moment, and his smirk widened, revealing his long teeth. She wondered if he would just eat her right then and there. "What should I relay to her? If I see her again, that is."

The Emperor leaned down, eyes burning into her, but Pen refused to yield her ground so easily. It was probably nine types of foolish because here in front of her was the man who killed because he could, the tyrant who'd taxed until people starved, the dragon who'd stolen far more than she ever could. He'd taken from everyone and more than just coin.

She fought to keep her hand steady and wasn't sure if her trembling came from her fear or her fury. Probably a little of both.

He huffed a little laugh at her. Then, suddenly, his hand shot up and caught her chin in his grip again. This time, the tips of his nails dug into her skin, and the bones in his fingers kept her head trapped at a painful angle. The urge to fight her way free made her jerk a little before she managed to make herself still. She didn't need him to rip her head off.

She wondered if he could hear her heart beating wildly in her chest, or if he could see it in her eyes. Her earlier fury felt just as trapped as she was.

He leaned in close, and she held her breath. "Tell her that dragons like fruit trees," he said lowly. "And that I look forward to eating up all the fruits again."

With that, he let go, then turned and marched off towards the door he'd entered. Pen watched as he lifted the key from the belt. He didn't detach it, simply pulled it up along its chain, and inserted it into the lock. He slowly pushed until there was a soft click, and then he turned the key heavily to the right. Halfway around the lock, the door opened.

The Emperor looked back at her with a raised eyebrow. "What is she offering you?" he asked. "A handful of coins? Oh, little one, I could give you *so* much more."

Pen paused. He couldn't possibly be offering what she thought he was. But he kept on talking. "I'll tell you what," he said. "You find this woman, and you tell my guards where she is, and I'll ensure that you get whatever your heart desires. Including a place…say, out of the city. Where you'll always have as much gold and good food as you could want."

"What if I have higher aspirations than that?" she asked, and the Emperor let out a laugh.

"Then I'd say find this woman first, have her brought to me. Then…

yes. You and I will have another conversation, little one. I have a feeling this isn't the last time we'll talk."

He headed out the door with one last pointed look at the guard. "Until then, see to it that this woman is given coin for delivering her message with such dignity."

The door clanged behind him, and another door echoed behind her. She spun around and realized that the guard had left her in the room alone, locked in. She was alone.

Pen expected to have to sneak back in to do what she wanted to, but if they were going to give her an opportunity now, she wasn't going to ignore the chance when presented to her.

She dashed over to the door the Emperor had left through and pulled the wax sticks from her purse. Her hands squeezed them together as fast as she could, making the wax warm and malleable. By the time she was done, it was wider than the keyhole in front of her.

Everyone always tried to steal the key and replicate it, to draw images of its likeness and get a measurement of the length and size of the dragon claws. No one had ever bothered trying to work backward, making a key that fit the lock.

She pushed the wax into the holes slowly, carefully, until she met resistance. Then she began to turn it a little from side to side, just enough to make sure it fit into every little groove. Time was running out, she could feel it, making her heart race, but this wasn't the sort of thing that could be rushed. She had one chance to do this right.

Carefully, oh so carefully, she pulled the wax back out. There, etched perfectly in wax, were four long talon shapes, as sharp as the real dragon claws. And in the very center was a long cylindrical shape with a notch at the end.

Pen stared and turned the wax around. With the claws as long as they were, there was no way to even *see* the long stem in the middle. It was carefully hidden and almost invisible. No wonder no one had ever been able to replicate the damn key before.

She'd be the first. She'd be the only one who'd successfully stolen the Dragon Key.

Footsteps made her carefully put the wax mold into her purse and race back to the chair just in time for the guard to return. He glared at her as if she were dung beneath his foot, then threw a bag at her chest. She fumbled with the bag, surprisingly, and found that her hands were trembling with adrenaline. Her chin ached, and she could still feel the imprint his claws had left in her skin.

She'd *done it*.

"Let's go, out with you," the guard growled. "Before I see fit to toss you into a cell."

It was a serious amount of coin. Not just any coins but the ones where you could drop just one at any shop and pick up nearly anything you might need. These were the coins that the nobles hoarded, the ones the Emperor gave out as favors. And now she had a bag full of them, more than she'd ever seen in one place before.

It would be easy to get done what she wanted now. No one would refuse her with those coins. Well, Roche might, on principle, but even he wouldn't toss away this many of the Emperor's coins. And she could have more if she wanted.

Pen stood in the alley outside of Billie's backroom, pondering the two choices before her. If she'd thought she had a dilemma before, now there was an even greater one before her. There were multiple offers on the table, multiple ways to gather a mass of wealth and be well off.

She could, of course, take the Emperor's offer. The Emperor treated those loyal to him very well. She knew: she'd broken into enough of their places to see their wealth. And Catadina trusted her, which didn't exactly suggest she'd make a very intelligent ruler. Getting her to the Emperor would be easier than drinking a cool ale. And Billie's ales were very easy to drink.

The very thought of his yellow eyes and his toothy smirk just made her want to vomit, though. She had no love for the Emperor. He was a bastard through and through, killing people just to prove himself mightier than anyone else. He was a tyrant. He was cruel.

He was powerful. And he was rich. Two things she didn't exactly want against her.

Catadina was rich or would be after she resumed her throne. And having anyone else besides the Emperor would be a boon. If people were allowed to keep their money instead of being taxed, there'd be more to lift from people's purses.

With a groan, she tilted her head back against the brick wall. Princesses and Emperors: this was well above her pay grade. This was the sort of nonsense she didn't care to involve herself in. It required someone with far more stomach than she had.

She didn't wish Catadina harm. And the Emperor didn't deserve his title. The only thing Pen really wanted was to have gone back to the day she met the princess and *not* have taken her purse.

You can't unwish a wish, Pen.

"Wish you were here, Cam," she whispered. If anyone could've sorted this whole sordid thing out and had an answer, it would've been her big sister. One of these days, she'd find her sister, and she'd get some answers.

Another face came to mind, and she winced. Magnus. She hadn't found the prison, not exactly, but she had a strong inkling of where it was. She also now had a way to get down into it. The wax hung in her purse, heavy against her side.

An arm suddenly swung out at her, catching her against her upper chest, and she found herself pinned against the brick wall before she could retaliate. Even as she began to grab the arm and reach to free herself, she caught sight of the furious face and relaxed. She'd sort of been expecting this. "It's not nice to follow people, Gart," she said.

"Like I didn't see you comin' out of the castle with a bag, dressed like you're not just a common thief," he snapped. "You might not want to be a martyr for her majesty, but I'll be damned if I see her hurt because she's got this misplaced faith in you."

"I told you I had to get inside to do my part," she told him. "I did what I had to, and now we're a definite step closer."

Gart paused. "We're what?"

Pen jerked her head towards the door. "Inside. Just because *I'm* good at avoiding the guards doesn't mean you are." She'd ducked two tails in a matter of moments. Hopefully, Gart hadn't brought anyone with him.

It took a moment longer than she would've liked for Gart to release her, but he finally did so. "And next time," she warned him, letting a little fire into her own voice, "don't touch me unless you want to be touched back. Severely."

The backroom held only Catadina, though she had a fresh bowl of stew in front of her on another crate. She seemed to be sitting on the same crate of apples that she'd been on when Pen had last seen her, but her golden curls were pulled up onto her head, and wet tendrils hung about her face as if she'd recently bathed.

Billie had let her use her washroom? There had to be magic involved. Or a serious amount of coinage.

"Is there news?" Catadina asked excitedly.

Pen gave a nod and pulled the wax replica from her purse. "What is that?" Gart asked.

"You…had a replica made?" Catadina asked, but her enthusiasm had waned.

"Not a replica of the key," Pen corrected. "A replica of the *lock*. The one thing no one's ever thought to do before. Look: there's a stem in the middle. It's nearly invisible thanks to the talons, but when I pressed the wax against the lock, this is the imprint it made."

Catadina's eyes were wide and hopeful again, and even Gart looked impressed despite himself. "How soon to cast it?"

"A few days, most likely," Pen said. "I'll have a copy made up for you. Then we're good and even, right? You'll pay me what I'm owed?"

"You still haven't named your price," Gart pointed out. He seemed far less murderous than he had been before, though. Progress.

"I haven't figured out what I want most yet," she said. "When I do, I'll let you know." A whole slew of ideas came to mind, actually, but a larger image was beginning to take place.

The first thing she wanted had nothing to do with Catadina or the Emperor. Balls to them both: neither was a priority. No, she had her own arrangements made, her own plans for that key. And they involved breaking into the cells and freeing Magnus.

Catadina leaned forward, her smile soft and genuine. "I can't thank you enough. I know you're risking your life for this. The fact that you've made a replica already is closer than anyone else has come. I promise you. I won't forget it."

Pen found her face flushing a bit at the praise. "Yeah, well, when there's good coin involved, I guess I can be coerced into anything," she muttered. "I gave him your message, by the way."

The smile fell from Catadina's face. "You saw him?" Gart asked, stunned. "The Emperor?"

"It wasn't part of my plan," Pen admitted. "I expected to give them the broach and the line, then let them fluster themselves into a frenzy. I didn't expect to hand-deliver the message myself, but that's what happened." She managed to avoid a shudder, but only just. Whether he was really a dragon wearing a human's skin or not, she didn't care: he was deadly and creepy.

Slowly Catadina nodded. "What did he say in return?"

"He mentioned eating through the family tree. Slowly."

"Of course he bloody did," Gart growled. "I told you, you shouldn't have sent him a message."

"And I told you he needed to know that I was here," Catadina said firmly. "It takes the pressure off of a possible theft and more on an open-led rebellion." Her face fell slightly. "Though I would've liked to have kept the broach. It's one of the last things of my mother's I had left."

Pen reached into her purse and tossed an item at Catadina, who barely managed to catch it. Her eyes went wide as she turned the broach over in her hands. "How?" Catadina breathed.

"I saw an opportunity," Pen said, shrugging. In truth, Jorel passing by with the purse had been too good to ignore, and lifting the broach from the swinging purse had been as easy as tipping the edge of the purse and palming what fell out. She wondered if the Emperor had seen.

She wondered if he'd seen far more than she'd wanted him to.

There were honest to goodness tears in the princess's eyes, and oh, Pen hadn't intended on starting waterworks. "Thank you," Catadina whispered. "Oh, Pen, thank you so much."

Thankfully Billie chose that moment to hurry into the back room. Her eyes were wide and frightened. "There's guards in my bar," she said, "and they're looking for all of you."

Pen grabbed Catadina's arm in one hand, and Gart's in the other. "Billie, keep them in here for at least five minutes, then send them to the western side of the marketplace."

Billie nodded tightly and hurried back out. "With me," Pen said shortly. "*Now.*"

They raced out the back door, where Pen kept them flush against the wall. A few guards sat in the street, and Pen cursed at how close they were. They needed to get past and quickly.

"I need coins," she whispered. Catadina began digging for her pockets, but Gart handed over a fistful of random coins in a moment. It would do. "Stay here."

She began to climb up the side of the wall, scaling the brick with her fingers. She still had those dainty shoes on, not her boots, and it made climbing all the more difficult. Still, she didn't need to get up very high—she only needed to get over their heads. High up enough that they couldn't see her, and no one would look for someone, Pen gazed out into the open market. There were plenty of people around: good.

She cast the coins out, throwing them as far into the empty square as she could. The sound of tinkling coins landing amongst the cobblestones instantly caught everyone's attention, and there was a sudden frenzy as everyone raced to gather them up. Including the two guards at the front of the alley.

She dropped down and nearly stumbled. Stupid shoes. She grabbed Catadina's wrist and tugged the princess after her, knowing Gart would follow. She hoped he could move fast because there wasn't any time to slow down as they raced out of the alley.

They barreled down the streets, through the marketplace, and down to the lower end. Several people gasped as she hurried past them, but Pen didn't slow down. Catadina's hand was firmly in hers now, and incredibly enough, the princess hadn't tripped yet. And Pen hadn't heard a thunderous rumbling, so she had to assume Gart hadn't fallen yet, either.

Pen frantically scanned the area near her den, but there were no guards here. Hopefully, they were all still on the western end, but if they were coming down to Billie's, they'd clearly started spreading out the search. And that meant there was only one place that would keep them safe.

She hurried down the familiar alley and didn't even bother being gentle with the steel sheet, just let go of Catadina, pulled it back, and grabbed the candle inside. "Go," she ordered.

Catadina paused and stared at her incredulously as Pen fumbled with the matches. Ah, finally some of the royalty rearing its head. "Is it safe—"

"Yes, just *go*," Pen ordered. She got the candle lit and handed it to Catadina. "Go!"

After another moment of hesitating, Catadina finally, delicately, stepped inside. Gart stayed at the mouth of the alley, peering around them, and Pen rolled her eyes. "Would you just get in here?" she hissed. "Come on!"

He glared at her but thankfully went inside as well. Pen finally followed him in and pulled the sheet as tight against the wall as she could. Her breathing was rapid and harsh, and her hands shook slightly. She'd never felt so out of control before.

Stupid princesses. Stupid Emperors. Stupid her for getting wrapped up in it all.

Catadina waited ahead, candle in hand. Her face was pale but resolute, and Pen suddenly realized this wasn't the first time she'd had to flee for her life. Pen certainly understood the feeling, but it was usually far more invigorating, far less frightening. She also wasn't usually responsible for other people, just herself.

Inching her way forward, Pen took the candle from Catadina and led the way silently through the dark. Down the stairs they went, first beneath the floorboards, then under dirt and stone, and finally, it opened up into her cavern. It was blissfully quiet, even though it was broken by the slight echoes of multiple footsteps.

"Welcome to my home," Pen said, giving a low bow. "This is probably the safest place for you to be at this point. There's, uh, not much in terms of comfortable spaces to sit or lay, but you can have anything you'd like." After a moment, she gave a nod to the hammock. "It's comfy enough to sleep in, believe me."

Catadina immediately shook her head. "I couldn't take your bed—"

"Plenty of open spaces for me and your formidable giant," Pen interrupted. She reclined back against one of the stone spires that jutted from the ground, crossed her legs, and closed her eyes. "When you're done being ridiculous, let me know."

After a pause, she could hear small footsteps move across the stone. The sound of the hammock creaking made her grin. "There's extra pillows in a basket to your right, if your royal head needs a bit more cushion."

"My royal head is just fine, thank you," Catadina said, a bit grumpily. It only made Pen grin all the more.

Gart found himself a spot and proved that he was probably descended from stones himself, given how he seemed to blend in with the walls. Pen wasn't really intending on sleeping, there was far too much day left, but after the race from Billie's, a rest wouldn't go amiss. And it gave her time to think.

She needed to find someone willing to make the key for her. She needed to find someone willing to make the key and *not* call for the guards. She needed to find the prison and get Magnus out. Unfortunately, at the moment, she couldn't do much of anything. There were too many guards on the streets to let her get to where she wanted.

But time was running out. She had no idea how long it would take to craft the key she wanted. Dragon claws needed specific tools to carve them unless you wanted to break a blade or spend hours grinding one, from what she understood. So, who had the tools for the job? Maybe one of the jewelers?

"Pen?"

She blinked, then blinked several more times. Had she fallen asleep?

The ache in her back spoke of having been in a single position for hours, but she hadn't realized she'd dozed off. She sat upright and found Catadina crouched in front of her, looking concerned. Gart's eyes were closed as he slept against the wall.

"What's wrong?" Pen asked, shaking off the last dredges of sleep. "Did you hear something?"

"Oh, no, nothing like that," Catadina insisted. "I feel ridiculous for asking, but I wondered about getting something to eat. I didn't want to pry into your possessions."

Oh. That was a good reason to get moving again. "Back corner, in the two barrels. There's some fruit and dried meat. I don't know about bread, but I need to go out this evening anyway. I'll get some, check on Billie, make sure she's all right." Billie was bound to cause more trouble than she got, but still, Pen would be happy to cause trouble on her behalf.

Catadina waved her off. "All of that sounds just fine, thank you. You're very loyal to those whom you call friends."

It sounded far more noble than she really was. "Billie serves a good ale," she said, shifting uncomfortably. "That's all. If she stops being in business, where else would I go?"

She got a hummed response, and a smile like Catadina knew there was more to it. Pen wasn't going to elaborate and prove her right. "Let's do dinner then, shall we, your majesty?" She stood and headed for the barrels. There *was* some bread left, though she'd probably still pick some up. Bread made for a good alibi if she was found in the streets at a later hour.

"Who is Cam?"

Pen froze, hand still holding the bread. "You called out for Cam, in your sleep," Catadina continued quietly. "I have to imagine it's someone important to you."

She felt betrayed by her own body, unwittingly giving her greatest desires away. It took a minute to find her voice. "She's, um, my sister. My older sister. She went missing some years ago." Left, really, to find someplace safe for them both. She could still see Cam, two long braids in her hair like always, a wide grin on her face. *I'll come get you when I've got a safe place secured. Just the two of us, like it always has been. I promise, Penny.*

"You don't know what happened to her?"

"No," Pen said. She brushed her hair back from her face as she stared down at the barrel. She needed more fruit, too. Cam would've kept it better stocked. Cam had been better at everything except stealing. "Just that she left, looking for a better place."

"It's been some time, then. Since you last saw her." Catadina let out a small sigh. "I understand that. My brother is missing, too. I don't know where he is."

The dainty shoes on Pen's feet looked a great deal like Catadina's, now that she looked harder. They weren't as nicely tailored to her feet, but at least they had some golden thread. "Is he older or younger?" Pen found herself asking, turning to Catadina. The princess looked small, standing amidst the vastness of the cavern. For the first time, she didn't look regal or majestic. She just looked like an ordinary woman. One who understood what Pen felt like, missing a sibling.

"Younger. He's still out there," Catadina said firmly, but her determination faltered. "And if I can get the kingdom back, I know he'll come home."

Pen wished she was as confident. She had no way to draw Cam back. She could steal for the rest of her life, and none of the gold or jewels or coins would entice Cam to come back. It had never held her eye. But the coins could buy Pen passage to find—

She was suddenly very done with the conversation. She slammed the lid of the barrel shut, startling Gart awake, and tossed the bread at Catadina. Catadina jumped but managed to catch it. "I'd be worried about yourself, princess. The Emperor doesn't take kindly to the rebellious sort."

She caught her hooded jacket and her boots and began to get properly dressed. Her scarves came next, and she grabbed the nearby purse, pulling out the bundle of wax and the bag of the Emperor's coins. Both went into her scarves, as did the dragon claws and the vial, and only then did she feel secure. Back to rights.

"Wait, where are you going?" Catadina asked, starting forward. Pen backed up, putting a good amount of distance between them. Being around the princess was hazardous to her health. The last thing she needed while she had things to do was have Cam on her mind. She couldn't focus if all she had on her mind was her big sister. She needed to be Pen. No, she needed to be The Ghost. That was the person who could get the job done.

Not Penny, the little sister left behind.

"I've got an errand to run. Eat up and stay here. Don't go *anywhere*. You're the safest you can be in Silve Hollow down here, and if you get cold, there's blankets. You step outside, and I can't help you."

"But—"

Pen just turned and headed down the tunnel, grabbing the usual candle as she went. Catadina's single word echoed briefly before dissipating into nothing.

That wasn't nice, Penny.

"You're not here," she muttered under her breath to the Cam that stayed with her. "Shut it."

There was no response. Jaw set, Pen made her way back out to the streets.

Roche wouldn't let her in, so Pen did something she never did: she went in through the front door and graced Marina with a bright smile. She also gave Marina one of the Emperor's coins, and that was enough to gain her access to Roche's basement.

Once she got inside, Roche finally agreed to give her the name of someone who'd do the mold, no questions asked. It took another two of the Emperor's coins. "You're still stupid," he told her angrily. "Come back only when you're done being foolish. And don't come through my wife again."

The man, Corter, wasn't much for words. He did give her a glance up and down when he saw what she wanted done, so she knew he was breathing. "Can you do it or not?" she asked him.

His response was to hold his other hand out. She placed the entire bag in his palm and watched him rub his thumb over the side, feeling out the shape on the coins inside. His eyes widened slightly, and he gave a sharp nod.

She handed over the four dragon claws and the mold. "Can you have done it by tomorrow?" she asked. Roche had told her that Corter was the best, but that didn't mean it would be fast.

In response, Corter simply nodded to a nearby chair. Pen raised both eyebrows in surprise but dutifully sat down. Guess she got to wait. She let out a sigh and looked around as he headed into the back. There was no way he could be done while she waited, but she was willing to humor him.

Unfortunately, with time to think, her mind went back over the insanity that was her task. Making a real replica of the Dragon Key was one thing—actually using it and getting in and out of the most notorious jail in the world was another. She'd passed the bulletin board on the way over to Corter's and found another name to match Simms and Magnus: Alina for fighting back against a guard. They had their three, but Pen had just been grateful it wasn't Billie's name on the list. She hadn't been able to stop by the bar to see for herself, though. Hopefully, the list wouldn't be updated by the time she came back through.

She had two days left before the public executions. Two days before Magnus lost his life for simply giving a damn about her. If this didn't work, if she couldn't get the replica to work, then what was she going to do?

Cam would've known what to do.

"Stop it," she hissed at herself. She hadn't given this much thought to her big sister in years now. She'd learned to live by herself, live *for* herself, without someone else to take care of her. She'd been good at it before Cam had left, and now? Now she was the best. She was the best thief in Silve Hollow, probably in Silveland.

Stupid princess.

Less than two hours later, along with a hefty amount of grinding and clanging noises, Corter came back out and presented the new key. The replica looked...pretty good, actually, with the dragon claws shaved down to match the wax mold. The iron handle looked ugly as could be, but the long pin in the middle was a thing of solid beauty. She didn't have a lot of time to admire it, however, mostly because Corter immediately shoved her towards the door. All right, she could take a hint.

On the way out, however, she caught a glimpse in the back room and found a glimmer of something glistening and glittering like no jewel she'd ever known. Huh. So, it was true: pixie dust could get any job done in half the time. No wonder he'd wanted her out as soon as possible. The stuff was notoriously rare and *very* much a crime to have, let alone use.

The replica weighed a bit heavy in her scarves, and she had to adjust them twice as she headed down the road. To avoid suspicion, she did stop at one of the vendors who was just packing up and bought herself a fresh loaf of bread as well as half a wheel of cheese. Catadina had seemed to enjoy the cheese from Billie's.

Speaking of *The Sparrow's Rest*, a quick roundabout turn let her check-in through one of the windows. Billie stood behind the bar, wiping it down. Something in Pen's chest let go at the sight of the woman, safe and sound, not in the prison. Good.

Only because it would make it harder to have to rescue more than one person. That was all.

She headed back to the den and scurried inside. She wasn't at all surprised to find Gart at the end of the tunnel, blade drawn. In response, she stuck the half wheel of cheese at the end of his blade, making him draw back to rip the cheese off. "I got bread, too," she said as a greeting.

Catadina rose from the floor (of course she wasn't in the hammock, why would she do anything that made sense?) and hurried over. "Did you check in on Billie? Is she all right?"

"Seems to be. Here." She handed over the bread and moved towards her personal things. There were a few things she was going to need to take with her. She made sure she had the vial on her – never knew when that would come in handy – and grabbed a bag of coins. Never knew when a bribe would come in handy, either. Her usual packet of matches went in with the rest.

"And the key?"

Pen paused. "That's what you were out doing, right?" Catadina asked from behind her. "You were getting a replica made, right? So…is it done?"

"Tomorrow," Pen said after a moment. She turned around with her most trustworthy gaze, which probably needed a lot of help, but she could bluff and act with the best of them. "It's still being worked on. A few final touches to make sure it's done right."

Catadina watched her with a long gaze, and Gart's eyes were heavy with suspicion. The key hung against her chest like a brand, but Pen didn't waver. The princess could wait for her crazy plan: Pen had something to do with it, first.

"Eat up," Pen encouraged. "You're here for the night. I need to run out and do another errand, and then I'll be back."

"You're leavin' again?" Gart asked, eyes narrowing further. "For *what*?"

"You think a replica comes cheap? You think a replica of *that* doesn't come at a price? I've got something I need to do before that key lands in your hands, so if you want it tomorrow…"

Catadina finally nodded. "We'll wait. Thank you, Pen, for everything. You opened your home to us, and I'm very grateful."

"Of course," Pen said automatically, then gave a shrug like it didn't matter. "I mean, you can't pay me if you're dead, right?"

Gart glared at her. Catadina simply looked amused. "Of course."

Infuriating woman. "I'll be back," Pen said, and headed out again.

She did have an errand to do before the princess could have her key. And it involved a prison door.

Never before had Pen been so happy to have the nobles up so high. In this instance, it was going to help her drastically.

Or send her plummeting to her death as she missed the jump

between where she hung and the castle walls below her. Y'know. It was the small things.

She gripped her hands tighter onto the balcony rails. From below her perch, she could see the tops of the guards as they walked around. If she were the heroic sort, she supposed she would be jumping down right on top of them, striking her way through them and gallantly unlocking the gates for the princess to glide through, probably on a white horse.

She wasn't the heroic type, though. There was going to be far more stealth than that. And a far more unsightly landing, if she aimed right.

Her eyes cast inside to the noble whose home she was hanging off of, some six stories above the ground. The wind tugged at her, bending the tower of houses just slightly, but she could see inside to where there was a wealth of items. Besides the golden chalices, there looked to be a complete *shelf* of books. Never mind the crystals that hung from the chandelier. Her fingers itched to pick the door and lift them from where they dangled just out of reach.

She made a face and turned back to her imminent fall. "Being good just doesn't pay," she muttered.

One deep breath, two, and her breathing settled into a steady rhythm. Her heart surged inside of her, excitement singing through her veins. Her wide eyes settled on her target, seeing through the dark night.

Being not-so-good had its perks, too. And it was way more *fun*.

With one more breath, she pushed off and soared.

The night sky flew past her in a rush as she descended. The guards got closer and closer as she fell, and she extended her hands to her target. She could catch it. She could catch it—

Her hands caught the rope, and she winced as her arms jerked above her. Her body swung down and smacked into the corpse, the half-eaten body rancid even in the night air. How the birds found it appetizing, she had no idea. Damn it all. She'd been aiming for one of the skeletons.

There was a tearing sound that made her freeze seconds before she realized just *what* the sound was. A cracking sound followed, and then all of a sudden, the body tore free, leaving the head and neck attached to the rope. "No, no, no," Pen hissed as the body tumbled to the ground. It hit with a dull thud.

Instantly several guards above and below her ran around, alerted by the sound. Light from several torches shone above her. "What *was* that? Did another body fall?"

Pen went perfectly still, hanging from the rope with her head behind the corpse's. The smell was enough to make her gag, but she managed to hold her breath. Mostly. That was just *foul*.

"I missed it," another guard said. "I like when they fall. I had a bet as to which one would go next."

Her blood boiled at the laugh that followed, but she carefully pulled herself up when the chuckle began to fade off. Her hands found the edge of the castle wall, and she nimbly rolled over, landing without a sound. The guards were halfway down the wall and facing away from her. Everyone else was moving back to their posts.

Well, that had worked out better than she'd hoped. Even if the guards made her want to hang *them* from the walls. How they could find it funny, she had no idea. Clearly, the Emperor had found the right sort to guard his domain.

She made her way down from the walls, creeping down two sets of stairs and clinging to the shadows whenever the guards got too close. So far, so good. Only the courtyard, the stone hall, and finding her way to the prison. Oh, and a few locked doors between her and her destination.

Her feet made no sound as she made her way across the stones, eyes seeking out random guards in the dark. The patrol was light tonight—the rest were all in the center square, setting up three hangman's nooses. She knew. She'd passed them. It just made her movements inside the castle even easier tonight.

She reached the door and quickly scaled the stones to perch above the door. Leaning down, she knocked three times, then once, and then pulled back up. The door opened a crack, but there was no one there to see. She watched the guard move out, clearly perplexed, and when he offered her enough space, she dropped between him and the hallway and darted inside. She never made a sound.

The hallway was still lit by candles, making her far more visible than she'd have liked to have been, but that's what her boots were for. She made short work of the hallway as she ran, feet barely leaving a sound and certainly not leaving any imprints. If she did this right, they'd never find a trace of her.

The room with the chair waited just ahead. It held no lock, and there'd been no guard inside. She caught hold of the handle and pulled her feet up against the door anyway, just to be sure, and slowly turned the knob. The door gave and began to open, her weight gently pulling it aside.

Nothing. No sound, no raising of an alarm. Just silence. Pen put her feet back down and glanced inside.

The room was empty. Only the lone chair remained, as hard and ugly as she remembered, along with the tapestries on the wall. She headed for the one in the middle and gently brushed it aside.

A long staircase circled down to depths unknown. Secrets: her specialty. With a grin, she descended.

Halfway down, she heard someone cough and immediately pushed herself up against the wall. There was a sound like heavy boots walking, and they sounded like the typical boots that the guards wore, big and thick, and absolutely no good for running. There was going to be no way to do this quietly.

She came down the stairs, still as silent as could be. There at the bottom was a guard walking back and forth in front of a room that held a semi-circular line of black iron bars running from floor to ceiling. Three of the separate cells held dirty faces inside.

So, she'd been right. The prison had been tucked away down here, underneath the little interrogation room. Now to deal with the single guard.

She pulled the vial of pinesbury out and the packet of matches. Drinking pinesbury was a fast way to stop breathing, but inhaling its smoke was far less deadly and more like a very, very awful hangover. One that typically sent people running.

The cap came off of the vial, and she grimaced. Even the smell was enough to make her stomach churn. Breath held, she lit a match and dropped it into the vial, then tossed the entire thing around the corner and down to the middle of the room where the guard was pacing. He turned immediately at the tinkling sound, and Pen pressed herself up against the wall of the stairwell and waited.

She didn't have to wait long. There was a small popping sound, followed by a long hiss, and then exclamations. Coughing followed, and then, just as she'd figured he would, the guard came barreling at the stairs. She waited until he'd run past her, never seeing her lingering on the stairs, before she headed down into the prison. The middle of the room was filled with purple smoke that kept stemming from the vial on the floor. The smoke made her throat seize up, and her eyes water, but she hurried through and made it to the other side, where the cells waited.

Three pairs of eyes stared at her, stunned. "Pen?" Magnus whispered. "*Pen?*"

"Next time, just tell the truth," she said, suddenly so dizzy with relief that she almost lost her wits. She pulled the replica key out and headed for the cell. There were, indeed, four holes and a tiny pinprick in the middle. She slotted the key in all the way and held her breath as she slowly turned it to the right.

For a moment, nothing happened. Pen's heart stopped beating. She'd missed something. Maybe these locks were different, why wasn't it working—

And then, just like that, the door clicked open. She stared, her mouth dropping open slightly in shock. She'd done it. She'd done what no one else had ever been able to do.

She'd stolen the Dragon Key.

Her heart began to pound all at once, enough to make her stumble a little on her feet. No amount of deep breathing was going to get her to settle down now, so instead, Pen ran with it, letting the feeling seep into her limbs, feeling the tingling in her toes and fingers and relishing it with each pound of her heart that said *I'm alive, I'm alive.* She swung the cell door open wide and couldn't stop the grin.

Magnus stared back at her, still stunned. "Did you want to stay?" she asked when he didn't move after a moment.

That was all it took. He raced out, but straight at her, and suddenly her arms were full of a skinny kid. "You came for me," he whispered. "I knew you would. I *knew* it."

Startled, she found her arms coming around him and feeling his own breath was suddenly worth more than any coin she could've swiped. "Never stolen a person before," she admitted.

Magnus let out a laugh that bordered on crazy. "If anyone could do it, it'd be you, Pen."

The energy kept pushing through her, zipping up and down her spine, and she yanked the replica key out. There was Simms in the cell next to Magnus's, his beard not even able to hide the widening smile, and she popped his door open too. Then Alina, on the other side, long hair framing the tears in her eyes when her cell door unlocked.

Three people no longer on the hangman's noose, and she'd done it.

It was time to leave. She never lingered when she had her prize in hand, and even though her prizes could run for themselves this time, she still wasn't about to break her own rules. "This way," she said, and she led them up the stairs while shoving the replica key back into her scarves.

They made it to the interrogation room and found it silent and empty. She hurried to the door and threw it open, knowing they could easily overtake the single guard at the other door. Four against one were the type of odds she could put money on.

Suddenly the room spun past her, her body only registering the blow she'd taken after she'd slid to the opposite door. Stunned, Pen managed to push herself up on her elbows, her head still ringing.

There stood Jorel, a club in one hand, his other reaching for the sword at his hip. He was advancing on Magnus and the others who had backed themselves towards a corner near the still-open door.

"Don't worry, I won't kill you," Jorel said. "I wouldn't dare take the joy of a public execution from his majesty. Especially when it'll now include the famous Ghost."

"Hey!" Pen shouted, and Jorel spun towards her. She yanked her hood off. "You want me, not them."

Watching Jorel's eyes widen in realization was a thing of beauty. "*You?*" he gasped.

"Me," she said. She pushed herself to her feet. All she needed was another step. "And you haven't caught me yet."

Jorel snarled and took two steps towards her. "Go!" she shouted, and Magnus didn't wait, just took off with Simms and Alina behind him. Jorel turned to go after them, and Pen seized her chance to try and run around him. She was faster and far lighter.

Unfortunately, she was also unarmed. Jorel swung his club at her again, and she narrowly avoided him. Another swing, and she ducked under, bringing her arm up into a strong punch up towards his chin. She only glanced him, and he pulled the club back to catch her in the side.

Pain shot out across her body as she flew towards the hidden stairs, and she desperately tried to pull another breath in. Her hands slid across the cold floor, sweaty and trembling. She felt out of control. She felt weak.

Get up, Cam told her, the memory of her voice urgent in her head. *Penny, get up or you'll never get up again!*

It was enough to make her roll out of the way of the club coming down. Her back seized, and she gasped in pain. She wasn't made for battle. She was made for light feet and stealing. She was a thief, not a fighter.

And it didn't seem as if it would matter for much longer because when she managed to push herself up, it was to meet the tip of Jorel's blade at her chin. "You have no idea how long I've been waiting to do this," Jorel said. His lips slid into a nasty grin. "Now you'll be a real ghost, little pickpocket."

Hands caught hold of the sides of his head and twisted. There was a cracking sound, and then Jorel dropped like a stone, eyes already sightless. Pen fought to catch her breath as she stared up at her rescuer.

Gart stared back at her. "Should've told him you weren't a pickpocket, that you were a thief."

Pen let out a high-pitched laugh. "I don't think I need to tell him anything anymore. Remind me not to make you angry."

He smirked at her and held out a hand. It took a moment to not fall back over, but Gart was surprisingly patient, keeping her upright until she was steady. It also gave her time to find her words. "How did you—?"

His smirk only broadened. "You're not as subtle as you think you are."

"You followed me. Again."

"Took your advice and got better at it. It was easy after three people came runnin' out, lookin' for an exit. Your friend Magnus said you needed help."

Of course he had. "Is he all right?" she found herself asking.

Gart gazed at her for a moment, and she was surprised when he actually gave her a small smile, an actual genuine smile. She hadn't thought he knew how to do that. "Yeah, he's out safe, along with the other two."

Pen let out a long sigh. At least one thing had gone according to plan.

That was when she heard a loud booming noise, and a second later, the castle walls shook. She clutched at Gart to stay upright. "What is that?" she asked, bewildered.

"That'd be the rebellion," he said proudly. "I imagine her majesty's leadin' the charge."

Wait. "You left her *alone*?" Pen said, feeling anger well. How was Catadina going to stay alive if he was down here with her? "She needs you!"

"You needed me more," he said. "'Sides, she's with m'cousin."

"There's more of you?" Pen said, dismayed. Gart finally glared at her, which felt much better than the smile, and she felt some form of equilibrium. "Let me guess, is his name Bart?"

"It's Scarzine," Gart said curtly. "I've wasted enough time on you down here. We've a castle to take back."

He led the way out through the hallway, back outside to the courtyard, and Pen glanced at the remains of the door as she stepped through it. The guard wasn't there. She didn't ask where he'd gone.

There wasn't really a point, honestly, with the way everything looked.

The castle itself was in shambles. Several bushes and trees were on fire, and the clanging of swords filled the air. A shout went up, and Pen stared as Billie rushed past, several men and women behind her. She had that horrible claw in her hand as she went, and it looked red already.

Another something made a very large booming noise, and Pen startled back as one of the walls came down with a horrific roar. Were they *trying* to destroy the castle? "You know, you're not supposed to break the thing you're trying to steal," she yelled over the noise. "That sort of defeats the purpose."

"Not our fault the guards won't let it go," Gart said stubbornly. Pen rolled her eyes, then remembered he'd literally just killed a man with his bare hands. Subtly she stepped to the side of him.

A rallying cry went up, and Pen's eyes flew to the center of the courtyard. There was Catadina, golden hair flying wildly behind her, a long sword in her hand. Her eyes were bright and fixed on something high above, and Pen followed her gaze to the top of one of the walls. Amidst the smoke and fire, she could make out a familiar figure, surrounded by a handful of guards.

The Emperor.

The two stared each other down, and for a moment, Pen was afraid he'd turn into a dragon and fly down to eat Catadina whole. But he didn't. Instead, he glared with rage and hatred from his place atop the walls, even as he backed away from the edge. Pen wondered suddenly if perhaps he *couldn't* transform into a dragon, after all. Maybe it was all a myth.

Maybe he was really just as human as the rest of them.

Catadina raised her blade at him, steady and calm, and the Emperor's eyes went wide before he suddenly hurried down into the wall. "For the Princess!" someone yelled, and a group of people raced forward to chase after the Emperor.

Not that it was going to do anyone much good. It was over. The few guards left had dropped their blades and surrendered as soon as the Emperor had fled the scene, and just like that, Catadina had the castle back. Catadina turned away and found Pen's eye, and she grinned, clearly elated. Pen couldn't help but grin back, energy still flying through her veins.

Well, that could've gone worse.

"It wasn't exactly the night I had planned."

"I know."

Pen glared at the woman beside her. Catadina seemed unafflicted. "Shouldn't you be helping them?" Pen asked, gesturing to the people gathered in the courtyard. None of them seemed willing to bother them where they stood, leaning against one of the destroyed walls. The whole castle was going to need help being put back together. It was a wreck.

Pen, for one, was hoping Catadina had the funds to rebuild *and* enough to pay her.

Catadina shook her head. "No, I'm fine here. They have it in hand. I believe the people are far more capable of handling things. They don't need someone telling them everything they ought to do."

"I thought that's what royalty did."

"We're here to help supply justice and peace, to defend our borders," Catadina said softly. "Our greatest asset should always be our people."

And the coins in the vault that were sure to be inside the castle, but Pen wasn't going to argue with the princess. Not when the high of having actually managed to pull off the heist of the year was resting inside of her.

Speaking of. Pen reached inside her scarves and pulled out the replica key. "Not that you'll probably need it," she said, and she handed it to Catadina. "But I'm sure he's had everything locked up tight. It could prove useful."

Catadina didn't even look surprised, which honestly was just disrespectful. "And what do you mean, you knew?" Pen said. "I said I had errands to run! I didn't say anything about coming to the castle!"

"You were wearing your boots and scarves," Catadina told her. When Pen stared at her, she just shrugged. "It's a dead giveaway that you intend to be "The Ghost," which, truly, is a horrible nickname."

"I didn't pick it," Pen said sullenly. She scowled at Catadina, who didn't seem bothered in the slightest. It was just insulting, honestly.

Billie walked past with a group and gave Pen a hearty wave and grin. Pen gave a quick wave back and let her keep going. Whatever she was doing, it was far more important than talking with Pen. They could always catch up later. And by catch up, she meant interrogate Billie on how long she'd been a part of some ridiculous royal resistance.

Beside her, Catadina stayed, silently watching everything with a bright smile on her face. Pen rolled her eyes. "So now what?" she asked. "What comes next for you?"

"Reclaim the throne and my people," Catadina said decisively. "It's time."

"You don't have a throne. You barely have a castle."

"Then I'll get another chair. The hammock in your den was comfortable. I might get something like that to sit on."

Pen made a face. "You don't have any walls to your castle."

"Those can be rebuilt. There's always stone to be found."

"You'll have to undo everything he did."

"I'm looking forward to it."

"…Your fruit trees burned down."

"Many of them need a fire every now and then to bear new fruit."

"Is there *anything* that isn't making you sunshine and roses right now?" Pen finally exclaimed. Catadina smiled at her, that same enigmatic smile like she knew the answer to everything, and it was seriously beyond irritating.

And a little hopeful, too.

"You didn't get him," Pen said, and that dimmed Catadina's smile. It was followed up by a firm look of determination a moment later, however.

"Not today, no. He has more guards, more support elsewhere. But we broke his hold. I can get the whole kingdom back. And this is the first part of that."

The sounds of the city waking up began as a low murmur, but then the cheers began, echoing through the streets, and it was one of the best things Pen had ever heard. Somewhere in that noise was Magnus, and knowing him, the kid was probably leading the wake-up call that the Emperor had fled. It made her smile a little.

The nobles probably weren't cheering, and that made her smile a little more.

"What about your brother?" Pen found herself asking.

Catadina blinked, surprised. "I don't know," she said after a moment. "I hope that word will reach him that the Emperor has lost Silve Hollow and that we can take back all of Silveland. I don't have any other way to reach him."

Yeah, Pen knew that feeling. She knew it really well. "Well, I hope you find him," she said, stretching her arms above her head. She could sleep for a week and still be tired.

"What will *you* do?"

Somehow, she'd known she'd get that question. Pen began to answer, then stopped. It was a weird night already, why not add honesty to the mix? "I don't know," she admitted. After helping start a rebellion to put a princess back on her rightful throne, everything else just sort of paled in comparison. Not even stealing from the nobles was going to be fun anymore.

There wouldn't probably *be* any nobles after Catadina was done, and that just soured her mood even more. Now she really didn't know what she'd do.

"I picked you."

Pen blinked. "What?"

"I said, I picked you. Billie told me what to wear and what would catch your eye. I wanted to see how good you were, and I knew if I outright hired you, you wouldn't be interested. She said you don't take on jobs."

"I don't," Pen said absently, trying to process what she'd been told. "Wait, you *picked* me?"

"I hung out in the marketplace for a while, walking around, trying to find you," Catadina admitted. She kicked at a nearby stone and sent it across the pathway. "I'd nearly given up when Gart suddenly went into action."

"Why?" Pen asked, dumbfounded. Of all the things she'd expected, this wasn't one of them.

Catadina turned to her, that soft, sweet smile on her face. "Because I needed the best. And Billie told me that was you. The only thief good enough to do the job, and the only one she'd trust."

Something caught in Pen's throat, and she couldn't seem to find her voice. Around her, parts of the castle kept burning, and the constant cheering filled her ears. The tingling in her fingers and toes had traveled back up to reside in her chest, pounding in time with her heart. She felt dizzy.

Catadina pushed away from the wall and began moving towards a larger group of rebels. Pen swallowed hard. "I didn't get paid yet, you know."

The princess paused and glanced back. "You promised me anything I wanted, and I haven't gotten it," Pen continued. "I expect that, when this is all over."

Hope filled Catadina's eyes and broadened her smile. "What is it that you want, then?" she asked.

"I'll tell you later," Pen assured her.

"Good," Catadina said, and she headed off. Pen watched her go and crossed her arms around herself. She needed to go find Magnus. She needed to cash in a few more things with Roche before the whole world turned upside down. Well, turned upside down more than it already had.

Cam was still out there. She had to be. Pen would find her. And they'd get their home with space around them and sky above them. They'd have grass and a tree.

The Emperor was still out there, too. Pen was looking forward to helping hunt him down. After all, she was a thief. She'd helped steal a castle back: the only thing left to top that was to try and steal back the whole kingdom.

Pen tugged her hood back up and slipped away, leaving Catadina amongst her supporters. For now, she'd settle for stealing a few hours of sleep. She had a feeling that tomorrow, there'd be a princess coming to call with more noble and good things to do. Maybe one of those things could be a new nickname for Pen.

…eh, "The Ghost" wasn't too terrible. She could live with it.

With a grin, she began to make her way through the celebrations of a new day.

Fin

ABOUT J.M. RHINEHEART

J.M. Rhineheart is a long-time writer, first-time published author. A fan of fantasy from a very young age thanks to the likes of Roald Dahl, J.R.R. Tolkien, Patricia C. Wrede, and Terry Pratchett, she loves writing fantasy in any form. Heroes that come from unexpected places, villains that aren't always what you think, and fighting for what's right: it's all in her stories. When she's not writing, she's planning road trips and trying to run more races. She lives in Virginia with her husband, her daughter, and no cats or dogs (though the possibility of a fish tank continues to lurk in the future).

Website: https://jmrhineheart.wordpress.com

facebook.com/jmrhineheart

twitter.com/jmrhineheart

instagram.com/jmrhineheart

BAD REPUTATION

BY LILY LUCHESI

"Miss? You can't park there."

Bree Carson glanced up at the security guard who spoke. He was middle-aged, married, and probably had to take this job to supplement his police department income. A good thing, too, since he didn't recognize her from the wanted posters.

Glancing back at her restored vintage Harley, she smiled and flashed her red eyes, pinning the mall cop to the spot. "I think I can."

The man's eyes glazed over, and he nodded. "Of course, miss. Have a nice night."

"Yeah, you too," she said, chuckling to herself as she walked into the bar on the corner of Halstead and Armitage. It moonlighted as a hip cafe, but it had a dungeon only special patrons could gain access to. Patrons who had fangs or fur, for example.

Bree walked through the humans yukking it up, drinking overpriced fruity drinks, garnering appreciative glances from the men and a few ladies as she strode by in her liquid leggings and black leather jacket. Perhaps she'd grab a quick bite from one of them before leaving for the night. Just for fun.

She reached the locked door that led to the dungeon bar and came face-to-face with a security guard. This one was definitely not a rent-a-cop.

"Credentials?" he asked in a deep, growly voice.

Bree flashed her eyes at him, but didn't get him under thrall. That wasn't her intention.

"Go ahead." He unlocked the door, and she slipped into the quiet, dark hallway, descending a flight of stairs.

With each step, the pulsing beat of some pop song assailed her ears, getting louder by the second.

Who listens to this shit? Bree wondered as she hit the dungeon. It was as big as the club above, but with an entirely different vibe and clientele. It was dark, the only light coming from flashing multi-colored strobes. The bodies on the floor here were by far more alluring and interesting. Tall, lanky vampires mingling with squat hags; hairy werewolves dancing with hairless ghouls; succubi and shapeshifters sharing pints of Old Style.

It was a mish-mosh, but it was normal. For them.

Bree went to the crowded bar, and immediately a fairy spotted her and leapt off his seat to offer it to her. He wanted to stay on her good side. Staying there guaranteed your survival. Pissing her off consti-tuted your untimely demise.

"Miss Carson," the bartender said. He was a wizard skilled in potions, but he kept bar in his spare time. He could mix a mean Bloody Mary. Or a Bloody Mike. Or whomever the blood came from that particular night. "The usual?"

"Lay off the hucon. Make the drink a double," she said.

He fiddled around the bar, and the witch sitting next to Bree asked, "What's hucon? The werewolf over there asked for a double last time he ordered."

Bree looked the woman over and said, "You're one of the human apprentice witches, right?"

She nodded.

"Then trust me, you don't wanna know it or eat it."

The bartender placed her drink in front of her and said, "*Voilà*, a Bloody Vinny!"

Bree smirked. "Wasn't Vinny the name of the dude who owned the club upstairs?"

The bartender nodded. "He threatened to out the club to the mayor unless I paid triple, so I took care of him. Guess I own the club upstairs, too, now."

Bree held her drink out in a salute before downing half of it in one go. "Here's to your entrepreneurship."

Vampires can't get drunk, and while they couldn't eat most food, alcohol wasn't a problem for their systems as long as it was diluted with blood. Hucon was another thing they could eat, but not often. Solids didn't digest well in an Undead system.

The night before, Bree finished a job and barely beat the sun home to sleep the day away in her coffin. She lived in a basement apartment on a residential street, not far from a park and elementary school. Her neighbors didn't know her well, but she once saved the guy who lived above her's dog when it ran into the street, so she was fairly well-liked.

No one suspected that she wasn't human. Nor did they know that she made her money as a mercenary, offing victims for a hefty price tag. She wasn't picky about species, either. Werewolves, humans, fae folk, magicians, other vampires … all were fair game if the price was right. Bree was the deadliest person in Chicago, possibly in the country. And she was only fifty-six. A true baby in vampire time.

Most of America's government was aware of the paranormals and let them be as long as they didn't hinder humankind or reveal themselves in any way. However, not all lawmakers had the same benevolence. In Chicago, particularly, the new mayor wasn't happy with them. She already disbanded the Werewolf Police Corps, stopped allowing magical kids into regular schools, and destroyed most vampire nests. Bree was lucky. She was a loner, and thus harder to smoke out. But she knew that she was on the mayor's radar, not just because of her species, but because of her occupation.

Mercenaries were bad enough. Immortal mercenaries who drank human blood were unacceptable. The Undead were skilled killers, each and every one of them. Killing was as natural as breathing for their species. Bree figured, why not make some cash off her talents? After all, the world was advancing, and she'd live forever unless some hunter took her down. She needed a nest egg.

To be fair, she only killed assholes. Each job offer was heavily weighed, and she never killed anyone who could be deemed innocent. She had a heart and a strong sense of justice. If vamps were allowed to join the Police Academy, she would have made an excellent cop.

She even took on pro bono jobs: wife beaters, child molesters, animal torturers, all manner of scumbags met the end of her fangs, many taken on for free when an abused victim begged her to take over where human police and courts failed.

The mayor really hated that. Bree didn't give two shits what the mayor thought.

"Did you see *Stranger Things*?" the bartender asked her. Bree had some human fun, and most of said fun was pop culture.

"Nope. Work. I might binge a few episodes when I get home," she replied. "I'm still kind of in the zone from finally seeing *IT* last month. May do a King movie marathon first to get it out of my system."

He laughed. "You'd make the perfect girlfriend."

"Too bad I'm not interested," she replied, handing him her empty cup for a refill. She glanced down at the diamond ring that hung on a chain around her neck and sighed. Relationships, even flings, were dangerous. The last human she had loved didn't fare so well. Not that she was a vampire then. And magicians were, essentially, human. It was too risky for them.

Once she finished her next drink, she walked around the room, making sure that no one needed her. There were multiple ways to contact her, but if other paranormals required her services, they came or sent a messenger into the dungeon. Tonight looked to be a quiet night, and for that, she was glad.

Around midnight she left the bar and went to her motorcycle. It was a cold, clear night, not long before Halloween. She could smell car exhaust, smog, sewer, and other city things. But she could also smell anticipation and excitement. Halloween was a favorite time of the year for many people, and she couldn't blame them.

As she got her helmet from the side saddlebag, she heard subtle movement from behind her. She whirled around to face her assailant, but was one second too late because she had to drop the helmet first.

Two humans in black suits were pointing guns at her heart.

Smirking, she said, "You think those things are gonna hurt me?"

"Soaked in holy water, yeah, we think they might do some damage," one of them replied. "So, you can come with us, or we can pump you full of silver and holy water, see how quickly you heal from that."

Bree knew she was fucked. But she got taken in before. It never took long to escape. She was just miffed that her quiet night at home was now ruined.

The other one put his gun away and took out silver handcuffs, wrenching her around and cuffing her tightly. The holy water must've been soaked into those, too, because they burned like Hell.

"Briana Carson, you're under arrest for multiple murders in the first degree. You have the right to — "

"Oh, shut up. We all know the mayor doesn't give non-humans rights," she interrupted. "Just take me in before I eat you for a midnight snack."

They shoved her in the backseat of a black sedan as it began to drive toward downtown. Sighing and leaning her head against the black leather headrest, she thought, *This night cannot get any worse.*

The two men led a still-handcuffed Bree to an interrogation room at the police precinct downtown and unceremoniously tossed her into the rickety metal chair. She fought the urge to bite them, mainly because she didn't want a body full of holy water.

When they left, she glanced around to see if there was anything loose on the floors to pick the cuffs off with. Damned humans, they thought of everything. They even had cuffs that dampened most paranormal powers.

There was nothing. For a police station, it was pretty clean. Even the two-way mirror on the wall before her was spotless ... not that she could see anything in it except for cute clothes that seemed to be in the sitting position of their own volition. Vampires didn't cast reflections, but their clothes did.

She wasn't left waiting there for long, however. The door opened within minutes. She expected some detective who thought he was trying out for a part on *Chicago PD*, but she got a surprise. It was the mayor. A bluesuit walked in behind the mayor.

"Uncuff her, please," the mayor said to the bluesuit.

"But — "

"I said uncuff her," the mayor ordered. "Now, Officer."

"Yes, ma'am," he said, hastily removing the cuffs from Bree's aching wrists.

Originally, the moment she was uncuffed she was going to hightail it outta there. But the mayor's appearance piqued her curiosity, and she wanted to know what the lady wanted.

"Now leave."

The bluesuit looked like he wanted to argue, but one look from the mayor sent him scurrying away, closing the door behind him.

The mayor turned back to face Bree, her dark eyes hard and focused. Mayor Ilona Warwick was the city's youngest mayor at only thirty-two and was also the city's first single mother mayor. People looked up to and respected her. Bree thought she had a terrible stick up her ass and needed to take a few Xanax and calm down.

"Well, Madam Mayor, to what do I owe the pleasure of a false arrest and mistreatment by your goons? Didn't you know you could just call me if you wanted to chat?" Bree asked scornfully.

Ilona slid gracefully into the chair across the table from the vampiress. "Your attitude is tiresome, Miss Carson. And are you really going to sit there and claim to be an innocent?"

"Unless you've got hard evidence that I've committed a crime, yeah," she said. "So, what do you want? Why go to all this trouble?"

Ilona sighed, and Bree noticed that the usually beautiful and immaculate mayor looked haggard. Her olive-hued skin had a yellowish tinge, and dark circles caressed her eyes. There was a tremor in her left hand and a tic in her foot, making it jerk unprompted under the table.

"I'm going to level with you, Miss Carson: I need help. And I can't rely on the police or my personal security to do what needs to be done."

Nothing could have surprised Bree more. The mayor could have announced that she wanted to become a vampire, and it would've been more believable.

"Let me get this straight: you're telling me you want me to help you? … Professionally?"

Ilona nodded, not blinking. "I'm willing to stop monitoring your professional activities and drop all open cases the police have on you in exchange for your assistance. As well as cash payment, of course."

"Huh. Tempting. And what if I say no?" Bree asked. She wouldn't, but she was curious. She just didn't want the mayor knowing *how* tempting the offer was.

The mayor's gaze hardened. "Then I will turn you over to the FBI, and I can assure you that they'll be a lot less lenient with someone who has your rap sheet."

Okay, so the girl's got balls, Bree thought, not exactly upset over the threat. "You're going to blackmail me into helping you?"

The mayor nodded. "I will do whatever I have to do, Miss Carson. But it's in your best interest to take the first deal because I've heard paranormal prisons can be far worse than human ones."

Bree leaned back in her chair and said, "And if I decided to kill you right here and boogie out, who's going to stop me? I can make myself disappear, and make the city get a new mayor. Perhaps one who doesn't think we're all scum."

"You're a killer, Miss Carson," Ilona said. "And you've admitted that."

Bree shrugged. "I kill paranormals doing terrible things. And as for the humans … let's just say I clean up your cops' messes. The human justice system is fucked, and if my slaughtering a man who abused his wife and daughter makes me a bad person, I'll take the moniker."

Ilona actually had the grace to look ashamed at that. "Our system is far from perfect, but vigilante justice isn't the way, either."

"I gave up on morals and virtues decades ago," Bree replied. "Now, I am able to feed safely while protecting innocent, vulnerable people. I call it a win, and I sleep like the dead in the day. … Or Undead, if you prefer."

Ilona sighed heavily. "I don't have time for this. Will you help me or not?"

"You mean, 'will I willingly assist, or will you have to haul my ass to jail first?'" Bree corrected. "I can't just agree. I need to know what you want from me, exactly."

The mayor's mask slipped a little, for only a moment, and in that moment, Bree saw hopelessness, helplessness, and grief there on that usually impassive face.

"A nest of vampires kidnapped someone. I want you to rescue them," she explained. "By any means necessary. Including murder."

Okay, now this was really getting strange.

"Who did they kidnap to make you think *my* methods are your only hope?" she wondered. "You're the one with a vampire killing militia."

"It is not a militia. And I thought I had a penchant for over-exaggerating when I was your age," Ilona huffed.

If only you knew I'm more than twenty years your senior, Bree thought.

Ilona reached into her jacket pocket and pulled out a small, worn photograph. She slapped it down on the desk between them. It showed a little boy, maybe seven or eight, with two lower baby teeth missing as he smiled for a school picture.

"Henry. They took my son." And at that, Ilona's self-control broke, and a sob escaped from her lips, tears gathering in her dark eyes.

Bree silently berated herself. She should've known that. A woman like Ilona wouldn't have asked for her help if someone kidnapped the President. But a mother would do anything to save her child. Seeing the strong, resilient woman broken down and defeated like this was nearly heartbreaking for her to watch. And bastards of any species always went after the innocent and helpless, like children and mothers. It made her sick.

"Ilona," she said, the use of the woman's given name, causing her to look up. "I'm going to find your son. And God help anyone who gets in my way."

Once Ilona calmed down, Bree needed information. She had a checklist that would help her track down the child.

"I need to know where he was taken from, when, and anything you can possibly give me on the vampires who did take him," Bree said. "And how you even know it was vampires."

"I asked you here specifically. This precinct patrolled where I grew up, and the captain is an old friend. We can speak freely here without anyone raising the alarm that the mayor is consulting with a known paranormal criminal," Ilona began, leading Bree down the hall to a slightly more comfortable room. Decently lit, with a rickety table and chairs, some files spread out on the table, and a pot of coffee that smelled rancid to Bree's senses.

"Sorry, they don't keep blood on hand," the mayor quipped as she sat down. "My son was at the park with a friend and his mother. They often play there at night without incident. He likes … likes to play in the fallen leaves." Her throat caught. "The vampires came out of the trees, about an hour after sunset. She caught a photograph as they were leaving, because she knew she'd need to identify the kidnappers."

Bree opened a file, and there were four vampires, three of whose faces she was unable to see. The fourth had the boy under his meaty arms like a football, and his face turned back to snarl at the camera, flashing his fangs and reddened eyes.

That was the problem with modern technology: vampires could be photographed on most smartphone cameras. Bree made sure to keep her face covered when she went on a job, just in case. She was usually fast enough so that a camera wouldn't be able to capture anything but a blur, but better to be safe than sorry.

When Bree saw the vampire in the photograph, she was thankful she was sitting, because her knees went weak. She knew this vampire. Oh yes, they went way back. He was a criminal, a monster. She wanted to kill him for thirty years.

"Miss Carson? Are you all right?" Ilona asked.

Bree shook herself to loosen up and said, "Yes. I just … I recognize the kidnapper. He's a known murderer in the vampiric circle. He needed to be hunted down long before he kidnapped your kid, that's for sure."

"But why target my kid?" Ilona cried, anger and sadness mixing in her voice. "I know why he'd target me — all you vampires hate me — but why drag my baby into this?"

"Because evil comes in all shapes and species," Bree replied. "Humans and vampires think alike in how to hurt people. They go for the ones we love first."

The human's eyes squinted. "You're speaking from experience."

"Let's just say not all vampires are as sweet as I am," Bree said dryly. "This guy's nest has evaded me for years. Do you have any information on where he is, where I could start looking?"

"Not much, I'm afraid. They've flown under everyone's radar," Ilona said. "There's a paper in there with what I could scrounge up."

The vampire was going under the name Gary Orville, and the city census claimed that he owned acres of property far outside the city, in the rural area that surrounded Rockford. Nothing else was listed that could be of any use. The address he gave within Chicago was an abandoned building.

"What's out there at the address he gave the city? The one in Butt-Fuck Egypt?" Bree asked.

"I went on Google Maps. It's nothing. An old farmhouse," Ilona replied.

But that was just on the surface. For all her posturing and lawmaking, Ilona didn't know her enemies as well as she thought. Vampires weren't just superior in speed and strength. They were infinitely more intelligent than the average human. Not because of anything chemical, but out of necessity. They always needed to avoid the ever-evolving human population, and that would make them think harder and clearer.

"No, it's not nothing." She tapped the paper with a red-painted fingernail. "They're here, I'm sure of it." She checked the time. "It's too close to sunrise for me to go now. But I will as soon as the sun sets."

Ilona spluttered, "But — what if they kill him?"

"They wouldn't have taken him if they wanted him dead. They would have killed him then and there. It's you they want. And that means they'll wait for you to arrive. Little do they know, I'll be the one knocking on their doors. They'll probably send you a message, a threat. Don't worry about it. It will be just talk," Bree explained.

"Wait. If they'll be asleep soon, I should send human operatives there. Ones I can trust," Ilona said.

Bree had to force herself not to smack the woman across the face. "They're underground. They may not need to sleep. And even if they do, and your operatives wake them, chances are the vamps will eat them and send you the corpses via FedEx Express."

Ilona's face paled.

"Wait for me. You asked for my help, and you were right: I'm the only one stupid and reckless enough to agree," Bree said.

Ilona managed a small smile. "You do have a bad reputation."

"You say that like it's a bad thing."

Vampires can dream. No one really knew what happened in a vampire's coffin or tomb, but they could dream. Bree didn't know if they all could, or only ones who were human and then turned were able to. She'd happily give up dreaming forever if she could. Because vampires don't have dreams — they have nightmares.

Bree never dreamed of the people she killed. No, she was certain that every victim deserved it. She dreamed of her life before turning ... and the night she turned. The entire cul-de-sac torn apart, blood running in the gutters like rainwater, her friends and neighbors torn to pieces and fed upon before her eyes.

There had never been an attack like that by vampires in America, not since the vampiric revolt of the sixties in San Francisco. Four vampires caused the carnage, led by the vamp who now called himself Gary.

Bree could smell the iron on his breath, see his bloodstained face in front of hers, feel the bite as he turned her...

And she woke up, hitting her head on the coffin lid and letting out a scream that tore at her throat. It didn't take her long to realize that it was another dream of the man who murdered an entire neighborhood and ruined her life. She'd like to say that her new job from the mayor brought the dream on, but who was she kidding? She saw his face at least twice a week, always haunting her.

Bree hoped that killing him would end the nightmares once and for all.

She went about her usual waking routine but had to be quicker than usual: the vampires made the kidnapping of little Henry Warwick public, and people were starting to panic about a vampiric uprising.

Not on my watch, Bree thought. *Tonight's the night you stop being a disgrace to our species.*

She got on her bike and sped to the police station, where a worried Ilona met her outside. Instead of one of her pristine suits, the mayor now wore jeans, hiking boots, and a white leather jacket. Her face was streaked with mascara, but she no longer looked sad; she looked pissed. Bree thought it was an improvement.

"Did you see the news?" Ilona asked before Bree even turned off her bike's engine. "They said if I turn myself into them, they'll let him go."

Bree grimaced. "Tell me you don't believe that. They'll kill you both as quick as look at you."

"I'm desperate, not dumb, Miss Carson," the mayor scoffed. "Here." She held out a small leather attaché case. "Your payment is inside, along with some weaponry we've developed."

Bree cocked an eyebrow and asked, "Including the holy water bullets your security threatened to shoot me full of?"

"Yes." No embarrassment, no hesitation. Bree thought that if Ilona didn't have such a bee up her ass about paranormal creatures, she'd get along well with her. "Along with knives we soaked in holy water for two weeks, so they absorbed the liquid a little. I advise you to keep those gloves on when you use them."

"I prefer to kill with my own powers," Bree reminded her.

"And I have no problem with that tonight. But these will help you wound them, so you can kill them by fang … or claw," Ilona said, her eyes glancing down at Bree's black-gloved hands. Bree knew she sliced many throats and torsos with her vampiric claws, left many corpses that way for the police to find and the mayor to catalog.

She took the case and glanced inside. There was certainly quite a bit of cash inside. Considering this was technically a rescue mission and not an assassination, it was almost too much. There were also four blades and two guns. She removed the weapons and began to hide them about her person, secured so they wouldn't fall out as she rode to the farm, but easy enough to reach quickly.

She then handed the case with the money back to the mayor. "It's certainly nice to know my services are worth this much to you, but that's not the payment I want."

"Then what do you want? I'm already giving you legal immunity," Ilona said, exasperated. "This is no time for a price negotiation! My son is — "

"Going to be fine," Bree interrupted. "What I want from you is your time, Ilona. I want you to sit down with me and let me teach you … let me show you that most paranormals are actually good. I want to try to change your mind about us. Fair?"

Ilona nodded. "I suppose it's only fair to at least lend you an ear."

"Good. That's settled. I'll return with Henry, I promise," Bree said. She knew she had no logical reason to think she'd get away from her Sire and his nest with the boy alive, but she didn't want to disappoint Ilona. She didn't want to leave the woman with worrisome, uncertain words. No mother deserved that at a time like this.

"You mean *we* will," Ilona said.

Bree had already been ready to get back on her motorcycle. She whipped her head around and said, "Excuse me?"

"I'm coming with you."

She let out a noise that was somewhere between a scoff and a laugh. "Are you nuts? You'd never survive! No, no way. I forbid it."

Ilona scoffed this time. "*Forbid* it? I'm an adult and can make my own choices. And my choice is that I want to come. I have to come. I took self-defense. I'm great with a gun. You won't stop me. It's easier — and faster — if you just let me get on the back of that thing with you."

Bree was somewhere between shocked and admiring. The woman was brave. Or stupid. Or both. "And if I turned into a bat and flew away?"

"I'll drive there myself. You're not going to stop me, Miss Carson," Ilona said.

Bree sighed. *She sounds like a petulant teenager.* "I don't know if I can protect you and save Henry. As much as I hate to say this, if you come, you're on your own."

Ilona's eyes darkened. "I've been alone my whole life and have survived admirably until now. I don't see why tonight is any different."

"You know what? Fine. Your kid. Your choice. Take this." Bree held out her helmet. She didn't actually need one, but wore it so some do-gooder cop didn't stop her "for her own safety" and possibly recognize the mercenary for what she actually was and arrest her.

This is a terrible idea, her conscience told her. *You have to protect Ilona, not take her into a vampire nest! This was a trap for her, you know.*

Bree waved her conscience away. The woman was stubborn and determined. Short of knocking her out, there was no way to prevent her from going. Bree hoped that she was as good a shot as she claimed to be. It increased her chances of survival.

The ride up to the farm was fast and uneventful. Once you left Chicago, the rural suburbs didn't hold much interest. Either it was fields, farms, or strip malls with the same generic stores and restaurants. When the wind hit, Bree could smell cow shit. It reminded her why she chose to live in the city. Garbage and smog were better than this.

When her GPS told her they were about half a mile down from the vampire nest, she stopped the bike and told Ilona to dismount.

"Why?" she asked.

"Because if I bring this thing any closer, they'll hear it. I highly doubt they get much traffic out here on the country roads. Especially not Harleys." Bree walked the bike to a ditch and laid it on its side, proceeding to cover it up with loose hay. It would be dirty, but hopefully intact when they got back.

She went back to Ilona and said, "Get your gun ready. We don't know what we're walking into." Despite her misgivings about using human weapons, she drew hers as well. They began to walk along the dirt road, Bree using her senses to spot any kind of life. It was pitch black out there, and if not for the three-quarter moon, she was certain that Ilona would have been virtually blinded by the night.

"Is it normal to be this scared?" Ilona whispered.

"Yes, especially for you, considering what you have to lose," she whispered back.

Ilona stopped her, placing her hand on Bree's shoulder. "Listen to me, I need you to promise that, if it comes down to it, you'll leave me and rescue Henry. Please, don't let anything happen to him."

A noble sacrifice, and Bree knew she meant it, too. Swallowing what she *really* wanted to say, she replied, "I promise."

They continued walking, and the large, ramshackle farmhouse came into view, an ugly black silhouette against the impressive night sky. Bree's heart was in her throat. Not only were two mortal lives in her hands, she was also about to face her Sire for the first time, and she wasn't sure she could defeat him.

They stepped onto the dying grass, and their boots crunched it. They couldn't help it, and Bree hoped that the vamps' hearing wasn't that great if they were really underground as she thought.

Her senses were alert, and she thought she heard a creak. She put her hand out to stop Ilona's movements and said, "*Shhh.*" She stepped back, and yep, something creaked underfoot. She backed up two more steps and bent down to see what it was. That was when she felt a sharp pain in the back of her head, and all went black. The last thing she heard was Ilona's terrified scream.

Someone was playing a snare drum, loudly and repeatedly. It took a second for Bree to realize that the pounding was in her head. She opened her eyes, afraid of what she would see as her memories rushed back to her from before she'd been knocked out.

She was on a hard floor made of packed dirt. The door was in front of her, and it looked like sheet metal. A window with bars was set about three-fourths of the way up, about face-height. To her relief, Ilona was next to her, alive.

They weren't dead yet. That had to be a good thing.

"Hey, are you okay?" Ilona asked, seeing she was awake.

"Yeah, I just have Tommy Lee taking up residence inside my skull," Bree muttered, sitting up and dusting herself off. "What about you?"

Ilona nodded. "They didn't even knock me out. I guess they thought I wasn't a threat. And I wasn't: the vampire overpowered me before I could get a shot off. He left our weapons, though. That's good."

Bree nodded, wondering what the Hell they wanted. They could've killed them all and didn't. Did they really want Ilona tortured so much? What did they have planned? Too many questions, not enough time.

"Did you see where they took us?" she asked.

Ilona nodded. "The thing that creaked under us? It was a metal door. This is either an entrance to their crypt or a dungeon. Once he jumped down with us, it was a short walk here, and I couldn't see anything else beyond... This is why I have a problem with monsters, you know. Shit like this."

Bree smirked. "There are just as many psychotic humans as there are vampires, but you don't see the good vamps forming task forces to hunt you down. Besides, some vampires were turned, not born."

"Isn't that worse? To choose to drink blood and be immortal?" Ilona asked.

Not if you didn't have a choice, Bree thought, but didn't say. "Not always."

They were silent for a moment, each staring at the door before them.

"Do you know why I formed the Anti-Paranormal Task Force? Do you know my story?" Ilona asked after a while.

Bree did, but she wanted to hear the mayor tell it. "No."

Ilona straightened her back and appeared to psych herself up mentally to tell the tale.

"I was found in a house with my dead parents by police when I was six months old. I was the only living thing around, according to the cop who rescued me, once I was old enough to ask. I had blood on me. One of my parents', according to police reports.

"I was raised by nuns in a Catholic orphanage. Because, apparently, my birth parents had Catholic items in the house. I grew up alone, treated like shit by those hooded old biddies, knowing that monsters ate my parents. I vowed as a teenager that I'd never let anyone grow up like I did. Knowing I had the chance to make a difference was the only thing that kept me from killing myself as a young woman."

Ilona's face was impassive, and again Bree admired her strength.

"Naturally, I wanted to be in a position of power. To take my revenge and save people all at the same time," she continued. "I was angry as a teen, and that anger carried into my adult life. It's why my husband ran off. He thought I was unstable. Huh. If I was that unstable, why'd he leave our son, too? Anyway … now you know."

Bree was silent. There were a dozen things she wanted to say but couldn't form the words. Finally, she said, "I'm sorry about that. That you were suicidal, that your life was upended before it even had a chance to begin."

Ilona gave a weak smile. "I sense a 'but' coming."

"*But*," Bree said with emphasis, "what one or two or however many vampires did doesn't mean 'all vampires.' Some of us value human life."

Ilona was silent.

"Look, we all know that not all paranormals are good. But you humans aren't so great, either. Good and bad exist everywhere, in everyone. You can't let one or two or even ten assholes spoil your outlook on everyone. It's a big world, and bad people and bad creatures are around every corner. But they're outnumbered by the good, I promise you that." She placed her hand on Ilona's, and the mayor jumped, startled. Bree hadn't had blood in a few hours, so she was as cold as a corpse.

Ilona looked over at her, with eyes as dark as her own, and said, "How can you be so sure of good in the world?"

Bree smiled. "There are people like you in it. People who fight to protect others with everything they've got. You're disillusioned. And I'm sorry for that."

Ilona smiled uneasily. "You have nothing to be sorry for … unless you killed my parents?"

"Um, no. Thanks for that vote of confidence, though," Bree said, standing up gingerly. She was still sore, but the pounding in her head stopped thanks to the healing speed of vampires. Cracking her neck, she said, "Did he lock us in, or are the doors automatically locked?"

"I don't know — I was too scared to pay attention," Ilona admitted.

"Okay, let's see here…" Bree picked many locks in her career, and quite a few lately were electronic. However, she usually broke into them from the outside, not the inside. This was going to be interesting.

It was sealed into the doorjamb, so there was no space to even try to pry it open. And despite her strength, it was far too heavy to break through. Even if she could break the bars, the hole was too small for either of them to slither through.

"If there aren't cameras outside the door — I don't see any in here — I can get out and hack the lock much easier from the outside," Bree said.

"How can anyone over the age of ten fit through there?" Ilona asked.

Bree winked as she proceeded to use her vampire strength to tear the four little metal bars from the window with ease. "Don't forget what I am just yet, Ilona." She took a breath and closed her eyes. Unlike most of the vampire mythos, vamps can't turn into wolves or smoke or run exceptionally fast for long periods of time. But they can turn into bats. They're the only creature that crosses over from demonic to shapeshifter.

Bree hated turning into a bat. Especially for a short period of time. It fucked with her eyesight, hearing, and equilibrium. But if they wanted to get out of there, she had to suck it up. Closing her eyes, she reached deep inside her soul for the bat that resided there, calling it up to the surface. Unlike with werewolves, shape-shifting didn't physically hurt vampires. It was more like a smaller center of gravity, a change in sight and hearing, but no pain.

Ilona gasped as she transformed, hitting her ears with her new echolocation. Quickly, Bree glided out the small hole and immediately changed back into her human form. Shaking her head twice to get her senses back into gear, she bent down before the electronic lock.

"Now that's what I was looking for," she muttered, looking at the keypad. Almost all electronic locks can be overridden with an external key. Bree happened to have a skeleton version of the override key, thanks to a technician she glamoured a couple years back. She scanned the keycard, and the numbers grid lit up like she won big at a Vegas casino, and there was an audible clicking sound. Then the sound of air whooshing and the door was open, much to Ilona's surprise.

The mayor looked like she'd seen a ghost, dark eyes wide and unblinking.

"What?" Bree asked. "Never seen a skeleton key before?"

The mayor scoffed. "No, what I've never seen is someone turn into a fucking bat before my eyes!" In her shock, her city accent came out, replacing the artificial clipped tone she typically used. Bree liked the accent much better.

"Oh, that. Well, come on. There's a tunnel this way, and I can bet anything they didn't expect us to get out this soon." She didn't want to talk about her powers right then. The way Ilona was looking at her wasn't like she was a monster — that Bree was used to — but more as though she was a circus sideshow.

It was another reason why Bree chose to drive a motorcycle rather than fly: she never felt more like a freak than when she was transforming. The motorcycle was a connection to her former humanity, in a way.

She checked her pockets, surprised that, though her gun was gone, the vamps didn't take her knives. Then she remembered why Ilona told her to keep her gloves on: the holy water. The vampires couldn't touch the blades, or they'd be burned. Good. That was one thing in their favor on this crazy night.

The tunnel was lit every few steps with an electronic light that looked to be fed by sunlight from above. Bree calculated that they couldn't be more than ten feet below ground. Where the oxygen came from was a mystery, but one she didn't care much about as long as Ilona wasn't hindered at all.

The vampires were careful when creating this underground hide-away, and Bree admired their ingenuity. And then she wondered how many vampires actually lived in this nest. Was it only the same four who attacked her neighborhood, or did more join their ranks? And if there were more, could she and one human hope to defeat them all?

She didn't want to think about the possibility of failure. She didn't become the most sought-after mercenary by doubting herself. She bit and clawed her way to the top, taking down anyone who dared challenge her. It was that fighter, the woman who managed to go on living even after everything was forcibly taken from her, that she needed to be. Because now three lives hung in the balance, not just one.

The tunnel continued for a quarter-mile before breaking off into five different passageways. Four led deeper into the earth, and one led upwards. Bree was pretty sure it led inside the farmhouse.

"Which way?" Ilona whispered. "We can't cover them all before sunrise."

Bree held up a hand to silence her and closed her eyes, listening deeply. The earth hindered her hearing, but she got lucky: a thump, like a body being dropped, came from above. She turned toward Ilona and pointed upwards. "Knife ready," she whispered. There were metal rungs in the dirt for people to climb up. Bree took a breath and began to climb, hearing more and more noises every few inches, she moved upwards. Four male voices and one was pissed off.

" … can't keep a child contained … better off with werewolves…"

"Lemme go!"

That. That had to be Henry Warwick, and if he was strong enough to fight, it was a good thing. It meant he was unharmed. Bree took a breath. She'd been on hundreds of missions, but none had ever been as important as this one. Mainly because she never had to ensure anyone remain alive, just get dead.

If she screwed up, she'd never be able to live with herself.

I couldn't protect anyone that night, but I swear I'm going to do right by everyone this time, she thought. Giving a nod to Ilona, whose face was as pale as cottage cheese, Bree threw the cover for the tunnel up over her head, causing murky light to flood down on them. Using her free hand, she pulled herself up and leapt out of the tunnel, into full view of the vampires.

Between the kid struggling and her sudden appearance, the vampires looked a little shell-shocked, which was perfect for her. She wished she still had her gun, that could've taken care of two of them right off the bat. As it was, she threw one of the knives, hitting the closest vampire in the chest, sending the holy water through his bloodstream.

The vamp staggered, tried pulling the blade from his chest, and yelped as the holy water burned his hand. He fell, the holy water doing its job quickly as he began to decay from the inside out. One down. Three to go.

But where was the fourth vampire? Gary was nowhere to be seen, and that wasn't good. Henry, too, was suddenly MIA. Tendrils of concern wove their way around Bree's heart, and she fought them off. Worrying would only get her killed.

The other two vamps launched themselves at her, and she ducked, letting them both leap over her head, on the other side of the hidden tunnel's entrance. The smaller of the two was swifter, and he jumped again. Bree caught him, and they grappled, trying to find purchase to injure each other.

He turned Bree back around, trying to flip her, but that was his mistake. She went with him, reaching into her coat for another knife and slit his throat while she was still in midair. Dark, Undead blood spurted from his jugular as he choked. Bree landed and stabbed him again, this time from behind, spearing his heart from the back. She twisted the blade, bringing back another torrent of blood with her.

The vamp fell to the dirty ground, bleeding out and already decaying.

Bree looked for the third one, and when she found him, she felt her heart stop.

In her haste to get the vamps before they could make their moves, she forgot that she was technically supposed to be fighting with someone.

The third vamp had Ilona in a chokehold, his claws mere centimeters from her throat. She was helpless against one so strong, and one wrong move could get her decapitated.

"Let her go!" Bree commanded, holding her blade in one hand, letting the other hand's claws extend.

"Sorry, sweetheart, no can do."

Bree whirled to the left, from where the voice had come. That dark, familiar, evil voice.

Gary (what a normal name for a bloodsucking demon) was standing off to the side, holding little Henry the same way the other vamp was holding Ilona. Henry was dirty and looked terrified, but unharmed. That was good. This current predicament, however, wasn't so good for Bree. She knew, realistically, she'd only have time to save one of them, and that meant she had to let Ilona die.

"Briana, it has been such a long time," Gary continued. "You deserted the nest."

"What?" Ilona shouted in shock. "You were *with* them?"

Bree hated to see the doubt settling on the mayor's face. Turning to Gary, she said, "You know I was never part of your nest. I *never* wanted this! You destroyed my life, it was only fair I double-crossed your pathetic ass."

He gestured toward his injured eye. "After ensuring I'd never forget you. And I haven't. I wanted you the moment I saw you, and I will have you. You're not running away this time."

Realization dawned on Bree, and she said, "This wasn't a trap for Ilona. It was a trap for *me*."

"Aren't we the smart one?" Gary scoffed. "You disappeared after nearly tearing my face off. And even with your … illustrious reputation … I still had no way to find you. Until this one won the mayoral race. That brought everything together, all falling into place perfectly."

It was Ilona's turn to scoff. "You think she'll trade my life for hers? I hired her, you Undead Neanderthal! She's not here out of the goodness of her heart. She doesn't give a damn what happens to me as long as she gets to kill you."

Ouch, Bree thought. *That hurt, but I guess that's what a bad reputation gets me: a bad reputation.*

Gary's good eye glowed a gleeful, terrible red. "You don't know, do you?"

Instead of taking the bait, Ilona said, "All I need to know is that you're a psycho, and I can't wait to see you dead."

Gary chuckled. "You might look like your father, but you've just as bad an attitude as your mother."

As expected, that got her attention.

"What? You knew my parents?"

"'Knew' might not be the right word. But I can still remember the taste of your father's blood as the life flickered from his eyes," Gary replied.

Ilona screamed at him, looking like the angry teenager she claimed she once was, and tried to lunge forward. The vampire tightened his hold on her, and she whimpered as his claws pressed into the skin of her throat. A droplet of scarlet blood ran down one of them.

"Quit fucking around, Gary," Bree said. "Let them go. If it was me you wanted, then your plan was successful. The Warwicks aren't your pawns anymore. You've put the entire family through enough the past three decades."

Her fangs itched in her gums, and she let them show, afraid to do more than talk. The vampire inside of her wanted blood, and blood it would have. But first, she needed to get Ilona and Henry out of there. And that couldn't happen unless she convinced Gary. He tried this tactic on her once before, sparing a human life to get her to join his nest. Since she double-crossed him once, she had a funny feeling he wasn't planning on making another deal with her.

"If your problem is with me, let them go, and let's settle this like the monsters we are," she said. "You and this one here outnumber me already. Just the way you like it." The words kept coming, despite her trying to reign them in. She always did have a mouth that got her in trouble. "You're a coward, killing helpless humans just because you can. But never alone. Oh no, you needed goons to back you up. Because you never got anything through brute strength, you got it by intimidation, by inciting fear in others. You're nothing but a sharp-toothed supervillain: all talk and no balls."

His good eye narrowed at her, and his grip on the boy tightened. Henry whimpered, and Bree could see Ilona's face contort in sharing his pain.

"Please, just let them go," she said, hating to beg but not wanting them to be hurt because of her, either.

"You are under the misapprehension that you are in any position to give me orders or ask favors of me," Gary said, his voice so low it was almost a growl. "I brought them both here for one reason, to hurt you. And that's precisely what I intend to do before I finally take my revenge on you for shunning my nest and insulting my honor as a vampire."

"You have no honor," Bree shot back. "You're a common killer, nothing more. People like you give vampires a bad name."

"Vamps like you are who I'm trying to eradicate from my city," Ilona added, seeming to regain her courage a little.

Gary glared at her. "Aren't you a brave one? And what about Briana, who has a body count bigger than mine behind her? Is she on your kill list, too? Or are you loath to kill blood? … Oh, I forgot: she never told you."

"Told me what? Damn it, someone speak straight around here and *let us go!*" Ilona cried.

Gary smiled, long fangs flashing in the moonlight streaming through the broken slats in the ceiling. "All right, if she won't speak straight, as you say, I will. You're not an orphan. I might have killed your father, but your mother's alive … or should I say she's Undead?"

There was a beat of total, complete silence. The autumn crickets in the high grass outside were the loudest things to be heard for miles.

The mayor looked over at Bree, not needing anyone to connect the dots for her, and then she did something Bree thought only happened in old movies: she fainted, leaving herself even more vulnerable to the monster who had her in his clutches.

December 2nd, 1985

"Lookit her," said Jamie Warwick, looking down at his one-month-old baby daughter, Ilona, who was sleeping on the kitchen counter in her bassinet, wearing a onesie with a motorcycle on it. "I'll never believe how perfect she is." He ran a hand through her black curls, which looked just like his, careful not to disturb her: she was finally asleep after an hour of trying.

His wife of one year, Briana Warwick, née Carson, smiled at him from across the kitchen island. They were a young couple, just twenty-two and twenty-four, respectively, and their marriage hadn't exactly been given everyone's blessing. Bree was a record store manager, and Jamie was a budding rock star when they met. They married six months later, having fallen madly in love, and three months after that, they found out they were going to have a baby.

And now, when little Ilona Warwick was screaming half the night, and Jamie was exhausted when he went to the Harley Davidson dealership where he worked, and Bree was lucky to get three hours of sleep a day, they were still just as madly in love as when they first met. Jamie loved Bree's give-'em-Hell attitude, and Bree loved his poetic soul.

Everything was perfect. But in the real world, perfection was an illusion that habitually got torn to shreds by reality.

Bree was reading a book at the counter when there was a shriek in the distance.

"What the Hell was that?" she asked, shutting her book and going to try and peek out the windows.

"Don't worry about it," Jamie told her. "Some housewife might've seen a mouse."

"My mother used to freak if she saw a mouse. She didn't break the fucking sound barrier," Bree replied. Always one with great instincts, she knew there was something wrong.

Their cul-de-sac was small, recently built for new families and retirees sick of the city. There were nine houses on the street, but only four were occupied at the time. Everything still smelled and looked brand new, like a Christmas card. A horror movie junkie, she knew that the most horrific scenes usually took place in nice little neighborhoods like theirs.

She told Jamie, "Watch the baby, and get ready to call nine-one-one."

"Where are you going?" he asked.

"To get my gun, where do you think?" Bree's father was a retired city cop, and he taught his daughter self-defense and marksmanship when she was a teenager. As soon as they bought a house, Bree bought a gun. While not a fan of them on their own, she knew one was necessary when you lived in a crazy world like they did.

"Oh, fuck, come on, Bree. I — "

Another yell rang out. This one sounded like a man being strangled.

"You'll do what you're told," she said to him, gesturing to the phone mounted on the kitchen wall. She raced upstairs, the bad feeling in her chest intensifying. There was something wrong, and she was afraid to find out what.

The gun was in a locked box on top of the closet. She grabbed her desk chair and had to stand on it to reach the damn thing, losing precious time. If she hadn't been afraid of her daughter accidentally getting her hands on it somehow, she would've left it in a much easier place to reach in case of an emergency.

There was the sound of glass cracking and shattering, much closer than the screams had been. Was it here? She couldn't tell. They didn't seem to rouse Ilona, so maybe not. Her hands trembled as she tried to load the gun, nerves getting the better of her.

There was a thump, one she knew came from outside. Their bedroom faced the street, and she went to peer behind the red curtains to see what it might be.

At first, she thought that the people two doors down had their nutcracker statue fall, but then she realized that the nutcracker was still standing, its head covered in snow. In front of it, lying with his head twisted at a one-eighty angle, was their neighbor. Bright red blood dotted the snow leading up to his body.

Bree covered her mouth to hold back a scream when she saw movement from another house. The front door flew open, and the woman that lived there ran out, barefoot, in her nightgown. It was only thirty-four degrees.

Behind her came what looked like a man, but couldn't have been a man. His eyes were glowing bright red like fire, and he had long canines, looking more like a tiger than a human. He was behind her in the blink of an eye, almost as if he hadn't moved at all.

Bree was in shock as she watched him turn her neighbor around to face him and bit into her neck with those long fangs. She was unable to move or even breathe as she watched what happened in what felt like slow motion. Her neighbor had time to scream before the scream died in her throat. The man was nuzzling at her neck like a lover, and crimson trails of blood began to leak where the man couldn't drink fast enough, falling into the snow and staining it ever so lightly. It looked like abstract art.

The man pulled away from the woman, his mouth and chin covered in sticky blood. With ease, he placed his hands on either side of the woman's neck and twisted her head around. Her eyes bulged, and then she was dead, tossed away into the snow like garbage.

Bree was able to do quick math. If two out of four houses had already been hit, then only one remained before they got to theirs'. There might just be enough time to escape. Then her eyes caught movement in the house right next door. An elderly couple lived there, and she saw the man's head smashed against the glass, creating a spiderweb of cracks before it became splattered with an arterial spray of blood.

If someone else was already attacking that house, then…

She looked for the man who attacked the woman, and the street was empty.

Fuck, she thought, moving away from the window. Her knees felt like jelly, but she needed to hold it together. She had a daughter to think about. Just as she turned to go downstairs, there was a loud bang, and Jamie began to yell, his words unintelligible.

But his scream rang out clearly. Bree was frozen with fear until Ilona started to wail. That knocked her into action, and she raced down the stairs, gun cocked and ready. Her heart pounded in her ears, and her every nerve ending trembled, but she was determined to save her family.

The carpet hid the sound of her footsteps, and she managed to get to the kitchen, but she was too late.

The man she'd seen in the street had broken into her house and had Jamie in his clutches. This close, sounds of sucking were loud over Jamie's blood-clogged groans of pain. The smell of iron permeated the air, and Bree had to hold back her bile.

Steeling every nerve she had, she entered the kitchen and brandished the gun.

"Put him down now, or I'll blow your fucking head off," she said.

The man's fiery eyes turned to her, but he kept drinking. If she didn't know better, she'd say he was amused.

"Are you deaf? Put my husband down!" she cried, hysterics tearing at the edges of her voice.

The man lowered Jamie, who was no longer moaning but twitching in his grasp. He was smiling, smiling with a face covered in her husband's blood.

"As you wish … Briana."

How does he know my name? she thought. Unable to do anything but watch in horror, the monster twisted her husband's neck the same way he had the woman's.

Bree saw Jamie's face contort before she was staring into his bulging, lifeless blue eyes. The man threw Jamie's body to the floor and stepped over it.

Now able to get a shot off, she fired three times in the man's abdomen, but that didn't even deter him. Blood dripped from the wounds, but only for a moment. They closed before he even crossed the kitchen to get to her.

Now he was face-to-face with her, at the counter. Ilona's crying died down, but she looked terrified, and now Bree couldn't even pass the man to get to her baby. Horror fan as she was, she knew what this guy was, and she also knew that she had no holy water or wooden stakes to kill him. She was next to die, and so was her baby, and there was absolutely nothing she could do to prevent it. She wanted to cry, but refused to give this bastard the satisfaction of seeing it.

"A gun, *hmm*? Cute. But you have impressed me," the man said, his voice smooth and cold. "You were the only one to fight back."

"I want you out of here. Get out of my house, and maybe I won't come after you in the future," Bree hissed, not sure where this courage was coming from. All she knew was that she needed to protect Ilona.

The vampire's eyes shifted over to where the baby sat on the countertop, eyes wide and fearful.

"Did you know that baby's blood is the purest of all?" he asked, smirking as though it was just an average fun fact on the cap of a Snapple bottle.

"Stay away from her!" Bree lashed out and went to hit the man with the butt of the gun, but he was quick.

Her wrist was in his grasp, and he squeezed, causing her to drop the gun and moan as she felt her bones being centimeters away from snapping.

"You want me to spare her? Huh? And what will you give me in return?" he asked.

"You already took my husband and my neighbors!" She tried to pull away, but it was useless. She despised being helpless and at someone else's mercy.

His smile widened. "True… But there is something else I want."

"I'll give you anything, just leave my baby the fuck alone!" Bree said, somewhere between angry and panicking. Her heart was beating a rapid staccato in her chest, and tears fell freely from her eyes, smearing her mascara.

"I promise. I will leave the child intact … if you come with me."

Her mouth dropped, and she was positive she was hearing things.

"You are just what my nest needs. There's a fire in your spirit, Briana. You'd be one of the most formidable vampires to walk the earth. Together we'd be unstoppable."

Bree was conflicted. Of course she'd never want to be a vampire, a monster. But if she said no, he'd kill Ilona. It was the definition of being caught between a rock and a hard place.

"You must choose now … or *I* will make the choice for you," he said. "Turn, or watch her die."

Bree hung her head, more tears falling. As she did so, he released her wrist from his grasp, knowing he'd won. "What will happen? How long does this take? How do I know you won't hurt her while I'm turning?"

"I cannot … because you need me to turn. I take your blood, replace it with some of my own. And it is as simple as that, Briana. So glad you see things my way." He smiled again, and she thought that no smile should instill such fear and dread in someone.

"Fine. Turn me … and if you even make a single move toward her afterward, no shadowy corner of the world can hide you from my wrath," Bree promised.

The vampire laughed. "And that, my dear, is precisely why I want you on my side. Your courage is unmatched. I have seen grown men on a war-torn battlefield fall to their knees and cry before my kind. But not you. Your name will be legendary amongst every paranormal in existence."

He grabbed her by the back of her head, her long hair tangling in his fingers. He pulled her head back, exposing her neck.

Bree squeezed her eyes shut, unable to stop the tears from coming. Girls are taught from a young age about predators, people who will violate them in a myriad of horrifying ways. But nothing prepared her for the way she felt as she stood there while his needlepoint fangs sank into her skin, as he took her blood from her veins, stealing her life.

She felt the world go into a grayish haze, becoming dizzy and incoherent. She was vaguely aware of something cold and wet being placed at her lips, liquid fire, sneaking down her throat and filling her veins with some type of cold burn. It was electrifying. It was invigorating. It was terrifying. It was death and life and rebirth. And she still didn't want it.

Her eyes snapped open, still tasting cold iron on her lips and in her throat. The kitchen lights were so bright … too bright. Everything was too much. The smells of the kitchen, the sound of the radio that had been left on next door, the cars on the main street a block away, everything was hitting her anew.

Everything including her emotions.

Her eyes fell on the vampire — whose name she still didn't know. He was smiling, appearing proud of his creation.

"How do you feel, Briana?" he asked her. The nerve. He had the fucking nerve to ask her that, as if he didn't ruin her life with his ultimatum, as if he hadn't threatened to *eat* her *daughter*.

"You really want to know?" she asked, her own voice sounding deeper and clearer. Rage filled her heart as she stared at his stupid, smiling, evil face. She felt sharp pains in her hands and gums. Fangs sprouted, accidentally biting into her lower lip and making more blood appear at her mouth. She looked down to see what ailed her hands. Her nails darkened; they looked blackened and dead. As she stared, they began to grow and hook into claws at the ends, each nail now over six inches long.

Instinct took over, and she launched herself forward at an inhuman speed. The vamp's eyes widened as she reached out with one of her claws. The nails crossed his beautiful face, tearing skin and drawing blood. Four long gashes crossed his temple, nose, and left eye.

He clapped his hand to his wounded eye, which didn't seem to be healing, and began to back away. She didn't want that to happen and jumped forward again; this time, her claws caught his chest, tearing through the fabric of his jacket and shirt, shredding the skin.

He called out, but no one answered. His nest already left after having drunk their fill, or so it seemed. He and Bree were alone, and it looked as though he wasn't healing from her attack as quickly as he healed from the gunshot wounds.

The vamp avoided being cut again and leapt into the air. Mid-leap, Bree stopped cold as his form began to change shape and contort. He seemed to … shrink. Only a moment later, the man was gone, and a large black bat hovered in the air in his place. It flew through the broken doorway, and then it was gone.

Bree's adrenaline began to fade from her body, and her fangs retracted, as did her claws, as she sank to her knees in the middle of the floor and started to cry from fear and rage and despair.

Then Ilona began to cry.

She leapt up from the floor and dashed to her daughter, who

brightened at the sight of her mother. Bree's heart broke, because while she saved Ilona's life, there was no way she could raise the child. Not as she was now. She was spoiled, evil. A monster. And she didn't deserve to even look at the baby, let alone hold her and raise her.

"Oh, Ilona…" she gasped out, tears falling anew. "Oh, my baby. I'm so sorry. But I promise you, you're going to be safe. Safe from me, and from monsters like him." She walked to the phone and dialed nine-one-one, said there had been a break-in, and hung up without giving anything more than the address.

She needed to leave. She needed to do the last thing that would protect her daughter.

Bree ran a hand through Ilona's soft curls, kissing her baby one last time as the tears seemed as though they'd never stop. "I love you, Ilona. This is what's best for you. Better you never know what I've become."

Bree held back her own tears as that horrible memory resurfaced in her mind. It felt like her heart was breaking once more, that her turning and abandoning Ilona was yesterday instead of thirty-two years ago.

And Ilona was in just as much danger now than she was back then, and that was what Bree needed to focus on.

Once she ran off, cleaning out her bank accounts and hiding out in the heart of the city, she began to form a new way to live. The world as she knew it had ended for her, and she needed to find her place in it once again. At one time, it was as a mother and a wife. That world came crashing down on her far too soon, and she felt lost. She needed purpose.

Eventually, she found other creatures, witches and vampires, and shifters. She was led to the paranormal club and taught the ways of her new world. She learned that not all paranormals were like the ones that ruined her life, and she didn't have to choose darkness if she didn't want to. But she was warned: vampires were natural-born predators. She would need to kill to survive.

It was then she realized she could make a difference again, be someone in this community. While she was great with weaponry and general combat, it never entered her mind to be paid for murder, but it was possible, especially now.

She entrenched herself in her new life for decades, until she went to the club one night to find most of the regulars there in an uproar. A TV was on, showing political stats.

"What's happening?" she asked the bartender.

"The new candidate for mayor is some young bitch who wants us all collared and locked up or outright killed!" he cried. "Says vampires killed her parents, boo-fucking-hoo. Like that makes us all fair game?"

Bree looked up at the screen and saw a beautiful woman speaking, with olive skin and long, smooth black ringlets, clad in a neat — but boring — black pantsuit. The headline read: "ILONA WARWICK VAMPIRE SLAYER."

Seeing that, the vampiress dropped her glass, splattering lukewarm blood all over the floor and her new leather boots. She barely noticed, stunned at the woman she was looking at. She'd know her even without her name plastered all over the screen. Those curls, that skin, and those eyes ... she knew that was her daughter, even if her name was not splashed across the TV screen.

It was her fault Ilona thought the way she did about paranormals, but what could Bree do? She made the decision that would allow her child to grow up happy, healthy, and unscathed. Gary did the rest. He ruined everything with that one ultimatum.

And now ... now the secret was out, and her daughter was unconscious in the clutches of one vamp, while her grandson was held captive by another.

This can't be happening, she thought. *I can't lose my daughter again.* Her eyes darted from the vamp she didn't know to Gary, who was grinning like the fucking Cheshire Cat.

"Killing them only ensures your death," she said to her Sire. "I'm willing to walk out of here, leaving you both intact, as long as they're left alive."

He laughed again, and Henry winced at the sound. "You still don't get it, do you? I don't want you walking out of here. I want to hear you scream and cry as I force you to watch as your precious family dies right before your eyes … slowly and painfully. And then I'll kill you, ending this entire, godforsaken bloodline. It's just too bad this one fainted before the fun could begin." He turned to the vamp holding Ilona and said, "Now."

Bree had to think quicker than the vampires acted. She had one blade and could move across the barn fairly quickly. Henry was closer to her by about four feet, which helped make her decision.

She threw the blade across the room, just as the other vamp was about to tear into Ilona's throat. The blade hit the vamp between the eyes, sticking out like a macabre unicorn, and the claws fell from her throat to her stomach. To a vampire, the sound they made as they tore into the fabric of her clothes and through her skin was vile: a tearing noise, and then wet squelching as the bloody flesh was severed.

The vamp fell dead. Ilona also fell to the ground, bleeding profusely. But Bree couldn't worry about her. Henry was more vulnerable than she was right then. The moment she tossed the blade, she leapt over to Gary, claws extended.

In order to move away from her attack, Gary had to push Henry away from him. The boy fell to the floor, screaming for his mother, while Bree did what she should have done decades ago. She clashed claws with Gary, whose one eye was blazing with Hellfire.

Bree's mind was a blank slate of rage. All she wanted was Gary's blood on her hands and his body decaying in the hay. She fought without her usual finesse and just went for it, wanting only to end his miserable existence.

"Did I hit a sore spot, Briana?" he asked as he deflected a blow, only to have her land a punch straight to his jaw, loosening it a bit.

He hit back, slicing gashes into her face. Warm blood soaked her cheek and neck, getting stuck in her long brown hair, but she ignored it. It was a flesh wound. She kicked out, her sharp heel hitting the soft spot on his stomach and sending him flying back a few steps. It gave her the momentum she needed as she dashed forward, kicking out again, this time at his legs. There was a sickening crack as his knee broke, white bone peeking through his slacks as he fell on his back. That would take a while to heal, even for a vampire.

Still, he fought. She had to admire his resilience. The son of a bitch wouldn't give up the ghost that easily. But Gary had one major flaw: he was confident to the point of being cocky. Bree steadily trained and fought for thirty years. Gary did nothing but terrorize a few humans before eating them.

His claws ripped into the meat of her upper arm, but her heavy leather jacket helped the wound not be as deep as it could have been. Despite the pain, Bree grabbed his wrist before he pulled away from her and pulled him closer.

In a move taught in self-defense classes around the world, she used his momentum against him and kneed him right where it hurt — immortal or not, any man is vulnerable there. He gasped weakly in pain, and she elbowed him in the chest. He flew back into the barn wall, and the wood splintered and cracked under his weight, but held.

Sorry for what poor little Henry now had to witness, Bree sprang forward, fangs exposed, and she sank them deep into Gary's throat.

He let out a yell of either pain or surprise, she wasn't sure, and then proceeded to attempt to get her off, but she held fast, draining his blood with every second that passed. She could feel her wounds healing with each swallow, her weakened strength returning to her limbs. Gary gasped, trying to fight but unable to shake the vampiress' fangs from his throat.

When he was sufficiently weakened, Bree finally stopped drinking, looking down at the once-powerful vampire who stole everything from her. She thought it would give her pleasure to see him small and broken, but it didn't. All she felt was a distant pity for a weak man, having gotten to his position in life via intimidation and force.

"How does it feel?" she asked, tears coming to her eyes. "How does it feel to have everything ripped away from you with one bite, you monster?"

His good eye was glazed over from pain and loss of blood, but he still managed to laugh, a low chuckle Bree only heard because she was a vampire. "I may die … but you have lost … everything once again."

She ignored his words and reached down with her claws, easily and quickly severing his head from his body. She stepped back, blood dripping from her hand, as she watched as his body rapidly began to decompose until he was nothing but a skeleton with clothes on. Nothing but a husk, a nightmare.

"It's over," she said and jumped at the sound of her own voice. She hadn't meant to say that aloud.

"Mom!"

Bree turned, her heart in her chest. In the few minutes it had taken her to kill Gary, she nearly forgot about Ilona. Henry's pained cry jogged her memory, and she turned to face her daughter.

Ilona was still unconscious, her skin an ashy gray color with deep hollows beneath her eyes. The hay she lay upon was soaked in blood; her wounds were so deep Bree could see muscle and tissue pulsing with each labored breath she took.

"Back away," she said to Henry.

"Is she going to be okay?" the boy asked tearfully.

Bree looked at him, really looked, and her heart broke. "I don't know," she replied. "I'm going to do my best to help her, okay?" Usually blood excited her, awakened her hunger. Now it was making her ill as she watched it leak from Ilona's wounds.

God, I don't know if You still hear prayers from people like me, but please, don't take my daughter. I did so much to save her when she was a baby, please don't take her now!

Her pulse was weak, and her skin was cold. She needed blood, but there was no time to call nine-one-one. As far in the boonies as they were, it would take too long, and Ilona would surely die. Bree took out her cell phone and handed it to the boy.

"Henry, listen to me. Call an ambulance, tell them we have someone injured. Do not say who your mother is." She told him the cross-streets of the farmhouse.

"But … that will take forever!" Henry whined. "Please, you gotta save my mom!"

"I will — I am. But she'll still need a hospital when I'm done." *And I hope that's all she needs, not a morgue.* The boy moved away, and she heard him talking to the operator in the distance. Vampire blood didn't only rejuvenate other vampires if ingested, a human could benefit greatly from it. The problem was, Ilona would need quite a bit, and that would alter her forever.

Would she accept life if she had to live with Undead blood in her veins for the rest of it? Or was she so wounded that she'd rather die? Did Bree want her daughter to live that way?

The answer was no, but she also couldn't be the reason Ilona died. With one hand's claws, she cut deeply into her other hand, letting her blood flow freely. She placed the bleeding hand over the open wounds, watching as her dark, Undead blood seeped into them, closing them ever so slowly. Letting her hand heal itself, she then bit into her wrist to get a thicker blood flow and placed her wrist to Ilona's mouth, letting a few mouthfuls drop down the woman's throat. Ilona moaned lightly, but still didn't waken.

Bree sat back on her haunches and sighed shakily, tears falling from her eyes once again. This was all she could do. It had to be enough to save her life.

"They're coming." Henry finished his call and handed her phone back to her. "Mom looks better. Is she gonna be okay now?"

Bree nodded. "I think so. Are you okay, Henry?" She looked at her grandson, taking in his similarities to her daughter and her deceased husband.

He shrugged. "I'm scared. I'm worried. I'm hungry, too."

Bree smiled and ruffled his hair. "I bet. The hospital's going to take care of you both now. You're safe, the vampires of this nest are all gone."

"You're a vampire," he said.

She nodded.

"So why are you helping Mom? She said all vampires are bad."

"Not all of us. Your mom's been hurt, that's all. But I promise you that I'm not one of the bad guys. And if you ever need me again, I will be there. I'll keep an eye on you and your mom forever."

His eyes lit up. "Forever? You mean it?"

Pulling him into a hug, she said, "Yes, I mean it." She closed her eyes and let herself feel his warmth, let it sink in that this was her blood, her descendant, and then released him. "I'll stay until the ambulance gets here, and then I gotta go."

"But Mom will want to see you, won't she?" Henry asked.

"Probably not, kid." Bree brushed Ilona's dirty curls from her face and kissed the top of her head before standing up. "You were very brave, you and your mom. You should be proud." She ruffled his dark hair.

In the distance, sirens wailed.

"I have to go. But I'll always be around if you're in trouble," she reminded Henry. She left the barn, going to retrieve her bike. During the hour-long ride home, she never once allowed herself to think. It wasn't until she parked her bike, entered her apartment, and sat down on her sofa that she collapsed on herself, drowning in her own tears.

Bree never took a full week off without doing a job, but she did after saving Ilona. She needed time to think, to let everything sink in. It was an emotional shock, and she supposed had she been human, it would have taken a worse toll on her psyche.

As it was, she was barely eating that week, mostly scouring the news to be sure that the mayor was all right. Ilona's mysterious disappearance was reported as a severe bout of the flu.

Bree had smirked at that and said, "Yeah, straight from Romania: the vampire flu." At least she knew her daughter was all right. That was the important thing.

After a week indoors, Bree went out to go to the bar, get some normalcy in her life again. The moment she put her hands on the bars of her bike, she heard people behind her. Whirling around, she was in a familiar position: face-to-barrel with a gun. She recognized the blue-suit who accompanied Ilona into the interrogation room nine days ago.

"Oh, what the fuck do you want now?"

"*He* doesn't want anything. All right, Brandon, stand down. If she were going to kill you, you'd be dead by now."

Ilona walked out of the shadows to face Bree. She looked perfectly healthy, no sign that she got torn to ribbons a week ago. Dressed informally, in jeans and a white leather jacket, she looked more like Bree than Bree wanted to admit.

The two women just stared at each other for a moment. Bree wanted to rush to hug the mayor, but wasn't sure how welcome it would be.

"Was he telling the truth? Gary?" Ilona asked, getting right to the point. "Are you really…?"

Bree nodded. "Yes, I am."

"Why the Hell did you send me to live with nuns if you were alive all this time?" Ilona cried, hurt tears gathering in her eyes. "All my life I thought I was alone. You left me alone!"

"What did you want me to do, Ilona?" Bree countered. "I was a newly turned vampire, and only chose to turn so that *you* could live! I couldn't very well take you with me. What if I hurt you? I had no control over my powers for months. Being alone was better than being dead. I knew you had a shot at a normal life without me. Little did I know you'd purposefully enmesh yourself in paranormal affairs."

Ilona smiled a little at that. "Answer one question for me, please. If you could have taken me with you as a baby … would you have?"

"In a heartbeat," Bree replied. She took a few steps closer. "Your father and I loved you with everything we had. I changed in many ways, but I have always loved you."

"The blood you gave me to heal me — yeah, Henry told me about that — it changed me. Just a little. I'm not … you didn't — "

"Turn you into a vampire?" Bree smirked. "No. You just have a few drops of blood. You'll be more aware and alert, see better, hear better. You'll want your steaks on the rare side. Probably live longer, too, but not by much."

She nodded, appearing to process everything. "I guess you saved my life again. Giving your blood both times to do it."

"And I'd do it again and again, for you and for Henry," Bree said.

Ilona nodded again, rocking back and forth in her stilettos. Her fingers tapped the side of her legs in a steady staccato. "I came because you requested something specific from me as payment for your services, saving my son. You asked for an ear to listen. I wanna listen. I made mistakes in banning all paranormals and hunting them down. I need guidance, and I would like that to come from you." She paused and blushed as a smile appeared on her face. "After all, what are mothers for?"

Bree's breath caught, and she tried not to let Ilona see the tears in her eyes. "Of course. I can't believe you want me around."

"How can I not? You gave up humanity for me. I can't imagine another person could do that, even for their kid. And besides, Henry thinks you're some sort of superhero. You should know … I've seen the dark side of vampires now, and it's not going to be easy for me to change my views. But I want to. I'm willing to let you guide me and teach me about the world … this world," Ilona said. She stepped closer, closing the gap between them, and held her hand out.

Bree took it and said, "It won't be easy, you're right. But it's going to be worth it."

FIN.

ABOUT LILY LUCHESI

Lily Luchesi is the USA Today bestselling and award-winning author of the Paranormal Detectives Series.

Her young adult Coven Series has successfully topped Amazon's Hot New Releases list consecutively.

She is also the co-owner of Partners in Crime Book Services, where she offers a myriad of services alongside her business partner Annie Smith, including editing.

She was born in Chicago, Illinois, where many of her stories are set. Ever since she was a toddler, her mother noticed her tendency for being interested in all things "dark". At two she became infatuated with vampires and ghosts, and that infatuation turned into a lifestyle. She is also an out member of the LGBT+ community. When she's not writing, she's going to rock concerts, getting tattooed, watching the CW, or reading comics. And drinking copious amounts of coffee.

She also writes contemporary books for adults as Samantha Calcott.

Website: https://lilyluchesibooks.wixsite.com/lilyluchesi

facebook.com/LilyLuchesi

twitter.com/lilyluchesi

instagram.com/lilyluchesi

HERE COMES TROUBLE

BY K. MATT

The day had been a long, stressful one for Nicodemus Trouble Taylor. He had been in the midst of the application process for the FBI. Of course, he had a specific branch he wanted to join, but that would come after a couple years of exemplary service as a special agent. Today was the part of the hiring process where they subjected him to a polygraph. Even hours later, the butterflies in his stomach were restless. He was sure he'd passed, though, even after they asked him a few times if his real name was, in fact, "Nicodemus Trouble."

The man never knew quite why his parents gave him such a name. It wasn't like he ever got the chance to meet them; his parents were killed when he was only two, his sisters being taken in by one of Hell Bent's labs. Nick, himself, was adopted by a scientist. After learning about the sheer madness that was Hell Bent's lab system, where human experimentation was a part of their society, he felt it best to get the hell out when he could, which brought him to Quantico, VA.

For now, he was making his way back to his apartment to de-stress. Maybe there was some cheesy romantic comedy on TV that he could kick back and enjoy. From on the street, he could see that someone had their lights on and hadn't closed the blinds, but there was no way to tell more from that angle. Either way, that was the same floor he lived on.

Shaking his head at the nerve of some people, he entered the apartment building and waved to the security guard on his way to the elevator. Nick's home was on the tenth floor, and his apartment was the only populated one up there, now that he thought about it.

Passing by the fifth floor was when that little tidbit occurred to him. Did this mean he had a neighbor now or was there some particularly bold intruder in his place?!

Nick hated having to disrupt others, and he didn't have one of those fancy cellular phones yet. His instinct was to call the police. But then he kicked himself. He *was* the damn police, and he was looking to go beyond that. He had left his service weapon at home today, having taken off to continue his application process. But if he could bluff his way past whoever had broken into his home…

The elevator dinged as it reached his floor, and he moved with caution toward room 1004. Pressing his ear against the door, he could hear voices inside. Female, laughing, and somehow familiar. Wait, was this someone he knew? He pulled his key from his back pocket, going to unlock the door. Carefully, he stepped into the apartment, pausing as he noticed three pairs of boots beside the door. A light red holster and a turquoise scabbard hung on the coat rack, minus its sword. The smell of alcohol, nail polish, and fish-filled the air, and he could hear something on TV.

"I'm tellin' ya, there's *something* about the dad on this show that sets off some major red flags!" one voice said.

"Ivy, you say that about any positive father figure…"

"Well, yeah, 'Vette, when's the last time *you* met someone that freaking sickeningly upstanding?" Ivy replied.

Well, now Nick wasn't sure if he should feel relaxed or even less at ease than he had. He knew these people. And if the Sangre Sisters had shown up, that meant his own sister couldn't be too far off. She had a habit of hanging around those two. He'd met them all at the lab a few years back.

As the officer thought of how to approach the situation, he was disrupted by a hug from the side. The purring clued him in as to who it was.

"Hey, Beast. Been a while," he said, fighting the smile that was playing at his lips.

"Missed you too, baby brother," came the reply.

Nick looked to his right to see his older sister standing there, her dark hair pulled back into a ponytail. Her feline ears poked upward, and her fluffy tail swayed. But what grabbed his attention even more, was the red hunk of metal attached to her right shoulder. It was a bulky facsimile of an arm, with overly long fingers that extended to the floor. She noticed him looking and lifted the arm like it had been attached to her since birth. Modeling the limb a bit, she grinned.

"You like?"

Nick sighed, moving to the fridge to get a beer for himself.

"So, Beast...what the hell are you and your friends doing in my apartment? I sure as hell know I didn't invite you guys..."

The cat-woman chuckled, her ears giving a little twitch. "Yeah, Nick, we know that. It's just that we were in town for a job, haven't tracked down our target yet, and figured you wouldn't mind. Plus, it's way cheaper than a hotel."

"And no paper trail this way!" called one of the others.

"...Hello to you too, Ivy," he sighed, cracking open his beer.

The fact that the psychic hadn't drained his entire beer supply, he thought, was a miracle. He whipped his head back and took a lengthy swig of the amber liquid.

"You don't have to worry about me stealing that weak-ass beer of yours, by the way," Ivy said. "It's eighty-proof or bust. Or, ya know, higher than that."

She'd read his mind, hadn't she? Shotgunning the rest of the bottle's contents, he charged toward the liquor cabinet above his sink. What once held six bottles of rum, whiskey, and vodka was now whittled down to those two small bottles of peppermint schnapps he had entirely forgotten were there.

He turned back to the couch, shaking his head in disbelief. Ivy was not that large of a person. She seemed skinny enough that a single martini would floor her. And yet there she sat on his couch, a sword and whetstone on her lap, surrounded by six full-sized empty liquor bottles. He wasn't sure if he should commend or berate her over this.

Glancing to Ivy's right, he saw the third of the intruders, who seemed to have helped herself to a shower and his two good towels, as she had one wrapped around her body, the other being used for her hair. She was waiting, apparently, for her red nail polish to dry. Wait, did she carry that with her? Because Nick knew for a fact that he didn't have any nail polish around.

"Sorry about the shower, Nick," she said. "It's just that teleportation spells take a lot of energy on my part, and I felt sweaty and gross...and if that weren't enough, *someone* here saw fit to vomit on me as we arrived."

Ivy scoffed. "Hey, I keep telling you teleportation's not great for the gut, but do you listen, 'Vette? No, it's all 'Oh, don't be so dramatic, Ives!' and then *every freaking time*, you act utterly shocked when breakfast ends up on your suit. Also, if you could quit calling me 'Ives,' that'd be really helpful..."

Nick watched as Yvette's pale red eyes shot wide open. "You mean you've been doing this on *purpose*?!"

"Not really, but if you stop calling me that, I'd make more of an effort *not* to do it."

Well, that just left the question of where the dirtied outfit was. Did she at least make an effort to get it to the laundry room in the basement? He somehow doubted it, at this rate. With a groan, he walked to the bathroom to see what the damage was.

Amazingly, the room was spotless. It wasn't even that clean when he left that morning! The black catsuit, gloves, and stockings Yvette had discarded were hanging over the shower rod to dry.

"Hey, did you clean the bathroom while you were at it? Seriously, thanks for that!" he called as he walked back out.

"Yeah, used the same cleansing spell I use for after we carry out a job!" she called back. "I prefer not to use that same spell on myself or my creations, of course...I mean, would you use the same cleaning product on both the floor and your hair? I don't think so."

He couldn't argue that point. Though, he did still have some questions. The man sat on the floor, given that his couch was taken. There was an assassin on either end of it, and a highly noticeable amount of cat hair in the middle (now whose could *that* possibly be).

"Now, ladies...when you say you're here on a job...is this something that's going to bring you into conflict with my line of work? He asked.

"Depends," said Beast, moving to take her designated spot on the couch and crossing one leg over the other. "Been after anyone that's committed a series of bank robberies recently?"

Nick had heard about that happening, but nobody had a solid description of the perpetrator, aside from them being a woman. He hadn't been assigned to that case, though. They were, thus far, happening in a different part of town. His job was more in the vein of dealing with domestic disputes. And to his credit, it was rare that he ever felt threatened enough to fire. His fellow officers found him a bit odd, but he was more than willing to negotiate when things got rough.

"A little," he said. "What do you know about your target?"

Yvette snapped her fingers, and a small folded up paper appeared in her hand, surrounded by a red glow. Unfolding it, she read it over.

"Woman by the name of Yolanda Quigg. Long dark auburn hair, olive skin, tentacles for arms, known for her robberies having a ninety-nine percent casualty rate, and she's been at it for a few years now."

Ivy's brow furrowed, and she leaned over to look at the paper. She had to lean behind Beast to do so, but she was looking over the paper.

"Uh, 'Vette? That says 'Yadira,' not 'Yolanda,'" she told her, tone flat.

The witch scoffed. "Nonsense. I know what it says."

Beast also leaned over, head tilted. "No, she's right. It does say 'Yadira.'"

Her face flushing, Yvette crossed her arms. "I wrote that down in a hurry!"

Nick wasn't listening to their bickering, however. The description of this woman sounded familiar. It had been a few years back when he first fled Hell Bent for someplace that didn't have anything to do with human experimentation. He had a girlfriend at the time, and the two were trying to take care of a routine deposit at the bank. As it turned out, a woman with tentacle arms was looking to make a not-so-routine withdrawal and was set to be the only survivor.

He wasn't sure what it was that kept him alive when the bullet had hit him. It had hit his chest, and things were touch and go for a while. But he had survived. The robber, however, was never caught. This incident was what made him want to join the FBI in the first place, and it still haunted the man's dreams.

"Hey, Beast, you might wanna check on your brother," he heard Ivy say. "Picking up on something from him."

Beast's ears twitched as she got up, going to hug Nick. "Is everything okay?" she asked him.

Nick returned the hug, nodding. "Y-yeah. It's just that I've met this target of yours once. Came really close to killing me."

He yelped as he felt his sister's grip tighten. "...She did *what* now?" she asked, the menace clear in her tone.

"She, um...she--or rather, the guy she was using as a puppet with her tentacle...I think that's what she was doing? Anyway, I got shot in the chest. It was her fault..."

The rumbling that emanated from her as she continued to hug him felt markedly different from the purring earlier. No, this was an outright growl. Oh, hell, was she just going to find this Quigg woman, tear her to shreds, then bring her head to him like a cat presenting its human with a dead mouse?

Cautiously, he reached up and scratched behind her ear, the growl soon easing into a purr. Once they broke the embrace again, Beast smiled at him.

"Sorry if I got a little carried away, there," she said, chipper as could be. "It's just that this bitch hurt you, and she kinda needs to die for it. Want me to bring you her heart?"

Nick paled. Yeah, that would do wonders for his future: a humanoid heart in his fridge, presumably having taken its last few beats in his sister's big steely hand. That was definitely not a good look for anyone, let alone a guy that wanted to save lives. What was he supposed to do if anyone saw that, claim that he was on some new diet?

"N-no. That's okay..."

"You sure?" Beast asked, head tilted with a slight pout.

Was she *hurt* over that? Just what on Earth had the assassin business done to the woman?

"I'm just not sure I would know where to put it. I don't have the space in my fridge, ya know?"

She raised an eyebrow. "You sure? Seemed to be plenty of room..."

Nick shook his head. "I'd really rather not have a heart in my refrigerator, is all. Or freezer. Or really anywhere that's not in its host body, ya know?"

With a sigh, Beast nodded. "Yeah, yeah, I get it. Offer's still open if you change your mind, though."

He politely waved her off.

"No. Thank you for the thoughts, though," he said. "I'm just gonna head to bed now. Leave you three to your business. Please make sure there's no way this can be tracked back to me, all right?"

"Got it!" came the three women's voices.

Nick walked into his bedroom. It was small, but seemed to have been untouched by his uninvited guests. His own little sanctuary, even with the mice he could hear within the walls every night. Or rather, almost every night. He couldn't hear them squeaking, rummaging, or anything else this time. They must have smelled a cat.

He lay back in the bed. While he didn't really mind visits from his sister, this was not quite how he'd hoped it would happen. He'd had to hide the fact that she was alive during his background checks. As far as everyone knew, he was the lone survivor of a home invasion robbery back in the seventies, surviving both of his parents and his two older sisters. In reality, this was only half-true. But if they knew that one of his sisters was an assassin, that would sink his entire future. His other sister was fairly well-known in the scientific community, but it could be easily reasoned that Taylor was a common enough surname. And nobody had ever really gotten a good look at the woman, save for her feline features.

So as long as he could keep all that under wraps, he should have a chance.

Meanwhile, back in the living room, Beast had started pacing, her tail swaying as she did. Ivy was back to sharpening her blade, Yvette changing out of the towels she'd borrowed and back into her now-dry clothes.

"So, you're gonna do that right there in front of us, huh?" Ivy asked, chuckling somewhat.

"Oh, it's nothing you haven't seen before," the witch scoffed. "Anyway, any suggestions for how we take on our target this time?"

"Brutally and with extreme prejudice," Beast growled, her fingers flexing a bit. "We'd need to make sure she doesn't get out alive."

"Well, yes, that is generally the idea, Beast," Yvette said. "But what execution method would be best, would you say? And please, nothing about putting the corpse on public display this time. That sort of spits in the face of subtlety."

The cat-woman crossed her arms. "It wouldn't be the whole thing! Just the head and tentacles, and it'd be to send a message."

"And that message would be…?" Yvette asked, arching an eyebrow.

"You mess with one of the Taylor clan," said the cat-woman, her tone, firm, "you unleash the Beast."

Ivy laughed. "I dunno if that was awesome, cheesy, or some combination of both."

Beast glanced at her for a moment, before realizing what she had just said and burying her face in her hands with a groan. "Oh, *God*, how could you let me say that…?"

"I wanted to see where you were going with it. And I wasn't disappointed. So, anyway, tracking her down…ideas?"

With a shrug, Yvette leaned back on the couch, having finished getting dressed and settling beside her sister. "Well…if I had tentacles, how might I roam around to avoid suspicion? I mean, she'd have to find some way to. You specify someone's ethnicity, there's generally some margin for error, but if you say you're looking for someone with tentacles? People are going to remember that."

"Might also say that you're seeing things," Ivy said, inspecting her blade for a moment. "Beast could get away with the excuse of going to a convention somewhere, but tentacle-arms are a lot harder to fake convincingly. And we're in too large of an area for me to do a full, comprehensive scan."

They chatted about this the whole night through, not even stopping for breakfast. No, their discussion continued even as they raided what was left of Nick's food supply for their meal. There was still a bit of fish left, which Beast took to the microwave. There wasn't a working stove there, and even if there was, she didn't want to deal with two dishes when just a plate would suffice.

As she entered the time on the microwave, her ears twitched at the sound of someone clearing their throat. Turning around, she saw Nick standing there, complete with fuzzy bathrobe and crossed arms. There were heavy bags under his narrowed eyes.

"...Hey, Nick! Sleep well?" Beast asked with a nervous chuckle.

Her brother shook his head. "No, Beast. No, I didn't. I could hear you three yammering on all night about how to take out your target. And then I come out here to see you putting fish in my microwave."

The cat-woman shrugged. "Seemed fine with it last night."

"In my defense, I didn't *know* about it last night, or else I'd have chewed you out over it then!"

She glanced at him. "I'd have used the stove if yours worked."

He somehow doubted that (and would have been right to).

"There is a *hotplate* about two cabinets away from the liquor stash your friend, oh so generously, demolished!"

"And how," Beast asked, rolling her eyes in the most exaggerated manner she could, "was I to know that?"

Nick was more than ready to scream at her about how they had precisely zero qualms about raiding his kitchen the night before. But he took a deep breath, said nothing more to continue the argument, and went to make some toast for himself.

Beast's own breakfast finished cooking, and she pulled the fish out. She noticed Nick's somewhat judgmental glare and let out a sigh.

"Look, I'll defishify your microwave later, all right?" she said.

"If by 'later' you mean 'after breakfast,' then sure."

To be honest, he was a little surprised that she'd made the offer, to begin with. And since that was going to be dealt with, he could go to work without an issue. But there was still the matter of his depleted liquor supply. As he thought of how best to ask Ivy to replenish that, the psychic herself walked by him.

"Yeah, sure, I can get more for you," she said, having been reading his mind once again. "Gives me something to do while looking for Yadira."

"It's *Yolanda*, and the kitchen is probably the last place you should be!" called Yvette as she fast-walked to catch up to her sister.

"Ugh...'Vette, no. The target's name is frickin' Yadira. We've been through this."

The witch rolled her eyes, looking through the cabinets again. "Hm...we should probably get some breakfast while we're out. There's not much to go with, here."

Nick nearly muttered something about how there used to be food, but then his apartment was raided by three assassins. As he glanced at the cabinets himself, he saw that there was, in fact, some food in there. It just seemed that Yvette was a picky eater. Shaking his head, he finished his toast, grabbed a box of cereal, and went off to get ready for work.

He pulled his uniform from the closet with one hand, popping open the Cap'n Crunch with his other hand and tipping the contents into his mouth. He didn't even care that it was starting to go stale right now. His plan was to get showered, grab a coffee on the way to the police station, and go about his day without passing out.

Once he was ready, he stepped into the living room just in time to see a red flash of light. Beast was still at the microwave, humming a bit as she was cleaning it out. And the place seemed to have calmed down a bit.

"Guessing they left?" Nick asked.

"Well, yeah," said Beast. "There'd be questions if they took the exit, ya know?"

He couldn't exactly argue with that. "Fair enough, I guess."

Walking over to her, he gave his sister a hug and a little scritch behind the ears. "Thanks for actually cleaning it, by the way."

Chuckling and pointing a metal finger at him, she retorted with: "You'll get my bill later."

He arched an eyebrow. "Catnip, then?"

"You know it!"

Nick made sure he didn't forget his service weapon, grabbing that from its case on the way to his shoes. Hopefully, today would be a calm, low-maintenance day.

But then, he'd hoped that about last night, as well.

The city streets were busy as always, but nobody paid much attention to the red flash of light that appeared in the alley between the Blockbuster and the bank next door. The light faded, and Yvette took a moment to survey their surroundings. Ivy, however, was a bit preoccupied. The teleportation was once again playing havoc on her stomach, and she ran toward a trash can.

She ripped the lid off, her stomach emptying itself entirely. It took a moment for her to regain her composure, stretching a little as she returned to her full short height.

"Damn drunks…" a voice muttered from nearby.

The psychic narrowed her eyes, ready to defend her need to drink (it was a medical condition, dammit!) and tell this strange woman off. What she saw when she looked over was an olive-skinned figure of medium stature, her long auburn hair extending to her knees. She straightened out her red pleather jacket with the bell sleeves. Fixing Ivy with a glare, she crossed her arms.

"You probably shouldn't drink so much. Might not get so sick," she told her.

The psychic scoffed. "It's a *medical condition*," she replied. "Also, who the hell are you to tell me how to live my life?"

The woman stormed past her in a huff, not noticing the bluish glow in Ivy's eyes as she did. She shoved Yvette (who had been admiring the woman's jacket) on the way out of the alley.

As soon as she was gone, the witch pouted. "Well, that was rude. And she looked like she's a pair of tentacles away from our target…"

Ivy pulled her flask from her hip, taking a long swig.

"Damn good reason for that, 'Vette. That was Quigg."

Yvette smirked. Well, finding her would be easier than anticipated. They at least had a face. But it wasn't like they could just kill her right there. People might have been able to ignore their entrance, but a full-blown assassination out there in the semi-open? They'd have to track her down again later, away from prying eyes.

Nick nearly laughed when the assignment came through. He and his partner were to help investigate the scene of a jewelry store robbery. Well, as it turned out, that resulted in the deaths of all ten people in that store. The only trace of a perpetrator was the shop owner's fingerprints on the gun left behind. A few odd suction cup marks were found on the back of his neck. Given the prior night's conversation, he was able to put two and two together pretty effectively.

Not that he could bring this up to the taller officer with him. That would mean admitting that he had a family in Hell Bent. That he had been lying on his applications for the FBI. That he was a fraud and didn't deserve to wear any sort of badge.

And then came those memories again, of the bank robbery all those years ago. He may have survived, but it shook him to the core. He could recall his ears ringing, his vision blurring, and the pain just as vividly as he had that day.

"You all right, Taylor?" his partner, an Officer Winthrop, asked, holding a clipboard. "You seem kinda distracted."

The shorter man jumped slightly. He rubbed the back of his neck, giving an awkward half-smile.

"Yeah, Barry. Just thinking, is all. This scene's whole MO reminds me of...well, something that happened when I first moved here. Remember that bank robbery with only one survivor?"

Barry nodded. "Weird...they found the bank manager the same way as this poor bastard."

He gestured toward the shop owner on the floor. "Think we've got a copycat sort of deal?"

"I dunno," said Nick. "I mean, you saw the suction cup marks, right? Remember what they found on the back of the bank manager's neck?"

He wasn't sure if he should inform Barry of the woman with the tentacles puppeting the manager. While he knew it to be true, he also knew that it would sound excessively odd to someone outside of his hometown.

Barry's head tilted. "Wait...so it's *just* like that robbery?" he asked.

Nick sighed. "Only difference is the location. Most likely, the same person behind it."

"Any idea who this person is?" Barry asked him, eyes wide.

Nick refrained from answering that, as it would undoubtedly lead to more questions concerning how he had acquired that knowledge. It was doubtful that most people like this, people that would commit mass murders, would bother giving their names. And so, he simply shook his head.

As they investigated the area, they found that the cash register had been cleaned out entirely, and any and all ruby jewelry was gone.

"Why just the ruby stuff?" Barry wondered aloud.

Nick had no idea. All he really knew was that he, his sister, and her friends were after the same damn person. But it was all a matter of who would get to this Yadira Quigg first.

Meanwhile, the twins had made their trip to the liquor store, Ivy making a hefty purchase. She was, of course, carded. She handed over a fake ID, giving her name as Jennifer Something or other. The store owner had given her an odd look, but she gave her best ashamed face.

"Yeah," she'd said, "I've been looking to change it for a while. Doesn't really roll off the tongue that well, ya know?"

With the alcohol stash in two separate large bags, the pair took their leave. It was soon decided, though, that Yvette would get the purchase back to Nick's place while Ivy stalked the target. Sure, Ivy knew that the first rule of horror movies was not to split up, but she and Yvette both knew that she could handle herself in a fight. Could kill without laying a finger on her target if need be. Though she did sort of wish she'd brought her sword. But that would've gained even more stares than the skin-tight catsuit and gloves.

It didn't take long for her to find Yadira at a few locations. Passing by a bank, she could pick up on her thoughts. It was a potential target, as were the high-end retail stores a few blocks away. She picked up on the little rush of pride that crossed Yadira's mind as she passed by the jewelry store surrounded by yellow police tape, with various emergency vehicles outside. People were brought out in body bags, and a couple of officers could be seen through the window.

Which was when Ivy heard another of her target's thoughts. It was recognition as her focus settled on the shorter of the two officers. She heard one statement in particular: 'Huh. So, he survived, did he…?'

The psychic's eyes narrowed. Oh, she was *not* about to let her take down her best friend's brother… But she still couldn't just telekinetically snap her neck right here and now. They needed to be alone. If she could maybe nudge her away from the location…

'So, how about getting out of my mind now?' asked a voice in Ivy's head.

To say that Ivy was taken aback would be an understatement. Nobody had *ever* responded to her like that. She couldn't read her mind back, could she?

Yadira turned back to face her, arms crossed. Ivy mirrored her body language, eyes ticking to her opponent's arms.

"So...Hell Bent tech or magic?" she asked.

The other woman smirked. "I met this nice guy back home that does some excellent engineering work. Hopes to surpass that Dr. Taylor chick someday. And since he created these babies to work flawlessly with my tentacles, I'd say he's succeeded."

"Whatever," Ivy scoffed. "So, why were you creeping on those guys?" she asked, pointing toward the two officers.

With a dark smirk, Yadira got in her face, her piercing red eyes staring right into Ivy's unimpressed turquoise ones. "I think you know why, Sangre. You might wanna stay out of my way and let me finish what I started."

Her eyes glowing, Ivy smirked. "You really think you scare me, Quigg? The only reason I haven't dropped you right here is because of witnesses. But if I ever get you alone..."

Yadira held up one of her lifelike cybernetic hands, raising her middle finger, before walking off. Ivy huffed, picking up a piece of trash someone had just left on the sidewalk. She wasn't actually sure of the source, but she shrugged and chucked it at the other woman.

"Pick up your trash next time, wouldja?" she called.

The target turned back around, glaring. She just smirked in response, still making plans to hunt her down later. Thankfully, the other woman bypassed the jewelry store altogether for the time being.

She'd try to get Nick alone now. Give him some warning that the target had noticed him and wanted to finish what she started. But she had to wait for this other officer to leave. Taking another drink from her flask, she figured he'd probably be hitting a donut shop soon, anyway. That would be when she should strike.

***

Nick and Barry were the last to leave the crime scene, the latter taking the wheel of their squad car. He hadn't noticed the woman with the voluminous waves of hair that seemed fixated on their vehicle, but Nick certainly saw her in the passenger side mirror. His eyes narrowed. What was she doing there?

"You're zoning out again, there, Taylor."

Nick jumped again. "Y-yeah, it's the trauma. Sorry about that."

"Hmm. Yeah, I can imagine. How's about this: I'll grab a coffee for you at the next stop, all right?"

"Six sugars, three creams," Nick told him.

"Never did get your taste in coffee, Nicky," he chuckled, pulling to a stop outside of a coffee shop. "Comin' with, or just hanging back here?"

"I'll just wait, I think."

Barry exited the car, going into the coffee shop. He didn't notice the woman from before beginning to approach. But Nick did. His eyes narrowed...how did she catch up so quickly?

Rolling down the window, he leaned his head out. "Is there a reason you seem to be following me? I mean, first, I see you at the jewelry store, now here..."

Ivy nodded. "Yeah, Nick, there is a reason. Found Quigg, and she noticed you and probably wants to finish that bank job from however long ago. I'm not gonna go full-bodyguard or anything, but I have kind of a vested interest in telling you to watch your ass. Beast would probably yell at me if I didn't."

He rubbed the back of his neck, eyes cast downward. "Yeah, she probably would...thanks for the heads-up." He then cocked his head to the side. "Where's the other one?"

"Took the supply back to your place, and I went scanning for the target."

He nodded, not even noticing the driver's side door opening. Ivy, however, did and handed him a card.

"I hope you'll consider our offer, Mr. Taylor," she said without missing a beat.

She waved to Barry before sauntering away. The taller man waved back, coming dangerously close to spilling hot coffee on his lap as he did. Nick took one of the coffees from him and took a sip.

"So, what was that all about?" he asked.

Nick looked at the card he was handed, pocketing it. "Oh," he said. "Just some pyramid scheme."

His partner seemed to accept this explanation, as he drove them back to the station. As they went, Nick's trauma began to seep back in for the umpteenth time that day. He really wished he had that alcohol stash handy right now. Even if it was one of those forgotten bottles of peppermint schnapps.

Ivy had taken a break after that meeting with Nick, grabbing a quick bite from a food truck. Walking along with her newly purchased burger, she saw a flash of red light from the corner of her eye. She stopped in her tracks, taking a bite of lunch as she waited for Yvette to rejoin her. Beast had also come along, apparently done cleaning the microwave.

"So, how goes the tracking?" Beast called as they approached.

Finishing the current bite, Ivy shrugged. "Whelp, Quigg may be gunning for your brother--don't worry, I let him know about that-- and she might be somewhat psychic...knew enough to realize that I was reading her mind and broke out the last name."

Yvette cringed. "Well, *that* is just a tad un-good. She still alive?"

Ivy nodded, causing Beast to grin widely.

"Good...means I still have a shot at doing it," she said, that predatory glint in her eyes again.

Yvette handed Ivy's sheathed sword to her. The plan was not to go back to Nick's until this target was dead. She'd already teleported again to get Ivy's half of the prior purchase back home to their own place. So now all there was to do was go hunting. Ivy strapped the sheath to her back, and Yvette had already secured her own holster on her hip. Beast's weapon was the set of long, slim, razor-sharp blades at the ends of her glove's fingers, which she was more than happy with.

To avoid stares, Yvette had placed an illusion spell over the three. To any prying eyes, they looked more like a random trio of tourists than they did a group of potentially conspicuous killers.

Nick couldn't help but look over his shoulder every few minutes. Ever since Ivy had informed him of the threat against him, the slightest bump made him worry. He nearly jumped out of his skin as some kid on a skateboard sped past him.

The whole day had been like this for him, even as the afternoon sun began its descent. The rest of his day on the job was mostly spent with minor domestic incidents and traffic stops. He was ready just to go home and rest.

At the moment, he and Barry were parked on the side of the road, waiting for any speeders. Nick's fingers drummed on the dashboard as he kept watching.

"Sure you don't wanna talk to someone about your trauma stuff, Nicky?"

Nick smiled. He had to admit, he did appreciate his partner's concern for his well-being. But he nodded.

"It's fine," he said. "Besides, I go to a therapist, you know others are gonna start talking, and I need to have a good rep."

Leaning back in his seat, Barry nodded. "Right. The better you look, the better your chances at the FBI. So, which branch you going for?"

"The HRT," he said, adjusting his badge somewhat. "After that whole thing a few years ago, I wanted to work in a field that'd try to save people in that kind of situation. Much as I love my fellow officers, you have to admit, they're not really *great* at negotiations."

"Negotiations don't always cut it, Nicky. Sometimes, you find someone that won't listen, no matter what."

Nick shrugged. "Still always worth a shot, though, right?"

The two continued to watch the area, both leaping out of their skin as they heard a knock on the window. Barry's hand flew to his weapon, and Nick looked outside.

He saw nobody there. Check the rearview, and nothing. But he knew he wasn't just hearing things. No, Barry reacted as well. So not an auditory hallucination.

Nick tried to settle back into his seat, but that knock came again. And this time, he could see the olive-skinned hand that caused it. It was right there by the driver's side window. The window that was now smashed. His hand went right for the radio. If there was going to be an attack, he was calling for backup.

"I wouldn't do that if I were you…" came Barry's voice.

Nick froze for a moment, looking up to see his partner's Glock pointed right at him. The other man's eyes were a blank, solid gray. Behind him, Nick could see her there, a tentacle to the back of the man's neck.

Yadira had found them. And as Ivy had warned, she looked ready to finish what she had started.

Nick felt that he had three options here: he could either let himself be cowed by this woman that had nearly killed him (which would likely result in death), he could call for backup and get shot right there, or he could get out of the car and maybe get himself a fighting chance.

And so, without taking his eyes off of his partner or the woman using him as a puppet, he reached over and opened the passenger side door. Once that was open, he threw himself to the ground and rolled a bit, just narrowly missing the shot fired at him.

As he stood up, he drew his own weapon. If he could get behind Quigg, he could probably take her out that way. But he knew that firing at her head-on would only result in Barry being hurt, and he didn't want that on his conscience. Keeping low to the ground, he made his way around the car.

He was met by the Yadira-controlled Barry once again, just managing to avoid another round from the firearm. A pair of discarded prosthetics lay at their feet. He could try to negotiate with Barry, but he wasn't in his right mind. But would Yadira listen…?

Clearing his throat, Nick began: "Please, you don't have to do this!"

He heard a chuckle from both Yadira and Barry, in perfect unison.

"Oh, but I think I do, Nicky. You weren't supposed to survive. Do you think I like my record being at only ninety-nine percent?"

Nick stood upright, glaring. "Just let him go," he said. "Barry did nothing to you."

He hadn't noticed the three figures charging their way. What he did notice was the layered scream of pain from both Yadira and Barry.

Looking around, he saw Beast, Ivy, and Yvette standing behind her, Beast licking a bit of blood from her claws.

"You wanna talk about having only a ninety-nine percent rate?" Beast asked, her ears giving a little twitch. "Bring it."

The target and her puppet both turned to face the three of them, beginning to open fire. Ivy had created a shield of telekinetic energy around herself and the other two, deflecting the bullets.

Nick took advantage of this opportunity to run at Yadira. Maybe he could rip her away from his partner. If that would keep him safe and open her up for the assassins to do their job, he was all for it.

He managed to get both arms around Yadira, pinning her tentacles to her sides as he pulled at the killer. He managed to pry her off of his associate, rolling on the ground with her. She yelped in surprise, and Barry fell to the dirt, limp.

Nick glanced in his direction, standing up.

"...Barry?" he called.

There was no response.

"Barry?!"

Yadira chuckled. "You can't just break a connection like that, Nicky," she said. "It's a good way to kill some--AGH!"

He looked up to see that one of her tentacles had been hacked off by a sword.

Ivy stood behind her, shaking the blood from her blade.

"Look, bitch. You really shoulda left well enough alone," she said. "Or at least get rid of someone if you truly want them out of the way."

Yadira seethed, placing her remaining tentacle over the stump where hers once was. Her red eyes narrowed in Ivy's direction.

"What," Ivy mocked. "Thought the threat would be enough to stop me? Please, I've seen more threatening in the mirror each day."

As the tentacled woman tried to think of a retort, however, her train of thought was halted by a single bullet to the back of the head. She dropped, and Nick could see Yvette standing there, casually twirling the gun on her finger.

"Okay, and that's one more target down. Yolanda Quigg can be checked off," she said.

"For fuck's sake, 'Vette, are you just *trying* to annoy me with that now?" Ivy sighed.

Beast had walked over to Nick, pulling him into a hug. "You hurt at all?" she asked, beginning to inspect her brother.

Nick didn't respond, just staring at the corpse of what used to be his partner. He knew that being killed in the line of duty was always a risk, but knowing that this other man, one he had seen as a friend, didn't even have control of his own mind before the end...

"I'm sorry..." he whispered, not taking his eyes off of the body.

Beast continued to hug him. "It's not your fault. She's the one that took control of him, and to be fair, none of us are entirely sure how her powers worked. Just relieved you're safe."

He nodded, returning the hug. Or rather, just sort of clung to her for a moment. She purred softly to hopefully calm him down as Ivy leaned against the squad car.

"So...how you wanna explain this to the station?" she asked, casually grabbing her flask and taking a drink.

Nick had no idea how he wanted to go about that, to be honest. He couldn't tell them about the assassins. That would have a whole host of problems (having his sister and her friends arrested, possibly experimented on by the federal government labs, getting on their bad side and ending up on their kill list because of this, and admitting that he had a living sister in the first place and jeopardizing his own future being the most prevalent in his mind). But the hacked-off tentacle would be pretty hard to explain away.

Yvette seemed to have a solution to that, crouching beside Yadira and reattaching the tentacle. Nick watched, and the story formed.

"Okay, so...should I say that she killed Barry, and I was the one that shot her in the back of the head, then?" he asked.

"Probably the most believable thing to go with," Ivy said.

Beast pulled away from the hug after a moment, tail twitching.

"We should probably get going," she told him. "Best of luck with the job. I'm sure you'll get it!"

Nick smiled at her, though he knew he would likely have nightmares about this day. He watched as the assassins gathered together,

Beast and Ivy standing behind Yvette. A red glow washed over the area, and Nick couldn't help but call over to them.

"So, what's up with the...well, that?!" he asked.

"It's a spell 'Vette came up with herself!" Ivy called back. "Gets rid of any traces that we were there."

He watched as the trio teleported away, heading back to the car once they were gone. Nick grabbed the radio, calling in to the station.

"There's...there's been an incident. Officer down, perp dead."

Once he gave the location, he sank back in the seat and rubbed his temples. On the one hand, he had to admire how well those three could handle killing someone else. On the other, he wondered how they could face themselves in the mirror, knowing that their sole purpose in life seemed to be to end others'. Granted, he knew a number of officers that brushed off their kills like nothing, but he knew them to be utter jerks, too. But his sister and her friends? They may have driven him nuts, but he actually *liked* them.

When the other officers arrived, he told them the story of what he and the assassins had agreed had happened. Aside from some paperwork, the fact that he'd "killed" a suspect had no bearing on his career. He was thankful for that one.

And after several more months, he would get the thing he had been hoping for most: his acceptance into the FBI.

END

ABOUT K. MATT

K. Matt is both an author and illustrator living in a rural part of New York state. When she's not drawing comics, she's writing stuff that may eventually become a comic. Sometimes, she's been known to procrastinate (her favorite procrastination activity being baking). Fairly often, she's known to be better communicating through text as opposed to verbally.

Website: https://kaylamatt.wordpress.com

facebook.com/HellBentBookSeries

twitter.com/MarieTwixie

instagram.com/kmatt666

HEROES AND VALLENEZ

BY ANGELA KULIG

ONE

I always say… a punch in the face is a great way to end the day.

All right, I've never actually said that, but I think it every time it happens, and for me, that's a lot. I chalk it up to the hazards of the life-style and buy boxes and boxes of Band-Aids. I hate running out of them; the guy at Quick Stop always looks at me weird when I have to buy cartoon adhesive bandages because that's all they have left. He never asks questions, though, so I keep going back. Maybe he doesn't speak English. I don't know.

The guy that stood in front of me looked vaguely familiar, but I couldn't decide if he was the one who paid to find out who his wife was seeing on the side or the son of that mob boss I accidentally offended last year. How was I supposed to know that horse was his daughter? How was I supposed to know she was anyone's daughter? Well, needless to say, he did not find my livestock jokes at all amusing. So I've been trying to sell him out ever since, and I can't be sure, but I think that only makes him angrier.

Only it doesn't really matter if this guy's the scorned lover, or the horse girl's brother, because he currently stood between me and my only escape route. Well, my only escape route apart from the ten-foot-tall metal fence I was backed up against. It had metal barbed wire up top, and signs reading *"Warning! Keep out!"* in about a dozen languages.

I eyed the rusted wire and wondered how much skin I'd lose if I had to depart that way.

The man was even closer to me then, and he was wailing on about something or another. Really, it's always the same thing from these people. They pay me for good information. It's not my fault that they don't always like what they hear, and it's not my fault that sometimes other people will also pay me for the same thing. It's just business, and I'm good at my job. Anything you want to know, anything at all, and I can find out for you. But don't shoot the messenger—or in my case, beat him up in a dark alley.

Some people just have a hard time letting go. *Oh, look at that,* I thought. *He's making demands now. Unreasonable demands. Isn't that cute?* It's probably just a part of the grieving process, the mourning over a woman, possessions, their control over the situation, anything really.

This is just your typical dark alley, off a typical dark street, and I've seen a few in my life. If I had listened to my mother, I wouldn't be here now. You know, I used to be a good kid. But things change.

The guy was right on top of me then. His blond hair was flattened down with perspiration. His angry eyes were dull and unfocused.

"You're gonna pay, Vallenez." he slurred. And gee—if I had a dollar for every time I heard that, I'd still have made far less money than spilling my dirty little secrets, or usually, other people's secrets.

I realized this man, in his present state, was capable of far less damage than the barbed wire. He had no knife, no gun, and no sword. He was just a mortal angry man, and bruises are always easier to hide than potential stitches—just a little tip from me to you.

It's not like I don't understand this guy's anger, I get that, I do. I've had all kinds of unpleasant things happen to me in life, and only the recent ones were brought on by myself.

Most people in the world aren't really good or evil. It's not just me, no matter what you think. Not everyone is a hero or a villain. Some people are, and I've met and pissed off a few of them, too. But for the most part, the lines are blurred, and people on either side love me, and then hate my guts. Whatever. I don't like them very much, either. It's just a paycheck.

I looked away from the blond and waited for a blow that never came. I hadn't closed my eyes, but I have this habit of mentally escaping unpleasant things. I've got this shirt that says, *I'm not here right now, I'm in Tahiti.* I've never been there, but I'd like to think I'd go one day. Or, you know, maybe just clip out some nice pictures from a travel brochure.

Right then, I was blocking out the guy in front of me. I'm pretty sure he had been shouting that he was going to kill me, but they always say that. Tough guy talk involves saying a lot of stupid crap loudly and thinking that you mean it, but really, they never do. And the guys that do mean it… well, I am too smart to wander around near them.

The blond's eyes suddenly looked semi-coherent, but his mouth puckered into a big stupid shocked expression. He was standing so close, at first I didn't see why. When people are about to pound you into the cement, you usually aren't looking *behind* them. Not even me, and I'm an expert at looking over people's shoulders.

Someone had pinned the blond's right arm against his sweaty back, and I recognized that face instantly. Short brown hair, dark eyes, and a dark complexion. The one hero in the world, I want to see the absolute least. Not that I really want to see any of them at all, but Richard Roca and I have a history, and not for any of the usual reasons.

Let's just say girls always want the hero and leave it at that. If you thought barbed wire and bruises hurt, it's nothing compared to what this guy did to me, and he did it all without even raising a finger.

And last time I checked, the feeling was mutual. So I had no idea why Richard was saving my hide in a dark alley in the middle of the night. Frankly, I was pretty sure that it was past the golden boy's bedtime.

You see Rich, and he hates it when I call him Rich, he belongs to an order of heroes, The Order of the Golden—*something.* Eggs? Was there a beanstalk involved? Or maybe it was a shield? No, I think that's an insurance company. Oh heck, it doesn't matter. What does matter is that even among the good guys, they are the good guys. So good, they should probably all be off being bishops somewhere, not saving a gray hat like me on the bad side of town.

Oh yeah, it was *The Golden Cross.* I remember now.

As good and noble as they typically are, however, by the time Richard had found me in the alley, that good-natured spirit no longer applied to me. The heroes in his order treated murderers better than me, and yeah, I knew why, but that wasn't really my fault.

I've done a lot of terrible things. I'd be lying if I said I didn't, and I never lie. So believe me when I tell you, I go out of my way to avoid those particular heroes. Besides, of all the horrible things I have done, there are many things I have not. I've never stolen from people who couldn't afford it, and I'd never killed anyone. Not directly, anyway. I can't be held responsible for what people do with my information once I deliver it to them. It's like trying to nix the Internet because some idiot looked up how to make bombs online. Watch your kids, people, seriously, and don't blame me.

Richard spun the blond around and deposited him lightly on the mucked up ground. It really stunk; I hadn't really realized it until that moment. Richard patted the angry and shocked man on the back and leaned down to whisper something in his ear. I couldn't hear him over the sound of the street, it's three a.m., but that's what it's like here. It never stops.

Richard wore an expression I can't read, but he looked miserable, and that made me feel a lot better about myself. He should be miserable. But he didn't look particularly angry, *so what gives?*

TWO

It was another day and another diner. They all look the same after a while, and this one had pretty standard 1980s un-renovated charm. Richard lured me here with one of my own best lines.

"I've got information that you're going to want to hear," he had said just above his breath. Since I was pretty sure he was morally against lying, I was inclined to believe him.

We sat at a small table for two in the middle of an empty section. Richard looked too big to be shoved into the seat against the wall. He seemed even bigger and brawnier than I remembered him being, which totally figures. Some guys have all the luck.

I was far closer to him than I would have previously thought possible, without us killing each other. Or, without Richard killing me and myself looking like a huge idiot.

I had figured out why he had hunted me down. He must have had heard some of the things I had said about his old man, or maybe his sister. So when he opened his mouth, I was shocked when that wasn't what came out of it.

"Emily's been kidnapped," he said.

And try as I might, I just couldn't make myself believe he would say something as awful as that, just for the sake of torturing me. My mind filtered through every sunny spot in the whole of my memory. All of Emily's blonde hair and bright smiles. I was really hoping I was wrong about that no lying bit. As much as I hated to admit it, I knew he loved her just as much as I did.

But he could never love her *more* than me, even if he was the one that got to be with her. It just wasn't possible.

When I was a kid, before my dad left, and before everything started to go wrong in my life, I lived in a nice house in a good neighborhood. Just three houses down from me lived the most beautiful girl in the world. That was how I would always remember Emily. She had crazy blonde curls and even wilder eyes. Some days they were green, some days they were brown, and some days you couldn't even tell what color they were at all, because her smile was too blinding.

I like to think I fell in love with her at the age of three. If not, then I defiantly sealed my fate when I made her cry on the playground at the tender age of seven and a half.

She got over it, though, and for a while, things were great. While she wasn't ever really my girlfriend, she was my best friend, and that meant even more. Those were pretty much the golden years of Vic Vallenez, but I know no matter how hard I wish for them back, it just ain't going to happen.

The year I started the ninth grade was the year my mother started to go blind. At first, it only made my family grow closer, but as time went on, and there were fewer options and almost no chance of recovery, we started to splinter. My life would have been completely awful, except for how Emily had still been my best friend. Even though she was a junior, and I was a freshman, and it was so not cool to hang out with me, she did anyway.

One day my father left for a business trip, and he never came back. He said, *take good care of your mother*. Then moved to Miami with his girlfriend, and he's been there ever since. My parents are still married, but my dad doesn't give us one red cent. Sometimes he sends me shoes that are two sizes too big, or clothes that have been out of style for years, but he won't send a letter or pick up the phone. Mom is still, to this day, convinced he's coming back, and I just don't have the heart to tell her about his new family.

Being blind meant my mother couldn't work, and being broke meant we had to move away from the good side of town and into a one-bedroom rathole next to the railroad tracks. Suddenly I was not only the loser freshman, I was the loser freshman with the ugly clothes, big shoes, and food stamps. Still, none of that mattered to Emily. She'd drive me home every day and stick around at least once a week. She always had nice things for my mom and junk food for me.

Then one night that had seemed so long in real life, and now rests so short in my memory, our lives changed irrevocably. Emily and I had both been drifting off on my pull-out sofa when she said she should probably be getting home. Reruns from some feel-good sixties comedy played in the background, and I offered to walk her to her car. She said not to and that she was just parked on the street. That she would be fine. Her voice was husky with drowsiness, and I longed to hang on to it, to use it in the place of desire in my dreams.

She said it would be fine, and ultimately I guessed it was. Emily met three men on the foot of the stairs to my apartment. I never heard her scream over the noise of the train, and I didn't find out about it for three agonizing days. Those guys were as bad as you can get, so bad even I won't do business with them, and honestly, I'm not that picky.

One of them grabbed her from behind, and I'm sure their imaginations were running a lot faster than they could while she kicked and screamed. Emily did everything she needed to do to get away, and no matter how much I hated the guy, I would always be grateful to Richard because he was the one who saved her. I'd even say it to his face if anyone dared say otherwise. I'd also say I'd wished every day of my life since that I had just walked her out.

"I said, Emily's been kidnapped," he told me again like I hadn't heard him, "don't you even care?"

"Do I care?" I asked him coldly, "I'm in love with her!" I would be for the rest of my life, but now really wasn't the time to go there.

Richard deflated as if his anger had been pushing him outwards. An easy listening channel went to commercial in the background, but neither of us really noticed. "Don't say that," he hissed, but he could no longer even look me in the eye. Fearless and brave, Richard Roca was too big of a coward to even look at my face.

"What does it matter if I say it out loud or not?" I asked, "We both know it's true."

Richard exhaled loudly, painfully, and slapped his hands, palm down, on the table. The waitress had brought him coffee, but it sat untouched. "I know, all right?" he finally said. "I know you love her, and that's why I'm here."

Why? I wondered. *Because misery loves company?*

"Vallenez… I need your help to get her back."

"Look. If I had information about where she had been taken, or even that she had been taken at all. I wouldn't be here talkin' to you. I'd be out looking for her!"

Richard furiously nodded his head, and I was starting to think there was a whole corner piece to this puzzle I wasn't getting yet.

"Wait," I said as it all suddenly clicked, "you want me to help you get her back, like physically go with you to find her, like lame hero crap. I don't do little adventures like that, Roca. I am strictly an informant. Besides, I know you belong to the biggest, bestest group of chivalrous asshats in like the whole world. Why don't they help you? Don't you have like a squire or someone to hold your sword while you do stuff like this?"

Richard's jaw was trembling by that point, and I don't think it was because he was fighting back laughter. Luckily the golden boy probably flosses three times a day, so the pressure wouldn't crack any of his perfect teeth.

"Why isn't there a search party, Richard? What aren't you telling me?"

"She's a hostage. They are asking for a ransom they know we won't pay. The Order does not negotiate. Ever."

See, I knew these hero types tend to live by stupid, pointless rules, but this one was ridiculous. Wouldn't you want to get the innocent back, no matter what? Clearly, I know nothing about what's right and wrong, and that's why I usually just stay out of it. People seem to hate when you get all logical about things.

I kicked the center table support. "So your Order would rather Emily, who is completely innocent, suffer for the sake of a stupid rule? The only thing that girl ever did wrong was associate with people apparently unwilling to save her."

Richard sighed and put down a fork he had nearly bent in two. "It's not like that, Vic. They want to make a plan, but they're just moving too slowly. You know what could happen; you know there is never time to wait."

Yeah. I was pretty sure there was a whole TV drama centered on just that. If Richard's Order was involved, we weren't likely dealing with B-rate career criminals, but something far more sinister—though probably no less likely to drop her body in the ditch to prove whatever their stupid point was.

Oh man, I really did not want to think about it, but my mind is as quick as my tongue. Before I could conjure up a distracting enough picture, the mental image of her beautiful, cold, lifeless body burned itself into my retinas.

I knew that wouldn't make these heroes stop. Something wasn't right.

"Who has her?" I asked Richard. But he was still looking away.

"I'm not certain," he said, "but—"

"But?" I pressed.

"It doesn't matter. We need better information."

Yes, I thought. *We really do.* I waited for Richard to ask me for advice in that area, but he never did. He sat there, making a sour face, still not drinking his coffee.

"She's been gone a day already," he confessed.

I looked at Richard, unsure of what I should really be doing. On one hand, I really wanted to tell him to go off himself. Nothing would make me happier, but on the other hand, this might be the only chance I ever got to win Emily back. If she fell for her savior once, it could happen again.

I'm not even sure I have one of those angel guys that sit on my shoulder, but I can tell you my devil guy liked the second idea quite a lot. The idea was crazy and would almost assuredly fail, but I had to try anyway, and no matter what, I couldn't just leave Emily lost.

"All right," I said. "But I've got to stop by my mom's first."

THREE

Richard and I walked down the dimly-lit sidewalk. Every third street light was on, the others burnt out or busted. Broken glass jutted from their fixtures, like jagged teeth in the mouth of silver serpents. I gave a second glance down the alley Richard found me in, but the blond was nowhere in sight. Hopefully, I wouldn't be seeing him again, and hopefully not because I die hanging out with Richard Roca.

I did, however, hear footsteps coming from not far behind us. Two sets and I know Richard heard them too, probably long before I did, and I was used to them trailing me by now. When he opened his mouth to ask me about them, I cut him off.

"Just keep going," I said. "They aren't dangerous." Okay, I didn't know that they weren't dangerous for sure, but they had been following me a while and had yet to do anything but issue a few threats they didn't mean.

"I should probably warn you," Richard said quietly. "My sister has stowed away in the backseat."

"Wait," I said. "What?" Because I couldn't remember how old his sister was. I knew she was about my age, was all. I had only seen her once before, and that time she had kicked me in the shin.

"She hid in the backseat. She hasn't even finished her Hero's Training yet, and she thinks I don't know she's there."

"So, what are we going to do with her?" Because something told me Richard would be totally against us leaving her on the street.

"I'm going to pretend I didn't know she was there until it was too late. The Order would never allow it, but since I am breaking all the rules anyway… She's a good kid. She will be useful."

He trailed off as we approached a mud-splattered SUV. It was white, and even with dirt all over it, I could tell it was still a sweet looking ride. Richard clicked the alarm on his keychain, and I slid into the smooth gray passenger's seat.

As I reached for my seat belt, I heard a gasp from the backseat. Slowly I turned around.

"Um, hi, Stella," I said, as I tried to manage a smile. But my heart just wasn't in it. It had been a while since I'd seen Stella Roca. I could tell she looked a lot like her father and brother, only much easier on the eyes.

"You!" Stella gaped at me as Richard climbed into the driver's seat. I watched as her eyes sharply focused on her brother next.

"What is he doing here?" she demanded.

"He's going to help us find Emily," he said calmly.

"I thought," she paused, "you came here to find Barneby Knotts!"

"I wish I knew where he was, sis, but he wasn't home, and his dad didn't know either."

"He's in the Caribbean," I said, and two sets of Roca eyeballs redirected their vision to me. "With Tyler, looking for something they aren't sure exists." I am sure that is where he is since that was what he told me he was going to do yesterday. Stella and Richard stared at me like I started speaking Finnish, and I couldn't get away. I tried to focus on something besides their gaze and realized that Richard's muddy SUV still has that new car smell.

"*You* are friends with Barneby Knotts?" Stella asks in an accusing disbelieving tone.

See, I get that a lot, so I am really not offended. Barneby Knotts is something of a hero legend, and at an obscenely young age, that is pretty damn impressive, even to me. And I honestly could care less about most of that garbage.

Barneby tells things like it is, and I respect that. So just because he became the youngest hero in America, oh like ever, doesn't mean I give him a hard time about it.

"Sure," I said with a shrug, "he's my friend."

"I don't believe you," muttered Stella from the backseat.

I just shrugged. I wasn't going to give Stella the satisfaction of arguing with her. My personal life was none of her business, and I really didn't want anything to do with her.

But Richard just wouldn't let it die. "I'm afraid he is telling the truth, sis. I've actually heard Barneby say Vallenez was his friend, and that he trusts him because he's never lied to him." Richard chuckled.

I have to admit, hearing that gave me a bit of personal satisfaction. I never have lied to Barneby Knotts—I try never to lie to anyone, but I would never lie to him. And of all the people in the world, there were very few that meant enough to me to keep me from selling them out. Barneby was one of them.

But Stella didn't seem to like this news. She was making a sharp clicking noise as she leaned back against the bench seat. I couldn't see her, but I got the feeling that she was staring a hole through the back of my headrest.

"What's the matter?" I teased her, "You got a crush on him or something?"

She definitely wouldn't be the first. If I didn't know better, I'd swear she had started drowning right there in the back of her brother's SUV. If you'd have heard her, you would have thought the same thing.

"Barneby Knotts is an arrogant jerk," Stella snapped. "Just like you. Actually, I can see why you two like each other."

"Stella," Richard said sternly, shifting gears into drive. "Father likes the Knotts, especially Barneby. Don't be so disrespectful."

I'm really glad Richard said something. I knew she was just lashing out because I'd embarrassed her, but no one insults Barneby Knotts on my watch. Except for maybe me.

I had Richard whip around a corner as I jumped out of the moving vehicle. We were still being followed, and I did not want them to know where I lived, or where my mother was.

I ducked into yet another dark alley. Really, it was amazing I hadn't learned my lesson by then. A metal clanging scared me more than it normally would have, and I spun a full circle before finally realizing it was just a stupid cat.

Returning my eyes to the road, I watched as a blue car with dark tint drove past, and I held my breath until they followed Richard into the next bend.

I ran the half-block to our apartment complex, and up the stairs, without looking back. My mother was already in bed, but she called my name when she heard the door click closed behind me.

When I walked into the tiny bedroom, she didn't budge from the fetal position she had curled herself into, head half on her pillow.

"Victor." She said quietly.

"Yeah, Mom?" I answered because she is the only one around who can get away with calling me Victor.

"Are you staying home now?" she asked, but I know what she really meant. She meant, was I staying home from now on.

I hated telling her no, but at least that time, I knew she would understand.

"No, Ma," I said, "but Uncle Erick is coming tomorrow, and I want you to go home with him."

"But surely you will come back," she whispered, "you won't be gone long." She said sadly.

"Of course I'm coming back," I assured her, "but I don't know how long I'm going to be gone. Emily is in trouble, mom, and I've got to save her."

Mom rolled over, but she still didn't sit up.

"Emily is such a nice girl, dear. It's a shame things won't work out for you two in the end."

Mom was always saying stuff like that. Like she knew what was really going to happen in the future. And sometimes, sometimes, I thought maybe she did. Right now, that thought was way too depressing.

I slunk back to my dresser, which was in the living room, and threw an extra set of clothes into my old ratty messenger bag before heading into the kitchen. I was looking for something, but it wasn't a snack.

I dug around under the sink until what I was looking for: an old box of mouse traps. Sandwiched between the stacks of wooden blocks was all the money I had in the world. Which I have to say, was not too shabby.

I found an envelope and scribbled *Uncle Erick for Mom*, on the top, and left her half. Just in case.

There were only five minutes until I had to meet Richard at the Texaco two blocks East of here. I was going to be late. Carefully, I pulled back the curtain on the front window. There was no blue car anywhere.

I was out the door and down the steps in seconds, and there was not a soul in sight. Just how I liked it.

It was January, and frost was forming on all the parked car windows. I was thankful for my leather jacket, which looked cool, but usually wasn't needed in Houston, Texas. Luckily the ground was dry and thus free from ice, as I was in a bit of a hurry.

When I got to the gas station, Richard was pumping gas, and Stella was walking out of the convenience store, clutching a tray full of hot drinks and a bag of candy bars. Instantly I disliked her a lot less. However, that feeling was short-lived: as she walked past me, she announced that it was my turn to sit in the back seat. I wanted to tell her where she could stick it, but it wasn't like I really wanted to sit next to her brother dearest anyway.

As Richard pulled back on to the street, the cabin of the SUV was temporarily illuminated by headlights from behind. I didn't have to turn around to know who it was.

"Your friends are back," said Richard, "Mind telling me who I am helping you run away from this time?"

Ha, so funny. Like Rich would really help me with anything, ever.

"Don't worry," I said, "it's just the Nigerians. They aren't dangerous."

"The Nigerians?" Richard asked me skeptically.

"Pax and Wilford," I said, as Stella turned in her seat to look at me. "I don't actually know if they are from Nigeria, that's just what their email said."

"Wait!" said Stella with a bemused expression, "You got an email from some guys who claimed to be from Nigeria?" I nodded. "Did they claim a relative of yours had died and left you a zillion dollars?"

"Well," I said. "Yeah, actually."

"And you believed them?" Stella and Richard shrieked at the same time.

"Of course not! I'm not an idiot, thanks."

Stella snorted and turned back. I got the feeling she thought otherwise.

"I told them, sure I'd send them four grand to cover legal expenses. I was just baiting them. I don't judge you for what you do in your spare time. Anyway, I said if they wanted me to send them the money, then they would have to send me fifteen hundred American Dollars to cover my early withdrawal fees, from taking money out of my retirement account."

"And they bought that?" Richard said in total disbelief.

"Well, then they said they would have to raise their fees to five grand, which means I had to ask for more to cover my higher fees, and somehow I got around thirty-five hundred dollars out of them."

"You got thousands of dollars out of two Nigerian scam artists?" Stella said, looking at me again.

Richard laughed and said, "That's really funny, actually."

FOUR

"Okay, I'm curious," I said over Richard's headrest. "Where are we going exactly? Do you even know where she is? Because you haven't told me."

"I have an idea." He said without looking back. "Luckily, we are in Texas, and we can consult *The Astrologers*."

I waited for a punch line of this obvious joke, but none came. He could not be serious. Emily was being held hostage, and he wanted to have his horoscope done. What was wrong with him?

"We always consult with a mystic advisor before a quest," said Stella indifferently.

Complete nutcases, all of them, I swear.

The Woodlands, on the Northside of town, went by in a blur, and that was the last of civilization for a while. When we were firmly driving through the middle of nowhere, Richard cut across two lanes of traffic and hastily exited the freeway.

I hadn't looked back in a while, but I assumed this meant we were still being followed.

Richard swerved onto a horrible gravel road. I hated the way it sounded, and I hated the way it made my teeth rattle around in my head.

The gravel road turned into a dirt one that led into a deep, wooded area. It snaked, and turned, and bent, and just when I was convinced we were all going to slam into a tree, and the woods were at their thickest, we were spat out into a perfectly circular clearing.

In the middle of the clearing was a small house with old white siding and a painted wooden porch. On the porch was a couple that was dressed like the days of hippies had never ended, or maybe just no one had ever told them. Boy, did they look grim.

I was really sure they were about to predict our gruesome and untimely deaths, but it's not like that would have been hard. A hero, a future hero, and a professional snitch—it wasn't very likely any of us would be dying of old age in our sleep. If that was all it took to be a metaphysical adviser, I was about to find myself in a new career. I'd love to sit around all day and predict doom and disaster. In fact, just thinking about it gave me a warm and fuzzy feeling inside.

When we parked in front of the house, the woman managed a small smile for Stella, but her husband gazed at Richard like it pained him to do it. No one was looking at me.

"Your father said you two had both run off," said the woman, whose name I learned was Mary. "We hoped you would wind up here."

"Sorry to put you in this position, Tom," Richard said, reaching out to take the man's hand.

"Not a problem, Richard. We do not recognize all the rules of man, because we know we are ruled by the movement of the stars."

Okay, I thought. Here it comes. Bad news, hippies. *Do they even believe this garbage?* I wondered as I followed the Rocas into the house.

The first thing I noticed about the inside was that the main room hardly had any furniture. There was a large wooden table, with dozens of circular shapes burned into the top of it, and more pillows than I thought could possibly exist in the world. In every shape and color imaginable—even pillows that looked like they'd make awful pillows.

Then I looked up. The ceiling was painted a very detailed version of space, like the heavens, in intense shades of blue and purple. There were glowing stars and planets, but not like the kind you would find in a kid's bedroom. These were beautiful and amazingly accurate.

Mary saw me staring at them intently, but she didn't mention it.

"Sit down, Richard," Tom instructed and lit incense on the wooden table. "Mary will see to the others in the kitchen."

I kind of wanted to stay and see the show, but I was also hungry. And old folks were sometimes good for cookies. But I glanced back to Mary again and thought she was probably going to try and subject me to some sort of all-organic health food. Bummer, because those candy bars were starting to feel like I ate them a million years ago.

Stella and I seated ourselves at the small kitchen table. This room seemed plain by comparison to the first, and relatively normal. It did have bright yellow curtains, though, and one of those cat clocks with the eyes and tail swinging back and forth, next to the refrigerator.

"How about we have a snack?" asked Mary. "Eat while Richard has his reading, and then maybe we can have an informal one of our own."

I wondered if it would be rude to eat, but avoid the psychic hotline treatment.

"I sense Victor here does not wish to eat health food."

My head snapped up, but that had to have been a lucky guess, though I couldn't remember telling her my name.

Also, she was *so* not allowed to call me Victor.

"How about some chocolate chip muffins?" she asked me.

"Yes, please," I said with a smile. If she gave me chocolate, she could call me whatever she wanted.

She allowed us to eat in silence, though Mary continued to stare at me.

"Mr. Vallenez?" she said, reminding me of a math teacher I'd once had. "Why do you enjoy your current profession?"

All right, this lady is really starting to creep me out. I have this thing where I really don't like to talk about my job. I forced down my last bite of muffin and wondered if she would notice or care if I just didn't answer her. But Stella kept kicking me under the table, so I had to say something.

"I wouldn't say I enjoy it. I make decent money, and I can help my mom. It's just a job."

Mary frowned, and there suddenly seemed to be a lot more lines in her face. "Victor," she reached out to touch my arm, and it was hard for me not to recoil. "You have such a psychic presence. Why has your mother not taught you?"

"Uh," I said. "I have no idea what you are talking about. My mother is blind and really just—unwell."

I could hear Stella swallow from next to me. All my skin itched to know what was going on.

"Mary," she said. "He doesn't know, and I don't think now is the best time to tell him."

"Tell me what?" I turned to her, demanding an answer. No one was listening. They seemed to be having a silent conversation across the table. Mary broke eye contact first.

"I guess you're right, dear," she sighed. "But it's just such a shame. Maybe you should bring him back here after you find the girl."

Um, no, I thought. Nice place to visit, but I could tell by the sound of Mary's voice she meant to stay for more than muffins the next time.

"Though," she said, "I can see he doesn't much care for that idea." Her eyes bored into mine. "But maybe he will change his mind when he understands."

I shrugged. It was really hard to know, since no one wanted to tell me.

FIVE

Later, I would wish Mary had never brought out that worn box of Tarot cards. She did Stella first, and they both got excited every time they turned a card over. Personally, I had no idea what an Ace of Wands or a Five of Pentacles was. I liked the idea of the money cards, but when I accidentally let that slip, I had to listen to the long and drawn-out version of what the card stood for, and in this case, it had nothing to do with money. It figures. How were you even supposed to know that?

Five cards later, we learned that Stella would get what she wanted if she worked hard and planned ahead, which sounded just like the kind of vague B.S. you would find in the astrology section of a magazine. Twenty minutes for one broken sentence—but then it got worse because then it was my turn.

Mary instructed me to clear my mind and think of only what I was seeking clarity in. She suggested possible lifestyle changes. I agreed, mostly because I did not want to object and have to hear about it.

My first card was the Devil, and I couldn't help that I immediately tensed. Mary was quick to assure me that it doesn't mean what one would assume. Of course not. It means new beginnings, or shedding old habits, or something. I thought Mary might keep that card up her sleeve, just to torment people like me. I assumed she wouldn't get many visitors out here, but there was a slight chance I could be wrong —I was about every card in her deck, apparently.

So the Devil was my problem or situation card, or whatever. My next card was The Fool in my past position. By then, I was starting to wonder if Mary was trying to tell me something on a personal level. Once again, she assured me it did not mean what I thought it meant. Are you noticing a trend?

My future card was a guy that looked like he was planting sticks in a field of mud. It was called The Seven of Wands. I waited for a long-winded explanation, but none was provided. Yet this card couldn't mean what I thought it did, because my only idea was that it wouldn't be very profitable to plant sticks. Maybe someone should have told him.

"Find your courage, Mr. Vallenez," Mary grumbled. "Find it and never let it go." And that was when my reading ended because Mary re-stacked the cards and put them away in their box.

I remember thinking that was pretty interesting, considering I was a bit of a coward. I never stick around the see the action or the consequences, and I never stick my neck out for just anyone either. Not even this quest, which looked innocent enough on the outside. I was doing it for purely selfish reasons. Actually, I do most things for selfish reasons.

Still, I didn't much like basically being called a coward out loud by Mary. No one likes to hear the truth. Not even me, and not even when I already know it.

So far, that day had been particularly exhausting, and I was pretty sure the last time I slept was two days ago. I had laid my head on the kitchen table only moments before Tom came in.

"All done, dear?" asked Mary from the sink.

"Yes, Richard is meditating on the porch now."

Of course he was meditating. It made perfect sense, right? They weren't bishops. They were those weird little bald monks that sing chants in the mountains. I closed my eyes again, and I was looking at a vision of real mountains. It wasn't right, there was a lot of orange in my vision, and it looked nothing like I thought Tibet or those places with monks should look.

My perspective shifted, to trees, and then a cave? No. It was open. There were walls, but no ceiling. That was when I saw Emily.

I banged my knee on the table because I stood up so fast.

"What's wrong?" Stella asked from behind me.

"That wasn't Tibet!" I shouted. I knew that probably made no sense, but it was the only sentence I seemed to be able to form.

"Of course it wasn't, Victor. It was Utah." Mary wiped off the last of the muffin plates.

"Utah?" Now I was confused. I had never been to Utah. Heck, I'd never been further West than Texas, and I didn't understand why I would be daydreaming about it.

"How do you know?" I asked her, but Tom just steered me back to my seat. I really didn't want to go, but I couldn't make my legs protest. I wanted them to tell me everything they knew they weren't saying, and I was starting to think it was worse than my imagination was dictating.

"You don't realize—" said Tom, choosing his words cautiously. "You are projecting your psychic vision outwards. Anyone close enough to you with the gift of sight could see it now. Quite clearly, I might add."

"That sounds impossible," I said. I don't believe in psychics. Things like that don't happen in real life.

"Ever had deja-vu, Mr. Vallenez?" Tom asked, one hand on top of mine on the table. I fought the urge to rip it away. Gone are the days I have casual physical contact with other people.

"Everyone gets deja-vu," I said flatly.

But Tom said, "Not like you, Mr. Vallenez."

Richard was on the porch. Shirt off, sweat glistening on his back, he was such a show-off. I guess being a hero might have some advantages, though not the ones you would probably realize. Most of it seemed like way too much work. Muscles, though, would be nice.

I was scrawny and pale. My loser father gave me so little in life, it was practically an outrage I should get his white boy complexion instead of my mother's darker Hispanic one. But who cared? I didn't. I had already wasted far too much of my life comparing myself to Richard Roca.

He opened his eyes and smiled at his sister when she walked out.

"We're going to Utah," he said exuberantly.

"We know," said Stella as she extended a hand to help her brother up, which in my opinion, was rather unnecessary.

Richard looked confused, which was a good look for him. It was nice for me, seeing plainly that he does not know everything.

"How?" he asked. "Did Tom say?"

"No, Vallenez saw it in that messed-up brain of his."

Okay, that had been a bit mean, but they were both staring at me so bizarrely that I didn't even notice. I wanted to know what the heck was going on in my life. How suddenly I was the weird one.

We used Tom and Mary's ten-year-old computer to book airline tickets online. It would have been slow on its own, but their sub-standard dialup connection made that worse. I didn't even know you could still get internet from your phone line. That was crazy.

I opened my mouth half a dozen times, to say one of us should just book them from their cell phone. But it was so much fun watching the golden boy lose his temper over slow-loading pages. Then I felt guilty when I remembered Emily was waiting for us. Luckily, it ended up not mattering. It was just over two hours until the next flight for Salt Lake, which would give us just enough time to get back to Houston.

We left in a hurry, but not before Mary grabbed me in an awkward hug. She told me not to go looking for trouble, but I wasn't sure she meant it in the usual way.

SIX

Traffic was miserable, and we had to run for our gate, but that was fine since no one had any luggage to check.

Richard got the window seat, and I got the aisle. At least I didn't have to sit by him. I hated planes. I had only ever been on three my whole life, and they all ended with me puking in the little paper sack from the seat in front of me. There was no way I was vomiting in front of Richard. No way.

The plane was freezing. I don't think I had been so cold somewhere climate-controlled in my life. I wasn't sure exactly when I had drifted off, I didn't even remember closing my eyes, but I remember them feeling really dry.

I was in those same woods from before. Patches of rocks stuck out of heaps of snow and piles of pine needles. In my dream, I kicked a little hill of them, and they scattered like they would in real life. The air was colder than it had been on the plane, and the wind nipped at my nose and cheeks better than any A/C unit ever could. Shoving my hands deep into my pockets, I wasn't surprised to feel some relief from the brutal breeze on my fingers.

It was just a dream, so it didn't matter at all that I walked deeper into the forest. I could just as easily walk into the woods in Utah and come out in the middle of the Sahara Desert. That was preferable, actually. I hate being cold. It was just a dream.

The woods were so black I couldn't see anything until I practically walked into it. There might have been a bright moon and stars, but the trees had gotten so thick I had no hope of seeing them.

I thought I heard people talking, but there was definitely no one around. Not even a rodent moved in the stillness, but I heard talking again. This time I was sure of it, but it sounded garbled like they were speaking to me from the other side of a long tunnel or far away.

Wait, I thought. *Was that Stella?*

The nonsense words seemed louder now. They also seemed to be coming from directly over my head. Like some deity speaking to its people from above. I was almost positive it was Stella, though, and she seemed to be yelling and really upset by then when a sharp pain on my cheek startled me awake.

She had slapped me! She had actually slapped me in the middle of an airplane! She said I didn't wake up, somehow I managed to sleep all the way to Utah, and all the other passengers that were not going on to LA were already off.

Hastily, I retrieved my old messenger bag from between my feet and slung it over one shoulder. I stood out in the aisle and then followed the Rocas off the plane. Maybe I was losing it.

Even though there was no luggage waiting in baggage claim for us, we still had to walk through it, and the crowd in it, to get to the rental car place. Luckily, Richard's Order had a contract with one of the car companies. That was sweet because I was pretty sure at nineteen, he was still too young to be trusted by most of them.

Stella and I plopped down on a cold metal bench, while Richard talked to the squat women behind the counter. She batted her eyes and smiled a lot. It was pretty gross, really. I thought someone should do the humane thing and tell her she had no chance.

Richard rented a bright red Jeep, and that made me worry that there might be off-roading involved. I called shotgun before Stella could climb into the front. I was pretty sure I heard her mumble something about children and attitude adjustments, but she got in back anyway. Ms. Sour Puss would have to work on her attitude herself if she was going to be a super wholesome hero, just like the rest of her family.

"So, where are we going now?" I asked Richard as he spun the tires leaving the parking lot. I was really sure these Jeep things had a high rollover rate among teenagers. Great.

"Someone slept through the briefing on the plane." Stella's rude tone came through loud and clear from the backseat.

"Just so you know," I said. "And not that it's any of your business, or I care at all what you think of me. But I hadn't slept in two days. How did you expect me to function on this escapade without any?"

"Stella," said Richard softly. "You must try not to judge others so harshly. It's not our way."

Sure, it's not, I thought. Really, heroes were all the same. They say they don't judge others, but just try pushing their lines of what they think is good, and what they think isn't. Stella sighed, but she didn't say anything else. I was hoping she felt a little bit ashamed of herself, but if I were her, I would probably just be pissed off.

"We're going to Zion National Park, an area in the West Rim. It's going to require some hiking. Think you can handle that?" Richard asked as he eyed my Van's skate shoes skeptically.

"Sure," I said, nodding. "No problem."

Of course, I had never been hiking in my life, but I did not plan on telling perfect Richard that. Hero mommies and daddies were always taking their kids off on camping adventures, at least they were, according to Barneby Knotts.

I was in pretty good shape. I did a lot of running, even if it was away. This time I would be running to something important. I was sure I could wing it.

The thing about traveling back through time zones like we did, is it ends up being almost the same time as it was when you left. Even if your body is telling you otherwise, clocks are telling you you're wrong. I could only imagine how unsettled I'd feel if I hadn't slept.

Stella snored softly in the back seat, as Richard pulled off I-15 to stop at a huge chain outdoors store. I offered to wait with Stella in the Jeep. I really doubted I would be of much help in selecting our outdoor equipment, and the truth was I kind of wanted to nod off again myself.

My power nap was great and everything, but with dreaming about being lost in the cold woods and all, it just wasn't as restful as it could have been. I closed my eyes as soon as Richard was out of sight, but of course, I couldn't get comfortable. I wished I had let Stella sit up front; that way, it would have been me sprawled out in the backseat like she was now. I reclined the seat back onto one of her knees, but she was a heavy sleeper. She just rolled over and mumbled something sleepy under her breath. I wasn't vain enough to think it was about me. She wasn't my type anyway.

I had just drifted off when the wind tunnel voices were back. This time they sounded nothing like Stella. They were male and familiar with their strong accents. I wasn't in a forest this time, however, I was standing on a rocky ledge. Yeah, maybe I am a bit afraid of heights, but so what? A lot of people are.

For whatever reason, I kept looking down. My dream self did not want to cooperate with what my real self wanted. There was a huge roaring bonfire below me; I could feel the warmth from it all the way up to my face. I wanted to turn and run, but dream me wouldn't let me.

Then a horrific banging noise shook everything. Surely it should have made the rocks around me tumble to the ground below, but they seemed unaffected. Maybe my imagination was already used up on other things.

The broken voices continued, louder, and angrier. It was sort of comforting to know these voices did not belong to Stella, but weird at the same time. Hadn't I only heard them before when she was trying to wake me up? If so, then who was speaking to me now, because there was no one else in the Jeep with me? At least there hadn't been when I'd fallen to sleep.

I remember my dream self groaning. I was sure if I woke up just then, I would find some concerned citizen thinking we were sleeping in a stolen car, or living on the streets, or dead or something.

The only experience I have in waking myself up comes when I have already hit the snooze alarm three or four times, but this time it was easy. I opened my eyes, and I was wide awake, and that was a good thing as Pax and Wilford were beating on my window, and they were pissed off.

Granted, Pax and Wilford were always pissed off, but this time they were angry, and they effectively had me trapped. Richard was inside with the only key, and I was locked in a tight box with a sleeping girl who wasn't all that fond of me.

So the important question was, would they damage the vehicle in an attempt to reach me? I was pretty sure that would tick Richard off, and as funny as his face would probably be, I just could not deal with that right now.

I doubted they would. Pax and Wilford had been following me for months, but had never laid a hand on me. They had only been a bit of a nuisance. Then again, I had effectively evaded them until now. I had been caught twice in as many days. I was really starting to feel I might be losing my touch. Maybe I needed to retire. It could have saved me a lot of trouble.

Stella had awoken by then, and I was already thinking I would rather be outside with the two irate Nigerians than inside with one recently rudely woken Roca. At least, at the moment, she was pretending to be on my side, and all of her anger was being directed at the men by my window.

She cussed at them in Spanish, and admittedly that was hot. Pax and Wilford didn't seem to know what to think about Stella. I could tell by their faces they were weighing the pros and cons of an even-numbered altercation. Stella already had her cellphone out, calling Richard. She had a brief conversation with him under her breath and in Spanish.

"He's checking out now." She said louder than she normally would have so that Pax and Wilford could hear her. "He wants to know if he should come out now?" she said more softly. "Are they going to start something before he gets back?"

I shook my head no. I didn't think they would, and I really hoped I was right. I was just fighting the urge to blow a big raspberry at the two of them glaring at Stella and me through the windshield. They were still trying to decide what to do in a language I had never heard before.

Then Richard was back before they could decide. When I first saw him, I thought it was just a moving pile of outdoor gear. Surely we wouldn't need all that. I could make out what looked like a tent still in the box, and three sleeping bags which were essential. I had no what the rest of it was.

When Richard made it to the Jeep, he dumped all the gear to the ground and grabbed Wilford, the larger of the two Nigerians, by the collar and flung him into the side of the Jeep.

I had a lovely view of the man's sweaty backside.

"Look," said Richard to the man he had cornered, "I do not have time to deal with you right now. But since you won't stop making a nuisance out of yourself, I feel I have to set you straight, or you are just going to keep showing up. As far as I am concerned, you are the scum of the Earth. At least Vallenez here has the decency not to lie about what he is, or hide behind a computer screen. I don't even want to know how many elderly people you have taken advantage of, people who didn't know better. I don't know if you have ever heard the expression, you should never cross a double-crosser, but you tried, and it didn't work out for you. Frankly, I don't care. I need the guy you are following right now, so you can just piss off."

All I could think was, *oh my God, Richard just said piss*. Imagine that.

Pax and Wilford stalked off, shooting me agitated looks until they were out of sight. Richard quickly shoved the gear in the back with his sister without a word. Neither of the Rocas seemed too happy to be in my presence at the moment.

SEVEN

Richard had to go in and buy us all hiking licenses. He ran inside minutes before the office closed. I was a bit put off that he didn't tell me that most people do this West Rim hike in two days. Two full days and not what we were planning on doing. Which the Park Ranger went out of his way to tell Richard was a horrible idea.

So Richard wouldn't illegally trek through the darkness without a license, but he would do it against the advice of someone who knows better. Great to know where he stands on this whole rule-breaking thing. Good to know he has his priorities straight. We wouldn't be much help to Emily or anyone else if we all plummeted to our deaths off a cliff in the dark.

But we marched forward anyway. Me with my messenger bag and the huge hiking pack Richard had slapped on my back. It had my sleeping bag, gross dehydrated food rations, an LED camping lantern, water, and a bunch of other stuff I didn't understand the purpose of, other than to make the bag heavier and the hike more miserable.

The sun was already mostly set, and colder air was rushing in as the sky grew increasingly grayer. My hands were already freezing, just like they had been in my dream, but the scenery was all wrong. We were still on higher grassland, there was the occasional pine tree popping out of the ground, but none of them was a forest.

The terrain was still flat, but that didn't mean it was even. I shoved my hands deep into my pockets and tried to walk that way, but fell less than a minute later. I tore a hole on my jeans in the right knee. That was wonderful, now my hands *and* legs would freeze.

Then it started to snow. I had never seen it before, and I thought if it didn't intend to freeze me to death if I stood still too long, it would be beautiful. I stopped, just for a second, to look up.

"Gloves are in the mesh pocket on the left side of your pack," Richard said without looking back. "I just guessed your size, but they should be fine."

"Thanks," I said. I really did appreciate it, even if I hated saying so out loud.

When the last of the daylight filtered away, Richard pulled out a really awesome high-powered flashlight and started walking faster. I fell many more times trying to keep up, but fortunately, no one mentioned it.

By the time we stood on the edge of the forest, both my knees were torn open and bleeding freely. My ears were freezing, and I was shaking so uncontrollably, I could hardly stand up. Or maybe that was the blood loss. Richard had failed to mention there was also a hat for me in another pocket till just two minutes before.

Mostly my black leather coat was now just for show. The lining was thinner than I realized, and it did little to keep me warm. I had never imagined the need for a heavier coat while being in Texas, but I was jealous of both the Rocas' very warm-looking puffy ski jackets.

I was really looking forward to trying to suffocate myself in my sleeping bag.

I sat there freezing and miserable, as Richard set up the tent. I never offered to help because I never do, and not because I could hardly move. Or that is what I would have said if anyone bothered to ask me.

When Richard was done with the tent, which might have been some kind of record, he threw me a roll of duct tape from his pack.

"Did you poke a hole in your brand new tent?" I asked sarcastically.

"No, stupid, it's for your pants." He said, rolling his eyes. "Sorry, you aren't stupid, you are actually quite bright. You just insist on doing so many stupid things."

"Gee Richard," I said as I patched the rips in my pants with his tape. "Why don't you tell me how you really feel?"

Richard stilled. He looked at me with an odd sort of expression he had never given me before. He looked like he wanted to say something to me, but instead, he just climbed into the tent with a sigh—sleeping bag in one hand, his sister right behind him.

I guessed I should probably try and sleep too, even if I had almost forgotten how cold I was.

"Scoot over," I said to Richard. Because, of course, he wasn't going to let me sleep that close to his sister. Too bad, because she smelled a lot better than he did. I also happened to know Richard was a notorious cuddler, and it was nothing personal. He just wasn't my type.

I crammed my sleeping bag against the left wall of the tent, and I immediately wondered if there was any hope of me getting warmer this way. At least outside, I had been moving.

I climbed into my sleeping bag, coat, gloves, shoes, and newly acquired beanie hat and all. But I didn't feel any better, and I really had to pee. But man, I could not imagine a trip to the bushes at this temperature.

"Richard?" I asked, nudging him through my sleeping bag. "Are you still awake?"

"No," He mumbled. Turning his head to look at me. "What?"

"I have to pee," I confessed.

He rolled his eyes. "And why are you telling me about it? Go outside."

"Right, about that," I said. "It's freezing out there, got any tips?"

"You're kidding, right?" he finally said.

"Uh, yeah." I managed to lie. Honestly, I had really been hoping that he knew something that could have kept my anatomy from catching frostbite, but I wasn't going to say that out loud.

"Richard?" I asked.

"Now what?" he sighed again.

"What were you going to say earlier?"

in your life," he said, "just do what I ask you to." I couldn't tell if he was telling me or his sister.

"Aren't you going to draw your sword or something?" I asked when he was a few feet away because I didn't even think big Richard could go very long at wrestling a bear.

"I refuse to hurt an animal unless I absolutely must," he told me over his shoulder. *Sure*, I thought, *wait until he sees the glowing red eyes.*

Stella and I walked to the edge of the woods and perched ourselves on two rocks sticking out of a snowdrift. The Nigerians came running out of the forest moments later.

"Your friend!" shouted Pax.

And Stella instantly stiffened.

"He is crazy!" added Wilford. "Walked right up to de bear an' try to reason wit' it!"

They kept running back the way we had hiked in, and before long, they were out of sight.

No noise came out of the woods now, which was a good thing. I wasn't sure of much, but was a hundred percent sure that we would have heard the bear eating Richard alive.

"Don't worry," Stella said, more to herself than to me. "Richard is good with animals."

I nodded. Of course. Richard was good at everything, right?

"Well, what have we here?" a voice whispered in the night, "You've separated and made it so easy for us."

Stella screamed, and I turned started to see who had spoken. A girl of maybe fourteen, and a woman that could only be her mother, stood behind us. They were dressed so strangely, I wondered how they had not frozen to death already. But, the cold did not seem to bother them.

The mother wore a long purple gown with bell sleeves, and she stood barefoot in the snow. No hat, no gloves, no jacket. The girl was wearing a shorter purple dress, legs, and feet also bare. Both women had unruly black hair, but the girl's was shorter, like she had tried to cut it into something resembling a bob.

"I would stop screaming if I were you, Stella Roca," crooned the mother, "I would hate to have to persuade you."

See, they never really mean *persuade.* The true meaning can vary, but it usually hurts.

"You're a witch!" spat Stella from between chattering teeth.

I thought I could probably come up with a better word, even with frostbite, but when I looked back at the woman, I got the feeling that Stella meant she was an actual witch. And... well, that was just great, really fantastic.

See, sometimes heroes have to fight villains that do not exactly fight fair. I don't really have much experience in that branch of the business, but I knew Stella's family had fought all kinds of bad guys. I guess I figured she would know. I knew there were people who used magic, people who could turn themselves into animals and vice-versa, and demons and monsters that weren't like heroes at all.

Something told me these women weren't the common garden variety witches either.

"Richard will come for us!" Stella said defiantly.

"Trust me," said the younger witch, "we're counting on it."

The witches took us off in a direction I would have never considered going if I wasn't being forced. We had to slide down a steep grade and into a deep ravine. Rocks shifted, and ice cracked below our unsteady feet. During the non-winter months, this icy death trap was likely filled with water, but now it was covered in snow, some of it, quite deep. It was hard for me to walk in. It was worse for Stella, who was several inches shorter than I was, but she refused to let me help her.

I was pretty mad that the witches, who were obviously using magic to keep themselves from freezing, couldn't do the same for us. I really wanted to stop and check my pack to see if Richard had also thought to include snowshoes, but I was pretty sure I would have seen those already.

The only plus of the snow was, it was a great indicator of which direction we had gone in. The witches, who wanted Richard to find us, did not bother to cover up our tracks. I readily admit I am a selfish lad, and I didn't care so much that Richard was walking into a trap, so long as I managed to walk away from it. Besides, it was obvious these witches were the ones who had taken Emily. Stupid Roca hadn't wanted to tell me before, because he knew I'd be pissed off.

Trudging through the snow had given me time to be alone with my misery, and I had come to all kinds of awful conclusions. Emily being taken, the bear, the witches, all a setup to get Richard, and I had just gone along with it. Because no matter what, I couldn't just stop loving Emily, and he totally used me—for way less than what my normal going rate was.

The ravine narrowed, and suddenly we were walking under a huge natural arch. I wanted time to freeze between the beats of my stubborn heart, so I could pause just a moment to look without having to feel guilty about it. The odds of me seeing something like this again in real life were slim. I like to believe that one day I really could get away, but the reality was I'd probably live in the same rathole until I died, and that would be the end of me. Still, that was better than my new fear of dying here and never getting to live at all.

After the arch, we walked into a makeshift campsite in the belly of what looked like a caved-in cavern. In the middle of it, there was a familiar-looking bonfire. The closer we got to it, the better I felt. I was getting to the point where I did not feel too bad about being held hostage and trudging through the snow. I probably would have gone willingly if the witches had just told me I'd finally get warm. Every part of me was now numb, and I considered that to be a vast improvement.

I felt sleepy again. Stella didn't look like she had fared our winter-time parade much better. Her usually tan skin was pale and clammy looking. I couldn't imagine being wet in this cold, and I knew that had to be a bad sign.

"Sit over there," said the young witch, pointing up against the rock wall on the far side of the fire.

With pleasure, I thought, but I practically had to carry Stella all the way there. She didn't even protest, which was a huge indication of how bad off she really was. The usual Stella would have told me to go jump off a cliff if I even thought about touching her. Never mind doing what

I was doing then, pressing every inch of her body against mine in an effort to keep her from freezing.

"Vic," a voice called from the ledge above us, and I stilled. I knew that voice. Some things you can just never forget, especially when you dream about them every night of your life.

"Emily," I whispered. And then, I admit it. I dropped Stella Roca. But really, it was an accident.

NINE

Emily was in a cage, almost directly over our heads, and I was amazed I hadn't noticed her there before. As if reading my thoughts like no one else could, Emily said, "It's hidden by magic."

Of course it was. Why wouldn't it be? We were currently being held hostage in the middle of a national park, by a couple of broads who could use witchcraft for anything. Snow is hot pink, and the moon is made out of cheese. I would have believed almost anything.

"Emily," Stella whispered, still on the floor by the fire, exactly where I had dropped her. "Are those witches the Van Trapps?"

"Yes," Emily sighed.

Not that it cleared anything up for me.

"Who are the Van Trapps?" I asked. I hoped they weren't some top ten villain that everyone should know about; I'd have to turn in my professional snitch badge—if there was such a thing.

Sparks crackled and flew up from the bonfire in every direction. Some of them were normal oranges and reds, but some of them were purple and green. The off ones reminded me of Emily's eyes, and how I never knew what color they would be.

"Richard had a run-in with them a few months ago. In the end, he had to kill Jaden Van Trapp." Stella whispered only loud enough for me to hear. She didn't have to tell Em. I was sure she already knew.

"And Jaden is what? A brother? A husband?" I asked, seeking clarification.

"The older witch's name is Miranda. That's her daughter Bridget. Jaden was Miranda's son, Bridget's older brother."

I really wanted to be mad at Richard, and I was, but I knew it was an irrational anger. It's not like Emily would have been any safer with me. But while I am being honest about it, if Emily hadn't fallen in love with Richard, then I would have never ended up with this kind of life. We still would have been watching rental movies in my crummy apartment.

The witches weren't talking. They stood there with their arms out, waiting to spring into action. The snow and rocks were an eerie backdrop against the moonlight. I wondered what sort of instantaneous magic they were capable of. I knew that kind was harder. I also wondered if they had set many traps. I looked around, but nothing looked out of the ordinary, except for everything.

Either way, things weren't looking too great for Richard. Of course, as soon as I started feeling bad for the guy, he showed up and had to ruin it.

"Hello Miranda." said Richard calmly, "I guess it was you who sent the bear after us. I realized that when I noticed it was no longer alive."

Now, wait a second, I thought. I had seen the bear only moments before Richard had gone in after it, and I can safely say it was very much alive. All its teeth, and growling, and red eyes—hmm... maybe the eyes...

"That is what the Van Trapps do," Stella said. "Reanimate things."

"Reanimate?" I croaked. "Like animal zombies?" I asked, horrified.

"Not just animals," croaked Emily from above, "people too, but it takes more effort."

I sprang to my numb feet so fast I fell, but I had to check. Relief washed over me when I was met with her same green-brown eyes, even though I had to stand on tiptoes to get a good look. I sighed, a puff of white tumbled out of my mouth as I forced myself to refocus on Richard. He was outnumbered and unfairly matched.

In my mind, using magic was cheating.

Miranda snapped her fingers, and a flock of molting and decaying blackbirds appeared and begun frantically pecking at Richard. Feathers flew, and more and more patches of dead skin appeared on the birds, whose red glowing orbs made lines like lasers in the dark night.

Richard raised his sword, but it did little good. They were already dead, and I got the feeling they'd continue on long after the last of their feathers floated to the ground. Several of the birds managed to wrap their dead, disgusting feet around the blade and wrenched Richard's sword from his hand. It landed only a few feet in front of us, hilt dangerously close to the fire.

No one but me seemed to notice, but Emily was screaming and crying and begging for the women to call off their horrible birds, and I couldn't take it. Bridget and Miranda were laughing so hard they could probably wake the dead—without magic. No one was paying me any attention at all, which was just fine by me. Especially now when it came in handy.

Quickly and quietly, I picked up Richard's sword from where it had fallen. It was almost too hot to touch. I felt the intricate carvings threaten to sear themselves into my skin—I hoped they wouldn't, or I'd never be able to forget stupid Richard.

I crept up to the women and paused. Still, they did not notice me. The moment before I plunged the blade into Miranda's back, I remember thinking I had never killed anyone before—and that I'd never be able to say that again.

Shoving the sword through Miranda seemed to take a lot less effort than it should have, and suddenly everyone's eyes were on me. The witches never saw me coming, and the only noise Miranda made was the sound that echoed around us when she hit the ground with a thud, Richard's sword still in her.

Bridget screamed, Stella gasped, and Emily finally ceased to make a sound at all. At that moment that Miranda's heart beat its last cruel note, all the awful blackbirds fell dead out of the sky.

Bridget ran towards me, but Richard grabbed her around the middle before I even realized he had moved. He tossed her easily against the wall of rock, but in my opinion, he should have thrown her harder, because all she did was hiss at us before running into the night. Why can't that idiot ever make a clean job of things?

By the time we were almost back to the Jeep, the sun was rising, and Richard had mostly stopped bleeding. Nearly ripped to shreds, and the idiot couldn't even stop smiling.

I had the strong desire to wipe it off his face for him.

He and Emily walked up front, hands laced together, sweet in a really nauseating way. Stella walked beside me, giving me off glances from time to time, and as Richard plotted how to get most of the gear and an extra body into the vehicle, I got to talk to Emily.

"You saved Richard," she said, but I could only nod in response. "You don't like him." She said it because we both already knew it.

"Just jealous," I said, because obviously, it was true.

"Why?"

Why? "Because I'm in love with you," I said before I could stop myself. This was not coming out as smooth as I planned it.

"You aren't a bad person," she said.

I was pretty sure I knew where this was headed. I wish she would spare me the *it's not you, it's me* kind of pain.

"You would make a good hero," Emily whispered closer to me.

But I was no hero.

TEN

"Wait, wait, WAIT! Tell me again how you—you, Victor Vallenez— saved the day?"

Only Barneby Knotts would find my bleeding heart funny.

"And—what was Richard doing?" he wanted to know.

"Stealing the girl—again. Scolding me worse than my mother. Being a chivalrous moron."

The usual, really. But the familiarity of it did not stop me from being bitter, though I was almost too tired for it.

"He was about to have his lovely chocolate eyeballs pecked out! Does it matter what Richard was doing?" Barneby was gagging in an attempt to keep from laughing in my face—I guess it's the thought that counts.

I had been home three days and had hardly slept. I hadn't let my mother come home, partly because I had finally got her away from the hell shack on the tracks, but mostly because I knew she'd hear me scream myself awake.

Every time I closed my eyes or went to let my mind wander, I seemed to slip into an odd mist—a whole space full of it and nothing but it—a great and empty room of fog. Maybe like I really was in Tahiti and standing at the base of a waterfall so large, it seemed to be the only thing that existed in the whole world.

And that loneliness and isolation were better than what happened next. After the first few times, when I knew to expect nothing at all, horrible things started appearing out of the mist. Not monsters, or witches, or even angry men in dark alleys, but nightmares crafted especially for me.

Always there was Emily, and always she was doing whatever might hurt me the most. Sometimes it was something as simple as smiling. There was this little voice in my head—the one I was usually good at telling to shut up—that liked to say I knew perfectly well she wasn't smiling at me.

I did know that.

Which is why her beautiful smile could wound so much when she bent down to kiss a tiny baby in her arms. The bundle was so small it could be a wadded-up bed sheet. But there was that voice again, telling me the kid's got Richard's dark hair and eyes—and that they named it after his dad. Who had probably gone and gotten himself killed by then.

Some people might call that intuition. I like to call it hell. Trust me, that was one place I was quite familiar with.

"Vallenez?" Barneby called, "Vallenez? Are you in Tahiti again?"

Not even close. That was the whole reason I asked Barneby here.

"Look, I know you just got back—but..."

"But?" Barneby asked me slowly, his eyes slanting into all business.

"I need a favor," I whispered, glancing around like I always did—

this time, worrying that when secrets were let out, they would be mine.

Barneby relaxed into his chair, his smirk sprung back into place like a rubber band that had been snapped. It happened so fast most people wouldn't have even known it had gone missing.

"And who have you pissed off this time, V?" he chuckled, but his eyes followed mine as I scanned the room again, before pulling them away to push his bangs briefly out of his face. They were just like mine and wouldn't stay.

"No one—it isn't that kind of favor. It isn't even 'work' related."

Barneby frowned, "Well, you know things are bad when you resort to using air quotes."

"Seriously," I sighed.

"Seriously," he repeated.

"Do you know—Richard called them, 'The Astrologers'?"

"Jeez! More air quotes! Why?"

I could tell his curiosity was waxing. Barneby Knotts sensed maybe there was an adventure waiting to be had. He could sniff them out like the well-bred bloodhound he was.

"Just…" I wanted to explain without having to explain. "Do you?"

ELEVEN

"Your dad bought you a new car?" I asked. Because we were standing in front of a car that was so new, I was surprised the paint wasn't still wet. It was sexy, and it was edgy and black. It was what I thought Barneby Knotts would look like if he were a car.

Not that I think he is sexy or edgy, but he likes to think he his, and the rest of the world is usually happy to oblige him.

"No," he said, setting off the car alarm instead of unlocking the doors. "Well, yes. But technically, I paid for it. You know my dad wouldn't let me have a new pair of socks unless he thought I earned them."

Barneby's voice trailed away until he finally managed to unlock the doors. As I climbed inside, I realized I really didn't know Barneby's dad at all. I had only seen the guy once, and he had quickly left the room. I didn't take it personally; most heroes are smart enough to stay away from me. He hadn't tried to ban me from hanging out with his kid or toss me out on the lawn—not that it would have stopped me—but I appreciated it.

I love new car smell, even if I can't remember having owned a new car. I took big greedy gulps of air and briefly tried to daydream about owning such a thing. Its leather seats were probably heated, but I blinked a little too long, and the mist began to slide back into my mind, and I worried; was it always there waiting to catch me asleep now? Was it a part of me? I didn't want to think about it.

"Now, how will I make fun of you?" I said, poking Barneby. But my heart wasn't in it, and my own voice sounded somehow off-key. "This new Barneby Knotts is fancy, and no longer chained to Tyler's peeling purple minivan."

Barneby had gone to shift the car out of Park, but he abruptly stopped. His fingers were almost touching the knob of the shifter, and they were shaking. It was the closest thing I had ever seen him get to flinching.

"What's wrong with Tyler?" I asked.

Barneby rolled his head on his neck like he could shake out the funk that seemed to settle there. I mentally patted myself on the back for managing to sound like I cared. The truth of the matter was Tyler, and I did not exactly get along. Barneby Knotts is my best friend, but he's also Tyler's. Unfortunately, Tyler is also Barneby's sidekick—assistant—tomato, potato, whatever. There are just some things that pride will not let me do.

"Nothing is wrong with Tyler," Barneby answered.

That might have been the most unconvincing thing he had ever said, and I think he knew that too.

I asked, "Don't want to talk about it?" but I already knew the answer.

"Nope," and with that, he threw the car into Reverse without looking back.

Barneby and I really understood each other. But it had just

occurred to me—after the horn of an approaching truck sounded behind us—that I had never been in a vehicle he was driving. Barneby is one of those guys who is annoyingly good at everything—he's Richard Roca, but less of a jerk. So, it should have given me some satisfaction that he was awful of this, but mostly, it was terrifying.

He shot his shiny new two-door Acura onto I-45 like he was preparing to drag race on the Autobahn. Inside, I hoped that an early rush hour might slow us down, but I kept my mouth shut. Barneby had picked up the tab at the diner, and I really didn't want to lose a free lunch.

Awkwardly, I pressed random buttons until the A/C came on high. Barneby would have glared at me, but he was too busy sliding around slow trucks and miscellaneous buttholes.

I knew I could close my eyes and make it all go away, but I also knew what was lurking in the dark of my eyelids. As we passed the exit for the 610 Loop, though, I decided I would rather face the mist than any further lane changes.

At first, there was nothing, and I hoped it would stay that way. No nightmare could really be as bad as Barneby's driving. Even if I had to watch Emily run down the aisle to Richard Roca, at least I'd have to be alive to feel that kind of pain.

Highways in Texas are the sort of experience meant to inspire your life flashing before your eyes. I didn't think the mist worked the same way. All the awful things it showed me, and they all seemed to be things that could happen in the future—and over my dead body. None of them seemed to be horrors from my sordid past. None of them even seemed current. Sixteen-year-olds should not be worried about their friends getting married.

I knew this time, it would be no different, as things began to take shape in the void of thoughts. My stomach clenched with anticipation of the pain I knew would come. In a short time, I had been turned into one of Pavlov's dogs, drooling and about to be kicked in the gut. I was all too familiar with that feeling. The almost piercing pressure of the initial blow, and the forceful way the air shoots out of your lungs, all wrapped in a brief half-second of my dark mind.

Only it never came. The image that arrived somehow both slowly and suddenly wasn't one that I typically associated with pain—except when I was hurtling toward my doom in his brand new sports car.

It was stupid Barneby Knotts. I wanted to laugh at the absurdity of it because I really didn't care if he got married. I suspected, though, that he wasn't exactly the marrying type. My spirits soared; they pushed high and then higher before crashing to an abrupt halt, like a kite that had reached the end of its string.

There was something wrong with him. His body, from bangs to purple high tops, was limp. He seemed to be standing half asleep in the rain. His hair was very different, a deep dark red. While dying, his usually black do some obscene color was definitely not outside the realm of normal for Barneby Knotts, something in my emaciated soul knew that wasn't what it was at all.

All of his coloring was off, not just his hair. He was so white I could have been staring at the newspaper print of him, or a drawing where the artist forgot to color in the skin. He was even paler than me. Though Barneby might have the exact same ethnic background as I did, he was blessed with an obnoxious perma-tan. Something else I often found myself jealous of.

A pool of water was gathering under Barneby's feet. It was the same wrong red color of his hair. Fat fast droplets fell on his head and shoulders. They ran from his arms and neck like reluctant rivers, trickling to that ever-widening puddle beneath him. One of Barneby's shoes was untied, its white lace wicking away at the wetness in which it sat, and that was when I realized it wasn't raining at all.

"Barneby!" I shouted, pulling myself away from the mist—but I could not shake the image.

"What? Come on, Vallenez, I really don't need a backseat driver!" he snapped at me, but I can't bring myself to bite back.

So, "What?" tumbled out my mouth instead.

"Well, I guess you are more of a front seat driver, but still annoying. So shut up."

That wouldn't be a problem. I felt like the blood I had seen in the mist had begun leaking into my stomach. It was nothing I tried to tell myself, desperately clutching the door handle, just more of my personal hell.

Remember when I said Barneby Knotts was my best friend? Yeah, I lied. He's my only friend, besides Emily. Since I had pretty much (not in my dreams) come to grips with the fact I had lost her for good, wouldn't losing him be the next worst thing? Not that I'd ever admit that to the idiot out loud. Backseat driver? Seriously?

At least I knew he wouldn't run off with Richard.

Most likely.

To say I wasn't excited to see Tom and Mary again would be the understatement of my whole miserable life. For me, this was really a last freaking resort. A thought every bit as insane as the action itself, and if they were surprised to see Barneby and I driving up the rough road, they did not show it.

But it wasn't because they knew we'd be coming. At least, I didn't think so.

It easily could have been that they heard us coming up the road. While Barneby had driven through Houston like he was preparing for the next installment of *The Fast & the Furious—Rich Kids Drift*, once the road to The Astrologers had turned to gravel and red dirt, he began to crawl. We inched along so slow, every time we approached even the most meager dip or hill, I was convinced there was no way we were getting over it. Yet each time, the car surprised me.

Perhaps the tires were so new, they simply grabbed on and lurched over the little swells. Even at less than three miles per hour, they climbed. The anticipation was larger than altitude change, and it grew and grew until I considered getting out and walking. I was so tired I'd have tried anything.

I really didn't know why I thought I'd find answers there, but I think part of me might have known. Besides, I wanted to find out what the hell they were talking about last time. I'm usually good at finding out secrets, more so when they were about me. Only when I glanced back up at a grim Tom and Mary, they weren't looking at me at all.

Did they practice these looks in front of mirrors? How long did it take them to master the various degrees of awfulness behind their eyes? Was there one look for *avoid mirrors today*, and another for *sorry your dog is going to die*? If they had been moderately forlorn when looking at Richard, that was nothing to how they were looking at Barneby Knotts.

I shivered in my black jacket. Maybe they had seen him in crimson puddles, too. That would be crazy, but so was coming here in the first place.

"Hello, Barneby," Tom said.

It wasn't cold or malicious. I had been mildly concerned about their reaction to his arrival since he had refused to divulge their history together. Tom was kind of sad sounding, like the tone you'd use when saying goodbye to someone with a terminal illness.

The Astrologers catered to heroes, the people whose profession was their disease, and one that would likely kill them. They had been pretty sad about Richard, but in my opinion, Barneby had a lot more guts. That would loosely translate to him doing more stupid stuff. Half of the time, he even recorded it and put it on YouTube. At least when he does die, his thousands of Twitter followers will get to see it happen, at least until someone complains about it.

Mary finally moved her eyes to me, but she gripped the porch railing like she needed it to prop herself up. Like she needed its strength for what she was about to say. My sensitive ears listened to the wood groan below her fingers. I guess Mary is stronger than she looks.

"Mr. Vallenez," she began.

I thought she was for sure going to say something snide like, "Didn't think we'd be seeing you again around here," or, "I knew you'd be back." Maybe she'd just rehash whatever had happened with Barneby and save me the trouble of prying it out of him later.

But she looked away again.

"Barneby, I'm sorry that you have lost Tyler. I hope you understand it was for the best."

If I had a heart, it would have beat in my chest like it had while going ninety down I-45. My mind shuddered, flinching back to that moment in the car. So there was a good reason why Barneby didn't want to talk about Tyler.

"Tyler is *dead?*" I asked, doing my best to not sound too happy about it.

Barneby gave me a look that said I clearly did not pull that off—but it didn't say *hey, he got his best friend killed*—so I guess I was a bit off base. Bad things happen to sidekicks; I could only imagine what was waiting for someone dumb enough to roll with BK.

"Seriously?" he asked me.

Okay, no, not seriously. I don't really want him to be dead. I just want him to move to another state and be someone else's conscious for a while. The whole idea was happy, like a little light sparkling in my middle.

But Barneby growled at me. He actually growled! At me!

"What?" I snapped. Barneby knows me. He knows I didn't really mean it.

"Tyler has left me," he says, throwing his hands up like I should have guessed.

Mostly it sounds like they had broken up. And come on, it's not like I'm a freaking mind reader. Tyler put up with so much garbage I thought he was capable of withstanding a never-ending amount of it. I guess I was wrong.

"Great. I wasn't aware you guys were dating B—I might have to reevaluate our relationship now."

I heard his teeth grinding together, and I worried that it finally happened—that I managed to push him too far.

I really hate apologizing, but— "Fine! Man, I'm sorry. Forgive me for having no idea what you are talking about." That was the best I had.

Barneby has this thing he does when he is exasperated by the amount of stupidity around him—and since it's directed at me this time, it's a bit offensive. It is something like a gag, a groan, a sigh, and a swallow, all in the same breath.

"Tyler isn't a sidekick anymore."

Oh, so he's left the business is all.

"Don't you mean assistant?" I quipped. I haven't had a verbal filter in years.

"Whatever!" Barneby shouted. "He's gonna be a hero, okay? I'm supposed to be happy for him—but mostly, I'm just miserable for me! Are you happy now?"

I just shook my head. Barneby wasn't as inherently as selfish as I was, and I had no idea what to say to him. I'm not the moral support guy. Our friendship isn't like that, and suddenly I worried that neither of us can survive without Tyler. This was probably our first get-together since he left, and it was our first fight—ever.

My mind again raced back to that image of Barneby in a pool of blood. I didn't want to know to whom the blood belonged to. Tom coughed lightly, but I still couldn't completely pull myself away.

"It's all right, Victor, Barneby already knows."

Barneby already knew. Something inside me broke. The force of it could have fractured a rib or spine, but I was still standing; because this break was so much deeper. I didn't want to let go of that awful scene; I thought it was important, and something awful would happen if I did.

"Barneby knows what?" I asked, figuring the answer was that I was going completely insane—it's hard to say for sure, but I assumed it was pretty obvious at this point.

"He knows all about that bloody end. I told him three years ago."

Slowly, I counted back the years. Three years ago, Barneby was just thirteen. He might have already been a legend, but he was still just a punk little kid. He stepped closer to me as I was thinking of how small he was back then, and his voice was low when he said, "It's all right, Vic."

"It's not all right!" I lashed out. "You're my best friend, and you're an idiot! I knew you'd slip up eventually, but I didn't think I'd have to see it on constant repeat!"

As the words tumbled from my mouth, the images in my head flickered faster, faster. Barneby smiled at me, but I was about to hyperventilate. I hated that I couldn't decide if I should hug him or punch him in the face. They're the same thing to me anyway.

"You know me, Vallenez," he said, "do you really think I'd let a thing like death stop me?"

Just like that, the horror flick in my head stopped. I found myself wanting to know what happened next—needing to know.

Again, but this time on my own terms, I cycled through all those awful images. I looked for something I might have missed, knowing full well that nothing was there. Then I realized the images were flat, and all flat things have edges. In my mind, I reached for the images, like pages I had to turn. There should have been the rustling of paper, but instead, there was a soft eerie breeze. Like the breath of an old vault that had waited years for someone to open it.

At that moment, I was relieved and so very afraid.

"Don't!" Mary shouted.

I heard their footsteps seconds before I realized they were too late. I was falling, and inside me, pages were flying up in every direction, each of them covered with people and places I knew, and others I would know someday far away. I was going to hit the ground before all those images did. I waited for the feel of it, but it never came.

The stupid hero caught me. I was such a girl.

ABOUT ANGELA KULIG

Angela Kulig is an American gypsy and former pirate. She has been from sea to shining sea--and though she is currently trapped in the desert against her will, she escapes every day in the form of many books.

Website: https://www.angelakulig.com

facebook.com/authorangelakulig

twitter.com/angelakulig

instagram.com/authorangelakulig

MORE BY FICTION-ATLAS PRESS

Fiction-Atlas Press releases two anthologies a year. We hope you'll check out some of our past anthologies or sign up to be notified about future ones on the next page!

Chasing Fireflies: A Summer Romance Anthology
A Twist of Fate: A Twisted Fairy Tale Anthology
Counterclockwise: A Fiction-Atlas Time Travel Anthology
Beyond the Mask: A Fiction-Atlas Superhero Anthology
Unknown Realms: A Fiction-Atlas Press Anthology

THANK YOU

We hope you have enjoyed our anthology.
It would mean the world to us if you had the time to leave a review!
Reviews are what keep us writing!

FOLLOW FICTION-ATLAS PRESS FOR INFORMATION ON FUTURE PUBLICATIONS.

http://fiction-atlas.com

facebook.com/fictionatlas

twitter.com/fabookbargains

instagram.com/cl_cannon

youtube.com/clcannonauthor

He didn't speak right away, but I could hear his breath against the plastic coating on his sleeping bag.

"Vallenez, if you ever would just pick a side, I was going to say we could probably be friends."

I bit my tongue to keep from laughing out loud. I thought, *how could he even think that?* As far as I was concerned, he had stolen the girl I love, making us mortal enemies until the day we both died. I'd be angry and bitter even if he went before me, I just know it. We could never be friends, and then something else occurred to me.

"You mean if I picked the right side. If I picked your side," I said smugly.

"What do you mean?" he asked, his voice clearly showing confusion.

"I could just as easily, haul off on my own, and be a bad guy. A villain."

"No, you couldn't."

"Excuse me?" I said. Because I was pretty sure I was still in charge of my own life, thank you very much.

"Well," he said, rolling away from me again, "Emily doesn't seem to think you have that in you. I don't think you could live with yourself if you ever had to prove her wrong."

———

Stupid, stupid, Richard Roca. Who did he think he was telling me what he thought Emily would think about me? He didn't know anything about it. Sure, he thinks he wants to be friends with me now, but what about when we find her—and I tell her I love her and that I can't live without her. We will see if he still wants to be friends with me after that!

The good news was, I was so angry that I didn't even freeze my butt off while peeing next to a rather sick looking pine tree. The bad news was, I was way too angry to just go back and go to sleep.

I quietly walked back to camp, which was probably just wasted energy looking back. There was no doubt in my mind that Richard would have heard me, which is to say if he had been awake.

I grabbed my pack from the pile they were lumped in and waited until I was several yards away before fiddling with the LED lantern. It took a few moments because the gloves made it awkward, but suddenly an orb of clear, bright light surrounded me.

So I walked into the forest in front of me. Not very far, I didn't know what could be in there, and I didn't have a death wish. I was just starving, and I wanted to raid the emergency rations in my pack. Also, I needed some time to think, and I couldn't do that anywhere near Richard.

I pulled out several silver bags with white labels. These emergency dehydrated food products were the same ones used by the United States Army. Which means they probably tasted just like cardboard, if I was lucky.

On a field trip to the Johnson Space Center when I was younger and did such things, I was rather unfortunate to be offered some of my friend's strawberry dehydrated astronaut food from the gift shop. If it really was just like astronaut food, like the package said, I feel bad for those guys. It tasted nothing like ice cream and basically ruined strawberry anything for the rest of my life.

The first *Meals Ready To Eat*, according to the label, was a strawberry banana milkshake. So that one was definitely out. I ended up going with the second bag, which was labeled as chicken noodle soup. Turns out, it was more of a chicken-flavored toothpaste with chunks of what I guessed were peas and carrots. If you closed your eyes, it wasn't too bad. It actually reminded me of what soup usually tastes like when I eat it, and since it's almost always when I am sick, everything tastes funny.

I folded up the empty silver bag and put it back in the pack. Mostly because I was pretty sure Richard would kick my butt if I littered, but secretly because I didn't want to hurt the planet either.

The stars were amazing. That is what happens when you are used to living in the big city. Light pollution ruins the sky, and you can hardly ever see the stars, and even when you can, they are nothing like they were then. I was transfixed, I could have stood there for days, and as my neck cramped, I decided to lay flat on my back. I never stopped looking up. I didn't even mind the cold snow or the chattering noise my teeth were making.

I got sleepy really fast after that. My eyes got heavy, and I knew I should get up and go back to the tent. I knew if I didn't, I'd likely freeze to death in my sleep. But I drifted away before I could make myself get up.

Fortunately, I didn't end up staying asleep long enough to lose any toes. A tree branch crunched, and at first, I thought it had been ice on cracking on a limb, but there was someone or something there, I could tell almost right away.

I got up, tossed my pack on, and that was when I spotted them. Back the way I had come was Wilford and Pax, and they seemed to be dressed even worse for trekking through the wintertime wilderness than I was.

"Dare he is!" cried Pax.

I really had to hand it to those guys because not many people would be brave or stupid enough to directly defy Richard Roca. I was going to go with idiots until proven otherwise. Unfortunately, the two of them were forcing me deeper into the woods, and I would really rather avoid that.

Turning to walk away from them, I was gearing up to run if I had to, and that was when I saw it. I hadn't noticed it until it was eclipsing most of the stars in the sky, and now I was way too close to it. A huge black bear with fiery red eyes—eyes that could be mirrors reflecting the dawn, if the dawn weren't still hours away.

EIGHT

When we had been in the ranger's office, I had actually seen a picture of a bear. Underneath it, there was a little sign that reads: RARE black bear sighting. The bear in that picture had been standing up on its back legs just like this one. Only this one was bigger, meaner, and it had those glowing red eyes—which could not be normal.

There was also the seasonal difference. It was January; shouldn't this bear have been hibernating or something?

The bear growled, and I was pretty sure I was supposed to play dead. On a personal level, I would have much rather run away. So I did.

Honestly, between me, Pax, and Wilford, I knew I was the better runner, and I just couldn't make myself feel bad about that. If there was anything in the world I was good at, it was the hundred-yard dash. I could run almost any distance if it was far enough to get me away.

I sprinted through the gap between the two stunned Nigerians. They didn't spare me so much as a sideways glance. After I was far enough away, I looked over my shoulder, and I really wish I hadn't.

It wasn't like I really liked Wilford and Pax, but I was getting kind of used to them following me around, and if they didn't start moving a little bit faster than being completely stationary, they were going to be eaten.

Slowly, not wanting to turn their backs to the bear, they inched backward. I slowed my pace and made myself pay attention to where I was going. I had left my lantern in the woods, and it was dark, and now my eyes were unadjusted. It was a good excuse as any to avoid looking behind me.

"Vallenez!" a girl shrieked, and of course, it was Stella, "What the heck are you doing? You vanished! Richard!" She called in the other direction. "He's here! He hasn't gone off a cliff, or frozen to death, or—"

"There is a bear!" I screamed over whatever she had said then. For the briefest of moments, she looked afraid, then angry.

"Super funny, Vallenez," she spat, "You had me going there for a second, but bears hibernate this time of year, stupid."

But I didn't have to explain myself further because the bear growled from behind us, and the Nigerians screamed.

"Richard!" Stella screamed. "There *is* a bear!"

Richard was already beside her, staring in the direction all the noise had come from.

"Stay with Stella," he told me, but of course, she objected. "For once